Dear Stranger,

ENTER IF YOU DARE

ECHOES OF THE FORGOTTEN

Michael Nunn

If you found this book, please read it and, whether you take it with you or leave it where you found it, please pass it on for others to read.

If you enjoy it, please get in touch via instagram (@michaelnunnauthor) or email (michael-nunn@outlook.com) and let me know what you think and where you found it.

Michael Nunn

Left by the author at Hotel Pocillos Playa, Lanzarote

1

'Where have you been for the past sixty hours?' asked the man across the table. He had identified himself as a Detective Inspector but Will Campbell didn't catch his name. He hadn't caught much of what the Detective Inspector had said since he'd entered the small, brightly lit room containing only a desk with four chairs, two on one side and two on the other. His mind had been too busy searching for its own answers.

'I don't know,' Will said.

'What do you mean?'

'I don't remember.'

'You don't remember anything?'

Will shook his head. It hadn't even felt like sixty hours had passed. To him it was as though the time he was missing spanned a single night, one he had initially assumed he had lost due to intoxication.

'What happened to your friends?' the DI asked.

He gave Will a moment to offer something, which he didn't, before continuing. 'You and your friends – Nicole Wilson, Tom Appleby, Julian Thompson and Craig Richards – left the Tremont Museum in Treevale on Monday evening. None of you have been since, until this morning when you were picked up forty miles away, outside North Allerton. If you ended up there, where are your friends?'

'I don't know,' Will said. His voice cracked, almost broke entirely at the mention of their names. He swallowed, trying to moisten his throat but his mouth was dry. He reached for the flimsy plastic cup of water on the table with a hand caked in blood. He lifted it to his lips, took the water in his mouth and moved it around before swallowing. He looked at the blood that covered both arms from elbow to fingertip. 'When can I clean this off?'

'Soon,' the DI said without empathy. He was large and burly beneath his suit, his face hard. He looked at Will as though he were already deemed guilty of something. 'We need to get to the bottom of what happened first. Your friends are still missing. Our number one priority is finding them.'

Will looked down at the table. 'I don't remember.'

'Why don't we talk about that blood? Where did it come from?'

Will shook his head. 'I don't know. I don't remember.'

'You were seen walking across a farmer's field. Where were you coming from?'

'I don't remember.'

'When was the last time you saw your friends?'

'I don't remember.'

The DI sighed. He was silent for a while, a stretch of time Will filled with his own thoughts and frustrations. His friends were gone and he felt like crying for them. He feared the worst but couldn't fully mourn them without knowing. What if they were wandering around their own stretches of the countryside, yet to be found? He strained to remember anything from last – the other – night but there was nothing there. He found only empty frames in the film of his memories.

'Okay,' said the Detective Inspector. 'Let's start with the last thing you *do* remember. When was that?'

'Monday night,' Will said.

'And what do you remember from Monday night?'

So Will told him, starting with his arrival at the museum and ending with he and his friends leaving early. He was careful not to mention his plans for that night to be his last.

2

It was supposed to be a night to remember, although not by Will. It was his intention that it would be one of the last, if not *the* last night of his life. This, he thought as the car pulled up outside the museum, was a night for his friends to remember for the rest of their lives, long after he was gone. He had butterflies in his stomach.

Once, he would have been excited by the idea of a museum exhibition. It would have been the only thing on his mind, but he no longer saw the point in it. What he had come here for was not to further his education, but to say goodbye and create some great memories in the process. He gazed out of the window as they pulled up on the curb opposite, looking at his friends stood waiting for him. It would be awkward at first, to speak to them, having not spoken much to any of them in the three months since his last suicide attempt, but once they were passed that, they could have the kind of fun that they could recall every time they thought of him.

At the thought of what he was going to do, he pulled down the sleeve of his jacket to cover the deep red, puckered line that ran down his left forearm. He wasn't looking at Ian, his stepdad, in the driver's seat, but heard his breath catch. It had been Ian who had saved him and they had spoken little of it since. The closest they had come had been when Will explained his intention to return to university for his third year. Ian thought it was a very bad idea, that Will wasn't ready. But Will could not be deterred – how could he be? This was his chance to make amends with his friends, to make it so he left them on good terms – and Ian had eventually relented and agreed to drive him, but not before Will had missed his first day back. He was joining the class at an exhibition for a local photographer and designer.

'Are you sure you're ready for this?' Ian asked him now that they were here.

Will looked through the window at the misfits he called his friends, and his girlfriend. They were stood together in a small group, looking down at their shuffling feet. Nobody spoke. As soon as he was among them, they would speak again, he was sure, but they would be walking on egg-shells the same way Ian had for the past couple of months.

Still, the sight of them filled him with excitement and a sense of joy that had become more and more foreign. They all looked over and noticed him. He gave them a wave.

'I have to be,' Will said. He made to get out of the car but Ian grabbed his arm and stopped him.

Ian was a strong man with solid branches for arms from years of manual labour, but his face was soft as though his features refused to obey the tough guy physique. Unshed tears moistened his eyes and his face had dropped, becoming softer still. If his friends from the pub saw him then, they would have laughed him out of the room.

'If you're not ready…'

'I have to go back.'

'You can defer a year, you know. Take some more time to sort your shit out.'

Unlike his friends, Ian had never subscribed to stiff-upper-lip style thinking, but *Sort your shit out* edged dangerously close. The truth was, Ian had been most effected by Will's suicide attempt and he had nobody to talk to about it. He could barely discuss anything with Will's mum, let alone something that required her full attention, and he definitely couldn't turn to his friends.

'I'm not deferring,' Will said. Even if he wasn't planning to end everything, he would never have been able to defer. He wouldn't want to come back without them. They were the best friends he could ever have hoped for. Outcasts and weirdos each of them. Although he would never be graduating, he was thankful he had come to university if only to meet them.

University had a strange way of creating friends of the most mismatched people and the five of them, Will included, were a prime example. Will was a shy nerd, the quiet type but without the mystery that made quiet types in movies attractive and interesting. He was often more comfortable alone in his room than with people, at least before he met the group shuffling around on the opposite curb, none of whom looked like they should be friends with each other let alone Will.

Nicole looked like a grown up Wednesday Addams. Hair dyed black, black make-up and black clothes, but with a great deal more smiling than the daughter in the classic gothic family and she loved being around people. Craig was a knot of muscle, who looked as though he belonged with the popular kids, except for his double denim obsession. Unlike the popular kids, he spent a lot of free time reading and he hated bullies. Julian was a gangly geek with thick rimmed glasses and prematurely bald head. He had a mouth that wouldn't stop and which often got him into trouble. Then there was Tom, shy and overweight with too much body hair but a wispy disappointment of a moustache on his face. Before university, he had been part of a friendship group who sat in the same room together, staring at computer screens and rarely seeing one another's faces.

They each belonged to different social groups, if any, before they were thrown together. When Will first met them, it seemed unlikely he would get along well with any of them, except maybe Tom, who he thought might share his passion for comic books – he didn't – yet they had formed a tightly knit group. And Will and Nicole had started a relationship that was still going. Or at least he thought it was.

'If I defer, they'll all graduate this year and they'll disappear, and I'll have to go on without them.'

'It's not a race, you know, Will,' Ian said. 'You have to think about what's best for you. And what's best for your mother too.'

Will said nothing. Ian sighed, 'Well at least be careful. You know a woman went missing in town a couple of weeks ago.'

'It's a city. People go missing all the time.'

'Even so, promise me you'll not go out alone at night.'

'Goodbye, Ian,' Will said and opened the door. It wasn't the farewell he wanted for the two of them, but it would have to do.

'Your mother's worried sick about you, you know.'

Will doubted that. He had said goodbye to her before he left, leaning in to hug her and she had squirmed backward in her chair as though Will were an alien creature. She had felt something but it wasn't worry.

Will climbed out and closed the door.

All four heads darted up. Awkward, shifting grins gripped their mouths – most of them, anyway. Will raised a timid hand, hello, and dropped it swiftly before the sleeve of his jacket could slip too far down.

'Hey,' Julian said. It was a start.

'Weren't sure you were gonnae come,' Craig said in a thick Scottish brogue. His voice was normally so powerful, but now it was soft and jittery.

Will shrugged. 'Time to get back to it.'

He had messaged them all in the group chat they shared to let them know he would meet them here, but he couldn't blame their surprise. Had any of them attempted to take their own lives over the summer, he wouldn't have expected to see them again so soon, least of all for the start of the stressful third and final year of their degree.

His friends looked from one to the other, none of them wanting to address the elephant in the group and he was reminded of the first time they had all met upon arrival in their first student house. When individuals are pushed into a situation with strangers they are going to spend a great deal of time with, the conversation is awkward. Forced and unnatural, as each person – there were ten of them back then – try and get to know each other as quick as possible. What resulted between them all was a set of questions and answers that resembled the kind of gameshows Will's mother watched obsessively.

They all knew each other extremely well now but the uncertainty of what to say was the same as it had been back then, as though they were strangers again.

Finally, Tom asked the question they all felt had to be asked. 'Are you okay? Stupid question. Sorry. Course you're not. You...'

'Tom,' Will interjected before Tom could spin himself into a tight coil. 'I'm...'

Okay? Alright? Fine and fucking dandy?

'I'm getting there.'

A lie but a smaller one and it settled them a little. Behind him, he heard the hum of Ian's engine as he finally pulled away.

Nicole was the only one yet to speak and, besides the first look they had all cast in his direction, she had avoided looking at him, focusing instead on her cigarette. They couldn't have been out waiting for long but there was a great many extinguished ends around her feet. The four of them looked at her as though she were an actress in a play whom had missed her cue.

'It's good to see you, Will,' she finally said and gave him a smile that was clearly a struggle. Her emerald eyes were already shining, glazed in tears.

Will made as though to say something, an apology perhaps, when they were interrupted by Stevie Quentin, the tutor who organised the trip. He was leaning out of the museum doorway at the top of the steps.

'Today guys. You're not going to see anything standing out here talking about–' He noticed Will and trailed off. His face took on the flicker of hesitation, he, too, unsure what to say. His years of teaching had given him the ability to adapt his attitude quickly and he replaced his awkwardness with a smile, as though nothing had happened.

'Welcome back, William.' With a flick of his head, he beckoned the five of them into the building. He stepped aside to allow Craig, Julian, Tom and Nicole to go in ahead and then he fell in beside Will.

'It's really good to see you back, Will,' he said. 'I'm glad you're here.'

Here at the museum, or here on the planet, Will thought. Either way, he knew it was only the start of a sympathetic speech, the likes of which had been unending since he left the hospital. He had received messages on Facebook from people who had made his school years miserable, informing him they were there if Will ever needed to talk.

Frankly, Will was sick of it. He was sick of the hypocrisy.

Even if it were true, any of it, what they didn't realise is that when somebody reached the stage of doing what Will did, they weren't interested in having somebody to talk to. Will hadn't wanted to be saved. He still didn't.

Stevie taught the written side of the course and Will had always gotten the impression he would be more comfortable writing his thoughts than speaking them. To brace this subject with Will must have been extremely difficult, so Will let him speak. For now.

'You can come and talk to me, you know,' Stevie offered. His offer was genuine, Will knew. but he also knew he would never take him up on it, even if he had planned to be around tomorrow morning.

He continued, 'You know, I once…'

And here came the admission that he, too, had once tried to do something very similar. Will had received a couple of those and he had yet to work out whether it was meant to make him feel better, that he was somehow part of a members only club, or to convince him that he was nothing special; he was not the first to fail and wouldn't be the last.

Dr Phillips, Will's therapist, had talked about moving forward, talking about his issues and working to change what was in his control and accept what was not, without dwelling on thoughts of the suicide attempt for too long, yet everybody else seemed intent on reminding him of it with their own stories.

Will spotted a silver sign for toilets, above two doors.

'Sorry,' Will interrupted Stevie. 'I really need to go. I'll catch up.'

Stevie's disappointment was evident and Will couldn't help but feel guilty, when the guy was only trying to offer some comfort. 'Don't take too long. Charles King will be starting his talk soon.'

His words followed Will into the bathroom. Will went to the rows of sinks, all built into a stone slab counter. Above ran a long mirror. He rested his hands on the stone to relieve the weakness in his legs, which felt as though they were about to give way, and stared into his eyes, sunken and weighed down by large purple sacks. It was no wonder the guys – and Nicole, of course – hadn't known what to say to him. He looked as though he hadn't slept in the three months since the attempt. He was unkempt and unshaven. He looked, if he was being honest, like somebody who had given up on life.

Even though he was planning to try again in the morning, thoughts of his first attempt shook him.

Breathe, William. The way I taught you. Dr Phillip's voice inside his head.

In for one second, out for one second.
Think about your family.
In for two, out for two.
Think about your friends.
In for three, out for three.
Think about your design work.
In for four, out for four.
Think about your dreams.

In for five, out for five.

Think about somebody you puts a smile on your face, and say their name.

'Nicole,' he whispered to the empty bathroom and the briefest hint of a smile twitched his lips. His legs regained their solidity.

He found his friends in the gallery at the end of the corridor. The walls were bright, almost blinding pristine white. Perfect. Adorned on each wall were mounted photographs and posters, some so graphic they made David Bailey's classic anti-fur ads from the '80s seem tame.

At the end of the room, everybody had gathered in rows of metal chairs that looked painfully uncomfortable, facing an enlarged photograph of a burning building that wasn't empty. Beside the screen, checking something on an open MacBook, was a silver haired man in jeans and a t-shirt.

Will sat next to Craig. He had wanted to be next to Nicole so he could try and get her to talk to him but she was sat on the other side of the guys and a stranger had taken the seat on her other side.

'You alright?' Craig asked. There was no worry about it being a stupid question this time. They had slipped into a more casual mode of conversation.

Will nodded.

Craig nudged him with cannonball shoulders. He'd taken off his denim jacket to reveal his thick arms straining against his t-shirt sleeves. 'Ye not hot in that thing?' he asked, gesturing to Will's jacket.

The temperature in the room, with all of those bodies, was rising by the second and beads of sweat had already started to spout along Will's hairline. He shook his head a little too quickly and Craig nodded his understanding.

Will pulled the sleeve of his jacket down into his palm and held it there.

'Right,' called the silver haired man with a clap. 'Thank you all for coming. I'm Charles King.' He paused, waited for the crowd to applaud. Somebody sniffed. He cleared his throat and began talking, first giving some background to his work.

Will leant toward Craig and whispered, 'How's Nicole?'

Craig shrugged and screwed up his face. 'About as you'd expect. A little hurt you didnae talk to her. Mostly, I think she feels guilty.'

'Guilty? Why?'

Craig looked at him as though it were obvious, and Will figured maybe it was. She hadn't noticed his decline, hadn't been able to save him. He wanted to tell her it was not her fault; he had hidden it from everybody. What happened was down to him and him alone, but saying so wouldn't go down too well. He thought it might taint the memories they were going to create, once he was gone come the morning.

Nicole's eyes were set dead ahead, as were Tom and Julian's. Will glanced at them all, then checked Stevie, a few rows ahead, wasn't paying them any attention. He turned back to his friends and whispered, 'Hey, you guys want to get out of here? Go have some fun?'

'Did you really just ask that? *You?*' Julian whispered loudly. Their expressions all asked the same question. There had been a time when nothing could tear Will away from an event like this, even when it ended. He would normally stay to ask a handful of questions of the designer, photographer or artist.

Will nodded. 'Let's spend some time together.' He reached into his jacket and pulled a vodka bottle from the inside pocket, far enough for them to see. They each stared at him. He gestured toward the door and slid out of his seat. He didn't look back. He knew they would follow, be it through concern or curiosity.

By the time he reached the reception, all four of them were with him.

'Ye sure you're okay, Will?' Craig asked.

He was growing tired of that question. 'Yeah, fine.'

'It's just…'

'You've never drank spirits before,' Nicole finished.

Will sighed. 'I want some time with my friends.'

Their eyes met and there were tears in hers again. She nodded and they headed outside.

At the top of the steps they stopped in the growing dusk. They looked at him – not Craig, the usual leader of the group – for guidance.

The sound of a fairground drifted to them on the wind. Polluting the purple sky of twilight with bright colours, Will noticed the glow of the lights in the distance.

He smiled. A night to remember, he thought.

3

'A fairground?' the DI said when Will was finished.

Will nodded.

The DI jotted something down in his notebook, then announced for the sake of the record that he was pausing the interview. He left the small room, leaving Will behind with his thoughts. If there was anything he wanted to be alone with right then, it was not his own thoughts. He could not help but look at the blood on his hands and wonder where it had come from. *Who* it came from.

There was a laceration across his temple, running from the end of his brow to just before his ear but it was not deep, had already sealed itself. Any wound that created this amount of blood would have stayed open and continued to bleed without stitches.

He tried again to remember anything after that moment on the steps of the museum. He had been missing for nearly three days. There had to be something to remember.

Almost in answer, an image flashed before his mind's eye. A dark corridor and a figure ahead of him, long and thin. A man with a crooked smile, he could not see in the darkness, but the sight of which he could somehow remember clearly.

'*Roll up, roll up,*' the figure called after Will. Will flinched, alone in the little room at the police station. He was thankful for the bright lightbulb above him.

There were even briefer images from the fairground itself but nothing else. The other memories simply did not exist. One minute, he was stood on the museum steps, looking at the distant fairground spread its colours across the pale purple of the darkening summer sky, the next, he was stumbling across a field of hard mud and rocks, and the sun was rising again. His head had pounded and the rising sun had created a long, blinding light on the horizon, producing a throb of pain behind his eyes.

He had assumed it was a hangover. As Nicole had been so kind as to point out, he had never been much of a drinker, and the bottle he'd smuggled from the kitchen at his Mum and Ian's house must have hit his brain like a hammer against glass.

His foot had caught a rock, sending him to the ground. His arms had scraped heavily against the rough earth. It was then he noticed the blood for the first time. His jacket was missing and his arms were covered in it. He had searched for a wound but there was nothing but the shallow cut beside his eyebrow and the puckered purple scar of his suicide attempt.

When he had become aware of the missing section in his memory, he assumed he must have drank the entire bottle himself and blacked out. But the more important question on his mind was who's blood this was and where the hell he was. Empty fields filled the horizon in every direction. There was no sign of where he'd come from. The ache in his legs suggested he had been walking for quite some time.

His phone was gone.

Eventually, Will had come to a road. A vehicle approached from one side. A small hatchback followed the bend into view, a middle aged woman behind the wheel. As she saw him, her face turned to horror. Her engine jumped an octave as she sped away.

Will didn't blame her. He could imagine what he must have looked like. He had thought he looked harrowing as he stared in the mirror in the museum bathroom; he certainly looked more frightening by the side of that road.

He had continued walking until he came to a handful of houses and a corner shop. The shutters were halfway down across the door, the shopkeeper not yet open to customers. A sandwich board had been placed outside, the front page of the most recent paper slipped inside of it.

Will's own face stared out from the front page of a national newspaper, beside Julian, Craig, Tom and Nicole. It was a photograph of them all dressed up and smiling. It had been taken at the end of year student exhibition back in May, a month before Will's attempt.

Beneath them, the headline ran:

SEARCH FOR MISSING STUDENTS CONTINUES.

When he looked closer and saw the date, he notices he was not just missing ten hours of memory. He had been missing, along with the others, for nearly three days. Will had gripped the edges of the sandwich board with all his strength to keep from toppling. He had felt like screaming. Instead, he had wept.

He was still that way when the police, no doubt called by the woman who'd driven past, picked him up.

The DI came back in, breaking Will from his thoughts. He sat back down and resumed the recording, announcing the time. Then he placed a metal object on the table. A Zippo lighter.

'When you were picked up, this was in your pocket,' the DI said. 'Can you explain how you came to have it?'

Will shook his head. 'I don't remember.'

'This Zippo belonged to Nicole Wilson, correct?'

Will nodded. The lighter was custom, with a large *N* decoratively displayed on both sides.

'Have you ever smoked, Will?'

'No.'

'Then can you think of any possible explanation as to why you would have your girlfriend's lighter in your pocket, alone in a field miles from home, covered in somebody else's blood?'

Will swallowed. 'No.'

'You claim that when you left the museum, you saw and heard a fairground nearby.'

It wasn't a question. Still, Will nodded. He didn't like the detective's use of the word *claim*.

'In what direction did this fairground appear to be?'

Appear. It was said in the same tone as *claim*.

Will said, 'It was in Graham Park.'

'How did you know where it was all the way from the museum?'

'That's where we went. I can only remember bits, but we went to the fair on Monday. It was in Graham Park.'

The DI thought for a time. He said, 'What do you remember after this fair?'

Will shook his head. 'Nothing.'

'Until this morning?'

He nodded.

The DI stared at him with eyes that sought to penetrate his soul. 'Where are your friends, Will? Where did you go?'

'I…' Will started. 'I don't remember. We went to the fair, then… I… I don't know.' Tears gathered on the brim of his lower lids.

'Will, I want you to be honest with me. For the sake of Nicole, Tom, Julian, and Craig.'

'I am.'

The detective shook his head. 'Will, there was no fairground on Monday night. Not in Graham Park, nor anywhere else in Treevale. So tell me, where did you go?'

4
Eleven Months Later

There was a man across the road when Will left for his daily run. He had one hand resting casually in his pocket, while the other brought a cigarette to his lips. His eyes were on Will, although he couldn't be sure if that was simply because Will was the only other person on the street at such an early hour, or because the man was watching for him.

The house the man stood in front of was notorious for its array of visitors, as Will's new housemate had informed him, and while Beth couldn't be certain after a full year living here whether the woman who lived there was selling drugs or sex, this man was certainly rough enough around the edges for either.

Still, Will considered going back inside and skipping this morning's run. His routines were important. They were what kept him on an even keel, or so Dr Phillips argued, but one skipped run wouldn't do much harm, would it?

Do you want to take that chance? he asked himself, remembering the times in the past eleven months when he'd lost control of his mind and his actions.

It was only a run but it was too important to skip. No matter how little sleep his nightmares allowed him, or whether there was a strange man across the road, possibly watching him. He had promised Dr Phillips when she agreed to green light his return to Treevale to start his third year of university again that he would not let his routines lapse. He had hated having to make the promise but it was better than what could happen if he slipped out of control.

He pulled the door closed behind him and tried to ignore the watchful eyes as he set off at a steady jog toward the end of the street and around the corner. Once he was out of sight, he let himself forget about the man and focused, instead, on the fresh air. It was a little after seven in the morning so Will saw few others in the streets, which he was glad for.

Running was something Will used to consider as tantamount to torture inflicted upon him by PE teachers and he never did any exercise outside the mandatory time. He had always struggled to see what anybody enjoyed about it. It made your chest tighten until it burned, made your legs ache, and it was boring. What was the goal? He wasn't a fan of other sports forced on them, like football or rugby, but at least they had a point to them.

He was therefore reluctant when Dr Phillips suggested running as part of his therapy. Why would he add in something that he wouldn't enjoy? He was dealing with enough in his life already. His best friends and his girlfriend were missing, with no answers as to what happened. Will was a wreck and the undetermined trauma he had suffered could cause psychotic episodes with little warning, one of which included the brandishing of a kitchen knife and bought Will a month in a nut house.

And, as though that were not enough, there was the media presence, the journalists that waited outside his house and called non-stop for a quote or an exclusive on what really happened that night, as though Will was only pretending he couldn't remember. And there was the harassment from a great deal of people who believed he had killed his friends and escaped justice. Going running and getting healthy was far from his mind. He had wanted to find them, learn what happened to them, and to himself.

What changed his mind was his mother. She was once a strong woman who worked two jobs to care for her children but for many years, following the loss of her eldest son, she had been a shell of that woman. Evelyn Hilton was disconnected from all those around her, even her surviving child.

Will didn't want to end up like that. The house already felt like a prison, with Ian as his warden. It was worse than the "Mental Health Clinic" had been. The nut house had been less like a movie style loony bin and more like an old people's home, painted magnolia, pale greens and browns, and furnished with wingback chairs. Instead of shuffling old people, there were shuffling, medicated zombies, who instead of shitting themselves, cried and screamed and erupted into outbursts that made a toddler's tantrum seem tame. Every day was spent in group therapy sessions with these people. He was almost never alone, so he had been glad to get out.

And then he got home and Ian lurked over his shoulder at all times, making sure he was okay, checking on what he was doing. Will couldn't bare it.

Through running, he could escape, even if it was for only half an hour or an hour. He actually started to look forward to it. Now, months later, he was much fitter, the excess weight around his stomach had disappeared and the daily rush of chemicals the run released worked wonders on his mind.

Running through the countryside was vastly different from running back here in the city. Treevale, to somebody hearing the name for the first time, sounded like a lovely, woodland place, with pleasant residential estates for middle classes and with bustling businesses, but it was the opposite. It wasn't peaceful and it wasn't exactly pleasant for the most part.

Built almost solely around the university, Treevale seemed to alternate every hundred or so yards from areas of wealth to slums. One minute, there was a row of niche little stores owned by private owners, and the next, bars with broken windows, and broken bottles at the door; modern doctors surgeries, then an estate of terraced houses boarded up with large metal sheets that had been screwed in place during the last recession. It was an oddity of a place, one that was both moving forward, redeveloping and expanding, while also slipping away into a crime ridden hovel.

In the countryside, the only people he was at risk of seeing so early in the morning were dog walkers and farmers, which he would be able to see a half a mile away and avoid if he needed to but in a city, there was no way of knowing who was lurking around each corner.

He wasn't afraid of any journalists these days. It had been so long since there was any hint of progress in the search, the media's attention had moved elsewhere. It was the everyday, judgemental pedestrian Will was worried would recognise him. They would be far more damaging to him than a journalist. Journalists wanted to know the truth. Most people who recognised Will already thought they knew it.

He slowed and came to a stop opposite Graham Park, two miles north of Treevale University. He stared at the gate but didn't move. He hadn't planned to come here, on this or any of the three mornings he had been back in town. Yet he had found himself right here, each morning, pulled there by the park itself, or something. He wasn't sure what.

A black metal fence ran the entire perimeter of the park, containing two miles of grass, trees and a small lake, and a number of memories for Will. Most of them were good, but this park was also where he knew they had shared their last.

Although he couldn't remember anything beyond those handful of flashes, he could picture the fair on the other side of that large black arched gate, could almost hear the screams – a sound he could no longer associate with fun, instead likening it to the sound of a massacre.

The police found no sign of the fair. Nor any witness who could corroborate the fair's presence. Will had worked hard to accept they were right and the flashes of memory he had were wrong – Dr Phillips claimed he remembered a fairground because it was a place of fun and he could convince himself nothing bad could have happened to him and his friends – but standing there, looking across at the open gateway into the park and trying to catch his breath, he wasn't sure.

The lights appeared in his head, the image of the park. He saw a flash of the whole fairground from up high in a Ferris wheel. Game stalls everywhere. A dark corridor. A figure lurching after him.

He backed away from the park as though the open gate were going to lurch out at him like a giant metal mouth and swallow him. Fair or no fair, it had to be the place where they had met whatever befell them all.

He turned and starting running painfully, breathlessly back the way he'd come.

When he reached his street the man who had been there earlier was gone, having collected his drugs and left, or gone inside for whatever else the woman was offering.

Will checked over his shoulder one last time before he stepped inside. There was an envelope on the doormat. It was completely blank, a crisp white rectangle. He picked it up, and despite the lack of a name or address, he knew it was meant for him. He could feel it. He shivered as he realised what that meant. Somebody knew where he lived, and they had come here to deliver it in person.

'Morning Will,' Beth called through from the kitchen. She must have gotten up while he was out.

'Er, morning,' he managed. His attention was on the envelope. He looked at it and imagined Beth coming out into the hallway and seeing it. He couldn't let that happen. If she saw it, she would know too that somebody had delivered it by hand. She would know the kind of attention he had brought with him to her house.

He closed the front door and stepped swiftly through the first door on the left, into his bedroom. It was one of the larger rooms in the house but had the downside of being downstairs. Will was still getting used to the room, especially it's bay window that looked straight out of the front of the house. That anybody could look in at any time and watch him made him deeply uncomfortable and the curtains, bland, generic beige sheets of fabric, had remained drawn since shortly after his arrival a few days ago.

The colour of the curtains doused the entire room and its limited furniture – a small double bed opposite the window, a cheap flatpack wardrobe to one side and a desk in the alcove of the bay window – in a brownish tinge. Will didn't turn on the light, but closed the door behind him, heard the yale lock click into place, and sat down on the edge of the bed. He stared down at the envelope in his hands, the perfect white now tinged with the same brown gloom as the rest of the room.

His hands shook slightly. Any post that had come through the door in the past year had been opened by Ian because of the high chance the letter contained some form of harassment or malice and he was sure this would be worse; the sender had put in the effort to deliver it in person.

The messages had started online, accusing Will of murdering his friends, despite there being no evidence to that effect – except the blood. After Will shut down his social media accounts, only reactivating them recently to seek accommodation, the accusations didn't stop. They arrived, instead, by post. Ian had shielded Will from these as best he could, just as he tried to shield him from the questions shouted by the journalists who, for a few weeks, were a constant presence outside their house. And so, Will had not opened a letter in months.

Surely it was over now, he thought with little confidence.

His fingers hovered over the top of the envelope. He was afraid to see what the letter contained and he could already feel the fear seeping into every crevice of his mind. Soon it would consume it.

He tore it open and poisonous butterflies came to life in his stomach. Nobody should have known where he lived; he had only been here a few days.

Inside was a folded piece of card. He unfolded it. In the centre of the page, written in ornate calligraphy were two words:

Roll Up...

5

He didn't mention the letter to Dr Phillips at that day's appointment, the first of his twice weekly sessions. The therapy had started in the wake of his suicide attempt and had increased in the aftermath of the disappearance. He had begun with daily sessions before reducing to four times per week, but when she agreed to sign off on his return to Treevale, she had agreed to reduce their sessions to two, on a Monday and Thursday. The decision was made more for the ease of travel – each appointment would require an hour and a half on the bus each way – than it was because of his mental state.

Informing her of the letter he'd received, he feared would convince her she'd made the wrong decision and he would have to go back to daily sessions, or worse, return home.

Instead, they covered the usual topics. They discussed his nightmares. He had variations of the same one. A figure with overly long, skinny limbs like a spider chased him through a network of dark corridors. The figure, although more like a creature, was a man. Will knew, although he couldn't always see it, the man wore a menacing smile that raised higher on one side. Will referred to him as The Crooked Man.

They talked about how he was feeling, how he was doing with his routines, and then Dr Phillips raised a new topic. How was he settling in at his new student house?

Will told her it was going well and he was telling the truth, although only one of his three housemates had moved in so far.

Beth was the kindest person Will had come across

since the disappearance. He had posted on a student Facebook page seeking a place to live and Beth was the only person to comment with an actual offer rather than a question or comment about the disappearance. When they had started messaging privately, she hadn't asked him anything about that night. Instead, they had talked about themselves, movies and music. They'd got on well enough, Beth decided Will would be a good fit to their house.

When he had moved in and met her in person a few days ago, he felt as though they already knew each other and not once did he feel the discomfort he had come to feel around most people. That first night, she had heard him stir from a nightmare and offered him a mug of hot chocolate and some company in the living room until the nightmare passed and he could go back to sleep. She was a night-owl, which was her way of saying she suffered from insomnia, and so she was already awake when she heard him mumbling and calling out. She didn't ask what he had dreamt about.

He left the appointment feeling good about his new friendship but, as he always did when leaving Dr Phillips, he felt the weight of his old friends' absence more heavily. He did his best to focus on the former as he made his way back to Treevale. He had agreed to meet Beth at the student union. One of his other new housemates, Ben, was going to be there and was looking forward to meeting him.

After a therapy session, Will and Ian would normally have gone to a pub or quiet restaurant to grab lunch on their way back home, so going for lunch with Beth and Ben would cause no disruption to his routines.

The university was Treevale's golden heart and the primary source of the town's economy. It stood apart from everything in town, bright, shining and modern. It was the town's pride and joy. Almost directly in the centre was the student union building with both a bar and nightclub inside, sat beside the library as though it was presenting each student with a choice about what type of student they were going to be.

The bar was almost empty when Will entered. Undergraduate courses didn't start again for two weeks, leaving only post-grad students and those like Beth and Will who had returned to town early, for potential customers. Accordingly, the staff was a skeleton crew. One bartender and two chefs glimpsed through the open pass at one end of the bar, both on their phones.

The bartender, an acne scarred baby-face with bags under his eyes, had undone the top button of his shirt and was leaning over the bar, copying out passages from a textbook. He looked up at Will as he entered, nodded a hello and turned back to his book.

There were high chairs and tables immediately across from the bar and then rows of booths adorned in tasteful grey leather. The length of the opposite wall was made up of glass doors leading out onto a terrace, where Will had stood with his old housemates on their first ever night together. There had been ten of them during that first year and that first night, they were all one group, trying to get to know each other. Over the course of the night, however, the five of them had come together and the start of a great friendship had begun. Now there was only Will.

They'd asked each other about their lives before. Nicole asked them all about relationships. Somewhat ashamed, Will admitted he had only had one girlfriend, their relationship short lived, and he remained a virgin. He'd expected to be judged, but Tom and Julian had confessed they, too, had never had sex. Nicole had been surprised, and she'd assured them each that there was nothing wrong with that.

Will had stared at her smile and wanted to never look away.

Nicole had a way of softening the negative emotions encasing his heart with that smile. He could remember all the times she had calmed him down or made him feel better about a situation with a smile. He remembered–

–her smile in the shadows of a dark, cold room. People,

barely more than shadows themselves, surrounded them. Will was panicking, filled up with dread, shaking and rocking in terror. They were going to die. They were all going to die.

'Will!'

Will jolted out of his own imaginings and looked around, heart pounding. The pub was empty but for a single booth. Beth stood, waving him over. She was dressed down in leggings and a hoodie, her fiery red hair tied up at the back of her head into a pony tail like a downward flame, but to Will she was as stunning as if she were dressed up.

Will raised a hand and approached the bar. He needed his heart to calm and his adrenaline to dissipate before he headed over to the table. He hadn't realised how difficult being here would be. He had expected it to be difficult to return to the art building in two weeks' time but they hadn't spent much time in the union outside of their first year - they found places they preferred in town for their second year – so he hadn't spared a thought for the memories it would invoke.

The bartender seemed glad for the interruption to his studies and eagerly leapt up to see to Will. It was late afternoon and Will was starving. He ordered a Coke along with a burger and chips. The bartender poured the Coke and Will joined the others. His adrenaline wasn't back to normal but it would have to do.

Beth stood to greet him as though they were old friends of years, not mere days. 'I'm glad you came.'

She stood aside to allow him entry into the booth. If given the choice, Will would have taken a seat on the edge, so that he had an easy point of exit, but Beth hadn't given him the option. He took a seat and she shuffled in beside him. He placed his glass down on the table but his hand didn't leave it.

There were two men sat across from him. Will recognised the first. He had seen him around the Art, Design and Media building, known to most as the ADAM building. He had a scraggly beard with a line of beer foam on the hair on his upper lip, and a bright red beanie hat sat casually on his head, despite the weather not having turned yet. As if his wardrobe was in argument with itself, his t-shirt had no sleeves, exposing thin, pale arms.

The second guy was practically a giant. He had to be nearing six-five and he was a hulking mass of thick muscle. He belonged in action movies, not a student union. He reminded Will slightly of a taller version of Craig, except for the cocky look on his face. He was big, and he was strong, and could break anybody he felt like, and he knew it. While Craig had been a bit of an outcast, as they all had been, the giant didn't look like he'd ever had trouble making friends. The popular dick, through and through.

'This is Ben and Daniel,' Beth introduced respectively. 'Guys, this is Will.'

Will raised a hand, hello, and quickly dropped it back to the table. His other hand gripped the glass a little tighter.

'Hey,' Ben said.

Daniel grumbled something that could have been hi, or could have just been a grumble for all Will could understand it, and then filled his mouth with a large gulp of Guinness.

'Daniel's doing sport science,' Beth explained. 'We lived with him in first year. And Ben's obviously on our course. He's in the middle bedroom upstairs, the one next to mine.'

'Yeah,' Ben said, 'But I'm not back until this weekend. I've come for a meeting with Stevie about this year's dissertation. He's worried about my skills as a writer, hah. Anyway, I couldn't stop by without meeting the new blood, while I'm here.'

Will nodded, tried not to let on his discomfort at the mention of Stevie Quentin.

'New blood?' Daniel laughed. 'Careful what you wish for, mate. This guy'll turn *you* into the new blood. He's a killer you know.'

Beth fake laughed until Daniel looked at her, and her face dropped into a death glare. Despite his size and cockiness, he dropped his gaze first and passed the moment with another glug from his pint. Will had learnt during their conversations in the dead of night that Beth had grown up with three brothers so, despite her mother's best efforts, had spent more time play fighting and getting dirty in the mud than she did playing with dolls. Her mother had managed to instil in her kindness and compassion but her brothers had made her a force to be reckoned with. She was also trained in kickboxing. Will didn't envy anybody who got on the wrong side of her.

'Apologise,' Beth demanded.

'The fuck for?'

Something thudded under the table and Daniel called out, looked at Beth, ready to pick a fight this time.

'Apologise, Daniel.'

He attempted to stare her down but he could see, yet again, that he was going to lose this particular battle.

'Well?' Beth said.

Daniel looked at Will, head down and face screwed up like a five year old and mumbled, 'Sorry.'

'That's better,' Beth said.

Daniel grumbled something Will didn't catch.

'She's right, Dan,' Ben said. 'That wasn't cool.'

Daniel shook his head, twisting that big meaty neck like a cork lodged in a bottle. 'I can't believe you're siding with him. You not heard what people say?'

'Yes,' Beth spat. 'We've heard. Since when did you start believing everything somebody tells you, huh?'

'When it's fucking true.'

'Yeah?' Beth looked at Will as though to confirm he was still sat there and hadn't miraculously disappeared in a puff of smoke. 'Then why's he not in prison, yeah?'

Something smashed and Will jumped out of his skin. Over at the bar, the bartender looked down at his feet, cursing the glass that was no doubt scattered around them that he would have to clean up. He sighed and turned away from it to grab a broom, and Will turned his attention back to the table. All three of them were looking at him.

Beth leaned close and asked, 'Are you okay?'

No, he didn't think he was. He could do with running through his exercises but he didn't want to freak them out by breathing strangely at the table with them.

'Fine,' he said.

Beth gestured to his glass, and said, 'I think maybe we should put something stronger in that. You could do with it to put up with morons like *this*.' She nodded toward Daniel.

'Fuck off,' Daniel snapped.

Unable to stop himself, Will thought of that night a year ago. 'I don't drink. Not anymore.'

Daniel looked up and smirked. 'What's the matter?' the giant asked, already laughing before the punchline. 'You scared you might lose control and kill your friends again?'

'Whoa, what the fuck Daniel?' Beth screamed. The bartender turned from his cleaning up, eyes wide. At this time of year, drama must have been far and few between.

Ben flared, first red as though he were going to erupt greater than Vesuvius, and then he sighed, looked down at the table, shook his head and said, 'Dude, I think you should go.'

Daniel kept his eyes on Will and acted as though neither Ben nor Beth had spoken.

'Don't worry, killer. You haven't got any friends left to kill.'

He burst into wicked, howling laughter and threw his head back like a werewolf at a full moon. Beth threw her own Coke into Daniel's face and his laughter stopped. His head dropped and he glared at her with building thunder. His neatly gelled hair unfurled into loose, out of place curls and dripped down his forehead. The Coke ran down his face and chest.

Everything was still and then he lurched for Beth. But Beth was out of the booth before he could reach her. Then Ben's hand was on his chest, keeping him back. The giant must have outweighed him by a few stone and it should have been like trying to hold up a breaking dam, but the presence of the hand, alone, settled the huge guy.

'I really think you should go, mate,' Ben said in his ear. Daniel continued to glare at Beth, then, without a word, turned away from them all, slipping out from behind Ben's hand, and stormed out of the bar.

Ben slowly took a seat and exhaled deeply. 'He's not normally like that,' he said, which Will doubted. Everybody would always see the best in their friends, even when there was evidence to the contrary, but Will didn't argue it.

Instead, he put on a weak smile and said, 'I think maybe we could all do with something stronger in our drink.'

Ben and Beth laughed but it was weak and empty, both of them unable to believe the actions of their friend. Will wasn't surprised. Ben and Beth were the minority. Even his friends' parents felt the same as Daniel.

Will had tried to reach out to them after the disappearance and only Nicole's parents answered him when he called. He wished they hadn't. They had answered only to tell him he was the reason their daughter was gone and to ask why he had taken her from them. Nicole's father, whom had previously gotten on well with Will, had told Will he hoped they locked him up and lost the key.

'Ben's right,' Beth said. 'Daniel's never acted like that before. Normally he's a good laugh. The only reason we don't live with him is because he's closer to the other guys we lived with in first year. I don't know what's with him today. I'm sorry it blew up in your face, whatever it was.'

The bored bartender brought Will his food and silently mopped up the spillage. Beth followed him back to the bar to order a replacement drink. As Will ate, Beth and Ben discussed their summers, which, excluding a family holiday to Lanzarote for Ben, and a disastrous hockey game for Beth and her brothers that resulted in two lost teeth and a broken nose, none of which were Beth's, were mostly uneventful.

Will listened while he filled his stomach and learnt how vastly different Ben's upbringing was to his own. Family, Ben had been raised to believe, was the most important thing and he was close enough to his parents that he talked to them in some form every day and skyped them every other day. His mother was an architect, his dad a woodworker, and while neither of those were completely in line with graphic design, they were greatly involved in harnessing Ben's skills and his degree, but supported him in being down to earth and not too serious, too.

When asked, Will offered little information about his own family, mentioning only that he lived with his mother and step-dad and that he used to have a brother. He didn't tell them how David had died, nor the effect it had on his mother.

'You always so quiet?' Ben asked.

Will shrugged. He wasn't sure if it was an accusation or not.

'Your therapist must really earn her money,' Beth said with a nudge. 'Getting you to open up must be like getting blood from a stone, yeah?'

Will couldn't help but laugh. They all did. It felt good after the tension of their run in with Daniel. But the incident still hung heavy over them as he ate, and they tried to talk about anything else.

When he was finished, Will pushed the plate gently away from him and said, 'I didn't... I didn't kill my friends.'

Beth squeezed his shoulder. 'We know you didn't, sweetheart.'

6

After the letter he had received, along with the interaction with Ben and Beth's former housemate, Will had been a little more than shaken up. He had forced himself to continue with his routines – they were what got him through each day without an episode – but he couldn't shake the thought of the letter's meaning, nor the worrisome facts of its delivery. As he left for his run the next morning, he looked around for anybody who might have been watching, waiting for him to depart so they could post another note through his door.

His first thought was of the man who had been stood outside the potential drug-dealer, possible prostitute's house across the road, but the street was completely empty. It was the same on Wednesday. He allowed himself to feel as though the note was a one off, meant to shake him but nothing more – although an internal voice argued that the note contained information nobody outside his therapist and the police should know – and during the rest of each day, he continued as normal. It was an isolated thing, somebody trying to get a rise out of him but he wasn't going to let that happen. Not this time.

His days were spent drawing alone in his room. Back at Ian and his mum's, he had had to draw in the living room where Ian could keep an eye on him, but here in his new house, there was too much to distract him and he couldn't keep his attention on the art therapy. He had never had issue with focus before but since the disappearance it took a greater deal of effort to keep his attention on the page for very long.

The drawing was followed by a skype call with Ian on

the evening, and he spent his nights in the living room with Beth, watching tv and talking when sleep was ripped from them or never arrived.

On Thursday morning, he repeated the wary glance around the street as he left for his run. A figure in a hoodie passed by the end of the road, hood up, which would have seemed suspicious in the countryside but was commonplace here no matter the weather. The figure passed without a glance up the street and then he or she was gone. Will could see nobody else and so he closed the door and started to run.

He went back to the park and stared at the gate as he did each day, willing his mind to open up the secrets that it held of this place. It didn't, and as he always did when he turned back from the park and headed back home, he feared it never would.

When he returned home, he paused for a moment at the door, his key in the lock and his hand on the handle, and he closed his eyes. A slither of fear worked its way inside him, and he was certain he was going to open that door and see a bright white envelope lying by his feet on the doormat, a single sheet of folded card inside.

Roll up...

He imagined in his mind an empty porchway. No letters, no cards, as though visualising it would will whatever might be lying there on the mat to spontaneously combust before he could discover it.

Finally, he opened the door, and opened his eyes. Empty blue carpet met his gaze. He let out a sigh of relief and headed inside, feeling light. Beth called to him from the kitchen. He headed straight in, almost bouncing on the balls of his feet, he was so relieved.

She stood at the kitchen counter, waiting for the toaster to pop. She had a smile on her face but the smile on Will's face was short lived. In her hands was a bright white envelope, already half open. He could only watch as she pulled out a piece of card as bright as the envelope.

She frowned at it, turned it over again to see if she'd

missed anything.

'This is weird,' she said. 'I found it by the front door. There wasn't even an address on…'

She looked up and noticed how pale and unsteady he looked, as though he were about to collapse. Her eyes went wide and she tossed the card and the envelope down on the table.

'What's wrong?' she asked, and guided him over to one of the dining chairs and made him sit.

He couldn't stop his eyes from tracking over to letter on the table. He had to know what it said. It had landed face up and it took only a glance, then his world felt as though it was falling away.

It read:

… Roll up.
Do you dare?

He could hear the screams and the bells and an eerie, distorted music as though listening through water.

Will's breath caught in his throat.

'Will, what's wrong?' she asked.

He shook his head. 'Nothing. I'm fine.'

She appeared at his shoulder. 'You don't look it.'

Sharing his feelings didn't come easily, especially now he didn't know who he could trust, but he had so far got on well with Beth. She didn't express any interest in talking about what happened to him unless he wanted to, and she had even defended him against Daniel. She had seen the card and she had seen his reaction before he had even lain eyes upon the words; he owed her an explanation, and if he didn't offer one, her mind would run as wild as his.

Without explanation, everyone eventually invents their own.

'It was meant for me. I got one just like it on Monday. That one just said "Roll Up".'

She placed a hand on his shoulder and stroked it gently. 'What does it mean?'

He looked up at Beth and bit his lip, afraid to speak the words again and have yet another person refuse to take him seriously. He didn't want Beth to think him crazy. If he stayed silent that was exactly what she would think.

'It's the only thing I remember,' he said. 'We were on the steps outside the museum, and then I remember flashes of a fairground and I remember being afraid.'

'I didn't know there was a fair that night.'

'There wasn't. The police said so. But knowing there wasn't really a fair doesn't stop me remembering it. I can remember a voice, almost a whisper in my ear, calling out to me. It said, "Roll Up, Roll Up."'

She mulled it over and he felt sure she was going to ask about the words, and the man who spoke them. He had said enough to tie his stomach in a knot and put her opinion of him at risk, and he didn't want to tell her about *him* – the Crooked Man.

Instead, she asked, 'So what, the police think you made it up?'

He shrugged. 'Dr Phillips thinks it's possible I misremembered as a way to cover up something more traumatic.'

Dr Phillips's explanation returned to him. *'Fairs are places of fun and joy, and it would be more comfortable for you to think you went somewhere like that instead of the traumatic events that really occurred.'*

Beth was quiet for a moment. 'She thinks you made it up? That's insane. Isn't she supposed to be there to help you, not call you a liar. I mean I know I don't know psychology – I'm not smart enough for that, I mean, that's why we're designers, right? – but it doesn't seem to me like that's going to make you feel better to call you a liar. It's a bit…'

'Beth,' Will said, stopping her.

She nodded. She had a tendency to ramble on if nobody stopped her, a habit she was well aware of but unable to combat.

'Right. What do *you* think?'

Will looked at his hands and shrugged. 'Dr Phillips said she believes *I* believe the memory but that doesn't mean it's true. I'm not supposed to think about it.'

'Why not? How are you going to remember if you don't think about it?'

'I'm not,' Will admitted and it felt like giving up, like admitting to a heinous crime.

'What, ever?'

Will shook his head. 'It's unlikely. Dr Phillips thinks its healthier to look at the future instead of the past.'

'So there's nothing you can do?'

Will's head was shaking before the question was finished. 'If there is, she's not willing to consider it. She thinks the memories are gone, just like my friends.'

Beth reached past him and picked up the envelope from the table. She waved it in front of him and said, 'What if you tell her about this? Won't that convince her?'

He doubted it. If she thought there was a threat of any kind, she would fear another episode and he would find his time here cut short before he ever made it back into the design studio at the university.

'I don't know,' was all he said.

Beth looked at the envelope, her face thoughtful. 'And this is, what? Somebody trying to scare you?'

He nodded. 'People still blame me.'

'People like Daniel,' she said, nodding. She didn't turn her eyes from the envelope and Will could almost see the cogs in her mind working.

She looked at him with a curious look in her eye, and a smile. She said, 'I have an idea.'

7

Will boarded the bus and made a beeline for the back seat, where nobody could sit behind him. He scanned the faces of all who climbed aboard after him. There were no faces he recognised and nobody's attention lingered too long on him, but he didn't allow himself to relax too much. To let his guard down was foolish.

Eventually, the bus arrived in Newcastle and Will could breathe, for a moment. While everybody climbed off, he worked the stiffness out of his muscles and only once the bus was empty did he get off. He kept his head down and headed to Dr Phillips's office. He thought about the letters in his pocket.

When he reached the building and headed up to the correct floor, he entered a waiting area with chocolate coloured walls and rich, cream carpeting. There were plush chairs around the edge of the room, even though there would never be any more than a single patient waiting. Hanging on the walls were large paintings of woody landscapes. The whole thing was designed to be as far from the clinical coldness of a hospital waiting room as possible but the stack of magazines on the coffee table in the middle of the room, along with the large plaque in the centre of the only other door, which read Dr Phillips MD, were unavoidable reminders of what this place was.

Fixed to the wall on one side of the room was a computer screen with a welcome message across it. Will pressed it and, when prompted, entered his first and last initial followed by his date of birth. The screen faded to white and *Welcome Will, Please take a seat,* faded in across the screen.

He did as he was told, and wondered as he always did, if in ten years there would be any kind of person-to-person customer service left. Would his therapy even be with a person, or would he be forced to talk to a computer who would run his life issues through an algorithm to determine the correct response?

Would his memories still be missing, along with his friends?

He sat with his hands clenched in his lap and stared at the painting hanging beside the office door. It depicted a broken tree in the woods. Each visit, he would stare at it, trying to decipher if there was supposed to be some meaning to it or if it was just a painting. There were times he felt it was a representation of himself particularly on those days when he felt so broken he could never be fixed, but there were days, more frequent as the past summer wore on, when the broken tree was the furthest from his own well-being. He was returning back to something resembling whole, while the fallen tree would rot and wither away.

Dr Phillips had worked hard with Will to assure him that he could be fixed, although he may never be whole in the sense of his memory. If he was supposed to be a tree, then his memories were to be considered branches that had fallen away and while he could grow new branches, those ones would be lost forever.

But he didn't know if he could accept that.

Dr Phillips poked her head out into the waiting room and invited him in. She offered a warm yet professional smile, the kind that let him know she cared but that if he saw her on the street, he was under no circumstances to approach her.

She closed and locked the door behind them. There was another door on the other side of the room through which her previous client had left and through which Will would leave in an hour's time.

Dr Phillips's office was not like the psychiatrist offices in the movies, where the lights are turned down low and a

Chaise Longue stretches out across the room, for patients to lie back on and stare at the ceiling, dramatically telling their deepest darkest secrets, while the doctor asks them 'how does that make you feel?' It was light and open, with a large window across the left wall, illuminating oak bookshelves and an oak desk. In the corner of the far wall, far enough from the window so the patient wouldn't be distracted by what was going on outside, was a small sofa, beside which sat an armchair, turned so Dr Phillips could be both beside him and facing him.

The room could easily have been a home study instead of a medical practitioners office.

Will took a seat on the sofa and Dr Phillips her usual place in the chair.

She looked at him through her pink tortoise shell glasses and said, 'It's good to see you, William. And a little more alert than last time. Are you sleeping better?' Her pen was poised over a notebook.

'A little,' he said, although he wasn't sure that was strictly true.

She nodded, wrote something down. 'Have the nightmares settled down?'

She looked at the point where her dangling pen met the page and waited for him to answer. When he didn't, she looked at him.

Will said, 'No.' The answer felt like the wrong one, even though Dr Phillips had persistently told him that there were no wrong answers, except untruthful ones.

'Is there any change to them?'

'No. It's always the Crooked Man coming for me.'

She nodded and wrote something down before moving on with their usual run of questions. The same ones every time, usually with the same answers.

Then she asked, 'How have the past few days been?'

'Okay.'

'And things with your new housemate? Beth, is it?'

Will became still a moment at the mention of Beth and

his eyes brightened a touch. 'We've been getting along well. She likes to talk.'

She made a couple of notes on her pad and nodded. Now he was giving her the right answers, he thought.

'And have you been talking, too? I know you're not one for many words but I hope you're not leaving this young woman to do all of the talking?'

'Some.'

'Have you talked to her about your family? Or your friends?'

'A little. I met Ben, too.'

'Another housemate?'

He thought of what had happened at this particular meeting and cursed himself for opening that door when he had such a pressing matter for discussion. He had the majority of his hour still remaining but the letters were itching to be revealed.

He opted not to mention the incident unless asked, and nodded.

'How did the two of you get on?'

He thought of Ben's hand pressing against Daniel's chest and said, 'Good, I think.'

'Very good.' The pen scurried across the page in large, hurried scrawls. 'Remember your breathing exercises if things get a little too stressful. Being put into a situation where you are required to get to know strangers can often be a scary experience, sometimes even claustrophobic. For somebody with your particular set of circumstances–'

Blah, blah, blah, and on, and on. Back to the same old questions.

'Now,' she moved on, 'I understand Beth has not asked you about your disappearance but I want you to keep in mind that she still might. If that happens, it's important you stay calm and answer that you don't remember.'

'But when will I be able to give another answer? What if we could find a way for me to remember?'

Dr Phillips sighed and put down her pen, looked directly at Will. 'We've been over this. In a case of dissociative amnesia such as yours, it's possible the memories may never return. They might return over time, but it's been almost a year and yet you still remember nothing about that night except for a fairground that didn't exist. I'm not optimistic. I know that's not what you want to hear. I understand you want to remember because of the guilt you feel. But you are not responsible for whatever happened to them, and yourself. Remembering the traumatic events that occurred is not going to change that, or make it any easier to accept.'

He had heard it many times before. She had urged him over the past eleven months to focus on moving on, but his disadvantage, as she had once explained to him, was that he was aware of the blank space in his memory. Most people with dissociative amnesia, including those that included a fugue state, like Will's, weren't often aware of their missing memories unless somebody brought it to their attention. They could go on as though nothing were amiss. Will, however, had a memory gap of sixty hours brought almost immediately to his attention when he'd stumbled upon the newspaper, along with the knowledge that something bad had occurred during that time.

Had things been different when he turned back up, he might have lived his life like the others who had suffered the same condition, unaware of the missing time, aware only that his friends had gone missing. He might never have known he was involved in whatever befell them.

But that wasn't how things were, and Will knew his missing memories held the secret of what had happened to his friends. But not only that. They would explain the change to his outlook on living. He had been committed to his plans of suicide when the night started but when he turned back up a few days later, he possessed a will to live that felt conflictingly foreign. It was like the flicking of a switch but without knowing what flicked it, he couldn't understand it.

'What's brought this on? You haven't mentioned recovering your memories in months. I thought we were making progress.'

He stared down at his hands, thought again of that phone call with Nicole's parents all those months ago, and mumbled, 'I need to know what happened to them.'

'I understand your reluctance to consider the likeliest possibility. You've lost four extremely close friends, one of whom you were in a relationship with. One of the main steps of grief is denial and that can sometimes last for quite some time. There are some who are there when their loved ones pass who still can't accept it's happened afterwards. I'm not so sure knowing how your friends passed would help you accept that they're gone. That kind of progress comes from talking here and now.'

Will clenched a fist behind his leg. He hated when people referred to his friends in this way. He snapped, 'How can I grieve, if I don't even know what happened to them? I don't know that they're gone. And neither do you. Nobody knows anything because I don't remember.'

Dr Phillips wrote something down on her pad before she replied. The scratch of her pen punctuated the quiet. She was probably writing he was mentally unstable or something similar. He hadn't meant to come at the subject with such anger but it had happened now and there was no going back.

Remaining calm, she asked again, 'What has brought all this on, William?'

He removed the letters from his jacket pocket and held it out for her. He had placed both cards into one envelope for ease. Dr Phillips took the envelope warily and pulled out first one card and then the other.

'They came on Monday and this morning.'

She nodded as she read them. 'Is it the wording that affected you, or the arrival of them as a whole?'

He swallowed. His throat and mouth were growing dry from all this talking. He didn't know how Beth managed to say so much without a glass of water constantly at her lips.

Finally, he said, 'Those words are pretty much the only memory I have, and you tell me it's not real. But I don't know what is real.'

There hadn't been a single day in the eleven months since the disappearance that he didn't think about his memories returning, of discovering what had happened to his friends. Hell, he spent a good hour of every evening searching the web for any possible shred of evidence of his friends showing up, looking at missing person reports, police social media and every news website he could find, both national and local, and he searched for any possible answer as to why he remembered a fair that left no shred of its being there. Nobody but him knew about this part of his routine, especially Dr Phillips.

'I *need* my memories,' he finished. He was becoming irate and animated. He could feel himself moving without thinking about what he was doing and only when Dr Phillips's hand appeared on his shoulder and he slowed, did he realise he had felt the same way he had that day in the kitchen at his mum's, grasping for the sharpest knife in the block and brandishing it before him as he cowered from Ian. His hands were clasped tightly around the edge of the sofa cushion beneath him.

'Breath, William,' she ordered, and removed her hand.

He did as he was told and a minute later, his hands had unfurled and he felt calmer, but his entire body felt heavy from the near-episode.

'You've let these notes get under your skin, haven't you?' she said, once he was calm. 'Remember that's what the sender wants, okay? He or she wants to rile you up because they'll know the fair was disproven. They're goading you with these because there's no greater reminder of your missing memories than something you remembered incorrectly.'

'But how can I know that if I don't remember what happened?'

'Because the police told you so, William. They found no evidence of any fair having been in that park. Nobody living near the park could remember there being one, either.'

He shook his head, hurt that she had written it off so easily.

'That doesn't change what I remember.'

'I'm sorry, but your memories might never return to you and the focus of our therapy sessions is on shaping a positive future. Memories don't work like in the movies. We can't know where you're going in the last scene of your memories and press play, and have the whole thing keep on going. Recollection is often complicated and fuzzy.'

She watched him for a minute, probably trying to work out if she had convinced him. She hadn't. She went on, 'Think of the first time you met Nicole.'

He didn't want to think of something so bittersweet, but he did. He saw her sat on the worktop in their first year kitchen, all in black, right down to her lipstick, and the way she smiled across the room at him.

'Now tell me what you remember.'

'She was beautiful, sat there in our kitchen,' he said. 'She stood out from all of us, all in black. The others had looked at her nervously, like she was going to perform a ritual to Satan or something, but she was so cheerful and she smiled at me.'

'What did she say?'

'I don't know. We all talked about ourselves. But we really connected.'

'Do you remember what she was wearing, specifically? Or what you learnt about her life on that day?'

He tried to, but he couldn't. He could remember so much about her, right down to the way she took her coffee – two sugars and the tiniest dash of milk – or the way she chain smoked when she was nervous; the way she held her cigarettes all the way down at the webbing between her index and middle fingers, and how it made her practically hold her chin in her hand in order to take a drag. He remembered that she'd grown up in Chessington in London, that she'd got on well with her dad but not her mum; how everything in her bedroom had been pink, including her clothes, until the age of ten when she decided she wanted it all black and red. He could remember it all without hesitation but he couldn't remember when she told him any of it.

'The point of that little exercise, William, was to show you how your memories are never clear. It may have happened as you say, with Nicole smiling at you across the room and you feeling a connection form, but your memories may have been skewed slightly by the relationship you later shared, as well as all of the things you learnt about her over time. Memory is not an exact sequence of facts and events. They are ever changing based off other experiences and knowledge.'

'But what about repressed memories?' he asked, timidly. It was all he had left. 'Don't people recover memories of abuse and stuff during hypnotism?'

Dr Phillips's lips formed a thin line and she became stern. 'Hypnotism is a dangerous practice and it is unethical.' The insult he had caused was clear and he half expected her to end the session right then and force him to leave. 'I will not practice it, nor will I even entertain the idea. Understood?'

He nodded, a scorned child, and he wished she *had* ended the session. The comforting dynamic between them had been sliced in two and he felt disconnected. A stagnant silence settled between them that neither wanted to be the one to break.

Eventually, she said, 'You've made great progress this past year, William. But there are going to be some challenges up ahead, particularly when you return to university in a couple of weeks. Stressing over these missing memories will only strain your mind even further. The last thing we want to do is to risk another episode. It's okay to miss your friends. I know you don't remember what happened but that doesn't mean the loss you feel is any less real. I'm sorry, but I don't think you're ever going to remember what happened to them.'

8

Empty spaces accompanied Will all the way back to the bus station, as though somebody had cut the silhouettes of his friends from the very fabric of space. Even as he walked through the crowds of the busy city streets, he could feel the emptiness where they would have walked beside him, so close he could have reached out and touched them.

The next bus back to Treevale wasn't for another fifteen minutes, yet there was already a large mass of people gathered at the stand. There were no spare seats left and people hovered around them, awkwardly waiting to swoop in if any were vacated. A futile effort given they were all likely awaiting the same bus. Will found a space against the wall opposite the bus stand and leant against it.

Although they took up no physical space, the negative figures of his friends, they weighed a great deal atop his mind and he slowly sank to the floor, his head in his hands.

It went against caution to draw attention to himself in such a public place, as though he were asking people to look at him, to recognise him, and to accost him for what they believed he did to his friends, but he couldn't help it. If they were going to accost him, then so be it. Let them come, he thought. So far as he knew, they might have been right. He didn't think so, not really. But that didn't mean they weren't right to hold him responsible. He had, after all, led his friends away from that museum and toward what happened to them.

Had his behaviour not been so out of character on the night of the disappearance, and had he not recently attempted to commit suicide, they surely would have shot down his suggestion of leaving the exhibition, and, in the end, convinced him to stay, too.

Will had always been a good student. He attended every class, even those that were optional. He was always the first to be ready in the morning, the last to call it a day and go home at night, and he never missed a day if he could help it. He had been branded a nerd, a geek, a bookworm, a lame-arse, and the like throughout his life, but it hadn't really bothered him because he actually enjoyed doing the work and the success of it mattered to him. He attended guest lectures every chance he got and always had a question. The Will they knew would have been there until the end, and even tried to shake the designer's hand.

And so he had known to leave the exhibition as it had only just begun would concern them enough that they'd follow. He had counted on it. Had he not manipulated them then they would still have been around today.

He could recall the moments on the steps of the museum and the way they had looked at him to decide what they were going to do, as though he were their new leader of sorts, instead of Craig. He could remember Julian telling one his untrue stories nobody could tell if he actually believed, and he could remember them all laughing at this sign things could return to something resembling normal. He could see all six foot one of him, towering over them all from the top step as Will started down them and, with a crushing weight, there came the flood of memories, not of what happened next, but of what had come before.

He remembered the kitchen of their second year house, Julian flitting from counter to counter. They had all moved on from the processed frozen food they'd lived on in first year – besides Craig, whose diet had always been slightly more disciplined – and were now all eating meals made fresh, and Will remembered the way Julian acted like he knew what he was doing, but was always oblivious to the meat in his pan turning black and crispy.

He told them stories about what he cooked for his girlfriend back home, a girl that none of them had ever met in the two years they'd known him, and whom Will still had not witnessed the existence of in the aftermath of their disappearance. Will could almost hear Julian's voice floating to him in the bus station, from the empty space where he should have been.

He was surprised to find himself remembering Julian and feeling his absence hit so strongly. He and Julian had not been close the way Will and Craig had been, or Will and Nicole. They had been great friends but they rarely spent time together without one of the others present, and there were times when Will actually got quite irritated by the constant flood of untrue stories. He was never sure whether Julian just enjoyed telling stories or if he actually believed some of them, so he always kept from arguing the point when they started to grind on him.

So focused he had been on his routines and his exercises and moving forward, he had almost forgotten how unpredictable grief really was – because he *was* grieving, no matter what he'd told Dr Phillips. He thought of his friends all the time but he could go long stretches of time in which he didn't feel their absence as a crushing weight. And then something would happen or somebody would say something that reminded him of one or all of them and it was like a hammer to the side of the head.

Not a month ago, in the break between two programs on tv, through which his mum decided to use the bathroom instead of fast forwarding, Will noticed an advert for a horror film.

He had thought, *Nicole would love that.* And *Wham!* He was struck with the overwhelming recollection that she was still missing, and she might never get the chance to watch that film, or any film, for that matter.

Nicole loved horror movies, while Will hated them, and always had. Since the disappearance, he hated them even more, because now they didn't just scare him, they smacked him with grief.

He should have been an expert by now, he thought.

The bus arrived and he climbed on, taking a seat, as always, at the back, but he didn't pay much attention to the others aboard. They were all paying him more attention than he would have liked, enough to normally make him suspicious, yet he had just climbed from the floor where he must have looked like he was crying his eyes out.

He should have been an expert, he thought again. He had been through it all when his brother died. Yet he still couldn't see the tricks of his own mind coming. Couldn't see the triggers of grief approaching and avoid them. And he was always left surprised by them.

Thoughts of his friends and that hole inside of him stayed with him the whole way back to Treevale. The only relief came in leaving behind his fellow passengers. Rain was starting to fall from the sky, which had remained grey almost since his arrival in town days ago. He rushed through it with his head down.

He wasn't able to fully tear his focus from the empty hole in his heart until he rounded a corner just before his street and saw the man stood at the end of his street, hovering. It was the same man he'd seen on Monday morning. From where Will stood unseen, he looked more closely at the man than he had been able on Monday.

He was in his late thirties or early forties. It was hard to tell because of the rough unshaven cheeks and unkempt hair. To match, his clothes were scruffy and torn. He wore a dark denim jacket with rips in places that couldn't be by design. The stub of a cigarette protruded from between his lips. While Will watched, the man stomped it under his shoe, and pulled out a fresh one and lit it. It reminded Will of Nicole chain smoking when she was stressed.

There it was again.

Wham!

Even in the panic of finding somebody lurking at the end of his street, grief found a way.

It was possible the man was waiting on the prostitute-drug dealer woman, as it had seemed the other day but then why was he stood at the end of the street instead of at her door. Why was he stood directly in the now pouring rain, instead of under the awning of any of the doorways along the terraced street. Will didn't like the look of him or his presence here. It unnerved him, especially considering all that had been going on already and Will didn't want to be seen by him.

The house was near the middle of the row of terraces. The back of each house led into a locked alleyway where the bins were stored, for which none of them had a key, which meant Will's only way into the house was through the front door. He had no other option but to allow the rough looking man to see him. Walking a little too fast, Will stormed toward the street and up towards the house. As he came into view, the man's eyes locked onto him and he watched Will, taking a long drag of his cigarette, all the way to the front door.

As he worked the key into the lock, he was overly aware of the man's gaze. Only once he was through the front door did he feel any better.

'Hello?' Beth called, groggy, from the living room.

'Hey,' Will said without moving from the door. 'There's somebody watching me.'

There was a pause and then Beth came out into the hall to join him. Her eyes were puffy as though she'd either just woken up or just stopped crying. Or both.

'What?' she said. 'Who?'

'I don't know. I don't recognise him. He was here on Monday too.'

Beth stepped past him, without giving any consideration to how sodden his clothes or hair were. She opened the door and rushed out into the rain. He peered out after her. She looked around and, seeing nothing, looked back at him, questioning. She didn't seem to care about the quickening drops of water striking her from all angles.

'Down there,' he said, pointing.

She looked, shook her head. She walked into the middle of the road and looked again, for good measure, before returning to the hallway and closing the door.

'Whoever it is, he's gone now.'

Beth walked back into the house and shook water from her hair with her hands. Will followed her as she headed through to the kitchen.

'Are you okay?' he asked. He had assumed the puffy eyes were from sleeping, given Beth's irregular sleeping habits but she was quieter than normal. He thought he might have walked in on her crying. She leaned into the bathroom at the end of the long kitchen and emerged with a grey towel, which she used to rub dry her hair. She had only been outside for a short time but her red hair was wet through.

'I'm alright. Don't worry about me,' she said. She handed Will the towel and gestured for him to use it. As he ran it over his head, she asked, 'Why would somebody be watching you?'

Will shrugged. 'For the same reason Daniel accused me of...' He cleared his throat. 'It's the anniversary coming up. People will be interested again.'

They were both silent for a spell, then Beth said, 'How did it go with the doctor?'

Will didn't want his concern to be dismissed so swiftly but it was clear she didn't want to discuss it.

He dropped his head and shook it. 'She won't help me remember.'

Hypnotherapy had been Beth's idea and she was as disappointed as he was at the rejection of it.

'You're joking?'

'No. She wouldn't even think about it.'

'Why not?'

'She says memory is unreliable and hypnotism is unethical.'

Beth placed her yogurt on the arm of the sofa. 'That's

bollocks. My friend Amanda is going to be doing a dissertation about hypnotherapy. She's been researching it for the past year. It's where I got the idea from. It's a pretty common practice for like repressed memories and stuff. I mean, if your therapist won't try it, I can ask Amanda if she will? She's starting her third year at the same time as us, yeah? So I know she's not like finished her degree and everything but she knows a lot and she's like the smartest woman I know. She…'

She continued trying to justify and defend this friend, as though Will had outright refused.

He nodded. 'Ask her,' he said.

9

Beth's friend Amanda agreed to help and they set a time for seven o'clock the following evening. The possibility of finally getting some answers filled him with excitement, but he had the worst night sleep in months as his excitement leant toward fear and anxiety.

As day broke, he was awarded no respite. Even as he struggled through his morning run and returned home to find no further notes lying on the doormat, he was unable to settle. He couldn't stay in one place and couldn't focus on anything – more so than usual. Beth had some CVs to hand out and Will's fidgeting and pacing got so bad, she practically dragged him out of the house to join her.

Given the weather of the past twenty four hours, Will expected the streets would have been empty and reluctantly agreed. The rain had stopped sometime that morning – although the sky remained a thick and depressing grey – and so the streets, although collecting water where the pavements were most uneven, were a great deal busier than he expected. To his relief, people seemed to pay him and Beth little heed, possibly because they didn't care but Will thought it more likely that Beth's presence made him stand out less. Still, it was an effort to not let his discomfort show and he caught himself more than once, even before they reached the first business for Beth to submit her CV to, with his head down so as to keep his face from view.

For a time they walked in silence until Will felt the need to speak, if only to distract himself from the itching touch of eyes creeping up his back.

'Why are you looking for a job?'

'Ha, I know right. Like, when am I going to have the time?' Beth chuckled, humourlessly.

Beth had already admitted that she had spent the majority of her second year the way he had, which meant spending almost every hour of the day slaving away in the studio, working on her projects at the sacrifice of her sleep – 'What sleep?' she had joked – and a portion of the social aspect to university. Although Will hadn't gotten as far as actually starting his third year, they both knew that it was going to be more of the same. A lot more. This was the year their degrees, and their futures, would depend on the most. It seemed crazy to be looking for a job that would take away precious time from her work.

'But I'll just have to make time, you know. I could do with a little extra money.' The words came out like they depressed her, as though she were really struggling for money. But she had plenty of food in the fridge, and there had already been a couple of amazon deliveries to the house since Will moved in, and it was only a couple of weeks until they were back at uni and their maintenance loans would come in.

Will asked, 'Do you need some help?'

Beth gushed gratitude but refused the offer. 'I'm not desperate by any means, but it's just nice to have a little bit more. For emergencies and stuff, you know?'

Will nodded, although he didn't know at all. He had controlled his loan with a strict budget, which allowed for nights out and spending on new clothes and games and books, but without coming anywhere near running out before the next loan day. Craig had been less careful, running out a week or two before the end of every term, leaving him with nothing for at least a month before the next payment, and Will had never been able to understand how he did it. He hadn't seemed to buy anything more than Will did but still he ran out. He figured Beth must have had the same knack for wasting money.

'Are you nervous?' Beth asked, changing the subject. 'About tonight, I mean.'

Will nodded.

'It is what you want, right? To remember? Because if not, we can call it off and just forget about it,' she said. 'Sorry, poor choice of words, but you know what I mean.'

'I do want to remember.'

'So is it because Amanda hasn't graduated yet, that you're worried? Because you haven't graduated either and you've designed things for real clients on the side, haven't you? I know I have. I did a little bit of freelancing over the summer and I was part of the Creative Conscience competition last year, which has actually been used by Oxfam. So think of Amanda treating you like freelance work. If we can create at a graduate level, then she can do the same, only in psychology.'

He shook his head. 'It's not that.' It was a concern, but it wasn't *the* concern. 'I'm afraid of what I'm going to say. Or not say.'

'Whether this works or not, it's better to try it than not to, right? And no matter what, you'll get no judgement from me. Or Amanda. Amanda's really nice. I think you'll like her as much as I do.'

To his own surprise, she made him feel better.

The anxiety was not squashed entirely but rather pushed to a deeper recess at the back of his mind where it could fester unobserved, until seven o'clock came and went and there was no sign of Amanda.

'Will you calm down? It's like you got bloody ants down there,' Beth said. 'She's coming. Don't worry.'

It was quarter past seven. Will had always been one for arriving on time, even before he started living his life as a series of schedules and routines, and he was growing increasingly more uncomfortable with every minute that passed without a knock at the door. There had been no messages to say she wasn't coming, but still, she wasn't here.

Will had already skipped out on a large portion of his

routines for the walk with Beth and was skipping further parts of it for this. Every second waiting was a second he should have been doing something else and, as Dr Phillips would no doubt say, a second closer to an episode.

Beth tried to convince him that Amanda was just a typical student and that she was never on time for anything. While Will could relate on behalf of his friends, whom had been in their own little world sometimes, irrespective of what was going on around them, it didn't make the wait any easier.

'She'll be here. She lives on the other side of the uni. It'll just be a little longer, I'm sure,' Beth said now, trying to set his mind at ease once again.

Amanda had, among others, including Daniel, lived with Beth, Ben, and Will's other new housemate, Xander, whom he had yet to meet, in their first year, but when the rest of the group split into two before second year, the three designers going one way and the rest going off into another shared house, Amanda had moved alone to a flat, which she now shared with her partner, Grace.

Grace wasn't a student and this time before the start of university was meant to be their quality time to spend together, so Beth had little room for argument when Amanda informed her shortly after returning from her and Will's walk that she would be forced to bring Grace along, which only added to Will's fear. He didn't know what was going to happen tonight and now there would be a tagalong. Could Beth promise this extra person wouldn't judge him for what he revealed tonight?

What was next, he thought, *they post an open invite on Facebook for a hypnotherapy session, so everybody can come and hear what really happened to the Treevale Five?*

As he waited, he couldn't escape the possibility she had had second thoughts. What if she had googled him and learnt what people thought of him, and come to the same conclusion? Had she changed her mind because she was afraid he would describe during the hypnotism how he killed them?

Beth placed a firm hand on his incessantly bouncing knee and he looked up to find her staring deep into his eyes.

'She'll be here,' she repeated. There came a knock on the door and she smiled. 'See? Told you.'

While Beth went to answer the door, he did his best to calm his movements and sit naturally. The result was closer to the rigid positioning of a poorly made waxwork. Down the hall, Beth welcomed their guests into the house and introduced herself to Amanda's girlfriend, who said hi in a way that made it clear she didn't want to be here.

'Hey you must be Will. I'm Amanda,' said the first woman to enter. She was pretty, with blonde hair tied messily at the back of her head. She was dressed in ripped jeans and a red plaid shirt. There was a smile on her face that lacked the cold professionalism of Dr Phillips. She proffered her hand. Will shook it. 'Beth told me a little about you. It's good to meet you.'

He wondered how long into her career she would lose that warmth and adopt a clinical demeanour. At what stage would she avert her gaze if she noticed a patient anywhere outside of her office, as he was sure Dr Phillips would?

'This is Grace,' Amanda said, and looked to the woman begrudgingly following behind. Her age was the first thing that stood out. She was in her late twenties or early thirties, and appeared older between Beth and Amanda's youthful faces, although she had made certain efforts to look as though she were still young. There were four inches of blue at the end of her long blonde hair and she was dressed in jeans and a hoodie with a leather jacket draped over the top, but Will thought she was trying too hard and it only emphasised her age. She took off her jacket and tossed it over the arm of one of one of the two leather sofas as though this were her own house. She didn't say hello.

She turned her narrow hook-nose up as she scanned the small living room. Like the rest of the house, the living room walls were painted magnolia, cheap vinyl flooring made to poorly imitate wood. The living room was furnished with two black leather sofas that were harder than they looked and a small table, upon which Beth or Ben or Xander had placed a television. No matter how hard Grace was trying to convince the world, and even herself, that she was still young, it was clear she despised their lifestyle, with a snobbery that could only come from somebody older.

'So,' Amanda said, and clapped her hands together. 'Do you want to be in here, or if you want to lie down and be comfier, we could go to your bedroom? I know from experience those sofas aren't comfy for about anything.'

She looked at Beth and the two smiled at some shared memory. Will couldn't deny that the sofas were achingly hard but he hadn't had a girl in his bedroom since Nicole. Even though Amanda was going to analyse his brain and not what was in his trousers, it still felt wrong.

'Here is fine,' he said.

'Okay, cool. Beth, Grace, if you two could wait in the kitchen with the door closed?'

'You're joking, right?' Grace snapped.

Amanda shot her a look. 'No. I'm not. Therapy is private.'

Grace huffed and marched into the kitchen. Beth followed but lingered in the doorway.

'You want a drink or anything, Manda?'

'If you wouldn't mind. Just some water, babes,' Amanda said. Through the open door, Will noticed Grace's face tighten. Beth poured a glass of water from the tap, handed it to Amanda, wished the two of them luck and disappeared behind the kitchen door.

Amanda took a seat on the other sofa, upright and ready.

'So, shall we start with your diagnosis?' she said. Straight to the point. Maybe she had the clinical coldness in her after all.

'Dissociative amnesia,' he said.

'Were there any drugs or alcohol involved?'

He nodded. 'Alcohol.'

'What about a head injury?'

He nodded again.

'And we're assuming, because of how long you were out and the fact your friends are still missing, a traumatic event?'

A third nod.

'A full house,' Amanda said with humour he didn't share. 'And how much is missing?'

'About sixty hours.'

'Wow. And none of it has returned in the past year?'

'No.'

'Okay, well, shall we see if we can change that? Have you ever been under hypnosis before?'

'No.'

'You believe in hypnotism?'

He shrugged.

'Because, if you don't, there's a high chance it might not work. If you're sceptical about it, you may be less susceptible to trance states.'

'I don't believe in the stuff they show on tv. But I believe in the therapy kind.'

'Good. Well let's get started. Sit back for me, and make yourself comfortable.'

He did as he was told.

'Close your eyes and listen to the sound of my voice. Take a deep breath in, and out. In. And out. You're becoming more relaxed. You feel yourself becoming weightless.'

10

('Take me back to the night you disappeared.')

We're at the Tremont Museum a couple of miles from the university at an exhibition for Charles King. Tonight is the opening night, and it's the first day of our third year of uni.

('Who is there with you?')

The whole class is here, as well as Stevie. He booked tonight for the third years and any interested second years because Charles King is going to give a talk on his work and answer questions and he thinks it will be good for our self-promotion modules.

('Your friends are there?')

My friends are all here. Craig, Nicole, Tom and Julian. We're watching Charles King start to talk but I'm not really listening. I'm talking to Craig about Nicole. I hurt her, broke her heart. I want to make it up to her, and to them, but I can't do it here at a boring exhibition.

('So what do you do?')

I suggest we leave. I have a bottle of vodka in my jacket pocket. I show it to them and head for the door, knowing they'll follow.

('Why did you want to leave?')

It's a special night. It's the first day of third year, their final year, and it's the first night I've seen them since my suicide attempt. Most importantly, it's the best chance I have of giving them a great night to remember me by when I'm gone.

('Gone? Where are you going?')

Once I've made my amends and given the four of them a night to remember, I'm going to slip away and end things.

('You're going to kill yourself?')

I only had two regrets when I tried in July. The first was that I failed. The fact I'm still here hasn't convinced me life is worth living.

('What's the second regret?')

The second is that I never said goodbye. I hadn't seen my friends for two months and their memories of me would be tainted by that. We should have had meaningful conversations near the end, shared some last great memories. That's what tonight is all about.

I convinced my therapist that coming back was about moving on with my life but it's really about tonight. I want one last night of fun with my friends, as a way to say goodbye without them really knowing, the way terminally ill people spend their final hours with loved ones, making the most of their time left.

('How do you know they will follow you out of the museum?')

Leaving is out of character for me. I regularly volunteer for optional lectures and I would never leave any of them until the end. I don't even look back to make sure they follow. I leave the building and they fall in behind me.

At the top of the stairs, outside the museum, they look at me, waiting. The look on their faces, it's as though they're waiting for me to start levitating. I do nothing out of the ordinary.

Howls, screams and cheers, the sound of exactly the type of fun I had in mind sing to me on the wind and we can see brightly coloured lights flashing and spinning in the distance. It's coming from the direction of Graham Park.

'Is that a fair?' Julian asks. 'I used to know somebody who lived in a fair, you know. Came to my school in the winter. Asked me once if I wanted to come with him for the summer.'

I laugh, and say, 'Sure you did.' Julian's nonsense breaks the stagnant silence between us and for a second, everything feels normal. Everyone is still staring at me, though, waiting for me to tell them what we're doing.

I take out the bottle of vodka and we pass it around. Then we set off down the stairs.

('You head for the fair?')

We follow the screams as they grow louder. It's like they're beckoning us nearer with the promise of fun and excitement. I feel a rush of exhilaration. No matter what, they will have a good night to remember me by.

('Do you talk as you walk?')

Julian insists he really did know somebody who lived at the fair. He says, 'His name was Doug. He worked an apple bobbing stall with his older sister, who was old enough to be allowed to handle the money. I would have gone, too, but my mam wouldn't let me. She said I was too young.'

Craig punches Julian on the arm and says, 'Maybe he'll be at this one and you can introduce us.'

Julian is so skinny that the punch sends him stumbling a few feet.

'What was that for?' he moans.

'Don't be a baby,' Tom says. The way he says it, it is as though it were he who had swung the punch and not Craig.

'I'm not being a baby,' Julian says.

'You are,' Tom says.

Julian shouts, 'Fuck off' and they both stop walking to face off against one another. Two polar opposite figures, a stick thin nerd towering in the mid six foots, facing down a five-four overweight guy with a wispy orange seventies moustache. We all stop and turn to take in the comical sight. Craig and Nicole sigh but it makes me smile.

They continue arguing and Tom shoves Julian. Julian is about to shove back when Craig steps between them. Craig's the unofficial leader of the group, not because he could kick any of our arses without breaking a sweat – although that helps – but because he speaks with a weighty authority.

('Is there anybody else around?')

It's just the five of us. Or I think it is. The noise of the fair gives us the illusion of there being others, and there's a feeling of being watched but I can't see who by.

('Where are you while all of this goes on?')

I'm left with Nicole. I look at her, allowing my half smile to fall away and I try to meet her gaze. Our eyes meet for only a second before she looks away and makes her hair fall over her face so I can't see her.

('She's angry at you?')

She has yet to speak to me since we left the museum. I never told her about my depression and definitely not what I planned to do about it. She was hurt, more than either of us know how to say. I wish I'd told her, but if I had, she would have stopped me.

('Do you either of you say anything?')

I make a joke about the guys being the 'same old guys'. Nicole shakes her head and says, 'Can we not?'

It is one of the first things she has said to me, not just tonight but since the attempt.

('How did she respond after the attempt?')

After I left the hospital, I tried to contact all of them. They were all reluctant but none more than Nicole. I don't know how many messages I sent before she finally replied to one of them. "Killed her inside" were the words she used.

Nicole is fascinated by dark and morbid things, but she's one of the most cheerful people I've ever met. Tonight is different. There's no cheer left and I don't know how to make it better. Until I can find the right words, I'm afraid we'll never get back to being more than friends. If we're even that any more.

('You separated?')

('What are you doing, Babes? I'm the only one meant to asking questions. Will you go back in there?')

('Sorry, I...')

We fell into our relationship and the way things feel, it's as though we've fallen out of it.

('Listen to my voice, Will. Follow it carefully, and only my voice. Listen to no other sound. Now, you're going to continue on with your night. You were heading toward the park. Do you continue to go there?')

There's darkness. I can make out the shapes of my friends beside me by the glow of distant lights. There's somebody else here in the darkness with us. His footsteps clap against the ground, coming closer. Between every other step there's a different sound, of something else striking the ground.

We look around at each other but we can barely make out the each other's faces. I can see it in them though. They're nervous. The man is close to us now. Coming toward us. He's coming *for* us. And there's nowhere we can go.

('Where are you, Will? Who is coming for you?')

He owns the fairground.

('Who? Do you know his name?')

The Crooked Man.

('Follow me, William. Listen to me very carefully. You are in no danger. You are in a safe place, from which you can watch events unfold. No harm can come to you in this place. Now, let's move backwards a little. Julian and Tom were fighting. How did you get to the park?')

Craig stops Julian and Tom from fighting and we set off walking again. We are not far from the park. The sound of the screaming and shouting and cheering is so loud. It is as though we are already there.

Nicole walks a few steps ahead, still not willing to let me see her face. I speed up, not to see her but to be near her, and our hands brush. She doesn't look at me but she doesn't move away either. Our hands brush again and she hooks my index finger with hers for a second and then she is gone.

('Where are you? Describe your surroundings.')

We're heading down a row of terraced houses, expensive looking ones with small front gardens with walls and metal fencing, and large windows, some of which are patterned. We turn a corner and we can see the lights of the fairground stretched out in the sky ahead. They're so bright and they glisten through a thin layer of mist like a mirage. I'm a man walking through the desert but what I crave is not water, it's fun.

('Fucking creative types. Can't you just say you see lights? Not everything is beautiful.')

('Grace. What did I just tell Beth? Absolute Silence. Get in the kitchen.')

The mist seems to move closer to us and the lights seem somehow brighter, blinding.

('Stay with the walk to the park. You're walking as a group. You can see the fair lights in the distance.')

The colours are bright and enticing in the sky ahead. We're close enough now to see the shape of some of the taller rides instead of just their flashing and spinning lights. Tom and Julian continue to bicker between themselves but they speed up when I quicken my pace and the excitement is enough to dampen their argument.

('What happens when you reach the fair?')

The screams are so loud as we turn the final corner. On the other side of the road stands Graham Park, closed off from us by seven foot tall black railings, like prison bars. There are four gates around the park. We follow the road along to the closest gate and then cross over to where two men stand. They're both dressed in large suits that look as though they belong in a different era. There are ruffles on their shirts that look Victorian. Across their faces they wear wide grins that stretch impossibly from one side of their face to the other.

And then...

Everything goes dark. The lights disappear and so do the men in front of us. There's a crooked doorway filled with a smoky green glow. A figure steps forward. It's him. He fills the doorway, he's so tall. He's made taller by the top hat on his head and as he reaches for the rim to tip toward us, an unnaturally elongated arm separates from the silhouetted shape of him, like a spider's leg. He leans forward to reveal a flash of his face in the green light. The hollows of his skull fill with shadow and a wicked smile stretches across his lips, higher on one side, as though he knows something I don't.

('Where are you now, Will? Are you at the fair?')

I am at the Crooked Man's house.

('This man took you home?')

It is his house, but he doesn't live here.

('What does this "crooked man" do?')

He pulls his face back into the darkness where he is only a silhouette again, and he whispers, 'Roll up, roll up.'

Then he is gone. Red replaces green, surrounding me in long strobes. I'm sat on a cold, hard floor, shivering. There's something wet on my hands. Everything is red in the light but I'm certain what covers my hands is really red. And it's everywhere.

('So he did kill them. Can we go now?')

So much blood. It's spattered across a table in the middle of the room and pooled on the floor all around me. And it's on my hands.

('Will, I'm going to count down from five and then...')

So much blood.

('On zero, I'm going to click my fingers and you're going to wake up.')

So much...

('Five. Four.')

It covers my arms.

('Three. Two.')

What have I done?

('One')

(Snap!)

11

Will's eyes snapped open. He was trembling but he couldn't understand why. He wasn't cold and he had been fine a second ago. Although it seemed as though it was a second ago. More than a second had gone by since he closed his eyes. Beth and Grace had been in the kitchen before, but now they both stood watching him.

There was a scowl on Grace's face but it contained a level of disdain and utter disgust that hadn't been there before. Beth looked at Will in a level of shock that bordered on terror.

He had actually been under hypnosis, and, for a moment, he had no idea what had been said or remembered. He had not awoken with a flood of memories as he'd expected. They drifted to him, slowly, like the recollection of a dream shortly after waking.

He looked down at his hands, expecting to find something on them but not knowing what. And then he realised. He realised before the recalled memories came back to him – his hands had been covered in blood as he had walked through the fields the morning he was found – and he knew he must have recalled what had happened to them, at least in part.

'Will?' Amanda said. She was sat where she had been before, when he had closed his eyes, but she wasn't relaxed anymore. She leant toward him, watching closely.

Will's face tightened into a knotted mask. He remembered the last thing he'd recalled. The blood, the red lighted room. He looked at her and asked, 'Did I kill my friends?'

Amanda turned to the other two women. 'Can I have a few minutes?'

They didn't question her, not even Grace who only a moment ago – or so it seemed – had been so resistant to everything. They headed back into the kitchen and the door closed behind them.

'How do you feel?' Amanda asked Will, once they were alone.

'Did I kill my friends?' he asked, again.

'What happened to your friends, I can't tell you. I'm sorry. When you reached the fair, your mind resisted. It pushed back, likely as a form of defence. So you were only able to reveal glimpses of what happened.' She placed a hand on his knee. It was cold and distant but it offered a slither of comfort. 'But no, I don't think you did. I know you cared about them. That much was clear from the way you talked about them when you were under. You sounded guilty for how you made them feel by not saying goodbye. I don't think you'd turn on them. I don't think you're capable of killing in cold blood.'

'You think I'm capable...' the words caught in his throat, 'if it wasn't cold blooded?'

She took a deep breath and let it out slowly. 'Those aren't the kind of thoughts you should be focusing on, I don't think. It'll put unhealthy ideas in your head.'

'You *do* think that.' It wasn't a question. Enough people had expressed the belief before but Amanda was different. She was studying psychology. Whatever she said could change the way Will saw himself and the disappearance.

She thought it over and said, 'I believe everybody is capable in the right set of circumstances. Most of us will never find ourselves in those circumstances but it's ingrained in our instincts. Mostly, it's about self-preservation, or the need to protect a loved one.'

They sat in silence for a minute before Amanda continued.

'We might not have found out what happened to your

friends, but we found out one thing for sure and that is, whatever happened, it happened at the fair.' She squeezed his knee and offered a smile before withdrawing. 'I'd like to come back and try again, if you're still interested? I have some stuff to do tomorrow but I can come back on Sunday night. I'll do a little bit of research in the meantime and work out a way we can skirt around your defences.'

Will agreed.

Amanda got to her feet. 'I'll come alone this time. I'm sorry about her.' She opened the kitchen door and called through that they could go home now.

'About fucking time,' Grace muttered. She slapped the glass dining table and climbed to her feet. She marched through the house without even a glance at her partner or Will. She was out on the street before Beth had reached the living room. A draught ran through the house and filled the living room with a September chill.

Amanda bent down and gave Will a quick hug. Startled, he slowly returned it. 'Nice to meet you, Will. I'll see you Sunday.'

'You're coming back?' Beth said, with more than a little longing.

'Yeah, babes. I'll see it through as far as Will wants to go.'

The two of them hugged, holding the embrace for a little longer than Will thought Grace would have liked. When they broke apart, they looked at each other for almost as long, until Grace shouted from the front door, 'Are you fucking coming or what?'

Amanda apologised for Grace again, and showed herself out. Before the front door closed behind them, both Will and Beth heard Grace start to shout.

'How could you make me sit in a room with *her?*'

They both pretended they had heard nothing.

Beth asked, 'What do you say we go get a drink?'

Will had already diverted enough from his routine with the hypnotherapy and he was reluctant to divert any further by going for a drink, especially considering he didn't drink alcohol. But his mind was spiralling. The fair had really existed, despite what he was told by the police, Ian and Dr Phillips. There was no evidence or record of it but it had existed. He *remembered* it. He wasn't sure what to think right now. He supposed a trip out to the pub would give him time for things to settle in.

He noticed the slouch of Beth's shoulders and remembered the way she'd looked yesterday, as though she'd been crying. He thought she could use the trip as much as he could.

His routines could wait a little longer.

12

From the gloom within his car, the man watched the house. His face was dimly illuminated by the ghostly glow of his phone screen, working as a cover in case anybody glimpsed him sat in his car, unmoving, as the night descended around it. Mobile phones were the most convenient and natural disguise for the modern world. Nobody ever questioned somebody hooked on their phone, even behind the wheel of a parked car.

The man was known to many as The Stranger, a name given to him by those who despised him and who he despised in return, due to his unlikability and inability – or perhaps just unwillingness – to connect with anybody else. He was the Stranger, he was once told, because, the way he treated those around him, even those whom had known him his entire life no longer knew him at all.

The name described him well and so he had taken it for himself, turning the insult into a badge of honour against all of those who had given it to him. He didn't need friends. He worked alone and his work was all there was for him now, all that was important.

A woman stepped out of the house, huffing and puffing and the Stranger watched. It was what he did best.

He had been watching William Campbell, the surviving member of what the media branded the Treevale Five – now renamed the Treevale Four in recent mentions – for days, patiently waiting for the kid to show him something. The kid remembered more than he was letting on, of that the Stranger was certain.

He had allowed himself to be noticed more than once

and he had observed a change in the young man's behaviours. It would not be long before something shook loose.

The Stranger had watched with growing interest tonight as two women arrived at the house. They were inside for around forty minutes before the older of the two stormed out in to the street and started huffing beside the open front door. He had been more interested in the younger woman, who seemed young enough to be a fellow student, when they had arrived but something had happened in there, a fight of some kind, and this older one was now a great deal more interesting.

A few minutes later the younger woman came out and closed the door. The two of them started arguing immediately as they started off down the street. The Stranger buzzed his window open a couple of inches and listened.

'You are *not* going fucking back. Are you kidding me?' the older woman said. 'What for?'

'We're not finished,' said the younger.

'He took his friends to a fair. And. He. Killed. Them. What more does he need to remember?'

So the kid remembered something after all. That was interesting. Very interesting indeed. He waited until the two women were at the end of the street, then climbed out of the car and followed.

He followed them a couple of miles across town and the argument grew hotter the further they walked. When they reached a large set of store fronts with luxury flats above them, the women stopped. The Stranger hung back. The stores were all closed so he stepped up to the curb and pretended to wait for a break in the traffic in order to cross the road.

Outside a doorway he presumed led up to their flat, the two women continued to argue. He couldn't hear what they were saying but he watched as the younger one stormed through the door and the older one started off down the street, marching like a pissed off soldier.

The Stranger followed the older woman. A few minutes later, she disappeared inside a pub. The Stranger waited half a minute and went in after her. She could be useful, he presumed.

13

They each headed for their bedrooms to get ready. Will changed into a smart checked shirt, buttoned all the way to the top. Once, he would have rolled his sleeves up to the elbow, but now, as with all his tops, his sleeves were kept long so as to keep hidden the red line along his forearm.

He met Beth back in the living room, her hoodie now replaced by a black t-shirt and leather jacket, leggings swapped for jeans. They didn't talk as they walked in the direction of the university. Will thought more than once about trying to start a conversation, feeling in the current situation an echo of his walk with Nicole toward the fair, but thought better of it.

On the other side of the campus, across the road from the Arts, Design and Media building where they had both spent so much of their time in the past and would spend much more in the future, was a pub called *Eastside*. It was a relatively small place where people primarily went for food, with only a select few visiting to drink. It had been a favoured place for Will and his friends when they finished up in the design studio in time for last orders. It was always quiet enough that they could decompress and disconnect from the work, although they often found themselves critiquing the labels on beer bottles, never quite able to switch off.

As Beth led them toward it, Will froze.

'You okay?' Beth asked.

Will shook his head and said, 'Yes.'

She gave him a look.

'We used to come here.'

That was all he needed to say. She nodded. 'You want to

go somewhere else?'

There was nowhere else, he thought, looking at the beer garden stretched out before the building, brightly coloured round wooden picnic tables, like the lights from the fairground. There were going to be memories of them everywhere. Remembering them would, at least, keep his mind from replaying the events of his newly recovered memories.

He shook his head and they headed toward the building. One of the tables closest to the door was red, which in the artificial lights brightening the garden, was much deeper than it would have been during the day. It appeared almost like blood. Like it could have been stripped straight from the room he'd remembered.

He tensed, but forced himself to go inside, away from the table and the flash of memory.

The pub was a ghost town. There was less than a handful of other customers filling the large space. It was furnished with an eclectic array of different seating and tables, as though it had all been bought at car boot sales, including high tables and stools, long tables and benches and old miniature sofas and armchairs, only two of which were taken.

Beth went to the bar, which was the only part of the pub that actually looked modern and consistent, and Will went off to find a seat. He found a table with a small black sofa on one side and a scuffed brown suede one on the other. He took a seat on the black one.

He looked over at Beth at the bar, and continued to track toward the pool tables on the far side. Craig and Julian played at that table any time they'd come here early enough to have a couple of games. Julian usually won and Craig, always too competitive, would argue Julian had an unfair advantage because of his gangly height and longer arms. A few feet from the pool tables were long tables with benches instead of chairs, where Will could remember them sitting along with a number of their class and some third years after the end of year exhibition. A couple of the tutors had joined them, celebrating the end of another year. One of their favourite tutors, Isabelle, a woman both harsh but constructive, announced it was her last day, much to everybody's disappointment. Nicole's especially.

The look on Nicole's face at the announcement made Will's heart ache, both then and now.

The memories were bittersweet, painful in the same way grief always is, but it was a better pain than remembering what he'd glimpsed under hypnosis. Before his mind could take him back to that dark place, Beth joined him at the table and placed a Coke in front of him. Her own glass was a large goblet filled to the brim with orange juice, although there was clearly something stronger mixed in. She took a long pull from the straw and looked at the glass, lovingly.

'I bloody needed this.' The way she looked at it, it was as though she had just experienced the first orgasm after a months long dry spell.

'Are you okay?' he asked. While he waited for her to respond, he swigged from his own drink. He couldn't remember having spoken very much tonight at all, yet his throat had turned to sandpaper and his gums cardboard.

She shrugged and nodded at the same time. 'Yeah, I guess. I mean, well, tonight was tough, you know?'

There was no doubting her statement to be true, especially after witnessing what he remembered from the end of the session, but he felt there was something more she was holding back.

'Being shut in the kitchen with that *bitch* was a nightmare. Sorry,' she continued. 'I don't normally talk about people behind their back but it was so awkward in there. There's no good blood between us. Even if she didn't look down her nose at me, and Ben, and Xander, we still wouldn't get on because of Amanda.'

Will thought of the way Amanda and Beth had held their embrace as though they might never see each other again. 'Babes,' Amanda called Beth, despite it clearly pissing off Grace.

'You were…?' Will started. He didn't know how to finish.

Beth nodded. 'How did you and Nicole become a couple?'

Reluctantly, because he didn't think she would start talking until he told her, he said, 'We sort of fell into it. We started spending a lot more time together just the two of us, even just watching tv in her room. Then after a night out, we all sat down in the living room and she cuddled into me. When the rest of the guys went to bed, she kissed me and then she went to bed too. From then, we became a couple.'

'That's not too far from what happened with me and Amanda. She told me she liked me one night in the first term of first year. I said I liked her too and we started going out, until part way through the summer. Four months is a long stretch of time to be hundreds of miles from each other, you know? What'm I saying? Course you know. Anyway, by the start of second year, she'd met Grace and by Christmas, they'd started going out. Grace knows about us and she won't let it go. Amanda and I are still friends but Grace is convinced I'm trying to steal Amanda back from her.'

Will wondered if maybe she would like to do exactly that, but said nothing.

'I'm happy for Amanda. I wish she'd found somebody that's not so snobby but I guess that comes with the territory of coming from London.'

Nicole had come from London and there had never been a more down to earth woman, without any sense of entitlement, a rarity among their generation.

'The posher parts, anyway,' Beth added, as though she had read his mind. 'Obviously, I'll always have feelings for her. She was the first girl I was ever with and there's something special about that you don't lose. So it sucks having to sit in *my* kitchen with *her* new girlfriend.'

Ten months together hardly made Grace new, but Will didn't comment. Beth's drink was almost empty. Her talking had only paused for her to take long draughts from the straw. Noticing how little was left, she tossed the straw down on the table, lifted the glass to her lips and threw back the contents. She slammed the glass back down with such a *thud*, it was a wonder the stem didn't crack in two.

Will took a sip of his own drink to moisten his mouth and lips. He needed to say something to keep her talking, because as soon as she stopped it would be his turn to talk and he wasn't ready to discuss what he had remembered tonight.

He said, 'When I came home yesterday...'

Her head dropped and she sighed. She had been waiting for this moment and, he suspected, hoping it wouldn't come.

'I'm fine.' She didn't sound as though she even convinced herself. 'I was just tired and a couple of things got on top of me at the wrong time. It's nothing really.'

He looked at her.

She huffed. 'I got a phone call from my dad. He's a bit of a shit. He's not around and he only comes around when he wants something. Usually money.' She chuckled but it was without humour. 'He's an efficiency manager, so he tells companies how to run better and manage their money. But he never seems to be able to take his own advice.'

She exhaled slowly and looked into her empty glass. Will could relate. He had issues with his own father, only one of the big issues was that he never came around, even for money. The guy had turned up to his oldest son's funeral but only because Will's grandfather had made him. When Will had tried to kill himself, and his grandfather was no longer around, his dad was nowhere to be seen. The same could be said for when Will disappeared.

She started playing with a beermat. 'It's more often now, past couple of years. Since I started uni. Used to be, he would come to me or my brothers not long after our birthday, 'bout a month later or something, when we'd still have some of our birthday money left, and he'd try and get us to loan him some. I was stupid enough to believe him a couple of times. Now that I'm at uni and have student loan and stuff, he's called a few more times. I stopped answering for a while but, I figured, this time, student loan doesn't come in for another few weeks so maybe it would be different. He knew I'd only have enough money to live off.'

She trailed off, which was unusual. It normally took a lot longer for her to run out of steam.

'It wasn't?' Will said, to get her talking again.

She picked at splintering piece of wood on edge of the table. 'No. It was the same as always. Worse even. He got married a couple of years ago. Not the first time. He's a gambler and sooner or later, he loses too big and fucks everything up. Things seemed to be going alright with this one. But he's lost his wife's savings and she threw him out. He asked for some money to try start paying her back so she'd take him back. Wants me to give him as much of my loan when it comes in at the end of this month as I can afford.

'When I said no, he started screaming abuse at me, blaming me for him being homeless and wifeless. Said if I ever loved him, or cared about him, I'd help him get his life back. Then he said he wished he'd never had me. That my brothers would say yes, because they were good kids.'

'I'm sorry,' Will said. In a way, he felt slightly thankful for the absenteeism of his own father. 'Is that why you're looking for a job?'

Beth laughed. It was a dry rasp, barely more than a breath. 'Yeah. I know everything he said isn't true, or at least, it's not something to take to heart. It's his problem not mine, yada, yada, yada.' She threw her hands in the air. 'But I still can't stop myself from feeling obliged to help him, even though I know I shouldn't. He'll probably not even use anything I give him to pay his wife back. It'll just be gambled away like the rest of it. But he's my dad, you know? As shit as he is, I still want him to love me and to feel I love him too.'

She buried her head in her hands for a second, then ran her hands through her hair. 'Fuck. I sound like such an idiot. He really knows how to push my buttons. You must think I'm a real sucker for even thinking about giving him money.'

Will shook his head. 'You can't choose your parents.'

Beth shrugged. 'No, I guess not. So what about you?'

Will shrugged. He had done enough talking for one night, and the subject of his own father and hollow home life was something he didn't want to go into. It had all contributed to his decision to kill himself a little over a year ago, and it was something he still had not delved too deeply into with Dr Phillips, particularly his father's absence.

'Do you want another drink?' he asked.

She forced a smile onto her face but it failed to hide the sadness she felt. 'Yeah. Yeah, that'd be nice.'

He ordered her a fresh vodka and orange at the bar, ignoring the niggling thought in the back of his head about his routines, about what he should be doing at that moment.

He returned to the table and she took another long pull. When she'd finished, she said, 'Now come on, what's your story?'

'I don't know,' he said and shrugged. 'I was born. I live. I didn't die. Twice. I live still? I guess that sounds a bit Dickensian, don't you think?'

She chuckled. It was good to see a smile on her face after the hurt that had been there before. She put on an overly posh voice. 'It was the best of times. It was the worst of times.'

'That'll be uni, one day. When we look back,' he said, with more sorrow than he intended.

Those first two years with his friends, and with Nicole as his girlfriend, really had been the best times of his life, regardless of a the crippling depression he had felt, bad enough he attempted suicide. And now, he was preparing to go back for his third year without them, having escaped a traumatic experience they hadn't. He couldn't imagine he'd ever be able to think of those "best of times" without also thinking about the worst night of his life, even if he never remembered anything more than what he'd recovered tonight.

He cast a dismissing smile at Beth and looked down at the table. The topic of his life, or of him, in general, was forgotten. Instead, Beth filled the silence with stories from hers and Beth's first and second year.

Once the second drink was gone, neither of them suggested another. They climbed to their feet and headed back home. It had started raining while they were in the pub and they rushed through it before it could get them too wet.

Back at the house, they each said goodnight and went to their rooms, although Will doubted Beth would be sleeping and he had no plans to do so himself. He loaded up his computer and started to search. He wanted to find any record of a fair in Treevale, anything the police might have missed, so he scrolled online news websites, personal blogs, and social media pages, searching for any shred of evidence to support his memories, now that he knew them to be true.

For hours, he searched. He backtracked through the past decade of events in Treevale. In the age of the internet almost any information was available and yet he found nothing.

That didn't mean the fair hadn't been there, though. He remembered it, and the Crooked Man with it.

14

Will awoke to the sound of knocking. At first he thought it must have been Beth knocking on his door, waking him from what must have sounded like a nightmare, but as he groggily sat up in bed he saw the figure in the window silhouetted against the dull orange of the streetlights through the curtain. It was a woman, knocking on the window. Wisps of long hair blew in the wind. He couldn't make out anything more than the height and slim build, but he knew it was her. Nicole.

She had come back.

He rushed out of bed and out into the hall. He grabbed the front door and yanked it open but the woman who had been knocking was already heading off down the street. Rain was falling and he was dressed in only a t-shirt and shorts with no shoes, yet Will couldn't let her slip away. He rushed after her.

'Wait,' he called.

She didn't turn, nor give any sign that she had heard him. She reached the end of the street and turned the corner. Will broke into a run, his bare feet splashing painfully through the growing layers of water lining the pavement, but even as he reached the corner, he saw that she was far ahead of him, about to turn another corner. He watched as she left the spread of light from one streetlight and waited with bated breath for her to reappear in the glow of the next one. It was really her, and as she stepped into the each shadow, he was sure she wouldn't come out again.

He chased her, desperately, wanting only to look upon her face and know that it was her, that she had returned to him, but each time he thought he should have caught up, she was the same distance from him as she had been before the last corner.

He didn't know where she was going until he turned another corner and saw her beneath the streetlight closest to the gates to Graham Park. She slipped into the darkness beyond the gate and into the park. At this time of night, the gates should have been locked but they remained open, welcoming her into the deathly blackness beyond.

Will continued running until he reached the spot across the road from the gate where he stopped each morning on his runs, and he stared at the darkness within, torn between his fear and his desperation to catch Nicole.

The faint sound of screams and ringing and music sang to him on the breeze, coming from inside that thick blanket of darkness. He found himself crossing the road. But as he reached the open gate, his body froze. No matter how much he wanted to go in there after her, he couldn't.

He continued to stare after her as though he would be awarded a glimpse of her in there. The noises were louder, like the ghost of the fairground he remembered was in there, shrouded in darkness and waiting only for him. And then he saw the figure coming toward him.

Long limbs stretched out from a small body, clambering over one another as they scuttled in his direction, the creep of a man-sized spider, meaning to wrap him in a web and take him from this life. It reached the gate and stopped short of where Will stood on the other side, a black figure against the pitch dark. It looked at him with eyes that shined out of the darkness and it's crooked pincers twitched.

The creature lifted a long, twisted leg, slick and black like oil and reached for Will.

15

When the alarm on his phone woke Will at seven o'clock, the echo of the nightmare still bounced around his head. He groggily rolled over to turn off the alarm. The nightmare was different to the usual kind, which always involved some variation of being chased by the Crooked Man through some form of maze, but the feeling it left behind was very much the same.

He was shaken and tired and strangely vacant, as though part of him were still in the dream, watching the shadowy creature reaching for him. He considered resetting the alarm for an hour's time. It was what he would have done once upon a time, especially after a late night with his friends. He would change the alarm, spend a little longer in bed and then awake fresher, and with enough time left to still get to uni on time if he rushed a little or skipped breakfast.

But he had already skipped enough parts of his routine in the past twenty four hours and if he skipped anymore, it would set off a domino effect that ended with his routine completely in tatters. He didn't want to explain to Dr Phillips the reasons why when he began to spiral. He wasn't even sure how to tell her about his discovery about the fair. She had outright condemned hypnotherapy; he didn't think she'd be happy he'd gone behind her back, and with a student, no less.

He pulled back the covers to get out of bed and was startled to find his body completely bare. He had gone to bed in pyjama shorts and a t-shirt. Even though it was still hot, and it was not uncommon for him to awake drenched in sweat in the night, he had never slept naked. He didn't like the feel of it.

So where the hell were his clothes, and why wasn't he wearing them?

Confused, Will got out bed and went to get his running clothes out of the set of drawers. Next to the drawers stood his thin washing basket, beside which were his pyjamas from the night before. Next to, not in it. Tidiness was another of those important things Dr Phillips had instilled in him. He couldn't keep to his routines if he left a mess. Yet he had dumped the clothes – when or even *why*, he didn't know – as he would have done before the disappearance.

He picked them up. They were wet through, too soaked for it to be sweat. He threw them in the basket. He pulled back the duvet and touched the bottom sheet. It wasn't even slightly damp. He ran a hand over the full area that he might have touched in sleep, but it was bone dry.

None of it added up. Or, at least, it added up perfectly to something he didn't want to consider. It wasn't happening again! It *wasn't*. He hadn't had another episode, he told himself. He had just got too sweaty last night because of the heat and the nightmares, and he had removed his clothes. It had been a strange night, that was all, brought on by the hypnotism and the disruption of his routines.

He stripped the bed and added the sheets to the wet clothes in the basket, before retrieving his running clothes. As he dressed, he noticed the souls of his feet were grubby as though he had been walking outside with bare feet. He thought of the nightmare and wondered. He swiftly shook the thought away. He couldn't have had another episode. If he did that, he would have to go back to the clinic, and then back home, where Ian would never allow him any control over his own life again.

Before leaving for his run, he put his sheets and sodden clothes into the washer-dryer and set them to wash, removing all evidence. Then he set off running. He ran his forty minutes, focusing on his breathing and the feeling of his feet against the concrete, and cleared his mind of the sodden clothes.

It wasn't until he arrived back home that he realised he had not visited the park. The pull the park had had over him had unnerved him to begin with but that he had passed it by completely this morning after the possibility of an episode unnerved him more.

He reminded himself there would be a rational explanation, that he had shown no signs of having an episode in months, and went about getting himself fed, showered and dressed. Then, putting thoughts of the night and morning behind him, he set about the rest of his routine.

16

On Sunday morning, Will returned to Graham Park. Without even thinking of where he was going, he found himself stood across the road from the park gates the same as he had on his previous runs. His thoughts as he had set off running had been on his recovered memories and they must have pushed him toward the park with each step.

He stared at the gaping mouth of the gate and shivered. He had been right all along. There had been a fair within those gates after all but he didn't feel that was something to celebrate. What he'd found in the depths of his brain was confirmation that this was where it had all gone wrong.

He had once considered the park welcoming and calming, but it felt foreign and wrong now. He wasn't a believer in any of the mystical horror things that Nicole loved and believed, so the idea that a place could feel wrong was ridiculous. But he couldn't stop the thought as he approached the opening. There was something evil about this place.

It was just a park, he told himself. There was no fairground there now, no disproportionately tall men with crooked smiles. Yet he could not step across the threshold.

'You've got nothing to be afraid of. Nothing's going to harm you,' Nicole said in his head but even the sound of her voice couldn't give him the strength to go in.

He set off down the pavement that surrounded the park, and looked in through the bars at the expanses of grass and the sprawling, nonsensical spiderweb of pathways where he and Nicole had walked hand in hand. It should have been a pleasant place, filled with brightness and light, where he had created so many memories with his friends but he could feel only darkness, as though the park were filled with ghosts.

He followed the fence, looking in through the bars, and idly watching the handful of people inside. There was an elderly woman walking a dog only slightly bigger than a cat, who yapped repeatedly at her knees until she caved and gave it another treat. A couple of women in running gear that didn't cover a great deal of skin ran side by side, their pony tails bouncing back and forth, almost in unison. An old man shuffled around, pushing a pram in front of him at increments of an inch. And another runner, wearing a thin hoody, his hood propped up over the top of his baseball cap. He was leaning over, hands on his knees, breathing deeply.

Then Will saw him, strolling along one of the paths that followed the edge of the park, a few metres back from where Will, himself, walked outside the park. Will hadn't been looking behind him so hadn't seen him until now. He might have been following Will from the other side of the fence the entire time, while he chain smoked his cigarettes.

It was the man he'd seen hovering in the street.

Will pretended he hadn't noticed. He started walking again, faster now, until he reached the corner. It was the furthest point from any of the four gates and Will seized his opportunity. He darted across the road, away from the park. In seconds, his legs were shooting like pistons and his feet pounded the floor as though he were trying to take off with each step. When he got back to the house, he stopped at the corner and tried to catch his breath. He needed to compose himself before he went inside and faced Beth's questions, provided she was up.

He never had the chance to compose himself. There was a car parked at the curb outside the house that he didn't recognise and their front door hung wide open. There wasn't a soul in sight.

A self-proclaimed coward, he thought of calling Beth and finding out if she was in the house, but if she was, what could she do? It was too late for phone calls. Whoever had come here – an accomplice of the man in the park, perhaps? – they were already inside.

Feeling so light headed, he might pass out at any moment, Will moved slowly up the street, toward the house. Had he locked his room this morning? How secure would the door be if somebody were determined enough? There was a MacBook pro on his desk, and a Bluetooth speaker and an iPod on his bedside cabinet, a games console and tv in the living room.

There was every chance this was a regular robbery, with nothing to do with the man following Will.

He came to a stop short of the door. There were voices coming from inside, drawing closer. There was nowhere for him to turn. He was too close and his energy was depleted. He swallowed, took a deep breath and waited for the assailant to emerge and come for him. A moving target was harder to catch, so he charged forward.

The man stepped into the street, almost colliding with him and Will let out a little whimper of a scream.

'Whoa, mate, careful.' It was Ben, holding up his hands and chuckling. 'You're coming at the house like a bloody freight train.'

Will released a wobbling breath.

'You okay?'

Will nodded. He had forgotten Ben was moving back in today. He cursed himself. Ben was far from threatening and, dressed in a beanie and sleeveless t-shirt as he was the other day, he was far from terror inducing.

'You sure you're all right?' Ben asked, stepping further into the street to free up the doorway. A short, plump woman with sandy curls of hair followed him outside.

'Is this your new one?' she asked Ben. She turned to Will. 'Hi, there. I'm Bev.'

Will held up a hand in a nervous wave and let it drop swiftly back to his side.

'This is Will, Mam,' Ben said.

'Pleased to meet you, Will. I hope my Ben doesn't get too on your nerves with his messiness. I know it gets on Beth and Xander's nerves.'

'Ma-am!' His cheeks flushed.

'Sorry, love.'

Will forced a flash of a smile and, with a nod, he passed between them and went inside.

'Not much of a talker, is he?' Bev asked Ben.

Will unlocked the door to his room, stepped in and closed and locked it behind him.

17

The Stranger itched for more information. He craved it.

The woman, Grace, had been unwilling to speak to him until she saw the money he was offering. Then the words had flowed faster than from a drunk. She had told him William Campbell had been practicing hypnotherapy with the other woman, an unqualified psychology student and had remembered being at a fairground with his friends, and then a room covered in blood, which was on his arms and hands too. Grace had taken this to mean William had taken his friends' lives.

The Stranger didn't correct her. His interest was piqued, but Grace had only overheard some of what was said, having been in another room to begin with. He had left the pub after his conversation with the woman and made a phone call.

'It's me,' he said, when it was answered. 'William Campbell's remembering things. What do you know about the fair?'

The recipient on the other end had been reluctant to help him, another name in a long list, but had relented. It would take a couple of days to gather the information he wanted.

The Stranger spent that time watching the house and following William Campbell whenever he left the house, mentally recording the growing irregularity of his behaviour. When he had moved here, William Campbell had gone running at the same time each morning and for the same amount of time, without discrepancy but the time he left the house was becoming more lax and the time he spent out grew longer and longer, as he lingered at the park longer each day.

He was unravelling. It was slow but this morning had proven it. The kid had not lingered at the gate as he normally did. Instead, he had walked around the edge of the fence, looking in as though searching for something that wasn't there. After the information he'd gotten from Grace, he wondered if the kid was trying to imagine the fairground in there.

Shortly after Campbell spotted the Stranger and sprinted away from the park, the Stranger received the text he'd been waiting for. There were no hellos or goodbyes, no pleasantries of any kind in the message. It contained only a time. He knew the place.

The Stranger walked back to his car in a nearby side street, and set off out of Treevale. For twenty minutes he drove west on the motorway, before taking a turnoff onto a country lane, where trees and hedges surrounded him on all sides. He followed it for a few miles before turning onto a road scarcely big enough for one car to drive along, let alone two. Trees gave way to views of the Durham countryside.

It was a beautiful view that would amaze most people, the kind that most could only dream of living amongst, and those that did would appreciate daily. The Stranger didn't even look at it as he drove. He had seen it too many times and it held for him nothing but pain. It was a view that provoked images of a young child running through fields.

He passed through a village and continued for half a mile on the other side, where a residential estate backed onto farmland. The houses were large and expensive bungalows with big gardens in front and behind, most of which were filled with well pruned flowerbeds and scattered with children's toys, discarded bikes. It was a great place to raise children. Cute homes to live in, great stretches of countryside to play in, with a small woodland a short way down the road and country footpaths to walk or cycle down.

One house, at the end of one of the streets, stood apart.

The grass out front was overgrown and the flowers had long since died and shrivelled, replaced by weeds. The grass hid the garden but the Stranger knew there were no toys amongst the tall blades.

While the other bungalows were bright white, their doors and frames painted pristinely, the walls of this house had begun to crack and the blue of the door and the frames surrounding it and the windows had started to flake some time ago and had not been retouched. This house was not good for child raising. Not anymore.

He climbed out of the car and approached the front door by skirting around the edge of the overgrown grass. He tried the door. It was unlocked. He stepped inside, into the remains of his old life.

The house entered into a small hallway where an empty shoe rack sat next to the door. The first door on his left led into a living room that was still furnished despite the clear signs the house was abandoned. There were no electricals but there was a sofa set and a number of units.

On one of the sofas sat a blonde woman staring at the far wall. She didn't turn to look at him as he entered.

She said, 'You know I hate coming here.'

'I know,' the Stranger said. 'I do too.'

'Then sell it.'

He shook his head, more to himself than to her. 'I'd rather see it burnt to the ground than know somebody else was living here, filling it with their own memories and happiness. Besides, if I sold it, where would we meet?'

'We wouldn't. We shouldn't even be meeting now. Do you not consider how much I put my neck on the line for you?'

He didn't respond.

Finally, she got up from the sofa and turned to face him. She was as beautiful as the first time he had ever seen her. Her face wore more lines but they defined rather than aged her and her body was in better shape than it had ever been. She was taking good care of herself.

The Stranger couldn't say the same. He had never looked worse. He was ungroomed and wearing tatty clothes. She looked at him for a moment, considering him. He knew she was likely considering everything that had happened between them, before he became a stranger to the world, including her.

'Do you have what I need?' he asked.

She huffed. 'That's it? No pleasantries? No "hi, Sally"? No "how you doing?"' She threw her arms in the air. 'Why should I have expected anything else?'

'Would you rather we stay here longer? We could sit on that sofa and catch up like it's old times. Pretend nothing happened. We can ignore the stains on the carpet from the leak during the last storm and we can look over there where the TV should be and just pretend she's asleep upstairs.'

She looked down and shook her head. 'You know that's not what I meant. Don't think you're the only one who still hurts. You're just the only one who can't move on. You're even still wearing that jacket.'

She reached out and prodded her finger through one of the rips in his right shoulder. 'Look at the state of it.'

He stepped out of her reach. He curved his middle finger toward his sleeve and traced an embroidered heart on the cuff.

'Have you got what I need, or not?' he said.

She shook her head again. It was a gesture of disbelief rather than an answer to his question. It was the kind of expression he had gotten used to from those who used to know him well. It meant they were failing to believe they'd ever cared about him, ever thought they knew him.

Sally walked across to the window. From the windowsill, she picked up a folder – a nondescript plastic wallet but what was inside of it, he knew, were confidential documents. She held the folder in her hands but didn't hold it out for him.

'What's your interest?' Ever the police officer, the Stranger thought.

'That's not your concern.'

'Are you kidding me? I could get into serious shit for giving you these, even for taking them out of the station, and you're going to stand there, in *this* house and give me that shit? Like I don't matter?'

She slapped the folder down on the arm of the sofa in front of him. A plume of dust exploded into the air around it. 'Maybe I don't matter to you anymore. But *I* still care.'

The Stranger picked up the folder but he didn't open it. He looked at Sally. She was upset and angry but she was looking at him the way she had many years ago, the way nobody looked at him anymore and he knew it was true. He was a stranger to many, in most ways even her, but she still cared like she knew him.

He sighed. 'The kid's remembering things.'

'You said that on the phone. So what?' Her anger was still burning but her tone had softened. She had won whatever battle was going on between them. She had reminded him she could still get through his barriers.

'So I need to know what there is for him to remember.'

'Why?'

'You know why,' he barked. 'The kid and his friends disappeared without a trace and then miraculously he reappeared as if from nowhere two days later. He's the key to finding out how somebody could disappear without a trace.'

She nodded her understanding. 'Okay. I get it. But you know it's not going to change anything.'

'It could change everything.'

They were quiet for a time and the Stranger headed back into the hallway, making for the front door.

'Wait,' Sally called after him. He stopped and she joined him in the hallway, their bodies close together, the air between them pregnant and electric. 'I'm sorry.'

'So am I,' he returned. Neither said what it was they were sorry for, but neither needed to.

She leant in, placed a hand on the back of his head and kissed him on the corner of his lips. She pressed her cheek against his and, in his ear, she said, 'Don't be a stranger, okay?'

He breathed in the scent of her and wished she'd place her lips on his again, but before he could reach for her, she slipped away. She opened the front door and stepped out into the quiet street.

The Stranger lingered a few moments in the hallway, the ghost of her touch on his head and lips, and listened to the sound of a car starting up down the road. Silence returned and wrapped itself like a shroud around him. From beyond it, he heard a child's laughter. He looked at the dust covered stairs leading up toward where the sound would have come from if it had been real and smiled sadly. Then he left the house, locked it and got into his own car. But he didn't start it.

He turned his attention to the folder. He pulled the thick wad of papers out and started reading, then read them again. The documents included multiple statements from William Campbell, a statement from Stevie Quentin, a university lecturer who organised the trip the missing students had disappeared from, and a number of reported sightings, along with reports regarding various investigative directions.

He focused on the statements from William. In each one, he reiterated the same thing: he did not remember. The last thing he remembered was the lights of a fair and then he was suddenly in the field miles away two days later, covered in blood. All he recalled in between was a scene of being chased through a dark maze. A psychologist had explained that the image of a fair could have been an unintentional fabrication on William's part, in order to give his missing memories some direction and to convince himself that there were at least some pleasant experiences before whatever happened to him and his friends.

The police found no evidence that a fair had been anywhere near Treevale and they had considered other avenues, of which there were few. With a psychologist supporting the police's findings, or lack thereof, he wondered how far they'd looked.

The Stranger would not be so easily deterred.

He started the car and left the bungalow behind. He drove back to Treevale but he didn't go to the street where William Campbell now lived. Instead, he parked in the town centre. He headed into a couple of shops, followed by the library, searching for somebody who had been in town long enough to know its history, but as a university town, there were few who lived there more than a few years.

Changing tack, he headed to the local newspaper. The Treevale Gazette had been around since the turn of the last century, when it was started as a small family business originally publishing once a week. Now they published three times a week, and every day online. They were not a large paper, nor was their building particularly large either.

He walked inside as though he owned the place. A bored looking woman sat at the reception but she didn't pull her eyes away from her phone.

'I need to see your archives,' he said.

The bored woman looked up and, startled, shoved the phone out of sight. Then she realised it was not her boss that had caught her and relaxed.

'And you are?' she asked.

He took a business card out of his pocket and handed it over to her. 'Show that to your boss.'

The woman was unsure but she shuffled on anyway. A few minutes later, she returned and, after a large gulp, said, 'Right this way, sir.'

She led him through the building into a dark, windowless room lined with shelves and crammed with plastic boxes. An ancient computer sat in one corner and a table was placed in the middle of the room, beneath a flickering fluorescent strip light. The receptionist left him alone.

He powered up the computer, which held a digitalized version of every newspaper since 2007, and also allowed internet access. He sat down in front of it and plugged a memory stick from his pocket into the machine, from which he loaded the research he had already carried out, and by the light of a desk lamp as old as the computer, he got to work.

Campbell was not the first to disappear from Treevale last September, the Stranger knew. He was a connoisseur of sorts when it came to the missing; a collector. In his collection were the reports of hundreds of missing people spread over years from all over the country, none of them seemingly connected.

There were a number in Treevale who had disappeared in September, each on the same date as somebody had disappeared the previous year, and again the year before that. There were no threads between them. The people were all outsiders of a kind, with only a couple of friends, hardly the popular person, but none of them had known each other or shared any of the same friends or acquaintances. They were separate people living separate lives, until what appeared to be separate disappearances.

But now the Stranger thought he had something. William Campbell remembered a fairground that didn't exist. If there was something to find, the Stranger would find it.

18

Amanda arrived a few minutes before seven and this time she came alone.

With an extra person in the house, there was a life and energy that hadn't been there before. From the moment Ben said goodbye to his mum, noise was a constant, with music, banging, and boisterous laughter. He had not even taken the last of his bags upstairs to his room before loading up YouTube on Beth's X-Box in the living room and turning the volume all the way up, on a playlist of mainstream pop, indie and soft rock music. It was like Radio 1 without the presenters.

When it came time for Amanda's arrival, the house descended into a nervous quiet that, in contrast to the rest of the day, felt closer to a grave silence. The knock on the door tore through the quiet like an explosion and they all jumped. Beth got to her feet and rushed to let Amanda in.

Ben leant toward Will and asked, 'Are you sure about this, mate?' Beth had told him what they were doing earlier while Will was in his room.

'Yeah,' Will said, although he couldn't keep away a tremor of doubt.

Ben opened his mouth to say something more when Beth came into the room followed immediately by Amanda.

'Ben!' Amanda ejected and threw her arms around him. 'I didn't know you were back.' She released him but left her hands resting on his bare arms, as though she were a long lost relative getting a good look at him after many years apart.

'This morning,' Ben said. 'I didn't find out you'd be here until earlier today. I would have mentioned something. Maybe met up earlier.'

She waved away his comments. 'Don't worry. I was trying to make things right with Grace because of Friday, anyway.'

'I'm sorry,' Will said.

For the first time since entering, she turned and saw him. 'Oh, sorry, Will. I come here for you and here I am ignoring you. Hi, you alright?'

Will nodded and shrugged. She could believe whichever of the two answers she wished.

'You don't need to apologise about Grace. It wasn't your fault. Grace can be...'

'A bitch?' Beth finished.

Ben laughed until Amanda shot him a look.

'*Difficult.* Anyway, it's good to see you again.' She pulled off her mustard pea-coat and draped it over the arm of the other sofa and leant against it. 'How you doing?'

'Okay,' he said, unconvincingly.

'If the other night affected you, we don't have to continue. There's no pressure for you to go on with this, you understand? It might be best if we suspend things for a bit?'

Will thought of Nicole, of Julian, of Tom, and of Craig. He thought of their faces, the way they had shuffled their feet as they awaited him that night, unsure if he was coming and unsure what to say to him. Unsure, even, of the state their friendships would be in. He thought of his selfish need to create at least one last great memory with them before he planned on abandoning them for good, causing their own grief and creating their own heavy empty space to walk beside them.

He shook his head. 'I'm fine.'

'Something's wrong. I have eyes, Will,' Amanda said. 'Is it the memories or is it the anniversary coming up?'

Beth chirped in. 'You know we can organise something that night to take your mind off of it.'

'There's going to be a vigil,' Ben said.

Will looked at him. 'What?'

'There's a vigil at the ADAM building that night. Stevie's organising it.'

'But,' Will sputtered, 'aren't vigils for the dead?'

'Well, yeah,' Ben said.

'But...' Will started.

Beth rubbed his shoulder. 'If you don't want to go to it,' she said, 'we can find something else to do. Anything. Whatever you want.'

Amanda asked, 'Are you sure you want to do this tonight?'

'I'm not sure it's a good idea,' Ben said. 'I mean, he's clearly upset and, is this even safe?'

Amanda snapped, 'I know what I'm doing Ben.'

'I never said you didn't, but you're still a student, Manda. Isn't there some kind of ethics about this kind of thing in your psychology stuff. I don't want you to risk your future.'

'Yes, there are. Practicing hypnotherapy is quite hotly debated, and doing it as a student is probably crossing some line, but if his own therapist won't try it, then what choice do I have.'

Ben threw up his hands. 'If a professional doesn't think it's right, then surely you shouldn't do it.'

'There are debates about hypnosis, and there have been for decades. That doesn't mean that practice is altogether unethical. There are a lot of people who believe the practice falls firmly within the lines of ethics and those that think otherwise. Ultimately, though – *legally* – it isn't unethical.'

'That doesn't make it right. What if you get caught?'

Amanda took a deep breath. Neither of them had yet raised their voice. While Ben appeared genuinely concerned for Amanda's participation and what that could mean for her, it was evident Amanda's temper was wearing thin. 'Are you telling me you've never done anything that's even a little questionable? How about when you convinced a guy on your course to drop out of uni in second term because he was planning on dropping out at the end of the year and you "wanted to save him the four grand for the final term tuition"?'

'He'd made up his mind, I just helped him speed it up.'

Amanda nodded. 'So it had nothing to do with you not liking him? With him calling Beth a dyke?'

Ben huffed and pulled the beanie off his head. He ran a hand through his mop of dark hair before returning the hat to its rightful place. 'Fine. I didn't like him. I know he said he was only joking when he called Beth that but that didn't mean it wasn't wrong. He was a prick. He decided he didn't want to be here, so I convinced him to leave so we could all be free of him. Our course was a lot more peaceful after that, but I stand by my saying it saved him money.'

Amanda sat back, satisfied by her victory. 'I'm not saying you were wrong to do it, but I'd call it pretty questionable. Not everything is a black and white, right and wrong.' 'This still doesn't seem right. What if you're damaging his head?'

Will looked up, unsure what to say. He had considered the same question yesterday, while looking at his sodden pyjamas. He didn't know what to say. Maybe Ben was right, but he had to go ahead with this. How could he convince them of that?

Beth answered for him.

'Imagine if me and Amanda and Xander went missing, Ben. Imagine having to live knowing you were there when it happened and not remembering. Wouldn't you do anything to find out?'

Ben swallowed. He shook his head and bit his lip. A fresh argument was forming on his face but it was obvious Beth had him.

'Now,' she went on. 'Imagine that people blame you. People like Daniel outright accuse you of killing us.'

'Mate. This is so nuts,' he said.

'Maybe, but if it's what Will wants, who are we to argue?'

He sighed. 'Whatever. But I'm not going to be a part of

it.' On his way out of the room, he turned to Will. 'Good luck dude. I hope you come out of it alright.'

Beth asked Amanda, 'Do you want me to leave, too?'

'Will?' Amanda said.

He shook his head and smiled. Beth took a seat, crossed legged on the floor.

'Okay, then. Are you ready?'

The debate that had unfolded before him, in which he hadn't even participated, had left him feeling drained and he wasn't sure if he had the energy remaining to jump back to that night.

He nodded. If he didn't do it now, he never would.

'Okay, we're going to do thing slightly differently this time around, okay? Once you're under, I want you to focus on the feeling of lightness.'

Will closed his eyes and started breathing. Amanda talked him down.

19

('You're stood at the fairground. The ground is hard beneath your feet. Grass and mud. There are people around you, laughing and joking. On either side of you run game stalls, tents and food servers. There are rides further away and you can see the lights flashing, some of them forming shapes. This is the fairground from the night you disappeared. What can you smell? What can you see? And hear?')

The smell of sickly sweet sugar fills the air, mixed with the smell of cooking meat. Burgers and hot dogs and candy floss. Mixed together, the smells are sickening. There's a Ferris Wheel towering above me, slowly rotating. Inside the little huts are the dark shapes of people sat together, groups of friends and couples. A little way further on is a ride that looks like a great rod reaching into the sky. A row of seats rises slowly to the top and then plummets towards the floor to a chorus of screams.

In the other direction, there's another ride towering over the whole fair, with two pendulum shapes swinging in alternate directions, until they're moving so quickly they're flying in opposing circles. There's so many screams, it's like multiple murders taking place at once across the fair.

('Turn your attention to the people at the fair, having fun at the stalls and walking around.')

There are groups and couples all enjoying themselves, walking down the paths between the stalls. They're laughing and joking and talking. Having a good time. There's a wide mix of people – old, young, rough, soft, friendly, thuggish, happy, bored, ecstatic. A couple are arguing. The guy is trying to convince his yelling girlfriend to quieten down because they're in public. Around them groups run fleeting and excited toward the next stall, the next game.

I can see them. I can hear them. But for a second, it feels as though they are not really there. It is as though we are the only patrons at the fair, walking alone through the flashing stalls, like ghosts.

('*Are your friends there?*')

Nicole, Craig, Tom, and Julian are beside me. We're following the path that weaves through the various stalls. The stall holders are watching us intensely, urging us with their eyes to come close enough to be hooked into playing their game.

('*Do you play?*')

There are so many eyes on us. To play is what is expected of us, and I did come here seeking fun. We approach a stall offering a throwing game involving a ball and a bucket tipped to an angle.

Nicole's face remains partially hidden from me behind the silk of her black hair, which shines with the flashes of colour from the fair's lights around us. Beside her, Julian shuffles his feet, an action that includes large swings of each foot due to his gangly height. Tom lingers beside Julian, their fighting from the walk here forgotten. Side by side, they are stark contrasts, one tall and thin, the other short and fat. Neither of them is smiling but it looks as though they want to.

Other than me, Craig is the only one who dares to smile, maybe overcome with the atmosphere or resigned to the change that the night has taken and committed to riding with it. The smile, beaming out from behind his dark beard softens him slightly. He's got muscles upon muscles, and if any problems arose, he'd be able to handle them better than any of us. Perhaps because of that, he's able to relax more.

We look as mismatched as ever, even surrounded by such a mix of people and there is still an awkwardness to us all, as we decide who should go first, or if we should be playing games at all, all things considered. There's a sense of unnerving dread coming from Julian, Tom and Nicole, as though playing a game would cause something bad.

Blood. I can see blood. An entire room spattered with it. It's on my hands, down my forearms, covering the scar of my suicide attempt as though it's reopened.

('Will, listen to my voice. Hear the words I'm saying and return to fair. There's lights all around you of every colour. Everybody is having fun. You and your friends are stood at a stall. A throwing game. Tell me what you see? What do you do?')

The stall owner asks if we want to play and it's clear he's growing impatient at the group of us standing in front of his stall doing nothing. I look at them all again but nobody moves. I agree to go first, hoping they would follow my example as they had at the museum. The stall holder hands me three balls. I aim, throw, and the ball goes into the bucket, hits the bottom and bounces straight back out again.

The next two balls do exactly the same, even the one I throw with less force.

Craig puts a hand on my shoulder and guides me back. 'Let's show you how it's done.'

Craig receives his three balls. He readies his arm and throws. The first bounces out, as does the second. Julian and Tom laugh, although it's strained. Nicole's lips even curl up at the corners and it feels good to see them starting to enjoy themselves a little, although it feels wrong.

I'm going to die before the night is out and, even though they don't know my plans, death looms over us so heavily, it's as though the air is suffocatingly thick and we should be addressing it, not playing games.

The third ball lands in the bucket and bounces up to the rim, and, as Craig holds his breath, sinks back to the bottom with a dull *thump*. He thrusts his large arms in the air in triumph.

The others don't want to join in, yet, and we move on.

('Are you being watched?')

('*Babes!*')

There's a doorway filled by the figure of an overly tall man in a top hat. He tips forward into the light and I can see a flash of his large, grey teeth in a crooked smile.

('*Sorry.*')

('*Will, listen to my voice. You're at the fair, moving away from the throwing game. You're walking through the crowds of people enjoying themselves. Tell me where you're going. What do you do next?*')

We walk for a while, neither of us talking but there's less tension between us already. Not much, but it's enough. We look at the stalls as we go, following the path around. We walk aimlessly for a while, following along the paths between the stalls, walking the same paths we've walked a hundred times over the past two years, but the presence of the stalls make them somehow different. Foreign and unusual. It's like walking through a world that has flipped our own. A distorted mirror.

('*In what way is it distorted?*')

It's as though we aren't actually in the park. As though we stepped through those gates and were transported somewhere else, into the world of the fair. It's the same old park but it's different in ways I can't quite place, the way your own body looks different in one of the mirrors in a fairground like this.

('*Tell me about what happens next. You're walking through the fair...*')

Craig nudges me and leans in close. He says, 'Tell her how you feel. While you still can. I don't know what's going to happen, mate, but wouldn't you rather make sure she knew how you felt?'

I nod, but it's not so simple.

Craig continues, 'It would take time I'm not sure you have. I'm not sure you can expect her to forgive you and be head over heels with you by the end of the night, but you need to make a start.'

I say, 'You forgave me though?'

It isn't intended as a question but it's how it comes out.

Craig shrugs and says, 'Not completely. But me and you are different. I'm hurt and pissed off, but holding a grudge isn't going to make a difference to anything, is it? Nicole, though, she's a hell of a lot worse. You know?'

I nod. I can find no words to say.

He says, 'She's hurt and angry, too, but more, and she's not going to come around so long as she thinks you *want* to die. So tell her the truth. Tell her you don't.'

I do, though. More so than ever. For a reason I can't put my finger on, I feel a surge of darkness spread over me, the wish to no longer be here on this planet, despite the flashing lights and fun, and my friends walking beside me intensifies. My heart trembles with it.

('Do you talk to Nicole?')

We talk on the Ferris Wheel, just the two of us. She doesn't want to go on it. Neither do I. I don't think I want to be here anymore at all. But there's a man beside the wheel dressed in an old ruffled shirt, sleeves rolled up to his elbows with a band around his upper arms. He shouts to us, tells us to 'roll up'

Roll up, like the whisper on the wind of the one who lured us here.

('What else does the Ferris Wheel operator say?')

He insists that we're here to have fun, so don't disappoint them all. He's pushy in an almost aggressive way and I feel compelled to climb into one of the little huts. Nicole follows me in. The others are compelled into climbing into the next one.

As it slowly starts to climb from the platform, I can't help but feel a sense of dread, as though something terrible is about to happen. We travel a full rotation without a word. Nicole's arms are crossed over her chest and she's looking off to one side, looking at the trees instead of me.

Unsure how to start, I look over the edge, down toward the path we had taken through the fair to get to the Ferris

Wheel. Between the stalls, there is a man in a top hat, looking up. We are too far away for me to see his face clearly but I know his features and I know he is looking up at us with a smile on his face.

I say, 'He's watching us.'

Nicole asks, 'What did you say?' They're the first words she has spoken to me in what feels like an age and they are spoken in a dry voice a little above a whisper.

I look at her and for a second, the man is forgotten. Almost.

I tell her, 'I'm sorry.'

'For what, exactly? For trying to kill yourself, for not telling me what was going on, or for dragging us away from that exhibition and leading us... here.'

She says *'here'* with a disdain I don't understand. I thought she would love a night at the fair. It had seemed the perfect solution to the awkwardness between us all.

I say, 'For not telling you I was struggling.'

Nicole says, 'Why didn't you? Why didn't you say *something*? Fuck, you didn't even say goodbye, Will. Do you know how that feels? I know you do. I know you know what it's like to lose somebody you love and never have them say goodbye. So, why? Why didn't you say something to me, to any of us?'

I tell her, 'I didn't want to be saved. I couldn't say goodbye because I couldn't look you in the eye and still go through with it.'

Tears stream down her face, glinting in the coloured lights from all around us. She weeps that I didn't even leave a note.

I say, 'I didn't know what to say. I was afraid anything I said to anybody would... I was afraid you would keep me alive. Even writing a note to you, I wouldn't have been able to go through with it. I'm not afraid to die. I was afraid not to.'

She wipes her eyes but the tears don't stop. She says, 'Killing yourself doesn't end the pain. It just shares it out among the people you leave behind.'

I think of David. 'There's always pain when someone dies,' I mumble.

She shakes her head and says nothing. Her tears flow harder until she is sobbing into her hands. Nicole is such a strong woman that seeing her this way is like seeing a different person and I can see the pain I've caused written there on her face.

Through her sobs, she says, 'Yes, there's always pain, but when you commit suicide, that pain is worse. Because us, left behind? We know you chose to make us suffer. And you couldn't even give us an explanation.'

'I'm sorry,' is all I can think to say.

After a long pause, she says, 'If we get through this, you're going to give me the spare key to your room. We'll go back to sleeping in each other's rooms, but I need access to your room when we stay in our own rooms. And I don't want you leaving the house without one of us.'

It sounds closer to a prison than student housing, but I agree. It is better than every alternative.

She continues, 'If we get through it, maybe we can hope to be back to normal again.'

(*'What does she mean, if you get through it? Get through what?'*)

The night. She's afraid we might not make it through the night. So am I. I remember the glimpse I caught of the man watching us from the ground. The man in the top hat. It's him. He's coming for us.

(*'Stay with the Ferris Wheel. You're returning to the ground.'*)

The cabin begins to descend and I peer over the edge but I can't see him. I search everywhere as we get closer to the ground. He has to be there. I can feel him watching. Feel his eyes on me. Boring into me in the darkness.

(*'What darkness?'*)

I'm cowering and alone. The fairground lights are all

dead. Empty balls of glass that glint with the light from the moon but don't lessen the darkness of the night around me. The wind swirls around me, chilling me to the core. It whistles, taunting in my ear. I scan the darkness for any sign of movement. For signs of *him* coming for me. I have to get away before he catches me but I can't move. I'm frozen. Everywhere I look, I see the shape of him, getting closer and closer. Until...

(*'Stay with the fairground. You're with your friends. There's colourful lights all around you. You're climbing off of the Ferris Wheel.'*)

We reach the bottom and climb off. The operator calls after us, 'Go on, now. Go have some fun.'

The group of us walk through the fair again.

Roll up, I hear, a whisper on the wind, coming to me from nowhere.

I see the tall man in the top hat, with his crooked grin. The Crooked Man. Every instinct screams for me to run but I am drawn toward him, helpless to stop.

(*'Where is he, this Crooked Man?'*)

I don't know. He was here but now he's gone. We walk on and the screams around us get louder and more intense until they are so loud, my head bursts with painful electricity. I screw up my eyes against the pain but it only increases. My head grows light and the world seems ready to fade.

(*'Open your eyes, Will. Focus on the lights of the fair. The images of comforting joy, people enjoying themselves. You're enjoying yourself. Focus on the fun atmosphere, like the ones from your childhood.'*)

I open my eyes and for a moment, the sun is too bright for me to see anything. The ache is still there but it's softer.

(*'Where are you? What do you see?'*)

We're beside the Ferris Wheel and the carousel. There are children in the Ferris Wheel's pods screaming down to their parents. Behind them, the sky is turning an ominous grey, washing out the sun.

(*'Will, where are you?'*)

I am at the fairground, surrounded by families and groups of friends enjoying themselves. I'm looking at the Ferris Wheel, but I don't want to go on it. I'm not enjoying myself.

('Who is with you, Will?')

I'm with Ian. He's trying to convince me to go on the Ferris Wheel. He wants me to go on anything because I haven't taken part in any of the fair yet. He isn't happy. He huffs and we walk off down the path, through the other stalls and rides.

He suggests the bumper cars. His face is a mask of desperation.

('Who is Ian, Will?')

Ian is my new step-dad. He married Mum about a year ago. He hasn't got any kids of his own and he's still getting used to looking after me. Mum and I are both more than he signed up for, I know, and I think he regrets it, but he won't leave. He can't. Mum needs too much looking after to be left alone.

('Why is Ian at the fair with you, Will?')

It's meant to make me feel better. I've been quieter than normal and moody since David died and Ian wanted me to have some fun.

('O-kay, so where does Ian take you next?')

We follow the path lined with stalls draped in plastic with faded red and white stripes, until we reach an opening. Inside the opening, there's a large, black house with darkened, barred windows. In place of a door, a monsters mouth has burst through the brick and lies open, waiting for somebody to step in and be swallowed. Beside the mouth stands a grey wooden sign. Words are carved into it reading: Enter If You Dare.

I shudder at the sight of it. Then I see the Crooked Man.

Stood beside the sign is a man abnormally tall, leaning on a stick in front of him and watching me from beneath the rim of his wide brimmed hat. The pale grey light of the sky catches the hat and his face is cast in deep, skeletal shadow. He opens his mouth in a grin that stretches out only one half of his mouth. His lips part further and shape two words, which sing to me like a whisper, loud enough they might have been whispered right in my ear.

'Roll up.'

Without thinking, I turn and run. I run as fast as my legs will carry me, darting through the crowds and skirting between stalls. I run until I burst from the fairground into a grouping of caravans. Clothes hang on lines strewn between them and cars are parked nearby to each but there are no people. They are all behind me at the fair, along with the terrifying Crooked Man with his impossible whisper.

I clamber under one of the caravans and tuck my knees to my chest. There, I wait. I don't know what I'm waiting for but I know I can't go back out there. I can't face the horror of that man and his black house. I wait until the sky is dark and all I can see is the distant glow of the rides in the fairground, until the air wraps its cold fingers around me and caresses my skin with its stinging bite.

('How long do you stay there?')

Until they find me. The sounds from the fair eventually die down and then I can hear them coming for me. A large group of people, all coming toward the caravans. Terrified that they will find me and rip me from my hiding place, but unable to climb out without being caught, I hug myself tighter.

A torch beam passes over the earth around the caravan and is gone. A few minutes later it returns, and then it is shining straight into my eyes, blinding me where I sit, shivering and crying.

20

Amanda talked Will back and snapped her fingers. Will's eyes opened, stinging with tears. At first he didn't understand why and then he remembered, in the slow, probing way as before, as though remembering a dream. The flow of the tears threatened to increase.

Beth had shuffled closer so that she was practically by his feet. She looked up at him with tears in her own eyes. She placed a hand over his and squeezed. Amanda handed him a glass of water. Will glugged it down, greedily, wiping his chin with the back of his hand when he had finished.

Amanda took a seat on the other sofa and crossed one leg over the other. In that position she closer resembled Dr Phillips and Will dreaded what she was going to say.

She took a deep breath and broke the silence that had settled among them. 'That went a lot differently to how I expected. We seemed to be making some progress in the last session before you're memories shifted and I was expecting the same today. I thought there'd be some more progress, and if it was going to shift, I would have expected more flashes of the scarier parts that your mind's trying to keep you from.' Amanda paused for thought and Beth gave Will's hand another squeeze. 'But something seemed to happen a little way through there and things got a little muddled. Your memory shifted to something not from the disappearance but from your childhood. And this "crooked man" ' – the image of the half smile, lips bared, flashed in Will's mind, and he swallowed – 'appeared first in the memory of the night you disappeared and then again when everything seemed to have gone back further.'

She thought a little more, chewed the inside of her lips.

'What can you tell me about that other trip to the fair?'

Will shook his head and thought of Ian trying to comfort him and show him the world hadn't ended. The cold that had shrouded him under the caravan pricked his skin through time, as though he were being stabbed by thousands of needles.

He said, 'Nothing. I don't – didn't – even remember going to one. I would have been twelve. Ian did his best to make me feel less alone but Mum needed so much looking after, I don't think he ever really managed. The trip to the fair must have been one of his attempts.'

Amanda nodded, more to herself. 'We've gone looking for one memory and another appears but they seem intertwined. I'd suggest you talk to your step-dad and find out a little more about what happened at the fair with him. Then we can try and separate the memories from one another, and know what's real.'

'What's *real*?' Accusations from Dr Phillips returned to his thoughts, claims that he had imagined things to make sense of what had happened, and his blood approached boiling point. 'What I remember is real.'

'I'm not saying it's not. But memory is messy and confused. It might take a bit more work to figure it out.'

Will tried to order the fresh memories but the nature of how they had come back to him, slowly and as though they weren't new, made it difficult. The back of his eyes throbbed. He pressed his hands to them.

'Are you okay?' Amanda asked.

He nodded. 'Headache. I remember… I don't know.'

'I think we should leave this a couple of days. Let your mind settle, before we try again?' Although it was phrased as a question, she went on talking without leaving time to answer. 'It'll give you time to talk to your step-dad and we can go from there. Take some time to relax, blow off some steam.'

Beth chimed in, 'What if we all go out on Tuesday night? Xander will be back by then and we can all get together and try and have a good time. Like old times. But with Will.'

Amanda agreed it would be a great idea and said she would be there. As she excused herself for the night and said goodbye to Will, she asked Beth if she could have a minute at the front door. Beth nodded and followed her out. Will was sorry to feel the warm comfort of her hand over his disappear.

He remained where he was and tried to focus on anything but the pain in his head. Words floated to him from the front door.

'Interrupt...' '....Careless...' '...Danger...' '...Leading...'

'I'm sorry. I was trying to help,' Beth said, clear enough for Will to hear.

'I know, Babes, but...'

Beth mumbled something. But all Will could think of was the Crooked Man, and his part in both memories, and he started to shake.

How long had the Crooked Man been there in his life?

Beth returned from the front door, solemn until she saw the state Will had descended into and she rushed to help settle him with an arm around his shoulder and calming words in his ear.

'You're safe. Nothing's going to hurt you. You're okay. Listen to me, Will.'

Despite the warmth of her words and the help they would do him, his mind drowned them out and he found himself instead staring at the skirting board across the room where a spider was crawling slowly upward. Its strangely disjointed legs moved with slow, almost robotic movements as it reached the lip of the skirting board and stretched out a long, thin leg toward the magnolia wall.

He watched it intently, observing the scrambling motion of its legs, like that of the Crooked Man in his nightmares, but the shaking subsided and his body grew still.

'How about I nip to the shop for some more milk and

then I'll make us some hot chocolate, yeah? And we can put some crap on the tv and talk, or not talk?' Beth said. Will didn't respond. He never took his attention away from the spider.

She took his silence as a yes and left the house. The spider continued its slow climb up the wall. It's front legs stretched out first and it seemed to drag itself upwards with them, hurtling itself toward some prey only it could see. What seemed like a long time passed before the spider crawled even halfway up the wall. Then, suddenly, the front door opened and closed, startling the spider into motion. It shot forward, its legs both pushing and pulling its small body upward, rushing toward the ceiling.

Will saw the dark corridor from his dreams and the shadowy figure of the Crooked Man dragging himself toward Will using all four of his elongated limbs.

'Hey,' Beth said from the living room doorway and Will looked away from the area where the spider had been before it shot away. She was leaning into the room, no milk in her hands and she looked tired all of a sudden. 'If you're alright, I'm just going to go up to bed.'

21

A blanket of darkness was shrouded over him. Pinpricks of light seeped weakly through the thick fabric of shadow. All was quiet, near silent, but for the clap of approaching footsteps and with them, Will heard the echo of the screaming and the music, as though the spirit of the fair drifted behind the approaching being, dancing on his coat tails.

He looked around at the darkness, and the points of orange light in the distance and for a moment, he thought he was in the black corridors that had filled his nightmares this past year. Then he felt the chill of the breeze on his skin and realised he was outside. The tiny orbs of light were distant street lights glimpsed through gaps in the trees. He looked up and he could see the sky.

His feet were bare and he could feel tarmac underfoot, a painful, hard pressure against his soles. He took a couple of steps toward the lights and his feet met the crunch of grass. The park, he thought, and despite no more evidence to that effect, he knew he was right. He could feel it. He had crossed through the gate, passed beyond the threshold and into the park that plagued his dreams.

How had he mustered the courage when he could not even enter the park in his nightmare a few days ago?

And why was he here, where it had all happened, in the middle of the night, all alone?

He was not alone. There was another in here with him, coming for him. There was no fairground here nor any corridors through which he would be chased, as the dreams always went, but the Crooked Man was coming.

With barely any visibility, Will set off at a fast walk across the grass and the steps grew quieter. Then stopped.

Unsure how far he'd gone, or where he was going in the darkness, Will stopped, too. He turned his head, although it accomplished nothing more than offering him a different set of pinpricks of light. He strained for any sound. Why had the Crooked Man stopped? Was he as lost in the darkness as Will? Or had he not stopped at all, instead stepping from the path, onto the soft grass, which would make light whispers of his approach?

And Will had stopped, dead, waiting.

He felt a presence behind him. Somebody was mere inches away, close enough he could feel but not hear their breath upon his ear.

And the Crooked Man whispered, 'Roll up, William. Roll up.'

Will leapt and spun around to face his tormenter, but the darkness had been lifted and he was not in the park at all, but in the middle of his bedroom. The room was dark and tinged with an unnatural shade of brown from the street light passing through the curtains. It was the middle of the night. The bed covers were pulled and ruffled back on the bed, revealing the space where he should have been.

His clothes were drenched in sweat but his bed appeared completely dry.

How did I get here? he wondered. *Was I really in the park?*

He checked his bare feet. They were a little grubby but not enough to suggest he'd been walking outside. Yet he was sure he'd felt the wind against his skin.

He froze. There it was again. A breeze. Yet his window was closed, as it always was due to the room's vulnerable position downstairs at the front of the house. The pavement ran immediately outside the window and he never felt it safe to open. Not in Treevale.

Will took a step out of his bedroom and the breeze blew stronger. He tightened, not at the chill of the air blowing against him but at the sight of the wide open front door.

The silence in the house was suddenly suffocating. What if somebody had gotten in and gone upstairs? What if..?

'What have you got to be afraid of?' Nicole said in his head.

Without closing the door, Will made his way up the stairs. When he reached the top he peered into the gloom at Ben and Beth's bedroom doors, as well as casting a quick glance in the direction of Xander's. There was a slither of light coming from the bottom of Beth's door, meaning she was still awake, but all three doors were securely closed and Will knew they would have both locked them before they got in bed.

Will's heart lightened a touch now he knew nobody had come upstairs but that didn't mean there was nobody in the house. He crept back downstairs and checked the living room, kitchen and bathroom. Finding no sign of anybody, he returned to the front door, closed it, and sat down on the edge of his bed, where he was forced to consider a far worse explanation for the open door than a break-in.

He had had another episode.

22

Eventually, somehow, Will got back to sleep and when he awoke, the incident in the night was almost forgotten. Almost. Residue of the fear and confusion remained. The realisation that he likely had an episode crept up on him. In an attempt not to think of it, he focused on his routine, changing into his running clothes and setting off on his run. He didn't visit the park today. More than ever since he moved back here, he didn't want to go back to that place, which held so much pain.

There was another envelope waiting for him when returned. He shoved it, unopened into a drawer and moved on with the rest of his routine as normal. He had missed too much of his routines and it was messing with his head. He ate breakfast, showered, then grabbed his sketchbook and drew for an hour until it was time to leave for his appointment with Dr Phillips.

As he made his way through to Newcastle, it was a struggle to keep his mind focused on what he was doing, and where he was going, as though his mind were being pulled in every other direction. He kept thinking about Nicole and him on the Ferris Wheel. He could see her clearly in front of his eyes, cowering in the little pod, the shine of the moon the only light to penetrate the night and shine against her black hair. He could hear her heart beating as fast as his own.

No, that wasn't right. That wasn't how he'd remembered it. The lights had been on when he and Nicole were on the Ferris Wheel. And there had been no need to cower. They had been sat having a conversation. The cowering in the darkness had happened later, and he had been alone.

But no matter how much he told himself that was the case, he continued remembering the interaction on the Ferris Wheel both as he had recalled last night and the dark, dread filled way that had just come to him. He told himself it was just his anxiety, the same kind that stayed with him every bus journey he made from Treevale to Newcastle, making him see his memories tainted by the way he felt in this moment, instead of that one.

So caught up in his own head, he didn't notice they'd pulled into the bus station until most of the passengers had already disembarked. He paused until more had left and then did so himself, cursing how distracted he was. He needed to be more alert.

He managed to reach Dr Phillips's office without incident and input his initials and date of birth into the computer on the wall, although it took him four attempts. Inside the office, he barely heard anything Dr Phillips said. He answered with short, brief sentences, as they went through the usual motions and he tried to find where his brain had run off to.

It wasn't until she asked about the letter that he snapped back to reality.

'What, sorry?' he said.

'I asked if you've received any more letters since Thursday,' Dr Phillips said.

'No,' Will lied. In his haste, he almost told her about the episodes he'd suffered, as he knew he should, and his fresh memories of the Crooked Man and the fair. But he couldn't tell her about any of it without telling her what had led to them. Telling Dr Phillips about what he'd been doing with Amanda was a bad idea.

He made an extra effort to be present in the room for the remainder of their session, and was careful not to say anything that would make Dr Phillips believe he needed daily appointments, or *worse*.

Afterwards, he grabbed lunch, alone in a quiet pub

restaurant, before returning home to draw in his room. He worked tirelessly to stay on his routines, to stay level. He felt off kilter. When it came time for his three-times-a-week skype call with Ian, he made sure it was brief. What he wanted to do was ask him about the trip to the fair he had remembered but once he saw the smile on Ian's face, and Ian started expressing how happy he was that Will was doing well back in Treevale, Will couldn't say any of it.

Oh, if Ian only knew the truth, he thought, and treated the call as carefully as he had the appointment with Dr Phillips. He updated Ian on Ben's arrival, and told a lie about spending last night watching a film together. The lies tasted like bile on his tongue.

When Ian was gone, Will sat for a long time on the edge of his bed and finally turned toward his thoughts. He searched for some answer to the things he remembered last night. In the twenty four hours since, he had managed to gain a clearer view on the two memories and there were so many things he didn't understand. First and foremost was the presence of the Crooked Man in both of them. He could think of no rational explanation, yet he didn't want to accept it as a coincidence.

He thought again of the memory of he and Nicole on the Ferris Wheel. He saw her, scared and trying not to cry in the darkness, squatting low so as not to be seen from outside of the cabin. He saw her sat beside him, lit by lights of many different colours, tears flowing freely. Playful organ music playing all around them.

His head began to throb.

He cast aside the memory of Nicole. Regardless of which version was real, it was too painful to replay. Instead, he focused on Ian.   Will needed answers, and he would only have the courage to ask the questions in person. He would have to travel back home tomorrow and return in time for the night out with the guys.

A knock on his door startled him out of his thoughts. He got up to answer it.

'Hey,' Beth beamed at him. 'Ben's gone out for the night. A family thing. Do you want to come hang out?'

Will nodded and followed her tentatively into the living room. The light was switched off but the TV was already on, on mute, casting the room in a strange, flickering glow. Beth headed straight to the kitchen where she shoved some toast into the toaster. She asked him if he wanted any and he shook his head. He had had his fill at dinner time. Having watched Beth devour a frozen pizza, he had expected she would have. She must have caught a look in his eye.

She said, 'I know, I'm always eating. But who doesn't love food, yeah?'

'You should be…' He started and then stopped before he said something she might take the wrong way.

'The size of a house? Yeah I know.' She laughed and looked down at her figure. 'I'm by no means a Victoria Secret model but I know I don't match the amount of food I eat. I suppose my kickboxing helps. But then, maybe it's the insomnia. Don't sleep, always burn calories. I should sell it as a diet. What do you think?'

They both chuckled. Beth waited for her toast and then quickly ate it before sitting down beside Will.

'Are you okay?' she asked.

He shrugged.

Beth selected some music on the tv, something quiet and somehow both peaceful and moody. She folded her legs underneath her and turned so that she was facing him. 'If you don't want to talk about anything, that's fine. I'm sorry I pushed the other night at the pub, yeah? I just wanted to know who you were before you disappeared.'

'Not so different,' Will answered, lying to himself as much as he was to her. Who he was before was complicated. He had been the happy, quiet guy that laughed along with the group's jokes and occasionally joined in, but he had also been the guy who stared into space, alone in his bedroom, feeling as though there was no point to anything, and feeling the urge to destroy something. He was a passionate creative, an awkward romantic, a borderline manic depressive. He was the quiet friend, the remaining son. The one left behind. The imposter.

Beth said, 'Can I ask, who's David?'

He looked at her as though thumped.

'You mentioned him last night when you were hypnotised or whatever. Said you'd become moody since David died. That's about when you started to cry.'

He looked down and nodded, felt the tears trying to return merely at the thought of David. He remembered the way David used to let him tag along with his friends when they went into the trees to make dens, even when, looking back, he probably didn't want to, all because Will didn't have too many of his own friends. Will had never been the popular kid, and David had done his best to change that by including him. At least, with David around, Will had had one friend.

'He was my brother,' Will said. His mind sent him back to the nights when David had snuck him into his bedroom after their parents had gone to bed, and the two of them were supposed to be sound asleep, so that they could play video games into the early hours of the morning. Will would be exhausted all of the next day but it would be worth it, and he would do it all again the following night.

'Tell me about him,' Beth said.

Will took a deep breath and surprised himself with a bittersweet smile. 'He was eight when I was born, so we didn't really play together much for a couple of years. We were still close, but I spent a lot of time by myself. My parents argued most of the time they were around. I got used to listening instead of talking.'

'*No!* That doesn't sound like you at all.'

Despite himself and the pain of what he was saying, he grinned. The smile was short lived. 'When I was six, and David was fourteen, our dad left. He moved over to the next town and saw us every couple of weeks and then stopped seeing us at all. Mum took on a second job to keep the money coming in, so looking after me kind of fell on David.'

'You must have gotten pretty close then.'

He nodded, warmed at the memory of the two of them eating cereal for dinner while their mum was at work for the second shift of the day, of discarding their bowls in the sink and sinking onto the sofa to watch a film or going to David's room to play games. One night, they had sat down to watch a film that was far too old for Will, about soldiers fighting werewolves – a film that terrified Will but which he watched in order to convince David he was a strong boy like him. After the film, the two of them had erupted into a pillow fight from opposite sides of the room, each of them throwing cushions like projectiles at one another and using the sofas for cover, until they heard their mum's car pull up and they scrambled to set everything straight before she reached the front door.

Thinking of that night brought a smile to his lips, but he didn't share it with Beth. Nobody but Will knew about that night and he wanted to keep it, just for him.

He said, 'Yeah. We played together, watched films together. He got me food, kept me out of trouble and cleaned me up when I got hurt. We used to read comic books together. I have a box under my bed back at home filled with all the comics he collected. He started sharing them with me when I was six and it became one of our things. He had me keep them in my room because he said he wanted me to be able to go back to them whenever I wanted but I know it was because he didn't want to look uncool if he brought friends or a girl round. He still bought them, though. We read them together and then they went in the box. Even at the end he was still buying them, although we weren't reading them together anymore.'

'Can I ask what happened to him?'

Will nodded that it was alright and started. 'David was with me all day except when we were at school. But at night, after Mum came home, he went out and did what teenagers are meant to do. Chased after girls, messed around, started drinking. He also started causing trouble, and shoplifting. He fell in with the wrong crowd.'

He took a moment to moisten the inside of his mouth. Speaking all of it aloud, perhaps for the first time – he hadn't even talked to Dr Phillips about it – was harder on him than he'd thought it would be, and he hadn't even gotten to the hard part.

'Maybe it was because of Dad not being interested,' he theorised. 'I was too young to see through his excuses, but David wasn't. So he fell in with the wrong people and didn't realise until it was too late. I don't know if he ever did.'

Beth swallowed and the sound bounced through the quiet, loud and surprising. 'What happened?'

He wiped his cheek and found a fresh tear. He didn't think she'd seen it, given the blue tinged glow from the tv that lit the room, but he dropped his head, casting it into deeper shadow to make sure she wouldn't see any more than might come. 'He started taking drugs. Weed, probably. Then coke, and pills. Things me and Mum wouldn't notice right away. Then Mum met Ian and she didn't have to work two jobs any more. David spent a lot more time with his friends. He was eighteen. A year later, Mum and Ian got married. By then, David was barely around. When he was, he stayed in his room. Three months after the wedding,' he choked down a sob. 'David was found in a bus station toilet with a needle… in his arm. He was… gone.'

Beth threw her arms around him and held him tight. No matter how tempting it was, he kept the cries back. 'Sweetheart, that's horrible.'

He nodded against her shoulder, then pulled away.

'That's why he took you to the fair?'

'I think so. Mum broke down. She switched off. She was vacant most of the time. Ian had to take up Mum's job of raising me, just like David did. Weeks would go by when she would barely acknowledge us, and she would remind me of the characters from that Robin Williams film; I can't remember the name.'

'Awakenings?'

'Yeah, that one. Then, she'd snap out of it and be obsessed with both of us. She wanted to spend all her time with us, hear our every thought. Like if we were out of sight, we would be gone too. Then, something would remind her of David and she would disappear into herself again.'

'Oh god. I can't even imagine.'

Of course she couldn't, Will thought. She had a shit father but her brothers were close to her and the three of them had been raised lovingly by their mother to be both tough *and* caring. It was an upbringing Will could only envy. None of that was Beth's fault, though, and he bit back the slice of bitterness he felt.

They were quiet for a long time, just sharing each other's company, then Beth said, 'You didn't have to tell me all of that, but thank you.'

He nodded. 'I have to go and see them tomorrow.'

On some level, he wanted her to offer to come with him and stand by his side as he asked the difficult questions. He would feel infinitely stronger with her beside him, but no offer came and he knew it was something he had to do alone, even if an offer had been forthcoming.

Beth, normally so eager to talk and with a word always waiting on the tip of her tongue, said nothing. She only nodded her understanding and patted his knee, gently.

23

Approaching the house in which he and David had grown up was like heading for a foreign country he had seen only in pictures. He saw it the moment he turned onto the street and he could recall any number of memories he had made within those walls at a moment's notice but it was as though this house were not the same one from those memories, and he wasn't entirely sure what he was going to find inside.

Of course he knew he would find his mother sat watching TV and he would find Ian fussing over her. But another part of him knew that in there with them were the lies of the past decade. He had been sure he and his friends had been at a fair shortly after the disappearance, and yet, Ian had never once mentioned the trip to the fair years before, even to explain why Will might be remembering something the police claimed couldn't be true.

How much more did Ian know than he was letting on?

Will took slow, cautious steps up the garden path, which was flanked by a perfectly trimmed lawn but no flowers. He paused beside a tree to the left of the garden and he was struck with the first heart wrenching attack of grief, softened only slightly by the years gone by. The tree was made up of two trunks twirling together and although it was not particularly high, a number of thick branches stretched out from it, which he and David had climbed up and along. David could reach the top and Will had always wanted to be able to match him, but he was too short. By the time he was tall enough, David was gone.

He swallowed the sorrow and turned back up the path toward the house, a red brick bungalow that looked as perfect and beautiful as always in contrast to the lives that played out within.

He reached the door and knocked. As he waited, he considered turning away and fleeing before anybody saw him.

When Will was eight, David had introduced him to a game he claimed everybody played, called knock-a-door-run. Will didn't fully understand why it was fun to knock on somebody's door and run away but he had gone along with it, because his brother had been the one to tell him. David had knocked first and darted back out of the garden. He was off down the street before Will had even started to move. In an effort to catch up, Will had sprinted so fast his lungs burned.

They hid behind a wall down the street and watched as a man opened the door and looked around. David smiled but they hadn't reached the punchline yet. The man realised what had happened, although he couldn't see either of the boys, and his confusion turned to anger. He shouted something into the street and slammed the door on his way back inside.

David had laughed heartily. But Will felt guilty, as though they had done something worse than mildly disrupt somebody's day. Still, he had played along. Considering doing the same to his own step-father, tearing him away from looking after Will's mother to find an empty doorstep, he felt that hole in his heart deepen.

He stayed where he was, and waited.

Ian answered. 'Will? What are you doing here? Is everything alright?'

'I wanted to talk to you about something,' Will said.

Ian's frown deepened. 'You don't have to come all the way back to talk to me. We only skyped last night but if it's urgent, I would always answer.'

'I wanted to do this in person.'

Ian ushered Will inside. Stepping into the house was like stepping back in time. There were so many memories lurking around every corner and hiding in every object. To survive after the loss of somebody so close, without moving house, he had subconsciously taught himself not to see the memories as clearly or as often in the things around him, like a child learning not to see the shapes of monsters within the shadows. The ocean of grief stricken memories were still there, though, and every so often they would creep back up on him. Now that he had been away, even for only a couple of weeks, he could feel the full weight of the ocean flooding over him.

He remembered he and David running, muddy and laughing, into the house after playing in the rain. He remembered the two of them, some other day, sprinting into the street with water guns they would use on the neighbouring kids, and some of David's friends – the ones who weren't drug takers.

Once he was through the porch and into the hall, he remembered the knock on the door that had woken him in the middle of the night. He recalled watching from the end of the hallway, out of sight, as Ian answered it, and allowed two uniformed police officers to enter. Ian had noticed Will and told him to go to bed, and he led the officers into the living room, and closed the door.

Will had not gone to back to bed. He couldn't remember if he had heard any of the words that were spoken, but he could remember the gut wrenching wails of his mother, pleading 'no.'

Ian followed Will into the living room and Will remembered how Ian had ushered him into the same room the day he had come home from the nut house, a hand on his shoulder as though he were a flight risk. It was the way the orderlies had guided the more withdrawn and doped up patients at the clinic. Instead of being brought home, it was as though he had been brought to another clinic, meticulously recreated to look like the house he'd grown up in, right down to the scuffs on the doorframes caused by he and David playing a little too carelessly. For a time, he had been observed far more closely than he had in the clinic and he had grown to resent the sight of Ian, despite all his good intentions.

'Evelyn, look who's come to see us,' Ian said as the two of them entered the living room.

His mam was right where Will expected her to be, in the corner armchair, eyes fixed on the television screen, watching a show hosted by Warwick Davis. Will couldn't remember the name of it. She didn't turn away from the pyramid of unrevealed answers.

'Evelyn, it's Will,' Ian insisted.

On the day Will was set to return to university for his third year, she had been sat in the same position, watching some other game show. He had gone in to say goodbye, knowing there would be no response after so long with her. He had told her he loved her, hugged her and made to kiss her on the cheek, but she had turned away from him. She had faced the window and stared out at the back garden until he left.

'Evelyn,' Ian tried again, but there was no change.

Will considered standing between her and the TV. Then she would have to acknowledge him. What stopped him was an incident that happened last November, only a few weeks after Will had been discharged from the clinic.

He had been sat drawing in the living room while his mother watched some gameshow one evening when the power had cut out. They were both plunged into darkness, something that affected both of them a great deal. In the darkness, Will started thinking about what might be hiding in it and he began to shake, edging toward another episode. On the other side of the living room, his mother had not just approached but dived head first into her own personal episode, at the loss of the television.

Ian had rushed into the room, torch in hand. He flicked the beam between Will and Evelyn, trying to work out who he should try and help first. The streak of the light moving between them made Will panic even more. Each time the light paused over his mother, Will saw that she was scratching the arms of the armchair to shreds, digging her nails as deep as they would go and forcing her body further and further into the chair. Over and over, as her shrieking quietened, she muttered 'Jim Morrison, Jim Morrison.' She was still trying to answer the question that had been asked before the television switched off.

'Evelyn,' Ian said again, now.

Will sighed. The claw marks on the arms of the armchair on which his mother sat were still there, as clear as though the fabric had been torn only yesterday. 'There's no point. Let's just go into the kitchen.'

Without waiting for an agreement, he left the room. As surely as his friends had followed him from the exhibition, Ian followed him to the kitchen and instantly started making coffee. The kitchen was small, most of it crammed into one corner of the room, the other taken by a small round dining table and the fridge. Will took a seat at the table and watched his step-father go about making their drinks as though Will was a normal student returning home for a visit.

'Are you looking forward to starting Uni?' Ian asked.

'I try not to think about it,' he admitted. It was less than a week away now.

Ian finished the drinks and sat down at the table. He said nothing, only waited for Will to continue.

'I'm afraid,' he admitted. 'I was supposed to do my third year with Nicole and the guys. We were meant to graduate together. I don't know how I've managed the last year without them but this is different. I shouldn't be doing this alone. They should be here, and they're not. Because of...'

'Don't finish that sentence,' Ian said. 'I know exactly what you were going to say and I'm not having it. It is *not* your fault that they're gone. Okay?'

Will looked down at the steaming mug of coffee and said nothing.

After a while, Ian said, 'Are you sleeping?'

Will shrugged. 'Some'

'Nightmares?'

You could say that, he thought. He nodded.

'Have you discussed them with Dr Phillips?'

'Yes,' Will said, although it was half a lie. He hadn't mentioned the latest ones. 'That's not what I'm here to talk about, though.'

'Alright. So what's up?'

'I've remembered something,' Will said, getting right to the point. He was afraid if he didn't, he'd be too afraid to say it at all, or Ian's own words would get in the way. Ian had always done his best to assure Will that he could talk to him about anything, especially his feelings, but Will had never found it easy to broach any of those kinds of topics. It wasn't that Ian wasn't his real father, as Ian suspected, but more how invested he was when Will did start to open up. He was too eager to help, too quick with a solution instead of sitting and listening. 'It's a bit muddled but I remember a fairground.'

Ian sighed. 'I thought we'd been over this fairground thing already?'

'I don't mean that night. This is when I was a kid. I remember being at a fair with you.'

'I'm not sure I understand.'

'I was twelve, I think. It wasn't long after David died and I remember you took me to a fair. Why didn't you mention it last year when I remembered a fair from that night?'

Ian leant forward. Will examined his face for some sign that he was about to lie but all he saw was puzzlement. Ian said, 'Because I've never taken you to the fair.'

'But I remember it.' Will shook his head. 'It was after David died. You said it was to prove the world goes on. I remember I got scared and ran away. I hid for hours under a caravan until somebody found me.'

Ian shook his head.

Will continued, 'I must have forgotten, or repressed it, but I remember it now.'

'Will, that never happened.'

'But I *remember* it. And then I went missing at another fairground with my friends, and you said *nothing*.'

'I never took you to the fair. That never happened. Have you talked to Dr Phillips about this?'

'Why are you lying?'

For a time, Ian wasn't able to look at Will. He looked pretty much anywhere else and released a long sigh. Then he looked directly at him and explained, 'Think about it, son. I couldn't have taken you to a fair, especially not when you're saying. Your mum was at her worst back then. I never could have left her for long enough to take you out for the day. Whatever you think you remember; it never happened.'

24

Will drifted around his room, readying himself to go out. It was a ritual that each time he enacted, filled him with growing excitement and joy as he anticipated the night ahead. He would shower, shave, dress and apply the finishing touches to his hair as the beat of music through the house pumped through the walls like a heartbeat.

Tonight, however, was a far cry from those days of old. Back then he would have been in a room that felt entirely his own, with movie posters on the walls and Pop Vinyl toys on his desk, but he had not allowed himself to believe when he moved in that he would be here long enough, so he had yet to adorn the room with any of his previous room's personality.

His personal scenery, made up of magnolia walls that were painted an even duller shade of beige from the light through the curtains as well as the week light bulb on the high ceiling, was not the only reason for the dampening of his mood. His mind was off somewhere else, too distracted to even consider going out into a public place to attempt to have fun. If he could, he would sacked off the whole night and stayed in his bedroom where he could wallow.

His mind had been spiralling since his conversation with Ian came to an abrupt and devastating end. He had gotten up, paced a few lengths of the kitchen while his mind attempted to catch up with what he'd just learnt and then he had become overwhelmed with the need to be somewhere else, to be alone back in his bedroom back at his new house. He was so caught up in his thoughts, he didn't even poke his head into the living room to attempt to say goodbye to his mother.

The thoughts had not relented at any point throughout the rest of the day, as he attempted to get his routine back on track, *again*. And they were still there, swirling inside his skull when it came time to prepare for the night out he had agreed to. He had not even gotten further than showering. He paced in nothing but his towel.

If it were true that Ian and Will had never visited a fairground together then it meant he'd remembered something that wasn't real. And if that were the case, what did it mean for the wellbeing of his friends?

The rational side of his head argued the memories were real. He had recovered them using hypnosis, and people used hypnosis all the time to recover memories of childhood abuse, and surely they hadn't imagined *those* memories.

On the other side of his bedroom door, the front door opened and Will froze mid pace at the sound of a man calling through the house.

'Hey dickheads.'

The house was booming with music, coming from either Ben or Beth's room upstairs, and neither of them would have heard the call. Cautiously, Will threw a t-shirt over his bare chest and opened his door.

'Hey,' the man said, turning toward him. 'You must be Will.'

The man looked around Will's age, although he didn't look like a student. He seemed more like an excessively young business executive. He was clean shaven and wore his hair in a slick comb over. He wore a smart blue shirt with the top two button undone as though he'd come home from a long day at the office and had already removed his tie. There was a large black hold-all slung over one shoulder, the only indication he was moving back in.

'Good to meet you. I'm Xander,' he said and cast a long gaze over Will, sizing him up. Will could see the judgements forming in his eyes, but he couldn't tell exactly what the verdict was.

When he was finished, Xander said, 'The other two dicks upstairs?'

Will nodded. 'Getting ready for a night out.'

Xander chuckled and grinned. 'Which means Beth's probably having a nap. Lazy bitch.' The way he said it told Will he was fully aware of Beth's insomnia and wasn't being serious. Even so, Will wasn't sure he liked the joke. 'I'll come meet you properly in a bit. Once I'm unpacked and ready to go.'

With that, Xander disappeared up the stairs, yelling more profanity at his friends, until he was close enough for them to hear it.

Will closed his door and sat for a while, listening to the music through the walls and ceiling. Eventually, he dressed in an outfit that would have made Nicole proud: a black shirt he'd bought on his way back home, to replace the smart shirts that were too big now that he'd lost the excess weight he'd had the last time he'd had occasion to dress up, and a pair of skinny jeans finished with black Converse All Stars. He spent a great deal of time in front of the bathroom mirror, trying to form his thick hair, in need of a cut, into some kind of stylish doo. Eventually, he gave up and swept the waxy hair to one side with a messy parting.

Ready, but not feeling it, he headed into the living room to await the others. Xander came down first, dressed even smarter than before, but with messier hair, as though that made him look edgy and fun. He still looked like a business executive only now it was as though he'd rolled out of bed, late for work.

Heading for the kitchen to get a drink, he tapped his knuckles against Will's arm and whispered, 'Brace yourself, man.'

Will met his eye, confused, and Xander flicked his own eyes toward the living room door. A moment later, Beth stepped through it and Will's jaw hit the floor.

In the short time he had known her, he had only ever seen Beth in gym clothes, leggings, or jeans and casual t-shirts or hoodies. Converse or Vans adorned her feet at almost all times if she was leaving the house and her fiery hair was tied back or hung loose in unkempt waves.

Tonight, a black dress hugged her shape, cutting off just above the knee, where it showed her sleek, toned calves and teased her athletic quads, accentuated by the elevation of her black high heels. Her hair was straightened and hung over one shoulder. Her eyes were decorated with black eyeliner and her lips burned a brighter red than her hair.

It was not her beauty that stunned Will – he already thought she was beautiful in a way that had stirred feelings of confusion because of both her sexuality and his continued feelings for Nicole – but how feminine she looked.

She caught Will's reaction and blushed. 'You can close your mouth, Will. I can wear a dress and get done up, sometimes, you know. I'm not always such a boyish slob.'

'I... I know... I... You look... I....' he attempted and she laughed.

She thanked him and went into the kitchen for a drink.

There was a knock at the door and Ben bounced down the stairs to answer it. Xander returned from the kitchen with a bottle of lager, amused. He explained that Ben had always had a thing for Amanda, even though she 'plays for the other team.'

Will could relate but he refrained from saying so.

Ben led Amanda into the room and the group was complete. Ben was dressed in a shirt that actually had sleeves but Beth's own outfit overshadowed any surprise at this change.

They all grabbed a drink and took a seat in the living room. Within moments, they were all four caught up in a mile a minute catch up conversation, which Will listened to with amusement and interest. He actually managed to relax a little and cast from his head the worries of the day.

He was reminded of the times he and his old friends had gone on nights out, and the pre-drinks they had enjoyed before going out to the usual pubs or clubs. They would laugh and joke and there would be drinking games, which Will would watch with great amusement. His disinterest in drinking excluded him from the games but he never felt excluded. The conversations as Ben, Beth, Xander and Amanda caught up on old times was very much the same. He was not an old friend catching up, but he certainly felt welcome to call their group his own.

After finishing a drink and going to fetch a new one, Xander sat down beside Will and turned his attention away from the conversation with the others.

'Must be tough, being back?' he said.

'Yeah,' Will said. *Tough* was certainly a word for it, and he wasn't even *really* back. He was in the same town but in a new house and he had yet to start university. Only once he had stepped inside the ADAM building again would he consider himself truly back, and then things would be more than tough.

'Anything I can do, mate, just let me know,' Xander offered and he took a long pull from his beer bottle. 'When we start again, I'll introduce you around, if you want. Get you properly settled in, so you don't feel like we're your only friends.'

'Erm, yeah, sure,' Will felt very far from sure. So far he had been introduced to two of their friends with a fifty percent success rate. He didn't feel like being pressured into meeting more people, even those that would share his graduating class, but nor did he want to turn Xander down on their first night of meeting and make an enemy of somebody he would have to live with.

Xander chuckled, 'Not that you're going to need anybody else.' He nudged his elbow against Will's. 'I can already tell we're going to be good mates.'

A short while later, somebody suggested a drinking game, and, as the only one in the room not drinking, everybody turned to Will.

'Do you mind?' Amanda asked.

He shook his head and told them to go ahead. While Ben went to the kitchen to get the jug and playing cards required for Ring of Fire, Beth gestured to the can of Coke in Will's hand.

'You weren't responsible for what happened, so why go teetotal?' she said.

Will swallowed. It was the closest any of them had come to mentioning the night of his disappearance outside of the hypnotherapy sessions, but it was Beth's assurance that he was not responsible that formed the tumour in his throat. It was sweet of her to say, but it wasn't true.

All eyes were turned toward him, watching and waiting, ears pricked. Curious, yet without judgement.

He forced out, 'I wasn't much for it before... Maybe because of David, I don't know. But that night was the first time I lost control and I don't want to experience that again.'

That he had "lost control" was a phrase that shook them, although they tried not to show it, because of the implications, particularly when considering that he couldn't remember what had happened. Beth spread her bright red lips in a sympathetic smile and turned to the game prepared between them all, a signal that they should move on.

As the game started, Will watched vacantly, his thoughts occupied and his stomach doing flips. In that hesitant moment, he had felt their judgements, known they were wondering what might have happened when he lost control, and what had started as a comfortable night had taken on a darker weight. It grew darker still at the thought of all the judgemental eyes that would lurk in the shifting shadows of the nightclub. What if somebody recognised him?

He had never wanted to flee to his room and lock the door more than he did in that moment.

He headed into the kitchen and opened the fridge to give the impression he was getting another can of Coke but really he needed a moment. The cold chill of the fridge rushed against his skin and he took a few deep breaths, allowing the air to cool not only his body but his mind.

When he closed the fridge and turned back toward the open doorway, he felt that old smack of grief strike him again. Amanda, Ben, Beth, and Xander all sat around the jug, which was slowly filling with a mixture of each of their different drinks, but for a second, he was seeing Nicole, Craig, Tom and Julian in their place. As he grew drunker, Craig would start drumming along to whatever music was playing. Julian would tell an untrue story and he and Tom would argue. Nicole would laugh and spill a drink, and laugh even more.

Will missed them so fucking much. He wished he'd valued the time he'd had with them while he had the chance. He wished he'd savoured the glance Nicole would flash him when they were laughing at Julian and Tom, their eyes meeting for only a second but speaking volumes; the comfortable silences they all shared walking to the studio, or going to the shop around the corner and the way he and Craig would stand on either side of Nicole in an aisle and start dancing to embarrass her; the way Julian would speed walk to the pub so he could buy a drink for them all before they'd even reached the bar; Julian's bullshitting, and the moments when he told them something genuine; Tom's passionate ramblings about music, most of which the rest of them hadn't even heard of.

Will would have given anything to spend a single day with them again and to experience any one of those things.

Beth lost the game and started pleading, 'No, no, no, no, no. Please.' The group didn't relent and Beth picked up the jug.

'Oh god, that fucking smell.'

'Chug it,' Ben ordered.

'You can do it, babes,' Amanda said.

Beth downed it and coughed. 'That's fucking awful. Let's go out before I end up having to do that again. Once I lose, I always seem to lose again.'

The group agreed and they shoved their things in the kitchen and prepared to leave.

This was the last chance to protest and back out, Will

thought. As they headed for the hallway, Will shuffled slowly behind. The last time he was part of a group, heading out somewhere like this, he had been the only one to return. He couldn't help but fear that something bad was going to happen.

Perhaps sensing his trepidation, they all looked back. Xander clapped a hand on his back and said, 'Come on, mate. You'll be alright with us. It's going to be fun.'

Reluctantly, Will left with them.

25

The air was bitter and cold, but they took no jackets. Nobody wanted to be burdened with one when they got into the nightclub. Ben, wearing sleeves for the first time Will had seen, walked as though through the height of a summer day. Amanda huddled into him for warmth and Xander shot Will a smug, knowing look.

A sneaking envy crept through Will, and he allowed himself to imagine, just for a second, Beth huddling into him for warmth, the feel of her body against his. She walked close to him, her shoulder almost touching his. In a flash, he saw his hand brushing against Nicole's as they walked in the direction of the fair, and he felt guilty.

The walk was a couple of miles through residential areas, most of them abandoned and boarded up, in which Will was glad for company at this time of night, with so many places for unsavoury people to lurk in wait. They reached the town centre without seeing a soul, and then, when they reached the high street, brightly lit by harsh streetlights and illuminated shop fronts, they found only a scattering of people. The shops flanking them on each side were dark and empty, having closed hours ago.

It was like walking through an abandoned town, Will thought, and couldn't help but flash on him and his friends walking through an empty, partially lit fairground. He moved closer to his new friends and tried to focus on where he really was.

On the far side of the town centre, the nightclub was a large gothic building with two floors. As soon as the bouncers had approved their IDs and they paid their entry, they stepped into thick smoke filled with strobing colours that froze Will on the spot.

Within the smoke, dark figures moved. He couldn't see their faces, only the shadowy flash of their movement, swarming around him, closing in on all sides. Coming for him. He tried to turn and flee back the way they had come but behind him he found only more smoky shapes of people piling in toward him.

A hand plunged out of the smoke and grasped his shoulder. He spun toward it and felt his head grow light and start to tilt. Then he saw Beth's face, close to his.

'I got you this!' she yelled above the blare of the music, and he felt a flimsy plastic cup thrust into his hand.

'Come on,' she called. She grabbed his hand and pulled him through the smoke on which the strobe lights danced, to where the others were converging, their own drinks in hand.

They huddled in together.

'On Monday,' Ben screamed. 'We start our final year, guys. This is it. Here's to one last night of freedom!'

He lifted his cup and they all tapped them together. They moved as a group toward the dance floor, where they reformed their huddle and, in the beams of the strobe lights that caught on the smoke the way sunlight caught on dust mites, started to move in poor attempts at dancing.

Will kept his eyes trained on their feet and stood close to Beth. She nudged him, prompting him to look up at the smile on her face, but what he saw was the smoke and the lights. He didn't want to look at them but the colours were everywhere. He could almost hear the screaming, despite the loud, thumping music. A light passed over his face and everything was red.

He stumbled back. There were splashes of red on the floor, on the walls. There was blood on his hands.

A hand grabbed him and he spun, lurching back and almost fell. Whoever had caused all of this blood had come back for him. His back hit the wall and his feet gave way beneath him. The hand kept him from going all the way down and he was forced to look up at his assailant. He expected to see the Crooked Man leering at him through the smoke but it was Beth and Amanda.

He looked around at the room, which a moment ago had been much smaller and covered in blood. The nightclub was the same as it had been when they entered. The blood on his hands and the floor was nothing more than his spilled Coke. A couple of the dancing patrons eyed him wearily.

'Will?' Beth yelled.

'Are you okay?' Amanda shouted, although it was clear from the look on her face that she knew he wasn't.

Beth yelled something in Amanda's ear and Amanda nodded. Together, they started leading him somewhere. Instead of the exit, as he hoped, they led him down a corridor, up a flight of stairs, and into an area that more resembled a pub than a club. The music was quieter and there were chairs and Chesterfield Armchairs and sofas scattered around. The walls were dark and plastered with graffiti and guerrilla style band posters. Amanda and Beth sat Will down on one of the sofas, Amanda taking a seat beside him. Xander dropped into the nearby armchair, while the other two remained standing. All of them watched him.

'What happened?' Amanda asked.

Will swallowed. 'The lights.'

Amanda nodded as though it were the answer she had expected. 'We'll stay up here then, where it's brighter.' The large room they were sat in was well lit with overhead lighting, and no coloured strobes.

'I prefer it up here anyway,' Xander said, slouching down in the chair.

Conversations started up between everybody once again, now that they could hear each other speak. Will sat and listened, and tried not to think of the lights and the smoke. Instead, he returned to a night that now held pain for him, but which at the time, had been anything but painful.

He and Nicole had come to this same nightclub during the Easter break of their second year, while the others were back home seeing their parents. It was a rock night and Nicole had glammed it up all the way with her black make-up. She was in heaven as the two of them danced – or whatever jumping up and down to music was called – on the same dancefloor downstairs where he had almost lost himself, listening to the music Nicole loved and surrounding by people their own age, dressed head to toe in blacks and red. They were lost together in a world of smoke and bursting strobe lights and Will had felt happier than he ever thought possible.

Four months later, he had tried to kill himself and thus began the course of events that would lead his friends to their fate. Will had led Nicole into another smoky mist, pierced by colourful lights. And that one, she had never emerged from. In some ways, neither had Will. He was still floating through it, searching for her.

Amanda became very passionate and enthusiastic with her movements as she spoke to Ben about something or other, and her drink sloshed over onto the floor and Beth's feet.

'Sorry, babes,' Amanda offered and swigged from her drink to keep it from happening again.

'You sure I can't convince you to have one?' Xander said to Will.

Will shook his head.

'We'll look after you. Nothing bad will happen,' Xander assured. 'Beth will, definitely. She always looks after us.'

Will looked over at Beth, who was now deep in conversation with Amanda. The conversation between Amanda and Ben ended and he had run off somewhere. Amanda and Beth's heads were almost touching as they muttered to each other and laughed. Beth burst out laughing and pushed her hand against Amanda's leg, her head falling back.

'So, did you do it?'

Will jumped at the question. 'What?'

'We're all wondering it. The others are just too polite to ask.'

'Wha...' Will started.

Xander nudged closer. 'I won't tell anyone, mate. Did you?'

Will looked around but the others were not there to save him. Beth and Amanda were still forehead to forehead, talking low, and Ben was at the bar.

'Will? Will Campbell?'

Will followed the voice with a slither of fear. A man in his late twenties approached him and Xander. He was a Geordie Shore type, with perfectly styled short-back-and-sides hairstyle and toned, angular muscles that his short sleeves wrapped around too tightly.

It took Will a moment to place his face. He actively avoided Geordie Shore types – the show had been bad enough and the wannabes were even worse – but he realised he did know this one. Elliot Dillon. He'd been on the course with Will. He would have graduated this past July, when he and his friends should have.

'Hi,' Will said, warily.

'Fuck me, it really is you, in' it?' Elliot held out a hand for Will to shake. Will looked but didn't take it. Elliot dropped it and looked at Xander. 'Hey, Xander, 'ow's it going?'

Xander nodded and said, 'Not bad. Not bad. Good to see you. I'm just going to get another drink. You want one?'

'Yeah, sure mate. And get one for me old pal Will, 'ere. What you drinking?'

Will gritted his teeth at the second drink offer in five minutes, and this one wouldn't be as easy to argue with. Elliot was the type who was used to getting what he wanted. Be it girls, opportunities or grades, he never had to work too hard to get any of them.

'I'm not,' Will said.

'I'm offering ya a fucking drink, like, mate. Don't be

fucking rude.'

'Sorry, but...'

'No, no buts, mate. What you drinking?'

He looked to Xander to save him but his supposed 'new friend' did nothing.

Elliot waved his hand, dismissing the conversation. 'Whatever. Xander, just bring us two vodka and cokes.' To Will, he said, 'How you doing, anyway? Going back to uni?'

Xander slipped away, heading for the bar.

Will nodded. 'Third year.'

'You mean again,' Elliot laughed and then nodded as though that would make the joke okay. When Will didn't laugh, he shrugged. 'I'm just back visiting some mates, ya know. Speaking of which,' he looked at Beth and Amanda huddled together on the sofa. 'These your new friends? They're pretty fit. I'd definitely give'm one. Be a shame if they end up like your old mates, like.'

His eyes were fixed on them, neither of them aware of him, so he didn't see it coming when Will leapt from his seat and shoved his full weight into Elliot's stomach. Elliot lurched backward and tumbled to the floor. His glass spewed beer all over him, drenched his face and shirt. Will stood, breathing heavy like a bull, fists clenching and unclenching by his side.

'Will? What the...?' Beth started. By the bar, Ben and Xander turned toward the commotion, their mouths hung open in large O's.

Elliot started to recover and fixed his eyes on Will. 'You're fucking dead, mate.'

Will headed for the doors and clambered down the stairs without looking back.

26

'Whoa, whoa, whoa,' the bouncers yelled and tried to reach out for Will as he burst through the exit. He twisted away from their grasp and ran as fast as his feet would carry him. He didn't dare to look over his shoulder and see Elliot's progress, whether he was even still coming for him.

He was about halfway home when he was forced to stop, and lean against a nearby wall to catch his breath. He risked a glance back the way he had come, cautious to do so in case he saw Elliot right there, or worse, the Crooked Man; he wouldn't have the energy yet to flee. There was nobody around, yet with the thought of the Crooked Man, he felt vulnerable and exposed. There were too many places he could be watched from, and too many people coming for him.

Elliot, Daniel, the Crooked Man, and the chain smoking man in the denim jacket. Who knew how many others.

Alone and afraid, he removed his phone from his pocket. He had time to note the seven missed calls on the screen from Beth before it started vibrating again with a fresh one.

With pause, he answered and Beth's voice blasted from it.

'Will, what the fuck? Where are you?'

He didn't reply. Didn't know how.

'Will?'

'Yeah?'

'What happened? Whatever it was the guy did to you, that was really unlike you. I didn't think you'd... Are you okay? What's going on?'

He tensed. Heard Ian's voice in his head. The voice of doubt, making him question what was real and what wasn't. He wished he'd never listened to Beth when she suggested hypnotherapy. If he had told her no, instead of jumping at the chance for her ex-girlfriend to play around in his subconscious, then he could have continued with his routines and been fine.

Would he? He still would have never known the truth.

'I'm fine,' he lied. 'I'm going home.'

'I'm going to come back, too. I'll keep you company. Maybe we can talk about this? I'll bring Amanda.'

'No,' he snapped, a little too harshly. 'I'm fine. I don't need your help.'

He ended the call before Beth could say anything more and suddenly, he was, once again, shrouded by the chilling silence of the dark, abandoned street. He shivered, either through the cold or the fear, he didn't know, and he headed off at a quick walk.

There were eyes everywhere, shimmering little orbs hidden within every shadowy nook, in the cracks between all curtains towering above him. Their gaze prickled his skin, pulling up the hairs on his arms like static. There was no escape. No matter how quickly he moved, they followed. At any moment, one of the shadows with shining eyes would unfold itself into the elongated shape of the Crooked Man, and flash that crooked grin of tombstone teeth.

Around the next corner, a figure stepped from the shadows and he released a yelp. His heart blocked his throat and tears sprung to his eyes, but it was not the Crooked Man. It was a woman with skin of melted leather and hair of straw.

'Three quid for a blowjob?' she offered. If lung cancer had a voice, it was hers. She looked like the living dead, but she was nothing to do with the Crooked Man. No matter her haggard, skeletal appearance, she was nothing more than the typical Treevale prostitute.

Will declined with a mumble and scarpered around her,

careful to avoid any physical contact. She looked as though a single touch would spread to him whatever cancerous contagion had ravaged her life.

'Two pound?' she called after him. 'Oi, come on. Don't ignore me. You'll regret it.'

The implied threat in her words chased at Will's heels and he quickened into a jog. He reached the university, and the emptiness was even more chilling. He had always been used to walking through the campus in the middle of the night, either coming back from a night out or a late studio session, yet it was as though a vacuum had sunk atop it tonight, voiding it of all feelings of life.

The house was a half mile to the east and he covered the distance as fast as he could, his jog returning almost to an all-out sprint. He scrambled to get the key in the door. Calling up images from almost every horror movie he had been forced to endure for Nicole's sake, he willed himself not to drop the keys. That would certainly mean death.

The key slid into the lock and he fell into the house, thrusting the door closed behind him where it locked automatically. He sat against it for a time, and waited for his breath to slowly return and his heart to fall back into rhythm.

He realised how ridiculous he was to have been so afraid. He regretted the way he had spoken to Beth. It was something the old Will never would have done. Even if involved in a disagreement, he would remain calm and never come so close to insult or malice.

The only thing he could think of to do to try and make up for it was to text her an apology but when he removed his phone from his pocket he found no new missed calls on the screen and he put it aside. They were still out there having fun without him. In *spite* of him. A message from him would only disrupt their enjoyment. He had been foolish and stupid and violent, all things that Nicole would have scorned him for, and it was best if he left them to the rest of their night, undisturbed.

Will crawled into bed, guilt and loneliness mixing together into a perfect poison. Rest was kept from him as he tossed and turned. He was wondering whether he was going to be allowed any rest when he suddenly jerked awake, completely unaware he had even fallen asleep.

A shadow danced across his bed and his body became wired, as it had been when he had first crawled beneath the covers. He followed it to the bay window and watched in growing horror as the silhouette of a man climbed up it like a spider. A second man stood beside him, watching.

Will leapt from beneath his sheets and backed himself into the corner, watching, unsure what to do.

They – whoever *they* were – were coming for him.

Without thinking, he flicked the bedroom light on and the shape of the silhouettes disappeared. Over the sound of Will's heavy, quickening breath, came the faint tap of feet striking pavement. The front door exploded with five heavy knocks and Will felt his heart burst with each one.

There was nothing in the bedroom for him to use to defend himself if the men broke the door down. The best he had on offer was a stack of heavy design books that he could throw at them, but they were still boxed in the bottom of the wardrobe.

The only real option was the kitchen. They each had their own set of sharp cooking knives. Four different sets of large, sharp knives, but they were all at the back of the house and to get to them meant leaving his bedroom and coming a mere metre from the front door. He wondered how long the front door would hold if they tried to kick it open. His bedroom door with its thin wood and single yale lock would take considerably less time.

He took a deep breath in and held it in his expanded chest, a hand on the latch of the lock and the other on the handle. He pictured his set of knives, lying safely to one side of his draw, saw the biggest of the set, pure, shining and barely used. He tried to ignore the image that followed of the blood the knife would produce if used.

At the same time, he twisted both the latch and the handle and sprung out of his room, not turning to look at the front door, which still thumped with continued knocking. He rushed to the kitchen and grabbed from his drawer the biggest knife, a nine inch monster that he had only ever used to cut up a whole chicken. His hands were shaking and he threw the knife straight back into the draw in favour of a smaller one in the middle of the range, which he could wield with less chance of hurting himself.

He crept back to the living room doorway and watched the front door. The hallway and the living room were in darkness, but for the light from the kitchen behind him and the pool of light spreading out from his bedroom door but he felt more comfortable and safer in the gloom. If they got inside, they would follow the light into his bedroom first.

The knocking paused, commenced again. His grip tightened on the steel handle.

Minutes passed, in which there were more knocks, growing more powerful and aggressive with each bout. Each one reverberated through the hallway, sending a tremor through his already shivering body. And then they stopped.

He waited for a long time, rocking in the doorway with the knife gripped in two hands, peering at the two slithers of glass in the top half of the door, waiting for the figures to come back and start knocking again. But all that was visible in the frosted glass was the fragmented orange glow of the streetlights.

No matter whether the assailants were gone or not, there would be no sleeping tonight, so he flicked on the hallway light, and, reluctant to sit in any room with a window, he sat down on the stairs, brandishing the knife between his legs, like a broadsword.

He didn't know how long he sat there, but his muscles had begun to ache from being tensed for so long when the front door opened and, drunk and laughing, his housemates stumbled through the door. The laughter dying in their throats at the sight of him. Crammed into the small hallway like they'd been forced into a coffin fit for one, they stared at him with open eyes and wider mouths.

'What the fuck, dude?' Xander said, his voice weaker than he probably intended. 'Is this how you waited for your old housemates when they were out?'

Beth leant past Amanda and thumped Xander. 'Shutthefuckup,' she slurred.   Xander realised what he said, and closed his eyes. 'Do you want to put the knife down?'

Will became aware of the knife still in his hands and placed it down on the stairs like it was a snake he'd not noticed before.

'Dude, what is going on?' Ben asked.

Before Will could answer, Amanda moved to the front of the group and held out a hand for him. He took it and allowed her to help him up and into the living room, where she turned on the light and told him to take a seat. As he did so, feeling smaller than he had ever felt in his entire life, Amanda went back into the hallway and ordered everybody to go upstairs.

Then she took a seat on the arm of the other sofa and looked at him.

'What's with the knife?' she asked.

He swallowed. He felt on the verge of a great flood of tears that wouldn't stop until it drowned them all.

'There was somebody...' he started. 'I saw somebody.'

'Saw somebody where? In the house?' she probed and, despite the fuzziness at the edge of her words, she reminded him of Dr Phillips. It was the doubt. She wanted to know if he'd imagined something.

He shook his head.

Footsteps thudded back down the stairs and Beth came into the room, swaying.

'What... the... the fuck?' she said.

Amanda turned to her. 'Babes, not now. Will?'

The pressure increased with Beth in the room, especially after their phone conversation.

He told them what had happened.

Amanda and Beth looked at each other.

'Go up to bed please, babes,' Amanda asked. 'I'll help Will.'

Beth sighed and, in a whisper the volume of her normal voice, said, 'See if you can help him stop acting like a prick,' and she disappeared upstairs.

With Beth gone, Amanda put all of her attention back on Will. She sank onto the sofa cushion and leaned forward, resting her chin in her hand to keep it from falling down.

'There's nobody outside now,' she assured him. 'We didn't see anybody on our way back either, so whoever they were, they're gone. Tomorrow morning, we can call the police.'

He looked away.

'What's wrong with calling the police?' she asked, every word taking a bit more effort than normal.

'They don't listen. They didn't believe me,' he said. 'Before.'

Were they right not to? he wondered. How real was his memory of the fairground, of anything? He screwed his eyes shut against the sting of angry tears. He was filled with a boiling fury but it was the kind he didn't know how to release because it was directed at his own mind.

If he couldn't trust his memory, and he couldn't trust himself not to act out of character, as he had done by leaving the exhibition that night or attacking Elliot tonight, then what could he trust? He thought of his strange nightmares and his sleepwalking, coming to in the centre of the bedroom.

The letter he'd received really existed but was it really possible he could be jumping at shadows? Had the letters triggered another episode, one that never seemed to entirely end?

Amanda chewed her lip and nodded. 'If they come back, you call the police straight away, okay?'

Will nodded that he would.

'They're gone now, whoever they are, and we're all here if they come back. Maybe you should try and get some sleep? I'm too drunk to get m'self home, so I'll be right in here. If you need me, you can come and get me.'

It was more than a question, and, as though ordered by Dr Phillips herself, he obeyed. He closed and locked his bedroom door and climbed back under the covers.

You've really done it now, he thought. *Now they're all going to question whether or not you killed your friends. And whether they're next.*

As sleep finally took him, he had one more thought.

Did I?

27

The house was deathly silent when Will awoke. Despite having said she would be sleeping in the living room, Amanda was nowhere to be seen. She had either snuck out extremely early, or more likely had slept in the room directly above Will's and was still there now, sleeping off her hangover with Beth.

The thought of the two of them together made Will both uncomfortable and aroused, adding to his confusing mix of feelings. He was quick to turn from the thoughts out of respect. Beth was his friend, one that he was already feeling strange about because of his attraction to her, and Amanda was trying to help him with his memory loss. Thinking of the two of them together, even unintentionally, felt as though he were crossing a line, peering into somewhere his attention didn't belong.

He stretched out his tired limbs on the doorstep and his thoughts moved to the events of last night. It had been a bad night, that was for certain. He didn't regret the shove he'd given Elliot, the act that had started the near episode – or was it a full episode? – he suffered back at the house, but he regretted the way he had treated Beth on the phone. It wasn't fair the way he spoke to her. When he got back from his run, if she was awake, he would make his apologies and hope the two of them could return to how things were before.

All stretched out, he started off down the street. He had reached only a few houses down when he saw a car door ahead of him swing open and out stepped the rough looking chain smoker in the denim jacket. There was no doubt now that he was here for Will.

Will stumbled to a stop and his mind was torn, not between fight or flight – he was too much of a coward for that. He was torn between which direction his flight should take. Run the other way and keep running, or flee back into house?

'Hello, William,' the man said. 'I think it's time we talked.'

Will's mouth bobbed, trying to find words. He was frozen. If he returned to the house, the man would knock on the door and everybody in the house would be woken up and he would have to explain to them why they shouldn't open the door. After last night, he seemed crazy enough. If he ran away, the man would still be here waiting when he eventually returned.

'What do you want?' Will asked.

'Ten minutes of your time.'

'I... Who...'

The man closed the car door and stepped toward Will. The movement sparked movement in Will's own feet and he began shuffling backward, inch by inch. His decision was made, he would go back inside and call the police. But he didn't dare turn his back. The front door locked automatically when he closed it and he was afraid the strange man would attack him when he turned to get the key into the lock.

As though he knew what Will was thinking, the man put his hands out to either side, showing that he was carrying no weapon, and implied no threat. Not yet, at least.

'Look,' the man said. 'Talk to me now or talk to me later, but you will talk to me, because I have nowhere else to go. I'll still be here when you get back from your run. I can wait out here all day.' Will looked back at the door, considered going back inside. 'Hide in there all you want. I'll still be here tomorrow morning when you leave for your therapy session. Maybe I'll even come with you.'

Will gulped. How far had this man followed him? Had he followed him all the way to Newcastle, to Dr Phillips's office?

'What do you want?' he finally croaked.

'Just to talk.'

'About what?'

'Your memories.'

Will's head started to shake before he even knew he was doing it.

'Kid, I'm not very good at asking nicely. You can either talk to me or I'll go and talk to your friends. I'm sure they'd be interested to find out about your night time trips out of the house.'

That stopped Will's head mid shake and he stared at the man, transfixed. He thought of the dreams he'd had, the sodden clothes, and the ache in his feet like he'd been walking outside. He *had* suffered another episode. More than one. His friends couldn't be allowed to know, especially after everything that happened last night.

Don't talk to strangers, he'd been told as a child. But if he didn't talk to this one, Will would see the inside of a mental facility by the end of the week.

He said, 'Okay.'

The man nodded. 'Good. Now why don't we go somewhere we won't be disturbed. I don't want to bring your housemates into this unless I have to.'

Without waiting for a response, he walked around to the passenger side of the car and opened the door. He stood holding it, waiting. Knowing, deep down, that it was a bad idea – he wasn't just talking to a stranger, he was getting in his car – Will climbed inside. The man closed the door behind him and climbed in behind the wheel. So close to him in an enclosed space, Will felt a tremor of fear. The smell of cigarettes and coffee lingered bitter and choking around them.

They drove in silence to a café on the edge of town, far enough away that ensured Will would require a lift back home. It was a bland café, carbon copied from a number of others across the country. Dark wooden tables and brown leather chairs, posters displaying coffee beans behind various text stuck up here and there.

The man directed Will to take a seat in one of the booths and went to the counter. Will did as he was told. The point of no return had been passed the moment he climbed into this man's car. The man could drive him somewhere and kill him and nobody would ever know.

Only now that he was here did he think of an outcome worse than death. What if this man was connected to the Crooked Man and he was here to find out what Will had remembered, in order to cover the Crooked Man's back? And once he learnt everything Will remembered, would take him back to the fairground and back to the Crooked Man himself, before seeing to the others, who knew as much about the fairground as Will.

The man returned with two mugs of coffee as Will started to think about how he would get away. On foot. Miles from home. And this man with a car.

The man slid a mug toward Will before taking a sip out of his own and looking at it thankfully.

Tremoring, Will asked, 'Who are you?'

Will regretted it instantly. The man wasn't going to give him his real name, or if he did, it would definitely sign Will's death warrant.

The man looked at his drink for a few moments more as though deciding how to answer. Was he coming up with a fake name, or deciding whether Will was going to live long enough for it to matter?

'People call me the Stranger,' he said, finally. 'But my name's Peter Lincoln. I'm an investigative journalist.'

That he was not a murderer was only a slight weight lifted from Will's chest, for he had cause to fear journalists as much, if not more. They didn't kill people, but they could make a person's life not worth living.

In the aftermath of the disappearance, reporters gathered outside Will's house at almost all hours, shouting at Ian whenever he left the house and sometimes shouting at the house if they caught a glimpse of anybody in the window. Will and his parents started living with the curtains closed. Then the real vultures swooped in. Journalists called their phone non-stop, posted business cards through the letter box and knocked on the door at various times throughout each day, hoping for an exclusive, or even a snippet of a sentence.

On one occasion, a week or so before the episode that would land Will in the mental clinic, Ian had walked Will to the car to take him to his appointment with Dr Phillips, attempting to shield him from the reporters. One of the group had broken from the group, sprinted right at the two of them, across the lawn, not stopping until the two of them were cornered between the wall and the car. Seeing a rival seizing an opportunity the rest crowded in. Ian tried to push back when the first reporter got rough. Ian was thrust to the ground and the reporter's hands pinned him there by the neck.

'What did he do to them, huh?' the reporter screamed. He looked up, suddenly, into Will's startled, deer-in-the-headlights expression and asked him. 'What did you do? Tell us what you did to them?'

Will had cowered against the car, unable to save Ian as he had been unable to save his friends, and he had unleashed an almighty, gut-wrenching scream, so loud the journalists backed off, including the one on top of Ian.

It later transpired, after he was arrested, that the man was Tom's second cousin and he had taken the disappearance very badly. He wasn't even a reporter. But Will remembered the way the rest of them had watched him sprint forward and instead of an incoming attack, they had seen it as a reporter getting a head start on them, and they swarmed in to make sure they were a part of anything that transpired. And he remembered the story they had made of it, the photographs of him screaming at them like an animal, alongside headlines that branded Will insane, manic, and dangerous.

The Stranger, seeing Will's face light up with something resembling fire, said, 'Look, kid. I don't want to drag your name through the dirt. I'm not like the tabloid guys. I'm not interested in a quick headline. I'm more interested in the truth. I remember when the news had some integrity. Besides, you've come this far, so you might as well talk to me.'

'How did you find me?'

Annoyed at how things were going, Lincoln shook his head and said, 'The woman across the road from your parents' house. Months ago, I offered her money if she would let me know if anything noteworthy happened. A few weeks ago, she called to tell me you and your step father went out and he came back alone. It wasn't too difficult after that to find out where you'd moved to.'

Will sputtered, 'I don't know anything.'

Lincoln sighed. He looked down at the table and shook his head, smiling to himself. His previously stubbled cheeks now wore a thicker beard, which was messy and uncombed. Combined with his coils of dark, unkempt hair, and dark denim jacket with rips that weren't meant to be there, he looked more like a crazed murderer than a journalist. The index finger of his right hand rubbed slow circles on his right thumb, a tick not dissimilar to the one Nicole had had when she was in need of a cigarette.

'I'm trying, William, to figure out what happened to you. For your friends' sakes.'

'Why?'

Peter Lincoln took another drink and said, 'I'll ask the questions, okay?'

It might have sounded like a question but it wasn't and, aware of how vulnerable he was, out here with this apparent journalist, Will stayed quiet.

The Stranger continued, 'I wrote a story about you but I never published it. I spoke to your step-dad, although he wasn't all too keen, and I even tried to get into the hospital to speak to you – the regular hospital, I mean, not the clinic you were in later– but they wouldn't let me. I wanted to be able to tell your side of the story, in the wake of all the accusations flying around. I thought you should have a chance to be considered a survivor before a suspect. Innocent until proven guilty, isn't that the way? But the hospital staff thought I was just another leech come to bleed you dry. The blood suckers ruin it for us with integrity.'

There was that word again. If there was such a thing as a journalist with integrity, Will sure as hell hadn't met one yet, and he had come into contact with more than his fair share.

'I don't have a side,' Will murmured. 'I don't remember.'

'Nothing? Not even of being at a fairground?'

Will looked down at his drink, which he had yet to touch.

Lincoln said, 'Do you know how many people go missing every single year? It's a lot more than most would imagine, but most of them end in a fairly predictable set of circumstances. Death by misadventure, runaways, kidnappings usually by a parent or relative; your typical boring stuff. But every now and then somebody goes missing in the kind of circumstance they make movies about. Malicious kidnappings, murders and mysteries. Most commonly involving children. You understand?

'Sometimes the missing person is found dead, sometimes alive and sometimes not at all. Your case stands apart. Five people go missing without a trace at the same time, and three days later, one of them miraculously reappears with no memory of what happened. You weren't the first to go missing from Treevale, did you know that?'

Even had he not searched through missing persons pages online most nights, he would have known that. Ian had told him that night that a woman had disappeared on her way home from work a week before. He'd used the information to try and convince Will to stay in the car.

Peter Lincoln continued, 'There were others who disappeared just as perfectly, never to be seen again. You're the only one who came back. Locked away in that head of yours, you could hold the answer to what happened to all of them, not just your friends.'

'I don't remember what happened.'

'But you remember something, though. You remember a fairground.'

'The police…'

Peter waved his words away before he could finish speaking. 'Screw what the police said. I'm not talking about what you told them. I'm talking about what you recovered in your hypnotherapy with your student shrink.'

'I… I don't know what you're talking about.'

'With the help of Amanda Stinton, a psychology student at Treevale University, you have undergone hypnotherapy to recover your missing memories. Am I wrong?'

Hesitantly, Will admitted he wasn't.

'And am I right in saying you've recovered memories of you and your friends at a fairground that night?'

Will nodded.

'Yet there was no evidence to suggest that a fairground had ever taken place in that park, or in Treevale at all, last year. Or, in fact, any year you've been on this planet. I've even looked myself and I couldn't find anything either. The last time a fair took place anywhere near Treevale, was in Graham Park when Harold Tombes came to town in Nineteen-Twenty.'

Will swallowed. He had no idea who Harold Tombes was but it gave him a bad feeling in the pit of his stomach.

'So why don't you tell me what you remember. Start from the beginning.'

Will looked at the mug in front of him. The steam that had been rising rapidly from the coffee when it was placed in front of him was now gone. Not even a slither of misty water particles remained. He stared into the dark liquid, hoping to find any way out of this situation.

Peter Lincoln continued, 'We're going nowhere until you talk. Feel free to walk home though. It'll only take you about two hours, through all the people heading off to work, and I'll be waiting in the car when you get there.'

Will started talking.

He told Peter exactly what he had remembered from the first session with Amanda. He talked him through the walk from the museum to the park, omitting the conversation and points of contention between he and his friends. He told it in a matter of fact manner, going from one location to the next, until he reached the park, where he explained that his memory blacked out, and he saw flashes of things he didn't understand, and which could deter him from remembering anything further. There had, of course, been flashes but it wasn't that he didn't understand them. He didn't want this man to know what he'd seen.

At the mention of the black spot in his memory at the gate of the park, Peter Lincoln leant forward and placed a thoughtful finger to his lip. 'Interesting,' he said. He offered no further comment.

'The second time, Amanda talked me down directly into the fair,' Will paused. 'But I didn't remember anything of worth.'

Peter Lincoln eyed him curiously, as though trying to figure out if Will was lying or not.

The Stranger looked at him a long time before he dropped his hand from his chin and nodded. He said, 'What made you want to go to the fair?'

'I don't know.'

'Have you ever been to a fair before? As a child, maybe?'

Did he know? No, he couldn't possibly know that. He was probing, hoping that he would give something up.

'No,' Will answered.

'Really? Most kids go to a fairground at least once in their childhood, don't they?'

Will shrugged, said nothing.

'So you didn't recently remember a trauma at a fairground when you were a child?'

How did he know that? It wasn't possible. Only Will, Beth and Amanda knew that. It was possible one of them might have mentioned it to Ben or Xander but he trusted that none of them would have spoken to this shabby looking man.

He recalled Xander asking him the night before if he had killed his friends and wondered if maybe Xander had snuck away to tell this journalist what the others had told him, but he had only arrived back last night and there hadn't been time for him to meet this Stranger and share information. And it wasn't as though Peter Lincoln looked much like a journalist.

Yet somehow, he knew. Still, Will said, 'No.'

'Are you sure?'

Will swallowed the nerves building up in his throat. 'The first time I was at a fair was last year.'

Peter Lincoln studied him for a long time. Then, staring deep into Will's face, he said, 'Tell me about the Crooked Man.'

At the mention of him, Will almost threw up both from shock and terror.

'I...' Will prepared to deny all knowledge.

'Do you know his name?'

Will gave in, looked down, and shook his head.

'What do you remember about him?'

Will didn't want to describe him. He couldn't bear to picture him in his head, even in the light of day. All he said was, 'He owns the fair.'

Peter watched him for a long time before saying, 'A fair nobody has ever seen and come back from, except you.'

There was an implication in the voice that scared Will more than the possibility of the Stranger taking him into a dark alley and murdering him. He thought of the episodes he'd been having, in which he woke up with the feeling of having been outside, of his drenched clothing curled up on the floor, which followed a night of heavy rainfall.

The Stranger *did* think he had killed his friends.

'I...' Will started to defend but stopped himself. He told himself to stay silent. He didn't feel he could completely trust his mind, therefore he knew he couldn't trust his mouth.

'And yet only you remember it.' Lincoln ran an exacerbated hand through his beard. Then, as if musing to himself, he said, 'Not a single fair here in a hundred years.'

28

The Stranger thought silently for a while. The silence was worse than the talking. It presented a myriad of possible thoughts going through the Stranger's mind and Will couldn't read any of them on his face. He felt certain of only one thing: none of them would be good for Will. When the Stranger finally turned his attention back to Will, he felt sure he wouldn't be leaving this interaction alive, so intense were the Stranger's eyes as the bore into his own. Will looked away.

'I think you know more than you're letting on,' Peter Lincoln said. He reached into his pocket and removed something. Will's first instinct was that it was a knife, and that his time had come, that his life was to be brought to an abrupt end right here in public, without any fear of the handful of witnesses. But as the object became visible, he realised it was a business card. Lincoln placed it on the table and slid it toward Will. 'If you feel like talking, or remember anything else, give me a call.'

With a shaking hand, Will took the card only because he was being watched and he still feared that should he defy this man's orders, he would not be going home. Once the card was in his pocket, the Stranger led Will back to the car. Will's entire body tensed as they drove away. It didn't start to ease until they turned on his street and he knew Lincoln was actually taking him home.

Will started to climb out of the car the second it came to a stop.

'It was a pleasure meeting you, kid. It's been eye opening,' the Stranger called after him.

Will didn't stop or turn back, even to close the door. With every step he took, stretching the distance between them, the better he felt. He entered the house and closed the door, waited and listened for the sound of the car humming away down the street.

He slammed the front door closed behind him and rushed to the kitchen, eager to be as far from the front of the house, and the point outside where the Stranger was still parked, as he could get.

He was surprised to see Beth sat at the dining table on the far side of the kitchen, given how early it was, but then he checked his watch and saw that it wasn't early, after all. He had been out with the Stranger for longer than his run had been meant to last, the run he had not been able to go on.

He slowed, almost to a stop, unsure what to say. He ought to apologise but he thought of the questions the Stranger had asked, and he couldn't help but wonder if Beth would have talked to him. She was so good natured and warm that he sincerely doubted it, but still he wondered.

'Hi,' Beth said, catching sight of him through the doorway. It was clear from her tone that she, too, wasn't sure what to say. He had spoken to her cruelly and then she had returned home to find him in the hallway, grasping a knife before him.

'Hi,' Will returned. He should have gone on his run instead of coming back in the house, and he could have avoided this interaction.

He grabbed a bowl out of the cupboard and poured himself some cereal. Neither of them spoke as he added milk.

'I'm sorry,' he finally mumbled.

Beth shook her head and offered him a weak smile. 'Me too. Last night was a mistake. I think we all should have known it was a bad idea. The crowd, the lights, the people. *I* should have known, especially after what happened with Daniel the other day.'

He offered a weak smile of his own, still unsure of what

he should say. What could he say? Hell, he had known it was a bad idea and had gone against every instinct that screamed for him to bail. He knew he wasn't stable enough, but he'd wanted to be normal so much.

Beth continued, 'What happened to you shook all of us – I mean it could just as easily have been us that had gone out that night and disappeared – but when I think of you, I don't think of you as one of the Treevale Five. You're my friend, Will. So it's easy to forget other people only think of you that way. If I hadn't forgotten that, the shit last night wouldn't have happened.'

Will had not yet touched his food. The longer he held it, the less he wanted it.

He said, 'I chose to go. It's not your fault.'

Before she could say anything more, he left the kitchen, taking his untouched bowl with him to the bedroom. If he stayed, they could have completely reconciled and gotten back to normal, as he had wanted as soon as he got out of bed, but he had other thoughts fighting for his attention, mainly something the journalist had said about a fairground a hundred years ago and the name Harold Tombes.

Why had that name made him shiver? As far as he was aware, he had never heard it before.

Will locked himself in his bedroom and sat down at his desk. He opened his MacBook and started eating while it loaded up. Then, he set the unfinished bowl aside and started searching.

At first there was nothing obvious. He had spelt the surname the French way, with an e between the b and the s – somehow he knew it was the correct spelling, although he didn't know how – and a great many of the results were written in French. The rest of the initial results automatically changed his wording to *tomb* and offered up a news entry about where King Harold was buried.

He refined his search by adding *fairground.*

There were some more French results and then, on the

fourth page, one in English. It was an article on an amateur true crime website inspired by the tv show *Unsolved Mysteries,* which Netflix had rebooted a couple of years ago. The site was called *Unsolved Murders*, and the article documented the life of a man by the name of Harold Tombes, a suspected serial killer from the early nineteen hundreds.

The article was poorly written. Whoever had written it had attempted to make it seem as though it were prose, not a description of real events. Will slaved through it and learnt that in the early nineteen hundreds, The Harold Tombes Fairground Company had travelled around the north of England, leaving a string of missing persons reports in its wake. Harold Tombes, the leader and owner of the fairground, lured people into his House of Horror, where they were played with, and murdered by Tombes himself. That was, until nineteen-twenty when the police tracked him down to Treevale. The fairground was surrounded and the stall holders all arrested and questioned.

Harold Tombes slipped away, never to be seen or heard of again.

It was an interesting story, Will had to admit, and one which made him feel a little uncomfortable when he thought about it too much but he didn't understand why. Had he somehow heard mention of the story before, perhaps as a ghost story of sorts shared amongst drunken students at the end of a night out or party?

At the bottom of the page were photographs of the fairground, taken the night it was raided. They were all sepia toned and displayed various stalls being surrounded by police and men and women in show make-up, dressed in the kind of Victorian garb that reminded Will of the terrifying figure Will remembered from his own fairground experience, being led away in handcuffs.

The last photograph was of a man who stood freakishly tall as he posed for the camera but with a torso no bigger than Will's. His arms and legs stretched, elongated disproportionately from his body. His head was thin and skeletal and he wore a bowler hat atop it.

The caption identified him as Harold Tombes, but Will recognised him as somebody else.

Will was staring into the frozen eyes of the Crooked Man.

29

Will considered calling off any further sessions with Amanda. His mind was too scattered. He no longer knew what was true or not. He recalled a trip to the fair as a child that couldn't have happened, a fairground that had been disproven already, and the man he remembered as his wicked tormentor perfectly resembled a murderous fairground owner from over a hundred years ago.

He didn't go to his appointment with Dr Phillips. He was afraid if he spoke to her, he would give something away, something small. Anything. And she would force him into confessing everything that had occurred since his return to town.

Maybe that was what he should do. If he was really experiencing episodes again, he would need Dr Phillips's help to become stable again. It would mean he would probably end up back in a clinic for a while, but would that be so bad? Maybe that was the best place for him.

He looked at the drawer that contained the envelopes – there had been another one that morning, which he shoved in the drawer unopened – and he knew he couldn't tell Dr Phillips. His memory might have been distorted, part of it even untrue – if such a thing were really possible – but the letters were real. And the memory of the fairground last year was true. He was certain. If he confessed now, or backed out from the hypnotherapy, he would be throwing away the chance to find out what happened to his friends.

He had to continue. He would find out the truth tonight, no matter what.

When the time came, the air was so charged with fear and anticipation, pregnant with the topic they had all tried to avoid, that the sound of a knock at the door made them all jump.

They – Will, Beth and Ben – glanced from one to the other before Beth got to her feet and headed to let Amanda in for what they all knew was a bad idea.

Amanda entered the room, followed by Beth.

'Hey,' she said, 'How is everyone?'

'Xander's gone,' Beth said. 'For now at least.'

Amanda cocked her head in question.

'We had words. He wants Will gone. I don't.'

She didn't share anything more and although the argument they had had earlier had been in hushed voices, Will had still heard enough of it to know that Xander was convinced Will had killed his friends and was afraid they would all be next. When Will came out of his room, Beth and Ben told him Xander had gone to stay with a friend for a couple of days and they had acted as though nothing out of the ordinary had happened.

'He'll calm down,' Amanda said. 'You know what he's like.'

She draped a coat over the arm of the other sofa and took a timid seat beside it. While in the previous visits to the house she had been strong and confident, she now sat with the same uncertainty and unease with which Ben and Beth had treated Will. They tried to seem as though everything was normal but the image of Will sat on the stairs brandishing a knife was ever present in their minds.

'How are you?' she asked Will.

'Okay, I think,' Will answered, although he wasn't sure anybody would agree with that, even himself.

'About Tuesday night,' she started.

'I'm sorry.'

'Not after an apology, Will. I want to make sure you're okay. You said you saw somebody climbing your window. It shook you enough you felt you needed a knife. That's not just going to disappear.'

At least, that's what he thought he saw, but he was no longer so sure. Had he not already imagined being lured out of the house by a figure outside his window?

'I'm okay.'

Amanda didn't pretend to believe it, but she brought a chair in from the kitchen and placed it directly in front of him, which she had never done before. She sat, knees together, staring straight at him. She looked around at the others and back to him.

'Are we sure about this?' she asked.

'Yes.' Will said.

She looked at Beth and Ben, but spoke to Will. 'After Tuesday night, I think Ben and Beth would rather be in the room for this but I won't force anything on you if you don't want it. It's your decision.'

Will glanced at his friends, if they were, indeed, still his friends. He thought of the information the Stranger had known and considered asking Beth to leave, but it had just as likely been Amanda who had spoken to the journalist and Will couldn't exactly ask *her* to leave.

'They can stay,' he said.

Unlike last time, Ben sat down and settled in for whatever was to come.

'Okay then,' she said.

Amanda told Will to close his eyes and talked him down.

30

('You're at the fair with your friends. You're surrounded by stalls offering prizes for games, and rides. All around you, people talk, scream and yell. There are bright lights flashing and moving, bells ringing, and music. Describe where you are.')

We're walking through the stalls as a group. There was bright coloured lights all around. The smell of hot dogs and sweet sugary things waft to us on the wind. The stall holder's watch us go by, hungrily, as though desperate for us to come to them and play their game.

('Where do you go?')

There's a stall offering up a throwing challenge with targets to knock down with a cricket ball. The edges of the stall are lined with soft animals, most of which are dressed in clothes. In among them is a large, purple dog. It's a particularly dark shade of purple for a stuffed toy, lacking the fun vibrancy that a child looks for, and it makes me think of Nicole.

Although she wears black almost all the time, her favourite colour is actually purple and she loves dogs. I throw a few balls and hit a couple of the targets but there's no enjoyment among any of us. I can feel a sense of dread creeping over me. It's tight around my heart like a fist.

('What else? Is there anything else you go on, anybody else who speaks to you?')

All of the stall holders speak to us. They call to us desperately, pleading for us to play their game.

('Let's move forward to when you meet the "Crooked Man".)

I hear a whisper on the wind. Two words. 'Roll up.' I spin in the direction of the sound in time to glimpse a figure, the same one I saw from the Ferris Wheel cabin, as he disappears around a stall. It's him. It's the Crooked Man. I'm terrified but I follow him. We reach an opening in the middle of the spiralling maze of stalls and rides and we stop dead.

('*What do you see?*')

There's a large building, like a grand, gothic castle, except smaller and made of wood instead of bricks. The grey bricks are painted on, as are the windows, although there are real bars on them. Above the roof are the words *Tombes's Manor of Horror.*

The entrance is a tall and narrow doorway. The dark grey frame has been stained with dark red streaks. Fake blood.

'Now this looks like fun,' Nicole says.

I shiver at the sight of it. I have never been a fan of horror movies, although I have watched a couple for Nicole's sake. Each time, I sit trembling, hands clenched into fists, and afterward, it takes an age, long after the credits have rolled and the lights are back on, for my heart rate to return to normal. Going into the smoky entrance that glows a deep, disturbing green, is the last thing I would call fun.

Craig agrees but he seems afraid.

I protest, 'I can't go in there.'

Nicole shoots me a look but I can see she is afraid too. She says, 'You're not scared of dying. How can you be scared of anything without being afraid of death?'

'*Roll up,*' a hissing whisper sings to us from within.

A figure steps forward through the green glow and the smoke. He is nothing more than a silhouette but I know who he is. There's a top hat on his head and a cane by his side, which he doesn't use as he steps forward into the light. He is dressed in an old fashioned tuxedo with tails and a ruffled shirt.

'Roll up, roll up,' he repeats in the calm sing-song of an escaped lunatic. As the words travel to us, the skin prickles on my arms as though scratched by a painfully cold wind. A grin stretches across his face, one half more than the other, revealing large slabs of grey teeth. A scar curves from the corner of his nose, across his cheek.

He says, 'Roll up, and test your courage in my manor.' He swings his cane to one side, bringing our attention to a sign beside the doorway.

Enter if you Dare! the sign reads, the words carved deep into the wood and painted a sickly black.

The Crooked Man hisses, 'Do *you* dare?'

He steps closer, emerging fully into the light. His eyes are large and his irises completely black, like black holes, pulling us in. He descends the three steps leading up to the building. His limbs are so long, each step resembles the movement of a spider. He stops short of the group and plants his cane in front of him. He rests his humungous hands, one over the other, atop the handle.

He says, 'Roll up, roll up. Enter if you dare, and find out what's inside of you.' His crooked smile never leaves his face.

Dark and thick, the man reeks of mould and decay.

'What's in there?' Nicole asks.

'No,' I plead. With difficulty, I tear my eyes away from the Crooked Man and look at Nicole. She glances back at me for a moment before quickly returning her gaze to the house of horror. Her fiery hair glimmers brighter in the nearby flash of red and green lights.

('Wh...')

('Shh. What does the "Crooked Man" say?')

He turns his attention to me. His skin is deathly pale, wrapped so tightly over the bones of his face, I can see every line of his skull, and he is no longer smiling. 'You do not wish to see what is inside of you? Do you not dare?'

I shake my head, and my eyes sting with tears I try to fight. Locked in the man's gaze, I am petrified of what will happen if I refuse. The Crooked Man stretches at least six feet five, towering over my five-nine, and although he is thin, almost skeletal, I fear he will, at any moment, strike me down with that jet black cane.

He asks, 'Then why are you here?'

I stammer, 'I... I... w... wanted to ha... have some... f... fun.'

The Crooked Man grins his crooked grin. 'Your chance for fun has passed. You will find none within these walls. Inside my manor, you will find only terror and petrification. You can only hope to make it out the other side the same. If you make it out at all. Do not doubt me, friends, for I know. This is my manor and my fair, and many who have dared to enter my manor, have never been seen again.'

I look at my friends. 'I want to go home,' I tell them.

They all glance at me, and I know they feel the same. They never wanted to come here in the first place. They wanted to stay at the exhibition, as I should have wanted. Before they can say anything, the Crooked Man speaks.

He says, 'It is a little late for that.'

('Why is it too late?')

Because we can't go home. The Crooked Man has us now and he will never let us leave.

('What does the Crooked Man do?')

He looks at each of us in turn and says, 'Such young men and woman, and you're crippled by your fear.' He shakes his head, disappointed and says, 'The only way to go on with your lives is to face your fears, don't you see? Embrace it. *Dare* to enter, not only my manor but your own minds.' He steps aside and gestures towards the smoking entrance. He says, 'See what you are made of.'

As though it is a given we will do as he says, he turns and runs back up the three steps and plants himself on the other side of the doorway to the sign, waiting for us.

Nicole, who is scared of very little, heads toward the building on slow, nervous legs. One by one, the others follow.

I watch Nicole go in and I know I have no option. I climb the steps, slowly. The smile on the wicked face grows deeper. I think about turning and running, but it's no use. The only place for me to go is into that house.

(Knock, knock, knock.)

Darkness envelopes everything. Nicole, Craig and I run down a corridor as fast as we can.

('Babes, could you...?')

I glance back over my shoulder. Walking slowly after us is the dark figure of the Crooked Man, his cane in hand. I find Nicole's hand and we run faster. Her bright red hair is the only hint of colour in the darkness and I hold onto the image as we run.

('Wake him up.')

Red light bursts over everything, throbbing. I'm cowered in a corner, my arms slick with sticky liquid. In my lap is a long object that looks like a bone of some kind, slick with the same liquid that, despite everything around me being red, I am certain is blood. I drop it to the ground and scarper from it. My legs are too weak to get up. I crawl across to the only door I see. My knees slip on more liquid. Everything is red in this light but I'm certain this liquid, too, is really red. I push open the door and there is Julian. He stares at me from where he lies, with glassy, empty eyes.

(Snap!)

31

There came the sound of arguing from the hallway. Grace burst into the room as though it were she who lived here. Will looked at her, dazed, and tried to get a grip on the new memories present in his mind.

Grace looked at Amanda and crossed her arms across her chest, waiting for some kind of explanation. When none came, she said, 'Well? You told me you were going to see Greg for a drink. Not come here for this... crazy shit with your ex-girlfriend.'

Beth appeared behind her, and opened her mouth to argue. A look from Amanda closed it.

Amanda sighed and looked an apology at Will, then Ben. To Grace, she said, 'I didn't tell you because I knew you'd have issue with it. Beth is still my friend, and besides, I'm here to help Will.'

'Is that right, *babes?*'

Amanda sighed again and closed her eyes. 'Shall we take this outside?'

'Why? You seem to want to share your nights with everyone but me. Why not share this? I bet you've already told them all the little details of our relationship. Have you analysed everything you don't like about me with them, yet?'

Amanda stood and approached Grace. 'Let's go outside.' She skirted around Grace and into the hallway. Grace shot a dirty look at Ben and Will before turning to follow. As she walked by Beth, she glared at her as though she were about to take a bite of her face. Then she was gone.

Beth stepped into the room and hovered there. She was

grave and shifted from foot to foot. She took a look at Ben, who was even more shell shocked. His lips were pressed tightly together, like he was fighting the urge to be sick.

'Did I miss something?' she asked.

And Will realised what it was that had shocked Ben so much..

He saw Julian's eyes shining like a doll's. They stared at him, empty of life.

Will lurched from the sofa and sprinted toward the kitchen. He made it only a step toward the door before his body curled over itself and his stomach emptied its contents across the floorboards. He coughed and heaved and brought up more. Tears burned his eyes as the lining of his stomach scorched his throat. His sudden movements broke Beth from her preoccupied concern and she sprang into action. Her hands were on the sides of his kneeling body, comforting him and looking around at the mess he'd made.

She rubbed a hand on his back and turned her head away from the stench. He heaved but there was nothing left.

'I think we definitely have some things to talk about tonight, don't we?' she said.

The front door slammed and Amanda came back into the room.

'Oh my god, Will. Are you okay?' she said, rushing to his side.

Ben coughed. 'I feel like doing the same thing.' Will had his back to everybody, bent over his knees, but Ben's voice was muffled and he assumed he was covering his mouth.

'Julian,' Will muttered and his tears flowed.

Amanda put her arms around his shoulders and helped lift him to his feet and back onto the sofa.

'Babes?' she said to Beth, gesturing toward Will. Beth took over comforting him and Amanda set about cleaning up the mess.

Will continued to weep. 'I saw... Julian's dead.'

Beth squeezed his shoulder but said nothing.

Ben swallowed. 'So... all of that... That's what happened?'

'Of course,' Amanda said, kneeling up to look at them all. 'I led him through the memory to the house of horror, or whatever it was called. I think his mental defences kicked in again, trying to scare him off delving any deeper. This time, when things started to skip around, it showed him a little more. The body of his friend.' She huffed and finished up cleaning the mess on the floor.

'I'm not sure I agree,' Beth argued.

Amanda stood up and frowned. 'Excuse me?'

'I'm not sure I agree,' Beth repeated. Will looked at her. He couldn't believe she would say such a thing. Not now. Not after he'd learnt the fate of one of his friends. Her hand slipped from his shoulder and she stepped away. He had become little more than a leper to her in that moment and he couldn't understand why.

'And why not?' Amanda asked. Her professional integrity was hurt but it was more than that. She seemed closer to the edge than she had during the past few times Will had met her and he never imagined she would act in such a way toward Beth. Whatever had happened outside must not have been much better than what had happened in here.

'When he was talking about standing outside the house of horror, he described Nicole as having fiery hair. I tried to point it out to you, but you told me to be quiet,' Beth explained. When nobody said anything, she threw her hands out to her side. 'Nicole had *black* hair.'

'It's a slip up. A minor confusion.'

Ben stuck his hand up like they were in class. 'He did it again when Beth was at the door. He mentioned Nicole's red hair.'

Will looked at them and shook his head. 'No. No. I... I don't understand.'

'It's possible,' Amanda started. 'And I mean *possible* – I'm not saying it's what's happened – but it's possible that

Beth being in the room, maybe hearing her voice, has worked its way into your recollection, distorting the memory slightly. Memory is a fickle thing and it needs to be handled carefully.'

Beth shook her head. 'If his memories can be that easily influenced, how can we know what else has been distorted? How can we know whether any of it was real?'

Will stayed quiet. He thought of the face of the Crooked Man, a face that belonged to a serial killer a century ago. He thought of a trip with his step-father that never happened. He and Nicole on the Ferris Wheel, a memory he somehow possessed two version of.

Amanda leaned back against the wall, growing more annoyed. 'Look, I'll admit there have been cases documented where the repressed memories have been disproven.' Beth's mouth opened in argument. Amanda held up a hand and went on. 'But, in those cases, the questions asked were very leading and suggestive. I was careful in all of the sessions with Will. In this one, I barely had to guide him. Once we'd started, he managed to remember one thing after another pretty much unaided. I'm confident it's true.'

'If you knew all that, why would you agree to go through with it?'

Behind Beth, Ben said, 'I told you it was a bad idea.'

'I seem to remember it being *Beth's* idea,' Amanda spat. 'And I saw an opportunity to flesh out my research first hand.'

Beth shook her head. 'If you knew there was risk, why did you agree?'

Ben nodded. 'Yeah. Why didn't you say no? Your research can't be worth the risk, can it?'

'*Because I'm failing! Okay?*' Amanda screamed, stunning them into silence. Quieter, she continued, 'I barely scraped a third last year and if I don't find a way to really step things up this year, I'll barely scrape one this year. How many places do you think are going to hire a psychologist who *just* passed their degree, huh? I don't do better, I can kiss my entire life goodbye. And besides, I didn't lead Will to the fairground. He led himself. Unlike hearing your voice before or while he's under, I don't see what could have influenced his memory of a fair.'

Will muttered something. They all looked at him and Amanda said, 'What was that?'

Will tried again. 'I already remembered a fair. The lights and the sounds, nothing specific.'

'Which the police discounted,' Beth offered. 'They found no evidence for it.'

Will nodded. 'Dr Phillips said it was my way of attaching a happy location to the missing memories to convince myself nothing bad had happened.'

Amanda thought about it for a minute, then shook her head. 'But if you'd already been convinced of that, then it wouldn't have interfered with the therapy.'

'The letters,' Beth said.

'Letters?'

'They said "roll up" and "Do you dare?"'

'None of it was real,' Will announced, solemn. His head was down and he couldn't look at any of them, although he could feel them looking at him.

'Not necessarily,' Amanda started to argue.

Staring at his hands – hands which had been covered in blood when he had turned up that day so long ago – he shook his head and said, 'Ian said he never took me to a fair when I was a kid. He couldn't have left Mum for that long because she was a mess after David...' He choked up, even after so long. He had known too much death in his meagre twenty one years, he wasn't sure he could bear much more of it. 'The memories all feel real but they can't be. The police were right. There was no fair. I just wanted to know what happened *so* much.'

A heavy weight tugged Amanda's features toward the floor. 'So without knowing it, you combined this disproved memory of a fairground with the letter you received and created a narrative of the Crooked Man and the house of horror, in order to finally give yourself the answers about what happened.'

'But,' Beth said, 'who sent the letters?'

Will shrugged. He couldn't even begin to guess who might have targeted him. He didn't think it was Peter Lincoln, but it might have been.

Amanda pushed herself off the wall. 'I think I should go.' There were tears in her eyes. 'Some psychiatrist I'll end up being, huh? If I pass. I've messed up my own life and all of yours at the same time, and all so I can get a better grade. Sorry, Will.'

Without another word, she left the three of them alone.

The painful, confusing truth settled among them in Amanda's absence and none of them said anything. Beth's legs went weak and she slipped down onto the sofa, beside Will.

'I'm sorry, too,' she said. 'I suggested all of this. I wanted you to have some answers. God, I've fucked everything up. I should have just stayed out of all your business. You even told me you wanted to live with us because we weren't interested in what happened and now, here we are. I'm so fucking stupid. I understand if you want to live somewhere else. I'll talk to the landlord myself, let them know it's my fault and if there's anything extra like a deposit they need you to pay on somewhere else, I'll tell them I'll pay it.'

He started to say something but he wasn't even sure what to think right now. He had no choice but to be washed whichever way the drifting ocean took him.

'I'm really sorry. I never wanted… this. I didn't think it would end up that none of it was real but when I heard you mention Nicole's hair colour, I knew something wasn't right. Somehow, you'd confused the two of us but you hadn't even known me back then so I didn't get how you could. I didn't know about the risks involved when I asked Amanda, I promise.'

She paused. Will wasn't sure if she was waiting for him to say something but words escaped him. He couldn't get a grip on any rationale, logic or sense. Left was right, up was down, and he couldn't seem to slow the spin.

'If you don't want to talk to me again, I understand,' she said, and stood up. Without another word, she left the room.

'Beth,' Will croaked, but it was too late.

From the other sofa, Ben took a deep breath and climbed to his own feet. 'I don't know what to say, mate, except, I'm sorry. Probably doesn't mean much but…' He shrugged and headed upstairs, leaving Will more alone than he had been since his friends met whatever fate had befallen them. And he had gained only one answer from it all.

There was no fairground.

32

It had come out sounding sarcastic and snarky but Peter Lincoln had been telling the truth when he told the kid their conversation had been eye opening. The kid had held a lot back but Peter had still learnt plenty within that short space of time. The specifics the kid had shared slotted nicely into the information Peter had already gained from his sources, and there was a theory coming together like a jigsaw in his head.

Will had not been the first to go missing, nor were the two people who went missing in the two weeks before the disappearance of the Treevale Five. There were, in fact, unsolved missing persons cases dating back at least a couple of years and always on the same nights, each year, as though following a schedule. Until the mention of the kid remembering a fairground, Peter hadn't considered anything remotely on the same lines, but it made some kind of sense. Three people, each September, disappeared on a particular date, and in three different parts of the town, always near parks or fields where a fairground could have been erected.

All missing without a trace or a clue. Until William Campbell came back and remembered a fairground that supposedly didn't exist.

The combination of disappearances and a fairground rang familiar with Peter. His grandfather had once told him a story he barely remembered now, of a fairground that travelled around and took sad and lonely little boys away, so he should be happy and polite and show his appreciation for his parents. The story went that the owner of the fairground targeted lonely, quiet, and grumpy people of all ages and locked them inside his house of horrors. The ghost story wasn't too far from the truth.

In the depths of the newspaper archive, he had found the true story. Harold Tombes was not the boogeyman but he had kidnapped and murdered many people for his own amusement.

Tombes had been born with a deformity that meant his arms and legs grew to a much greater length than his body, leaving him freakishly disproportionate. In the late nineteenth century, he was deemed an abomination and kept out of sight by parents who loathed him as they would a monster. As a teenager Tombes joined a circus, where people would pay to see him instead of cowering at the sight of him in the street. As a freak in a travelling circus, he found a family who would accept him. It was believed that it was as part of the freak show he developed the love of terrifying people.

During a night in London at the turn of the century, the circus was attacked by an angry mob. While the rest of the freaks hid, Harold tried to defend himself and was said to have attacked a member of the public. To avoid arrest, Harold fled the circus but he was said to have been angered by the mob and his hatred for the closed minded normal people grew.

Three years later, Harold Tombes reappeared in the north of England, as the proprietor of a fairground, the heart of which was Tombes's pride and joy: a house of horrors intended for the cruellest of torments. It was designed specifically for him to play with his victims before he killed them.

It all ended one night in Treevale in nineteen-twenty, when the police raided the fair and arrested Tombes' friends and employees. He had followed the same schedule year in and year out, making it easier, once the connection was made between the missing and the fair, for the police to find him. There were fresh victims found on site that night but Tombes slipped away.

It was the same night on which William Campbell and

his friends would disappear a little more than one hundred years later.

The only other member of the fairground to escape capture was a woman who performed a mystic act dressed up to appear occult. And so the boogeyman story told by Peter's grandfather had started, claiming that the fairground owner was still out there somewhere, kept alive by the mystic woman's witchcraft, and he would come for you, lure you in with the promise of fun and then take you away. Unless you showed him you didn't need any more fun; you were happy enough, already.

Peter didn't think his grandfather had been the only person to tell such a story, and he didn't think it was a leap to consider that somebody had taken inspiration from it. It wasn't only the Treevale Five's disappearance that matched up with the fairground's schedule, but all of them. And more. In the hours since his conversation with the kid, he had found unsolved cases spread all across the north of the country, all on a night the Tombes fair had once been to town.

Peter was particularly intrigued by what William Campbell recalled about his first session with the psychology student, in which he and his friends reached the park where the fair had taken place, and where a hundred or so years ago, Harold Tombes's murderous game came to an end, and his brain forced him to skip ahead.

Maybe his brain skipped ahead, he wondered, because–

His phone pinged with a message, leaving his thought unfinished. It was from an unnamed contact but he knew who had sent it.

'There was no fairground. Will has serious mental issues. The hypnotherapy created false memories. Leave him alone and don't contact me again.'

Peter stared at the phone in amazement.

The kid had remembered wrong? Was that even possible?

He turned to the computer in the corner of his cramped

living room and started an entirely new string of research. It quickly became apparent that hypnotherapy was a topic of hot debate among psychiatrists. He read through article after article, then started calling psychologists in order to get some kind of grip on which side of the debate was right.

He was told of cases in which people recovered memories of abuses that supposedly had never happened, including one particular story of a woman developing a conviction her family, a group of normal, kind people, were the leaders of a child prostitution ring, all of which had been thoroughly disproven. But he was also told stories in which recovered memories had been corroborated by witnesses and supporting DNA evidence.

The mind was a fickle thing and easily led, Peter was told. It was able to mould new memories that never occurred in response to outside stimuli and the words used, even in regular questioning without any use of hypnosis. A couple of psychologists shared their belief that hundreds of parents convicted of sexual assaults had been done so wrongly, due to skewed testimony that came down to a psychiatrist saying one wrong word during hypnosis.

There were just as many who told Peter the opposite, that memories recovered under hypnosis were a truer version than any conscious recollection of an incident. Those who pushed the idea of false memories were doing so in order to maintain an appearance of innocence.

The phone calls left him with more questions than answers, and he felt as though he was back to square one.

He tried to get in touch with his contact but there was no answer. It seemed the last message had been serious. Peter was cut off and with no idea where to go next.

All of his research and his theories were based on recalled memories that might not even have been real.

33

Will's alarm went off at its normal time of seven o'clock on Monday morning but he didn't reach over immediately to switch it off or leap out of bed to get changed into his running gear. Instead, he stared at the screen of his beeping mobile and let out a deep sigh. The day had arrived and he wanted nothing more than to turn that alarm off, roll over and shrink away under his duvet.

It was the first day of his third year. Again. He had failed to attend the last one, instead turning up for the museum visit that evening. He had missed every day since. Not a single part of him wanted to attend today, either. He had spent the entire weekend filled with dread, amongst all the other mental issues he was forced to battle after Thursday night's shattering revelations.

He was doing his best to convince himself none of the memories were real but it was a struggle and he wasn't sure if he was even making any progress. This morning, that all took a back seat. Today, he felt the absence of his friends more than ever.

Things between Will and his new housemates had returned to something resembling normal. He had avoided them over the weekend, until he stumbled into both Beth and Ben on Sunday morning.

He had walked into the kitchen to find them eating breakfast and had turned to go.

'Wait,' Beth called after him.

He turned back and said, 'I don't want to leave. Not unless you want me to.'

She shook her head. 'No. Of course not. I'm...'

She was about to say sorry and Will didn't want to hear yet another apology. He was back a year ago, hearing it from every single person who had heard about his friends going missing. Before they started to accuse him, that was.

'It's not your fault,' he had said. 'It's nobody's fault. I... I know none of it was real. I should have known all along. Nobody remembered there being a fair that night. I should have listened to Dr Phillips.' He nodded to himself and sighed. 'If anyone's to blame, it's me.'

They stood there for a time in silence, just looking at each other.

'So what now?' Beth asked.

Will shrugged. 'I'll get back to my routines, and talk to Dr Phillips.'

'Will you tell her what happened?'

He hadn't had an answer for that.

After their conversation, everything went back to normal, as though nothing had happened.

Xander had yet to return from staying with a friend, but with the others, it was as it had been before the night out. It was that night out he credited as the turning point in his mental breakdown, and while he hadn't been entirely okay before it, he was definitely worse after.

If only it were as easy to pretend his mind had returned to before that night too.

Instead, he was confused and depressed and he would have to face the absence of his friends every waking moment of the day ahead. He would have to face the memories that filled the walls of the university building, and he would have to do so with the knowledge that he had failed them.

He would never find out what happened to them. He would never be able to fully stand up and take his share of responsibility for what happened. He could never speak to their families and offer them any kind of closure, only accept the blame they laid on him.

He flicked off the alarm and considered, again, climbing back under the covers, but if he skipped today, he would skip it the next day, and the next, until he was kicked out, and he would have to move back in with his mum and Ian.

Feeling sluggish, he forced himself through a slow, exhausting run, ate breakfast, showered and dressed. Then he took a seat in the living room and waited for his housemates to join him. While he sat there, another letter was posted through the door. He rushed for the door and pulled it open, peering out. But he found only an empty street. Whoever posted the letter was already gone. Will put it with the rest and returned to the living room.

At first, he had found the letters threatening but since he had stopped reading them, and nothing else had happened, he could see that they were nothing more than a tactic meant to scare him.

What he feared today, though, did not come in a crisp white envelope. It waited for him behind doors and large windows. When they came down, first Ben, then Beth, Will got up onto wobbly legs. Ben and Beth offered sympathetic smiles but could find no words to suit.

Eventually, Ben asked, 'You ready for this, mate?' He did his best to hide his own excitement at what was, for him, a very big day, but it showed. Will didn't blame him. He got the impression Ben had never imagined he'd get this far.

Will nodded and shrugged.

Together, they walked to the university, which was bustling with students. As they reached the Arts, Design and Media building on the far edge of the campus, Will froze, staring at the students passing through the revolving door into the building, as though this was just a normal day. Which, of course, for them, it was.

The others realised he had stopped and turned to check on him.

A guy with long hair and the kind of patchy under-beard that made him look Amish, walked around Will and shot him a funny look.

Will continued to stare at the building, crippled by fear. Ben and Beth came to his side. In the glass, he saw his own terrified face. Haggard, exhausted and unshaven. What would his friends have made of him, now?

Beth said, 'We're right here with you.'

Snap out of it, Nicole ordered in his head. He imagined her running a finger over the stubble on his cheeks. *This isn't what we would have wanted. We'd want you to put on a brave face, even when you don't feel like it, and live your life. For us.*

He had been living the last year of his life for them, and he was tired.

He took a deep breath and let Beth and Ben lead him inside.

The building was busy with other students, some baby faced and some who looked older, even, than Will. Bags were slung over shoulders and groups shifted from one place to another, the odd loner moved through the crowd.

Upstairs, the hallway opened into a large space with round glass tables and soft furnishings alongside large printers. It was deathly familiar to Will as he looked upon it but it was as though he were looking at a negative image. Everything appeared reversed and unnatural. Everybody went about their business, excited by their first day back, or their first day ever, heading into different studios. Other groups gathered on the soft furnishings, meeting up with friends they hadn't seen in months. It was a scene Will should have been a part of but instead, he walked through it, ghostlike.

Some things change without having changed at all. It was the same space as it always was, and would appear as such to almost all who looked upon it, but to Will there was a void, where the building's character, atmosphere, and joy were supposed to reside.

'Will you pack that in?'

Craig's voice rattled in Will's head and suddenly he was looking at them all sat around one of those tables, eating lunch but still working. Craig was poring over his sketchbook, waiting for a tutor to summon him for a feedback session he'd requested, while Julian flicked balled up paper wrappers from the sweets he was eating at Craig's head.

Each of them laughed as they watched Craig's growing annoyance. Julian passed his sweets around and they all joined in throwing the wrappers at Craig.

Beth and Ben led him toward the digital studio, his legs moving as though through treacle. There were five hexagon tables throughout the room, with a humungous iMac screen in line with each table edge, and a row of rectangular tables pressed against the far wall. Will glanced at one of the middle tables, where he and his friends had spent almost all of their time in second year, working and joking, and talking, and he felt the echo of those memories bounce back at him. He could picture them all there, himself included, wheeling their chairs around to each other when they grew tired or stuck and wanted to talk one-on-one. He remembered sharing opinions, advice, and making fun of each other.

Beth and Ben took a seat at the nearest table and wheeled out one of the chairs for Will. It was a struggle to tear his eyes from the next table, and the echo of his friends, but he took the offered seat. Around them, students piled in.

Xander walked through the door laughing with another student. As his eyes met Will, his laughter died, and he fixed Will with a hateful glare. Will was reminded of something the Stranger had said, the implication that he knew things he couldn't know, and, matched with the evil stare from Xander, he wondered if Xander was the one who spoke to him. He'd discounted him before because of the limited time it would take to have met the journalist and shared things with him since coming back. But how did he know the Stranger hadn't made contact earlier, and that Beth or Ben had not already shared what had happened with Xander before he moved back in?

Xander's gaze eventually tore from Will and he took a

seat on the other side of the room.

Finally, Lucas, a broad, athletic man with looks that would make most of the female students swoon, entered the room and took his place in front of them all.

In a melodic yet manly Irish accent, he said, 'I hope you all had a good summer and kept your eyes open and your minds active.' It was clear from the playfully accusing look he scanned across the room that he knew full well the majority of the class had switched off their minds the moment they were able to return to the easy life of Netflix and video games at their parents' house. 'You better have done, anyway, because you were all assigned to keep a design journal, and to start researching self-promo, which you'll need in order to get a head start on this module. You *will* be required, by the end of the year, to have created a set of self-promotional materials that adequately demonstrate who you are to potential employers. So I expect you to take a hard look at yourselves as designers and as people to find the right direction.'

Now more than ever, Will didn't know how to articulate who he was. Personality is a collection of experiences and memories, and Will could trust neither. A year ago, his life was greatly changed by a defining, traumatic moment, but of which he was left with no memory. Now, in the place of those memories, he had false ones. He couldn't begin to say who he was, or what had made him into that person.

Lucas finished his presentation in which he explained the two starting modules. Some of the students left right away, and Will watched them go, enviously. Before, he never would have thought of jumping up and leaving early. He would have started working and wouldn't have stopped until one of his friends or his stomach told him it was time for a break. Going against that basic part of himself had been what led him and his friends from the museum last year and to the fair.

No, not to the fair. To… wherever. *Somewhere.*

Will glanced over at the other table again. His gaze was pulled there as though by invisible hooks.

He pictured the five of them together on an evening. Nicole, Julian and Tom talking quietly among themselves, when suddenly, Craig started yanking Will's swivel chair the length of the room, toward the door.

Then Craig was kneeling before Will, his face bleeding, his face contorted into a mask of agony and horror. He tried to swallow, to say something but couldn't. The sound of fairground music and screaming drifted into the cold, dank room.

Will swallowed and shook his mind back from that false memory. He returned to the real one playing out before him. Craig pulling him toward the door. Will flailing for purchase on any passing object, laughing.

The other three turned their attention to what was going on and burst into their own bouts of laughter.

'Come on,' Craig said. 'Time to take a break.'

'No,' Will pleaded. 'I'm okay. Just another half an hour.'

'Nope.' Craig yanked a little harder. 'It's been five hours. Come on. Outside.'

'We need to get out of here. Before it's too late.'

Will winced.

When Craig had reached the studio door, he snapped it open and held it there with his back and one heavy foot while he continued yanking the chair out into the hallway.

Will could not help but smile as he observed these phantoms move across the room. His eyes grew moist.

How could he ever have dreamt of leaving these people without even having said goodbye?

Will tried to focus on the research but the thoughts kept coming. He remembered Julian's stories. Will was wheeling his chair around the table, stopping at each of his friends' computer screens one evening, when Julian had started in on a story. He'd been watching adverts on YouTube, as "research" for his project.

Will saw Julian's eyes, glassy and shining, as empty of life as a doll. Blood everywhere around him, and up Will's arms.

'You know, my ex-girlfriend was in adverts,' Julian said at the sight of a stunning blonde woman on the screen. 'It's not her. I can't seem to find the advert she was in but she was beautiful, man. You know? She did some modelling and then moved onto acting in a lot of British TV shows.'

'I used to know somebody who lived in a fair, you know.'

'Yeah?' Craig asked from beside him, without taking his eyes from the screen. 'Like what?'

Julian had shrugged. 'I don't know. I can't remember. But she was good and she was in a lot of them. A few Channel Four dramas and a couple for the BBC.'

'Sounds like she's had quite the career already. How old is she, like, thirty?'

'No,' Julian protested and frowned, scorned. 'Our age.'

'Our age?' Tom laughed from Julian's other side.

'Yeah, like, twenty.'

'And how long ago were you together?' Craig asked.

'It ended about two years ago because she went off to live in London for work.'

Will laughed along, knowing, as they all did, how full of shit Julian was.

'I could have gone with her. She even said she'd try and get me into some stuff as an extra, like, but I'd just got into uni. So we split.'

'Could you hell have been on tv,' Tom said.

'Could too.'

The back and forth continued for a minute before Nicole put her hands in the air and said, 'Calm down everyone. It's obvious that Julian's just a massive player. First the actress and now the current girlfriend. You've been with her, what, four years? And you were seeing the actress until two years ago. Fuck, that's impressive.'

All of them laughed, except for Julian, who sank back in his chair. He fixed his eyes on his screen and said, 'Fuck off.'

Nicole always knew how to prove Julian wrong. Julian

who had stared at Will with lifeless, glassy eyes reflecting the throbbing red of the lights.

'*Roll up,*' Will heard in his ear.

You're not real, he thought. *The Crooked Man is not real.*

Not anymore, at least. The Crooked Man had existed a hundred years ago. Will must have come across the story at some point and absorbed it into his subconscious, eventually using it to influence his false memories.

He couldn't keep his attention on the screen. Everywhere he looked, he saw their faces. He remembered the time they'd spent together. And he remembered the untrue memories of what had happened to them. He grabbed his bag and fled the room.

34

The news that the memories Will Campbell had recovered may have been false had left Peter Lincoln reeling, unsure what to do next. After weeks of watching and researching, it had all come to naught. He was back at square one with a notebook and computer files crammed with useless information connecting a series of potentially isolated disappearances to a historic murderer.

He had done exactly the opposite of what he should have done as a journalist. He had taken a shred of information and ran with it, forming a theory and diving headfirst down the road to prove it, only to find he'd wasted weeks. Now, he didn't know where else to go.

At the start of the weekend, he had pored over the information he had collected over the past year, doing his best to disregard any mention of the fairground, but he kept coming back to the dates, which matched perfectly to the schedule of Harold Tombes's fair. He despised coincidences, but had the timetable of missing people been isolated to Treevale alone, he could have easily disregarded them as such. Instead, he had found at least two years' worth of unsolved disappearances across the entire north of the country, all of which corresponded to Tombes's schedule.

It was too much to ignore, and so, despite what his contact had told him, he continued to pursue his theory. Even if the kid's memories weren't real, it didn't mean there wasn't still a connection to Tombes. The kid had flinched at the mention of the name as though he had heard the it before. It stood to reason that either Will had heard the same story as a child as Peter had, or the man who took he and his friends had mentioned him, influencing the memories of a fairground he later created under hypnotherapy.

If Peter's theory was correct, whoever was taking these people was a Harold Tombes fanatic. Such a man would have been unable to keep from mentioning his idol, perhaps acting out similar actions.

Whoever held such fanaticism, he thought, might have had some connection already to fairgrounds. Peter started making a number of phone calls to fairground owners, asking if they knew of any employee or owners who had expressed an unusual enthusiasm regarding Tombes. Most were not remotely pleased by his questions and responded with profanity. Others simply hung up.

If there was a potential kidnapper – and, he feared, murderer – among the fairground communities he called, they were not forthcoming, and without visiting each one, which would require him driving all over the country to visit the areas they had set up in for their last run, he could not hope to speak to every show person and narrow his suspect pool.

Instead, he put himself in the mind of a fanatic. Before coming to the point of imitation, what would he desire most? He would want a location to visit to serve his obsession. Like a killer who returned to the scene of the crime or a victim's grave, the fanatic would want a specific location, which he could visit in order to feel closer to Tombes.

It was done the world over. Celebrity fanatics aspire to eat at the same restaurants as their idols. The locations of famous murders garner a similar, morbid fascination within many people. Harold Tombes kidnapped the visitors of his fairground, which left a fanatic little more than a plain old park to visit. That wouldn't be good enough. A fanatic would want something bigger, something they could guarantee had been touched by Harold Tombes. They would want to stand where their idol had stood, touch something he had touched.

The end of September marked the end of the season for

fairgrounds and they would all soon pack up and store their stalls and dismantled rides in warehouses or rented industrial yards, where it would be safe during the autumn and winter. Peter wasn't sure if that was exactly how fairgrounds worked in the early nineteen hundreds, or if it was how Harold Tombes's fair had worked, given that he was unable, due to his startling and unnerving appearance, to fit in and live out six months of a normal life, but he had to assume Tombes had stayed somewhere during those months. If he was wrong, then there would be no hope of finding the truth.

He had gathered up a list of local archives across the north, which came to a list of more than eighty, and spent the weekend visiting them. He visited twenty-four archives, searched through countless pages of digitised documents and read through boxes of papers, flicked through pages of heavy books, until he found something.

A business by the name of The Harold Tombes Fairground Company, listed with an address. Peter took a photograph of the page with his phone – it featured a signature made by the man himself, which would do great for the story that lay at the end of all this – and he searched the address on Google Maps. The map showed a corner at the intersection of two roads but when he switched to satellite mode, it showed no buildings on the corner, or anywhere nearby for that matter.

Yet the spot had an address, as though a house had once sat there. If there was a place Harold Tombes had been, this was as close as he was going to get.

He left the records office in Durham as the gloom of dusk put an end to another day. He felt disappointed he had missed another day of potential surveillance of William Campbell, despite the possibility of his false memories. Watching the kid's house and following him had become a sort of habit, as creepy as it sounded even to himself, and he felt as though there may be something he was at risk of missing.

As he headed back to his car, he realised it was Monday.

He had missed the kid returning to university and the affect it had on him. It wasn't just for the sake of the story. Peter felt for the kid. He had lost loved ones and he didn't have any answers. He was the Stranger, but he could certainly relate to that.

There was nothing for it now, so he got in the car and started the drive toward North Yorkshire. When he reached the address on his phone's GPS, the sky was pitch black and the street lights had abandoned him some time back. Here, he was way out in the country. It wasn't yet the moors but it was as empty and unending. The last house was some fifteen or more miles back the way he'd come.

'You have arrived at your destination,' his phone declared. Peter pulled to a stop at the barely visible junction. He could see little except what was directly in front of his headlights. There were no other lights visible in any direction besides the moon, which traced the faint outline of trees in the distance, and those towering over one half of the road to his right.

He killed the engine, extinguishing the lights, and suddenly, he felt very vulnerable. He wasn't normally one for fear – he had already endured that which he feared most in life, and there was little else anybody could do to him to match that pain – but he was out here looking for a place a potential murderer used as a shrine for his idol, and Peter couldn't see what was out there in the darkness.

He took a deep breath to puff out his chest and calm him, even the tiniest bit, and stepped out of the car.

On his phone, he turned on the torch function and scanned the cone of bright white light around him. It pierced the darkness so harshly, the areas untouched by it grew impossibly darker. He crossed the road to the corner where the address had directed him, the light spreading out before him, carving his path.

He stopped on the corner and scanned the area, but he still saw nothing but grass, rock and trees. Beneath his feet were more rocks and dry earth. No sign of any building. Still, he took a few steps further down this next road, moving further away from the comfort and safety of his car. There were a good many metres between him and it now. He stood exposed to anything or anybody out here who might be waiting and watching in the darkness.

The cone of light passed across a patch of stone. Peter swung the light back. It was smooth and flat, and cracked in places, through which weeds grew. At the stone's edge there were points that rose half a foot from the ground, and upon closer inspection, Peter saw they were made of brick, not stone. There had once been a building here. Not a house, at least not of the habitable size of modern standards. It must have been the size of a single room.

He stepped onto the stone and cast the light over it, part by part. There had definitely been a building here, once. How long it had been since it had been knocked down, there was no way of knowing, nor by whom. To come here in search of Harold Tombes, decades after he would have passed, and find a patch of stone where a house had once stood must have been quite the disappointment to a fanatic.

Peter was definitely disappointed. The place was a dead end and he didn't know where to go from here. He never should have ran with his theories, especially after the news about Will Campbell, and now he was in the middle of nowhere, with miles behind him to retrack before he re-joined civilization.

Back in his car, he considered the right turn. There was nothing visible down there but he wondered if there was a chance he might reach civilization sooner that way. He took it. He was a few hundred yards up the road when he thought he saw something to the right. He slammed on the brakes hard enough for the seatbelt to strike the wind from his chest. The car came to a stop and, after a moment to recover himself, Peter turned it around, observing everything within the beam of the headlights.

There it was. A dirt road hidden among the trees that lined that side of the road. It was a blink and you'll miss it turn that wasn't signposted, and he had damn near missed it himself. He stopped the car with the dirt road in his beams. When he had looked at the map of the area, he had seen no other roads. It didn't look inviting.

He considered it for a long time. The part of his mind responsible for self-preservation reminded him how exposed, vulnerable and alone he was all the way out here. Even something as small as a puncture down that dirt road which didn't exist on the map, would be the end of him. He had already noticed his phone had lost signal a few miles back.

Screw it, what else am you going to do? he thought. He lifted his foot off the brake and eased forward, down the dirt road. He was immediately surrounded by tall trees, thick black shapes in the darkness, which made the road seem smaller as they collected and gathered shadows. Carefully, he followed the road for a little more than a mile until he came to a grotesque black gate. On either side, the headlights offered the glimpse of a towering grey wall.

He could not see anything beyond the black bars of the gate and the thick chains holding them together. He had found something, but he didn't know what.

35

Twenty-one year olds were not meant to suffer existential crisis but that was exactly what Will was suffering for the second time in a single year. He should have been a graduate trying to start a career and struggling to keep in contact with his friends now that they had scattered to their own separate corners of the country. He should have been trying to make a long distance relationship work with Nicole.

Instead, his friends were gone, with no signs of what happened even after an entire year. Will had started his third year for the second time, and just like the first, hadn't even made it through a full day. The pain was too much, and if that were not enough, he couldn't tell what was real and what wasn't.

Even after a full weekend of thinking, his mind, his whole understanding of his life, spun like a Waltzer at the fairground that more than likely had not really existed, and while he pleaded that he wanted to get off, his mental pleas were little more than screams. As the old saying goes, a scream means you want to go faster.

He had managed to slow it only slightly over the past few days but being around the ghostly memories of his friends in the studio today had sent him reeling once again. He was supposed to have a video appointment with Dr Phillips that afternoon, which could have helped to see things clearly but he had kept his computer switched off. He had missed Thursday's appointment and he couldn't explain to her why. He couldn't deal with that right now.

The memories he had recovered felt so vividly real, and

he could not escape the glassy-eyed image of Julian staring at him, unblinking. The way Nicole had looked at him, scorned him for what he had done to hurt them all. The sounds and sights were so clear, as were the lingering scents of candyfloss and toffee apples, of burgers and hot dogs frying on food carts.

Yet there had been no evidence a fair had ever been there. The police had found no witnesses, including those that lived in the streets surrounding the park, who could confirm that there had been a fair. No matter how vivid his memories, he still had no answer as to how that was possible.

Nor had he visited a fair with Ian when he was a child.

And then there were the episodes. He had sleepwalked, venturing outside under the belief he was following Nicole.

He was losing his mind. Hell, maybe he'd already lost it.

If he could fabricate things while he was under a psychiatrists guidance, even one who was still in training, how could he trust a single memory in his head? Had he invented the Stranger as well as the Crooked Man? After all, nobody else had laid eyes on the man, and who, in real life, referred to themselves as something as ominous as 'The Stranger'? It was the kind of name normally reserved for a comic book character.

'See you later, Will,' Beth mumbled awkwardly through his bedroom door as he sat thinking over it all, again. She and Ben were going out for a drink with a couple of people from the course and wouldn't be back for a couple of hours. They had asked if he wanted to come but he had refused.

He stayed in his bedroom for another hour after they left before stepping onto weak and wobbly legs, and headed to the bathroom. Once he had relieved his bladder, he moved to the sink and paused. On the windowsill behind the sink sat his razor. He stared at it for a long minute.

He had, he had realised, been staying alive for the sake of his friends, in the belief that so long as he lived, he might one day discover the truth of what happened to them and bring help to them wherever they were. But he had failed.

There was no way now he would ever find out what had happened. If they were still alive out there somewhere, they were beyond his help.

Will moved his gaze from the razor to the bathroom door. There would be nobody to stop him this time. The house was empty. Even if he decided to run a bath to ease the pain as he had done the first time, nobody would hear him. By the time either of them came home and realised what he'd done, it would be too late. Will would be gone.

He sat down on the edge of the bath but made no move for the razor, not yet. He first pulled up his left sleeve, all the way to the elbow, and then the right. He looked down at the reddish purple line that ran down the entire length of one forearm.

'You're lucky to be alive,' the doctors had said. He hadn't agreed. After the disappearance, although he was left with a desire to remain alive, he still did not quite agree with Dr Phillips's assessment. Things had not improved since the attempt. With the disappearance of his friends and the loss of his memories, they had gotten considerably worse. Although he no longer desired to commit suicide, he wasn't glad to not have died during that attempt.

Had he died, the disappearance never would have happened and his friends would have been around. What he was left with after the disappearance was not exactly the desire for life that Dr Phillips believed it to be, but rather the obligation to remain so, to stay alive for his friends, as the only person who knew – if only he could remember – what had happened to them.

Everything had become such a mess now, the chance of him remembering and helping them was gone. His friends were more lost to him now than they had ever been. He had been living for them but now, what reason did he have to go on?

He stared at the scar and saw the awkward shuffle of his friends' feet as they waited outside the museum for him, all of them nervous to have to speak to him and none of them wanting to address the elephant in the room. He wasn't even sure anymore if that memory had been real. It hadn't come from his hypnotherapy but did that make it real?

The void they left behind was definitely real and it was with him in the bathroom, the same way his own empty space would have haunted them had he been successful in his first attempt to take his own life. As it would have haunted Ian and his mother, as they mourned and searched for an answer to their pain, an understanding they might never be awarded.

'Killing yourself doesn't end the pain. It just shares it out among the people you leave behind.'

He didn't know if Nicole had actually said those words or if he had made them up but he knew she was right. Still, he made no move to pull his sleeves back down. Doing what he was considering would pass his pain to those around him but did that mean he shouldn't do it? There was so much pain, so much confusion, he wasn't sure how much more he could endure. He couldn't see the reason for it. To keep from hurting those that cared about him didn't seem a strong enough reason to continue living. The suffering would not be as heavy on their shoulders as it was on his.

Was it fair, he wondered.

Did it matter?

It was selfish and cruel but they didn't know what it was like to feel responsible for four people no longer being here, and to not remember how. Or what it felt like to not remember a moment which defined the person they'd become, to not know which memories were real and which weren't. Memories were what made people who they were. Without his, he'd lost his identity. Maybe he was the kind of person who was willing to pass his pain onto others, so as to not have to feel it himself any longer.

He had never considered suicide in such a way before. If he had, he wasn't sure he would have been willing to share his pain among Nicole, Craig, Tom and Julian. He had loved them each more than anything in the world. They had become his family, his brothers and his partner. He would never have knowingly done anything to hurt them.

Back then, he had not even thought of the effect his death would have on them, which was a selfishness in itself, but it was a far worse selfishness to think about the pain they would feel and then choose to do it anyway.

Was he capable of doing that now, knowing what his continued existence had brought his old friends? Was a little emotional aching not better than whatever horrors had befallen the last people who chose to care about him?

Could you live with yourself, people liked to say but Will wouldn't have to live with it; everybody else would.

Will pulled his sleeve back down over the scar and then covered his bare forearm, too. He could do it, of that he was certain, but not like this. He had had two regrets when Ian saved his life. The second of which had been that he had not said goodbye. Instead of them losing him, he had lost them, and he still had not said goodbye. Instead, he had stayed alive, clutching to the idea that they were alive and he would be the one to save them, that if only he could remember, they could be found and brought home, but the chances of that were nil. His memories were as lost as his friends, and it was time to let both go.

The vigil tomorrow night was the perfect place for him to finally give his friends the goodbye they deserved. Then he would come back here and end it all.

36

It might have occurred to Peter that he had stumbled on the property of a wealthy recluse were it not for the silhouetted profile welded into the top of the large metal gate. It was not dissimilar to the popular illustrations of Sherlock Holmes in his inaccurate deerstalkers hat, but instead of warm nostalgia, this image made Peter's skin prickle despite the car's heaters, for this was not the profile of a detective, but of a murderous fairground owner.

He recognised it from the photographs in the newspapers as the logo for The Harold Tombes Fairground Company, depicting the features of the man himself in a top hat.

The gates were secured with thick chains and a heavy padlock. Both would be too thick to break, even if Peter had any large tools with him. The black metal of the gate appeared thick and strong enough to obliterate the front of his car if he tried to gain entry by more forceful means.

He climbed out of the car without killing the lights and approached the gates. He tested them in his hands. As he'd guessed, they were thick and sturdy, just the way people used to make things in the days before mass production. There was no budge in them beyond the pull of the chains.

The headlights passed only a few feet beyond the gate, revealing nothing. Peter took out his phone and, using it as a torch, held it at arm's length through the gate. The spread of light extended another few feet. The light glanced off of a grinning face.

'Shit!' Peter yelled and jerked backwards, nearly

dropping his phone in the process. He heard no movement from within. 'Who's there?'

He cautiously approached the fence again and edged the phone with its beam of light back through into the dark space beyond. He focused on the same area as before, moving slowly. He started low, revealing a black pair of shoes, tracking up a pair of legs in black trousers. A ruffled, Victorian style shirt and suit jacket. The light revealed the face and he prepared himself to jump back again. But the figure didn't move. The man he was looking at appeared so real and lifelike but the eyes, open and staring straight ahead at him, didn't even flicker at the light shining directly in them. It was a model of some kind, one that was scarily realistic and wearing a creepy grin that stretched as far across its lower face as was humanly possible.

Peter took a breath and steadied himself, brought his phone back through to his side of the gate. He looked up with the phone's light. The gate reached a good five feet above him. There was a horizontal beam running through the middle. If he could get his foot onto that, he could boost himself to the top, he thought.

He took a cigarette and lit it while he considered. When the cigarette was burnt down to the filter, he tossed it into the treeline and stretched. He had spent too long in his car these past few weeks and it had been a while since he had made any kind of effort toward his physical health, so there were multiple pops and creaks from his muscles and joints. It was not going to be as easy a climb as it once would have been.

Without knowing how long he would be away from the car, he killed the lights and took out the key. So far out in the middle of nowhere, the last thing he needed was a dead battery. Then he grabbed the bars of the gate with both hands and heaved his body upward. As he pulled, he pushed his feet off the ground in a jump and threw one leg higher, aiming for the middle bar. His knee struck the bar, sparking pain through his thigh but he managed to force it onto the bar long enough to bring his other foot up, and stood up on it. He placed a foot against the wall the gate was fixed to and used it to kick himself upwards. Awkwardly, he mounted the top of the gate, swung one leg over and then the other, and began a slow decline on the other side.

As he reached for the middle bar with his foot, he slipped and tumbled. He landed on his feet but his right foot buckled.

'Fuck!' he winced as the pain shot lightning up his shins. With wobbling legs, he straightened and applied a little pressure to the aching ankle. It flared with pain, but he forced more weight onto it. Took one step, then another. It wasn't broken but there was a definite sprain. He didn't think he'd be walking without a limp for a couple of days, which meant there would be no quick escape if he found anybody in here with him.

Without the light from the car, Peter was shrouded in a suffocating blackness the moon could barely touch. He used the torch on his phone again. The white beam tore through the darkness like ripping apart a sheet of black velvet. A well-trodden dirt path led from the gate into the darkness. The figure he'd glimpsed stood to one side of it like he was there to greet visitors. On the other side of the path he found another one, looking almost identical to the first.

He reached out a finger and touched the shoulder of the figure, confirming that it definitely wasn't real. Something whirred and the arm shifted forward an inch. Peter jumped, sparked the pain in his ankle again. But the tiny movement was all that came from the figure. The man was not real, that was for sure but nor was it a mere model. This was some kind of animatronic, one that had long since ceased proper working function.

Even so, looking at that grin, Peter was eager to leave the pair of them behind. He headed down the path. The light before him revealed a wooden stall on either side of the path a little further up. There were three solid walls of red and white striped tarpaulin. They looked exactly as old fairground stalls would, although they were empty and bare inside.

Against the one on the right of the path there was a sign bearing the name of the fairground: Harold Tombes Fairground.

Between the two stalls, at the furthest reaches of the torch's beam, he glimpsed the shape of more stalls. They were each covered in tarp, decorated with white and red stripes. Slithers of red ran from the red stripes, as though they had been painted on instead of dyed. The tarps covered these stalls entirely, including the front.

Peter reached for the edge of one of the first stalls and peered behind the tarp. An explosion of light blinded him and he stumbled backward, unaware of what had just happened. When his vision cleared and his mind stopped reeling, he saw a row of bulbs were strung between each of the stalls. The bulbs of the closest stalls glowed bright and colourful. He waited for them to turn off, or for some irate show person to appear and attack him, but nothing happened. The lights remained on.

They must have been triggered by some kind of motion sensor, he presumed, and he knew he was on the right track. The motion triggered lighting had to have been an addition made by the Tombes fanatic he was searching for. The earliest motion sensors were invented in the middle of the last century and any kind of advanced system wouldn't have been available in Harold Tombes' lifetime.

Peter continued on. With each few steps, a few more bulbs came to life, lighting his way and leading him further into the abandoned fairground. He kept the torch on his phone switched on, ready for any point when the lights gave out, but kept it down, out of the way. When he came to other paths splitting off from this one, he shone his torch down it and took a few tentative steps along them, but no lights were triggered by his movements and he returned to the main track.

There came a grassy opening between the stalls, where something heavy had once sat. There were large rivets in the earth and the grass was flattened. The absence of whatever was supposed to be here unnerved Peter more than the abandoned stalls did.

As he limped onward, he found more of these open spaces where something had sat until sometime in the not too distant past. The path drew him deeper and deeper into a place he shouldn't be and he wished he'd never entered.

After what felt like a terrifying age, the path led him to an open expanse, where darkness reigned, through which he could make out nothing more than a dark shape. He lifted the phone and approached. The shape was a large wooden building, the size of a small mansion, but the walls were blackened and withering, the wooden beams of the structure crumbling.

The building was somehow still standing, despite the significant damage it had incurred from a fire long since extinguished. The front of the building was covered in soot and withered grey material that resembled rippling, scorched flesh. Metal bars clung to the walls as though windows had once been there.

Despite the damage, he knew what this building was. At the top, there remained the general shape of what had once been letters. Although there were only a couple of them still legible, he didn't need to read them to know they once read *Tombes's House of Horror*.

This was it. This was the house in which many had lost their lives as part of a circus freak's twisted game.

A set of three burnt and broken steps led up to what had once been a doorway. Now, the opening was obscured by the top half of the frame, which had collapsed across the doorway. Peter got as close as he dared and cast the light from his phone through the gap. There were more collapses within, too many to count. It was a death trap only a fool would dare to enter.

He squatted down and worked his way around the collapsed doorframe. He had come this far; he wasn't about to stop now.

Inside was laden with more obstacles, which he worked his way slowly around. He walked through the burnt building, stepping over walls that were no longer complete, heading deeper into the death trap. It was a maze, he realised as he observed the twist of the walls more closely, and he was thankful he was able to step through them.

He weaved through the burnt remains of the house of horror, not entirely sure what he was looking for, until he glimpsed an opening in the floor. It was perfectly rectangular, made by man, not fire. From the opening, a set of concrete steps descended into a darkness blacker than any he had ever laid eyes on.

The cone of light from his phone barely seemed to touch it.

He'd come this far, he thought again, and descended. When he reached the bottom, he cast the light around at his surroundings and swallowed.

What the fuck had he stumbled on to?

37

Peter fled the burnt building as fast as his ankle would allow. He eased under the fallen pillars of wood that blocked the corridors as quickly as he could, but in his haste he tore another hole in the shoulder of his jacket and felt the graze of the splintering wood against his skin. He couldn't tell if it had broken the skin but the pain was intense. He gave it only a second of thought; he was too busy trying to wrap his head around what he'd seen at the bottom of those stairs. Somebody needed to know what he'd found here.

He burst out from the collapsed doorway and hopped down the three warped steps on his aching ankle. Free of the building, he felt lighter. He paused to gather his breath.

This strange, abandoned fair was out in the middle of nowhere but Peter checked his phone signal anyway. It was hopeless. It didn't even show his network name in the top corner, let alone any bars.

Peter had come across a great many disturbing sights in the course of his fifteen year career, including dead bodies – which he never got used to – but what he had found at the bottom of those stairs was worse than any of it. The large room down there belonged nowhere near a usually joyful place such as a fairground.

While he had not managed to hold it together at some crime scenes – although he always threw up somewhere out of sight where there could be no contamination and few witnesses – he managed to hold it now. The entire fairground was a crime scene and he had no time to waste on vomiting. The police needed to be called in.

They were the last people he wanted to deal with, despising the entire institution after the way he and Sally had been treated, but this was no longer something he could do by himself.

He limped his way back through the paths to the locked gate. His ankle throbbed louder and he thought he'd probably done a fair bit of damage, after all. He wasn't sure he would be able to climb over the gate again. It had been difficult enough with two working ankles.

Unless he wanted to stay in here waiting for the Tombes fanatic to come back, he had little choice but to try. He started to climb.

Peter wasn't the biggest or strongest guy, so using his upper body and only one foot, the climb was slow and agonising. More than once his arms threatened to give way under the weight of his own body. He was unable to kick upward against the wall as he had on the initial climb, so he had to heave himself up with his arms and back. He pulled up until his stomach was resting on the top of the gate, then swung his lower body to meat it, twisting until he was practically lying across the inch thick metal. Carefully, he swung his legs down on the other side and slid them down to the middle beam. From there, he moved his hands to meet his undamaged foot and stepped down toward the floor. He was sure to land on his undamaged ankle but he came down off balance and had to grab the fence again to keep from sprawling.

He hobbled to his car and climbed behind the wheel, exhausted and sweating through his clothes. In the darkness, his body began to shake. For a few minutes, all he could do was sit there and wait for it to pass. When the tremors retreated into his chest and focused on his heart, he started the car and set his mind to the task of turning around in the narrow dirt road.

He pressed the clutch and screamed. He saw spots. His injured ankle had swelled to the size of a balloon. He forced it down and bit through the pain, getting the car into first. When he lifted it, it throbbed more than ever. The car inched a little to the right, until it was almost touching the trunk of a large tree. Then he forced his damaged foot down onto the clutch again and switched to reverse. Reversed until his back bumper was at risk of striking another tree. Back to first.

His gut wrenching screams filled the car, until, finally, he faced away from the gate. He made a final switch to first and set off down the road, driving slow enough he didn't need to change gear again. Once the car broke the treeline and the tyres hit the tarmac, he took his phone out and held it against the steering wheel, waiting for a signal.

He travelled a long and tiresome mile before a single, solitary bar appeared. He pulled onto the shoulder and called Sally.

It rang off, once, twice, a third time, and then finally, as he thought it was going to click off, she answered.

'Hey, Roxanne,' Sally said. 'How are you?'

Peter was about to ask her what she was talking about when he realised the time. She was at home, and with *him*.

He waited for her to get to a place where she could talk.

'Peter,' she said, almost a whisper. 'What... want?'

'Hold on,' he said. 'Signal's weak. You're breaking up.'

He braced himself before bringing his left foot back to the clutch and bringing the car back into motion, screaming through gritted teeth as he did so.

From the phone Sally shouted to know what was happening, if he was alright. The signal reached two bars and then three. He brought the car to a stop and raised the phone to his ear. He was panting. His brow dripped with sweat.

'That should be better,' he said.

'What's going on? Are you okay?'

'Fine,' he lied.

She paused for a moment, weighing up whether to probe further. She decided not to. 'So what do you want? You know you can't keep calling me any time you want something.

I actually have more in my life and more to do at work than steal files for you.'

'Sal,' Peter said with a tremor in his voice he hadn't expected. 'I found something.'

'What is it?' She made no attempt to quieten her voice. She was all go, all concern, ready to leap in her car the moment the call was over, no matter what she had been doing with her fiancé.

'I'm going to give you an address,' he said. 'You need to see this.'

'I'm busy, Peter. Just tell me, is it Amelia?'

Peter swallowed at the mention of his little girl and he felt sorry that he had made her think that, and would have to break her heart all over again by telling her otherwise.

He took a deep breath to level himself. Be the journalist, report the facts. 'It's about the Campbell kid. I'm sorry, Sal.' He gave her a second to accept it. 'There's a yard I've found in North Yorkshire, hidden down a dirt road and surrounded by trees. It once belonged to a serial killer from the early twentieth century. Inside there's an empty fairground, and among it, a burnt down building that used to be a house of horror. Inside,' his voice caught. 'Inside the house, there's a set of stairs going down into some kind of basement. Down there, Sally. It's horrific. It's our worst nightmare. A… a dungeon. I think somebody's been keeping people down there.'

'North Yorkshire? That's miles away Peter, and I don't work in that constabulary. You have to call nine-nine-nine.'

'Please, Sally. This is some serious shit.'

There was silence on the other end of the line for a long time. Then she said, 'Where is it?'

He told her how to reach him.

Peter sat in the darkness of his car for over an hour and a half before a set of headlights pierced the darkness in his rear view mirror. He watched as they grew larger into the shape of a Lexus. Sally parked the car in front of him and got out.

She moved with clear annoyance at having to be out

here in the back end of nowhere – she was supposed to be having a pleasant evening with her fiancé – but she was also worried.

She had changed out of whatever glamourous and sexy attire she had worn for her darling fiancé and into the pant suit she normally wore for work but her face still wore the delicate yet attractive make-up far too over the top for standard policing.

Peter rolled down his window, and flicked on the internal light.

'You look good,' he said, and he meant it.

'Steven and I were hosting a dinner party,' she said. Her tone was annoyed and standoffish but she blushed nonetheless. 'Why don't you give me the rundown of how you found this place, what you've found and then you can go home? Hop out. I'm not talking to you through a fucking window.'

'Is that an official request, because I don't see any probable cause.'

'Don't be a dick. Just get out of the car, or…'

'Or what? Are you going to manhandle me?' His usual snarky attitude felt uncomfortable even to himself and it came out without humour. The images from down in that dungeon continued to play in his mind.

Sally huffed. 'Get out or I'm leaving.'

Peter switched off the light and climbed out. He closed the door behind him and leant against it in a way that made him seem casual and uncaring, but allowed him to keep attention from his swelling ankle.

'Well, DI Lincoln,' he said.

'Don't do that. Just tell me what I'm doing here.'

'I think it's better I show you. Did you see a dirt road on your way to me, a short way back?'

'I saw an opening. I couldn't see if it was a road or not.'

Peter gestured to her car. 'Let's go back and head down it. You can drive.'

He limped toward the Lexus without waiting for permission. Sally caught sight of his ankle.

'What the fuck have you done to yourself?'

Peter waved the question off. 'Come on. I don't want you to miss too much of your dinner party.'

Sally didn't bite. Instead she got back in the car and turned it back the way she'd come. They coasted until they reached the dirt road.

'Do you want to tell me anything about what I'm going to find down here?' Sally asked after a quarter mile of dirt road.

'Getting a little wary, huh? Did your mother warn you about driving into the middle of the woods with a strange man?'

Sally sighed, and this time, reacted. 'Why do you have to be like this? After everything we've been through? Do you want to know the truth? My mam did warn me about this. She told me it isn't healthy for me to continue seeing you. For any reason.'

They both knew why he was like this, even with her. It had been the subject of many arguments at the end of their marriage. They had both been treated in such a horrendous way by the police in the wake of the biggest tragedy they could ever imagine enduring – the disappearance of their child – and yet she had remained one of them. After all these year, he was hated by the police as much as he hated them, and yet she was a part of that family, even after they had torn theirs apart.

He said, 'Your mother never liked me.'

They fell silent and a few minutes later, the car came to a stop at the gates of the fairground. No lights were on inside.

'Where are we?' Sally asked, making no move to leave the car.

'I think this is where William Campbell and his friends were taken when they disappeared. This is the fairground he remembers.'

She considered him and he could see her doing the math in her head. Was it possible? The kid had reported remembering a fairground despite there not having been one in town, but then the kid had turned up many miles from Treevale.

'You know finding out what happened to the Treevale Five won't help you find Amelia,' she said.

He nodded. 'Everyone deserves an answer. Even if we never got ours.'

Their eyes met, both of them glazed with shining moisture as they shared the memories of their tragedy through look alone.

Peter turned away first and got out of the car, putting the conversation to an end. After a moment to wipe her eyes, Sally joined him. Her make-up had run, drawing lines of grey from her eyeliner down her cheeks.

Peter explained how he had gained entry to the fairground. She gave him a look of disapproval intended to remind him that counted as trespassing, then took a set of hairpins from the glove box and used them to pick the padlock. She unwrapped the chains and pushed open one side of the heavy gates.

She stopped beside the figures that flanked the rough path heading into the fairground. She reached out as he had, but her finger pressed against the figure's cheek, which appeared solid under her touch. They looked so realistic but so grotesque at the same time, as though two freakshow participants had been transformed into animatronic dummies.

'Creepy,' she said. 'Very welcoming.'

Side by side, they walked and limped through the fair, following the same route Peter had taken. As before, the lights burst into life to guide their way.

'So what makes you think this has anything to do with the kid?' Sally asked.

'The dates line up.'

'What?'

He didn't answer. He didn't want to talk. His every

thought was taken up with a rising dread as they drew nearer to the burnt house of horror.

'This is it,' he said, as they reached the open space. He stepped toward it and lit it with his phone.

'You expect me to go in there? Without telling me why? Are you sure you're not out here to kill me?'

'You want to see this,' Peter said and ducked under the first collapsed beam. Reluctantly, Sally followed. One in front of the other, by the light of Peter's phone torch, they worked their way back to the opening he'd discovered. At the top of the steps, they paused.

Peter stared down into the darkness, unsure he wanted to go back down there. Sally misinterpreted his hesitation for concern for his swollen ankle and hooked his arm around her shoulder, and started down. Peter had no option but to descend with her.

At the bottom, he cast the cone of light around slowly so as to give Sally a good look. There were soiled, stained mattresses laid out on the floor at regular intervals. Trays of rotten food sat beside them, mere feet from metal buckets, the purpose of which was obvious. The stench was pungent in the air. Beside the mattresses were D-rings built into the concrete floor. From each ran thick chains ending in a large cuff.

'Oh my god,' Sally muttered.

She left Peter by the bottom step and took his phone, looking at each of the areas closely. Then she helped him back up the stairs and out of the building.

Sally looked flustered, wired. 'This is messed up. Once we get back to the car, I'm going to call this in. Then, you're going to get that ankle looked at. I'll have a patrol unit follow you to the hospital in your car. I'll come see you tomorrow and get a statement.'

38

Given his initial reaction when Ben first told him about the vigil, Ben and Beth were apprehensive when Will told them he wanted to attend, but still walking on egg shells around him, neither of them pushed him on the matter. Instead, they agreed to stand by his side as he said goodbye.

It was a hot evening, a hangover of the recently ended summer, which left the air thick and humid, in desperate need of a storm. Yet the atmosphere between them as they made the short journey from their house to the university was anything but warm. There was still a lingering hesitation. Conversations with Will had become a minefield and nobody had a metal detector.

What sent an added chill through their evening was the sense of death. No bodies had ever been found and, so far as Will was aware, none of his friends had received a funeral – a small, mournful gathering had been held by Nicole's dad, who had accepted his daughter was never coming home, but, being the one he blamed, rightfully or otherwise, Will was not invited – and he thought this would have been what one would have felt like.

Beth grabbed his hand and squeezed. And then her hand was gone. He felt a great comfort that it had been there at all. Only a couple of days ago, he had feared Beth may never even *talk* to him again.

He had no thoughts when she touched his hands of his feelings for her. Not tonight. Tonight was for Nicole, and Craig, and Tom, and Julian. He was even dressed in a jacket Nicole had left behind.

It was a navy cavalry style jacket with three rows of gold ball buttons running down the front and gold stripes on each bicep. Nicole had bought it – in a man's size because she preferred the fit that didn't accentuate her chest, or lack thereof – to wear on nights out. It fit her desire to stand out.

She had left it in Will's old room and it was collected together with Will's belongings when Ian collected them when he turned back up after the disappearance. When packing to come back, Will had found it and brought it with him. He had had no intention of wearing it. He'd brought it to feel closer to Nicole. Tonight, however, he needed that closeness with him.

He would wear it until the end.

He'd put on the jacket like a piece of armour and stepped into the living room.

'Cool jacket,' Ben had said.

'It was...' Will had started and choked.

Beth had nodded, understanding, so he wouldn't have to finish.

Xander had returned to pick something up before returning to stay with the friend who had welcomed him for the past few days and he wasted no time in making it clear he wouldn't be coming with them to the vigil. He didn't 'agree with honouring the dead stood beside their murderer', a statement which earned him a slap around the head from Beth.

At the sight of Will's jacket Xander laughed, cruelly. 'You're definitely a fucking serial killer, looking like that.'

Ben threw his arms questioningly out to the side. Beth shook her head and ushered Will and Ben out the front door. On the pavement, Ben told Will not to listen to Xander and assured him that it really was a cool jacket.

On campus, the cold, heavy atmosphere was thicker, almost suffocating. They waded through it to the arts building. As they grew nearer, the air grew thicker. They stopped a hundred yards short of the building, where they could still turn back without anybody noticing.

Beth turned to him and asked, 'Are you okay?'

Will nodded, although they all knew it was for show.

'Because, you know, there's no shame if you want to go back home. Nobody will judge you if you don't think you can do this, least of all us two, yeah? We're here to support you. I mean, we have no idea what you're going through, how you must feel, first losing them and then your head going a bit...'

Ben nudged her before she could spiral into her usual ramblings.

'Right, sorry. My point is, we're with you, all the way, whether you want to do this or if you want to go home and, I don't know, tell stories about them until the sun comes up.'

'I'm ready,' Will said. He didn't feel it but there wasn't a choice. Not really. The sun was setting, and it would not be rising again. Not for him. He had to say goodbye.

She examined his face a moment and then, still unsure, nodded. There was already a sizable group gathered outside in front of the building, made up primarily of their course mates, and a few of the second years, who had been starting their first year when the five of them had disappeared and so had never had the pleasure of meeting any of the four missing. Closest to the door were the lecturers, talking quietly amongst themselves.

Will, Ben, and Beth joined the back of the small crowd where nobody would notice them.

Above them, the lights from the digital studio blasted out into the descending night. From within, Will could feel their eyes on him, the spectres of his friends watching and judging him for what he was doing.

How can you give up on us? he imagined them asking.

I'm not giving up, he thought. He was saying goodbye. That wasn't the same thing.

Ben checked the time on his phone.

'Five minutes,' he muttered. The vigil was to begin at eight o'clock and given Stevie's obsession with scheduling, this would start on time and not a second earlier. He would want to give every chance for those not yet here to attend. They waited in deathly silence, shifting on the spot in a way that reminded Will all too painfully of the way his friends had awaited his arrival outside the museum.

Eight o'clock came and Stevie turned to the crowd. 'Listen up, everyone. I'm really glad to see so many of you here. I'm sure it would have meant a lot to Julian, Craig, Nicole and Tom. Now, the vigil will be taking place in the car park on the other side of the building. There are candles in boxes outside the back entrance. If you each take one and take up a position around the vigil.'

Like a herd of cattle, the crowd filed after Stevie, skirting around the building and passing away from the judgemental eyes of the four phantom students. The crowd swarmed toward the back door and retrieved a candle stick in a small plastic holder that reminded Will of the handle of a tiny toy sword.

The crowd came together in a large circle around a display in the middle of the car park. Lying on the tarmac was a humungous photograph surrounded by a circle of thirty or forty unlit candles in glass holders. Will felt a lump catch in his throat. It was the same photograph that had been used on first newspaper he saw following the disappearance, and on almost every bit of media coverage since, printed on a massive scale in full colour: Tom, Julian, Nicole, Will, and Craig, all beaming, genuine smiles of joy. They were five people having a great time, pausing only long enough for the snap of a photo.

Their names were written across their stomachs at the bottom of the print, all but Will's. Beneath the photograph read:

IN A BETTER PLACE BUT WITH US, ALWAYS.

A better place? Not only was it an overused cliché that only comforted the religious, of which Will was not one, but it struck Will as a preposterous assumption, given that nobody knew where they were. He took a breath and reminded himself why he was here. The vigil was to say goodbye and to accept that they were gone.

Will shrank back, not just from the photograph but from the glances that had already started to turn in his direction. He wondered why Stevie couldn't have photoshopped the photograph to remove him. It would have hurt to see the four of them in that photo without him, but it would keep the attention from him. He could only imagine what they were muttering.

'It's him.'

'He went missing too. How did he get away?'

'Do you think he did it?'

'It's like in the movies. Killer returning to the scene of the crime. Sort of.'

He tried to tell himself that this was all his imagination, distorted by the awful things Xander had said to him, when, to one side of him, he overheard, clear as day, 'Do you reckon he regrets what he did?'

It was spoken by a baby faced blonde girl with no comprehension of what muttering was, and who might as well have asked Will directly. Will was tempted to answer as though she had, but he held his tongue. He didn't want to draw any more attention to himself than was necessary, and, more importantly, he didn't want to disrupt a night that was all about his friends, not him.

Stevie wormed his way through the crowd and took his place in front of the large print. He had his own unlit candle in his hand. He turned a slow circle to take in the crowd that had formed. A bittersweet smile grew across his face.

'We're here tonight,' he announced. He sounded like a priest at a funeral. 'To honour the lives of four lost students. Tom. Craig. Nicole. Julian. A year ago, tonight, the Treevale Five disappeared without a trace, and, tragically, four of them still remain missing. What happened will, unfortunately, remain a mystery, but we are here to remember them, warmly, knowing that, whatever occurred, they are at peace.'

Will wiped tears from his cheeks. He hadn't even realised he was crying.

Stevie held up his unlit candle. 'We honour the lost with our light.' He lowered the candle and lit it with a lighter he took from his back pocket. When he spoke again, Will got the impression Stevie had rehearsed his speech more than a few times. 'The five people in this photograph were the best of friends and the best way to honour them is with a warm union of people. So I ask that you not light your candles with a match or lighter, as I did, but to pass the flame from one candle to another, sharing your light.' He stepped toward Will. Will hadn't even realised Stevie had noticed him. 'Who better to begin sharing the light with, than William Campbell, the fifth of these best friends?'

All eyes burned into Will. There was no hiding from them now.

Stevie continued, 'I had the honour of teaching this incredible group of friends, these five kind, considerate, passionate people who were always smiling and laughing. None of them deserved whatever happened. They were some of the best people to work in this building.'

Stevie let out a long breath that Will thought was to keep him from crying in front of all these students. He offered Will his candle and Will touched the tip of his own candle to the flame. The fire wrapped itself around his wick and split into two. Stevie stepped back and gestured to Will.

'Do you feel up to a few words?' he asked. 'It's okay if not. Just pass the flame on if that's what you want.'

Will opened his mouth and his chin wobbled. He forced it to steady. He didn't want to say anything but he would. For them.

He said, 'My friends were... When people die or go missing, everybody who knew them or even said "hi" to them starts talking about them as though they were best friends. It's always such *bollocks*. People say things like "she was always smiling" and "he never had a bad word to say about anybody," "he was such a great guy." But they don't know them. Not really.'

He felt the eyes on him, most of them confused, and Beth and Ben's, filled with concern, and his voice faltered for a second.

'Julian was a compulsive liar. He told bullshit stories that got him in trouble. In our first year, there was a girl called Zoe, who went to college with Julian. He told us a story where he was trapped in the dark room with her, and led her to safety through a crawlspace in the ceiling before she had a panic attack. Zoe heard about the story and threatened to cut Julian's balls off if he ever made up another rumour about her.'

Will laughed to himself. After they disappeared, Zoe had posted a sentimental piece about her friendship with Julian, and called him a natural storyteller, an all-round lovely guy.

Nobody else laughed.

'Tom was a flake. He agreed to go to parties and events and almost never showed up. Even when we were having pre-drinks at our house, he would make up excuses not to be involved. He would agree to do things for people, then pretend he forgot.

'Nicole was almost always smiling but she had a short temper. She didn't get angry but she got moody and she would hold a grudge for a lifetime. She chain smoked, without checking with whoever was around her, and sometimes she would go days without responding to a message. If she responded at all.

'Craig got rough if he'd had a few too many drinks, which was often because he couldn't hold his drink. He wanted to playfight all the time, and he didn't realise his own strength. He went too far and got into actual fights, or hurt his friends.

'They were my best friends, and my girlfriend. Don't tell me they were the best people, who never said a bad word or did a bad thing. They were flawed and imperfect, and I love each one of them.'

The crowd looked at him weary and worried. It wasn't dissimilar to the way his housemates had looked discovering him in the hallway brandishing a knife. They were here to honour people they didn't know but whom they could relate to more than any other missing report on the news, because it could just as easily have been them who went missing, and Will, one of the five, was bad mouthing them.

They all stared and for a time, it seemed as though the vigil would go no further. Nobody would take the flame from his candle, and everybody would finally slip away.

Then Ben stepped up to Will and offered his candle. Will looked up at him and returned his sympathetic smile, gratefully. Hs shared his candle first with Ben and then with Beth. The two of them then turned to the students around them and passed their flames on.

Will looked down at his flickering flame and thought of the friends he was honouring with it. He saw their smiling faces and said a silent apology. Suddenly, another candle moved toward him. He looked up into the face of a girl from Ben and Beth's year. *His* year, now, he realised. She smiled at him with the same sympathy he had felt from Ben, and he placed the burning end of his candle to the empty wick of hers. The flame grew across and split into two.

More stepped forward to share a flame with Will or their neighbours in the crowd, and soon, there wasn't a person present who didn't hold before them a lit candle. Stevie, once again, took up position in the middle. He moved his candlestick to his left hand and, with his right, lifted one of the candles in glasses from around the poster. To the crowd, he explained that he wanted them all to now, orderly and one at a time, use their candlesticks to light one of the candles on the floor, just as they had each other's candle. It was, he believed, their way of sharing the light with the four lost students.

Again, he requested Will go first. Will stepped forward, all too aware of the eyes upon him. Stevie handed him a glass. Will took it and tilted it almost sideways, and moved the candlestick toward this new wick. It took almost instantly and he levelled off both candles. Stevie gestured toward the circle around the photograph and Will crouched to place the glass down in the empty space. Looking into their smiling faces as he leant down to place the glass on the floor and thinking of the night that photograph had been taken and how happy they had been, made him feel as though they were there with him.

'I'm sorry,' he muttered to them. He placed the glass down and stepped back. He watched people he barely recognised and some he didn't recognise at all, step forward and light a candle, return it to the circle and recede back into the crowd.

Will's throat almost closed around his silent weeping. He looked on, his lit candlestick held before him, and spoke a silent goodbye to his friends, whom he would never see again.

From somewhere behind him, he overheard more muttering. A young man whispered to his friends, 'I heard there's a fair up in Graham Park tonight. We should check it out after this.'

A chill ran through Will's heart and up his spine.

Roll up.

Roll up.

Do you dare?

39

'So there it is,' Will muttered, staring across the road at Graham Park as he did when visiting the park on his morning runs. But while the park was practically abandoned and lifeless when he saw it normally, it was full of light and life now, bustling with noise and movement of a fairground in full swing.

Will, Beth and Ben had left the vigil at the same time as the majority of the crowd. He had led them back to the front of the building before asking them if they had heard the comments made by the students behind them. When they both reluctantly revealed that they had, he told them he was going there.

Beth and Ben both voiced their concerns but there was no stopping Will, and they soon realised it.

'I know it's nothing to do with what happened to me and my friends,' he said. 'I just want to go there and see if it'll help separate reality and what I remember.'

This was only partially true. What he really wanted to do was see if maybe there was more real in what he'd remembered than false. There hadn't been a fair in Treevale in more than a hundred years. The timing was too much of a coincidence.

Beth and Ben had exchanged a look before each relented and now, here they were, stood across the road from the arched gateway of the park, looking at the flood of people roaming about within, surrounded by the explosion of bells, blaring music, and screams of joy, which reminded Will of pain and suffering. A massacre.

They had been able to see the tinge of colour in the darkening sky half a mile from the campus, and heard the screams and booms of the music and calling. It was both haunting and alluring as they approached. Up close, it was a headache of senses.

'Yep,' Ben agreed. 'There it is.'

'How do you feel?' Beth asked. They were both walking on egg shells.

Will said nothing. Only stared.

'So what now?' Ben said. 'Are we going in?'

'No,' Beth said. 'We're going home. Right, Will. It's just a fair, see?'

'I'm going inside,' Will said. He felt drawn to the fair as though it were calling to him.

He pictured the Crooked Man in there, waiting for him. It wasn't real, couldn't possibly be anything more than his imagination because the Crooked Man had to have died many decades before Will was even born, and it had already been concluded that his memories were false. Still, he saw that smile, heard those calling words, 'Roll Up.'

He had been haunted by those words before the letters arrived but for a split second, he wondered if he had remembered them before or if he only believed he had, creating yet more memories with the use of hindsight. A fair taking place on the anniversary of his disappearance was a hell of a coincidence, unless he had seen something that told him the fair would be here and invented the memories to match. Had he created an entire conspiracy for himself?

Roll up.

He was going in, but he wasn't going to make the same mistake as last time.

'I'm going alone,' he said.

'Like hell,' Beth exclaimed.

Will turned to her. 'I know it's just a fair, but it's such a coincidence, don't you think? I can't risk leading you and Ben anywhere like I led the others.'

Beth sighed. 'You're not leading us anywhere. I'm making my own choice to go in there with you. You might think you're the reason your friends ended up… wherever. But they made the decision to go with you, the same as I am. You are not at fault. Now, if we're going in, let's go.'

On either side of the open gate, stood like bouncers outside of a nightclub but with far cheerier demeanour, were two polar opposite men. One was broad and a little short, making his bulk appear wider, while the other stretched over six foot and barely had anything on his bones. They were both dressed in Victorian garb, which made Will uncomfortable.

'Good evening, miss, and sirs,' the short, broad one said, as the three of them approached. He smiled and revealed a set of bright white teeth Will had not expected from somebody without the benefit of a fixed abode and the regular dentistry that came with it.

'They stop working around this time and spend autumn and winter in one place,' he heard Julian's nonsense echo through time – or perhaps his own fabrication of time, he wasn't sure. *'So this guy, Tim, was at school for six months and then he was off again.'*

Will didn't believe that Julian had gone to school with a show person any more now than he had then but it made sense, and it would explain the fine dental work.

'And to you,' Beth answered in a slightly amazed tone. She tipped an invisible hat toward them in a gesture that reminded Will of the Crooked Man tipping his top hat. The two men wore no hats but they returned the gesture. 'What's the entry fee?'

'Go right in,' the short man added and waved them inside, with an exaggerated sweep of his hand that almost became a bow.

Inside they were in the same old park but it had transformed into a bazaar of lights, bursting enjoyment, and noise. Immediately inside they came to another archway, erected across the path with no gates or fences attached to it.

At the very tip was a logo: the profile of a man in a top hat.
Beneath the arch, hung a sign which read:
JOY
FEAR
LIFE
YOU WILL FIND THEM HERE, FOREVERMORE

Through the archway, the path split three ways, left right and dead ahead, each direction lined with stalls. Beth led them left, and they were instantly surrounded by stalls offering food and a couple with games.

'Ooh, darts,' Ben said, excited but trying to hide it.

To Will, Beth said, 'How about we take a walk around the place first and then if you're up to it, we can play at some of the stalls, yeah? We'll do whatever you want. You're in charge.'

Will wasn't so sure power was such a good thing to be put in his hands. The last time he had been in charge, the group disappeared without a trace. He didn't know how to put that into words without them worrying about him, especially after what Beth had said outside the park, so he nodded.

The stall holders not already entertaining patrons called greetings to them from behind their counters or beside their stalls. Will attempted a smile back at each of them, feeling a slither of guilt at the thoughts that crept to the forefront, and he tried to ignore their faces. His gaze was snagged by a couple of them and he was certain he had seen them before.

'It's not real,' Beth said in his head. He spared a moment of confusion that the voice of logic and reason within his mind had changed from Nicole to Beth, but turned his attention quickly to the content of the thought, not the voice. He didn't recognise them, he tried to tell himself. He had not been at this fair before.

The fairground memories were not real.

He tried to dredge up any solid memory from which those faces might have originated, or one single solid memory from that night, but he couldn't. Anything he summoned to the surface, he couldn't trust.

Laughter rang out around them and he could feel it directed at him. Every guest who turned in his direction, laughter on their lips, bored into him with their mocking eyes. *Look at him,* those eyes said, *look at the moron who can't remember how his friends died. Look who's mind might as well be mincemeat.*

Will turned his eyes away from all of them. Inside a stall for candyfloss, a young woman looked at him with a smile that didn't reach her eyes. Her name was Amy. She had gone missing from Treevale a week and a half before he did.

Her lips were red like blood. She leant toward him and whispered, 'Do you dare? I did.'

Will spun away from her, knocked into one of the laughing patrons at the opposite stall and then there were hands on his arms and Ben and Beth filled his vision.

'Are you alright, mate?' Ben asked.

'Watch what you're doing,' the man who'd been knocked snapped, his temper rising.

Beth looked up at him. 'Sorry. He's a bit clumsy.'

The man huffed and walked away with his friends. Will looked around and found everything as it should have been. There was nobody turned to laugh at him. The woman at the candyfloss stall wasn't Amy Hargrave. She had darker hair and had to be in her forties, at least, while the girl who'd gone missing had been nineteen. The gentle slope of the woman's jaw and the cute, narrow nose looked vaguely similar to the girl in the photograph that had been published in the news at the time, but her eyes, untouched by her smile, were riddled with crow's feet and the rest of her skin was lined and loose.

Will's mind was playing tricks on him. He had stumbled into a minor episode without any warning.

'Breathe, Will,' Beth said, and he noticed he was hyperventilating. He turned away from the middle aged woman.

He started breathing.

In for one, out for one.

Think about your family.

In for two, out for two.

Think about your friends.

In for three, out for three.

He didn't have anything for that section any more, nor for the next, both of which would once have been about his creative work and his dreams for the future. He had no dreams for the future and his work no longer mattered, so he focused on his friends again, first the old, then the new.

In for four, out for four.

In for five, out for five.

Think about somebody who puts a smile on your face, and say their name.

He spoke Nicole's name in his mind and felt his heart tear. His eyes became moist, and the smile, which used to adorn his lips at the end of the exercise, was gone. He had skipped out that last part of the exercise for so long because of the pain it caused, but he had included it now, without even thinking.

'You okay?' Beth asked.

He glanced around at the other people, none of whom paid him any attention, and he nodded. 'Yeah. I'm okay.'

'It's just a fair, yeah? Nothing to worry about.'

He nodded his agreement and they started walking again.

'See?' Beth said, gesturing at the entirety of the fair around them, where people laughed and played and enjoyed themselves. 'There's nothing untoward. Even if there had been a fair last year, which I'm obviously not saying there was because we've already gone down that path and we know where it leads, yeah, and it's not good. But if there had been, then what would the chances of been that a fair would take place in this park on tonight of all nights?'

The words were designed to make Will feel better but

they made him feel the opposite. She was right, what were the chances?

Will had escaped and the Crooked Man wanted him back.

'It's you,' he heard somebody say beside him. He turned and locked eyes with a woman in Victorian garb behind the counter of one of the game stalls. She was staring right at him. She looked scared but weakly hopeful.

She said, 'Are you here to save us?'

'What did you say?' Will asked, thinking he'd misheard.

Beth and Ben, who had started their own conversation, turned to see who Will was talking to and the stall holder straightened and smiled.

'I said, Do you want to try your luck?' She gestured to her stall.

'Oh. No. Thank you,' Will said.

Beth and Ben gestured him on down the path. He glanced back at the woman running the stall and saw the same fearful pleading in her eyes, staring out of a joyful mask.

They strolled a short way down the path until Will smelt something and came to a stop.

The sweet smell of perfume, both floral and fruity, wafted in a cloud around them. An all too familiar smell, Will breathed it in, hungrily, and his heart trembled with loss and love. His jaw tightened with dread at the scent he'd smelt a thousand times before.

He wanted to scream. To himself, he muttered, 'I don't know what's real and what isn't anymore.'

A breath tickled his ear and he heard Nicole's sing-song whisper. *'I'm* real.'

40

Will spun, searching for Nicole. The hot echo of her breath was still moist against his ear but there was nobody there. The smell of her perfume was still there but growing weaker.

'Mate? What's up?' Ben said.

'I,' Will said, looking around. He cast his sights on the path, back the way they had come, where people walked in either direction. 'I thought I heard something.'

He had been so convinced Nicole was right behind him, her perfume permeating his nose with painful memories and the whisper in his ear had been so clear, that he had allowed himself, for a moment, to believe. Yet it had been no more real, he knew, than the recovered memories.

A throb appeared behind his forehead and he wanted to go home, to crawl into bed with the lights turned off, and wish away the last year of his life. He wanted to open up the scar on his arm and let it all come to an end.

He took another glance around, searching desperately for her. If she was here, really here... The thought brought bittersweet tears to his eyes and he turned away from Ben and Beth before they could see. If she was here, it meant she was still alive, which was, he knew, the reason he was so willing to hold onto the reality of his memories, despite any contradicting theories. It was the reason he had stayed alive this past year.

From somewhere up ahead, a voice called to them, 'What does the future hold for you?'

The voice was a woman's, loud and booming, and it tore through Will's thoughts like a ballistic missile. He searched around for the source. When the words repeated in perfect imitation of the first instance, his eyes found it. Coming up on the left of the path, separate from the neighbouring stalls by a couple of metres, was a glass cabinet, inside of which stood, erect, the upper body of a raven haired woman in an old fashioned, deep red corset, full with ruffles that made him think of the Crooked Man. Atop her head was a large hat, the same red as the dress. Staring directly ahead, she called out the same statement for a third time.

The writing over the glass identified her as Mystic Miss Nikita.

'Oh, cool,' Ben said. Without any of them discussing it, they gravitated toward the machine. Will hesitated, not so much because of whatever ridiculous, and clearly fake, mystic qualities the animatronic woman might possess – he wasn't going to wake up tomorrow morning in the body of Tom Hanks – but because it made him think of Nicole.

'She used to love this kind of stuff,' he said.

'Nicole?' Beth asked.

'Psychics, mediums, mind readers, anybody who could connect with either the future or with the past.'

'Yeah?'

'I never bought into it, but she loved it. She loved the idea that there were magical things in the world that couldn't be explained. That there was always a connection between the past, present and future. Nothing is ever lost.'

Ben clapped a hand on his shoulder. 'That's a nice thought that, dude. You had yourself a sweet woman.'

'You have no idea.' There were tears building in his eyes but he didn't try and fight them this time. Nicole deserved them.

'Maybe we should give it a try,' Beth suggested. When he looked at her sceptically, she explained, 'You've spent so long looking at the past, it could be good to see what the future holds. I don't believe in that kind of stuff either, just a bunch a hocus pocus, yeah? But it could be fun.' She chuckled through her sadness, and even though it was forced, it lightened something in him. A tiny flame in the depths of his darkness.

Will agreed. He knew exactly what his future held and how much of it he had left, but maybe doing it would make him feel closer to Nicole, somehow.

Even up close, the woman in the box appeared strangely, uncomfortably real, as though, instead of an animatronic, the fair had actually trapped a real woman inside the glass casing. It repeated the same phrase again, the mouth moving perfectly and fluidly, unlike anything they had ever seen, besides the real thing, and the eyes seemed to follow them. Were it not for the feeling that the eyes stared straight through them, he might actually have believed it was a real woman.

A sign on the bottom of the glass explained that it cost a pound for a palm reading, and there was a faint outline on the glass where a hand should be pressed, or three pound for tarot cards. There was a space in front of the woman for cards to be placed down and a stacked deck tucked beside her. Beth took a small little purse from her pocket, and started sorting through coins.

Beth shoved a pound through the slot in the bottom half of the machine.

'Welcome,' the mystic said, almost hissing in an attempt to sound seductive. Will felt like running as strongly as he would if she had said, 'roll up,' but he stayed firmly where he was. 'I am Miss Nikita. To what do I owe the pleasure of your company? A reading of your palm, perhaps? Or is it the cards you seek? Make your selection from the buttons below, but I warn you, not all of those who come to me like what they find. But no matter what is found here, nobody leaves the same.'

If they make it out at all, Will thought with a shiver.

Beth selected the palm reading.

'Please place your hand on the glass and I will examine your future,' Miss Nikita instructed.

There was a smile of nerves and excitement on Beth's face. She was enjoying this despite believing so little of what this machine was peddling. Will didn't believe anything like mystics, magic or the supernatural but the machine filled him with a sickening dread in the pit of his stomach.

Beth placed her palm against the glass. The machine woman leant forward so her eyes were almost touching it, and then, with a long, bony finger tipped with a jet black, pointed nail, traced the lines on Beth's hand. Will was overcome with a wave of Deja vu, stronger than any of the echoing feelings of familiarity he had experienced since stepping through those gates.

Had he come here before? Had Nicole used the machine when they had been at the fair?

'Let's see if there's a future for you and… and for us,' he heard Nicole's voice echo from some deep and buried recess of his brain, and he imagined watching Nicole place her hand against the very same machine. What had the mystic machine said? Had it known there would be no future for the two of them, not because of the tension between them but because there would be no future for Nicole?

'Hmm,' came the mystic's voice. 'Beliefs will be tested. Secrets revealed. Somebody close to you will find out something you have done. You will have to make a choice between two people you care about.'

Ben leant forward, examining the mystic. There was no mechanical whining, no gap between words that made them awkwardly connect. They connected with one another with perfect inflection and the emphasis on all the right words as though constructed by a human brain, voice box and tongue.

She suddenly leant back and righted her body, placed her hands together in front of her. The reading was done.

'A pound for that?' Ben scoffed. 'It was a bit bloody vague, and generic.'

Without a word, Beth shoved another pound into the slot.

'Welcome,' the raven haired woman came back to life. As she continued her scripted message, Beth turned to Will and ushered him toward the machine.

'Come on.'

He hesitated. The woman was too real.

'For Nicole?'

There was no way he was going to be able to ignore that, and he didn't doubt Beth knew it. He might have been angered by her manipulation but there was a phrase Ian had always liked about the pot and kettle, which applied pretty well here. He had done his own fair share of manipulating friends.

Will stepped forward, waited for the woman to finish her speech, pressed the palm button and then, when instructed, placed his hand against the glass. In a perfect mimic of the previous reading, the woman leant forward and traced the lines of his hand. He relaxed a little. The movements, no matter how realistic, were no more than preprogramed mechanisms.

'Hmm,' the mystic said. 'You will find nothing here that you seek. For there are no answers to be found.'

'What?' Will sputtered, as though the machine could hear him. He kept his hand against the glass and the mystic continued to trace her mechanical finger across it.

The mystic looked up and seemed to meet his eye. 'You should not have come. You should have stayed away. Leave this place. You will not find what you seek here.'

Will stumbled back from the machine. He looked down at the hand the machine had read and then back at the woman behind the glass. She was back into her original position, a dead stare aiming somewhere behind them.

Will looked to his friends, unsure if what he had just witnessed had actually happened. Both of them seemed shocked.

'That was a bit aggressive,' Ben remarked, but still, Will couldn't work out if he had heard the same thing as Will.

He glanced back the way he had come. In the crowd of patrons there was a woman watching him. A woman with dark hair and emerald eyes. He took a step toward her but she was already turning and walking away. And then, as quickly as she had been there, she was gone.

'Yeah. It was a bit strange,' Beth agreed. 'Sorry, Will. I thought that might have been more fun.'

Will said nothing. His eyes still fixed on the point where he thought he'd seen Nicole. He started toward it, searching everywhere with his eyes until he saw her, a solitary figure amongst the couples and groups, weaving down the path. He followed. Beth and Ben joined him, asking him over and over where they were going and if he was okay. Will wasn't listening to either of them or to the deafening music and calls through the speakers as they passed between large and small rides.

He had a mind only for Nicole. Up ahead the dark haired figure turned around a stall and he sped up. As he turned the same corner, Nicole was nowhere to be seen but Will stopped, frozen to the spot. They had arrived at a large, grey structure, which loomed over them. Had loomed over him for an entire year.

The Manor of Horror.

It was almost exactly as he remembered it. Down to the blood streaked doorway from which smoke and an unnatural green glow emanated. And the sign beside it, which read *Enter if you Dare*.

Voices filled his head.

'Do you dare?'

'You can only hope to make it out the other side the same. If you make it out at all.'

'You're not scared of dying. How can you be scared of anything without being afraid of death?'

He *was* afraid of dying. He hadn't been then, at least not that he'd been aware, but he was afraid now. His reason for living was gone and he had started the night planning to end his life just as he had been planning that night a year ago, but he was suddenly terrified of dying.

He was afraid of never seeing his mother again, or Ian, or Ben and Beth. He was afraid of the pain he'd share out among them all when he was gone.

Nicole had been right, if she had ever truly spoken the words; pain wasn't ended by death, only shared amongst those left behind. He was afraid but he knew that this all had to end where it had begun. He had to dare.

'That's...' Beth said, confused. 'That's just like...'

Will nodded. 'Like I remember it.'

It was the only place Nicole could have gone, through that smoke filled doorway.

As he expected, they were greeted by two words. A whisper on the wind.

'Roll up.' A dark figure shifted in the blue glow. Will glimpsed a top hat and a hand beckoning him forward, and then the Crooked Man was gone.

Will started toward the house of horror.

41

After hours in the hospital, Peter was diagnosed with a severe sprain but no broken bones. He was told to take paracetamol and rest his leg. He returned home in the early hours of the morning and crawled, exhausted, into bed.

The sun, which had yet to rise when he pulled the covers over him, was almost set when he was awoken by a hammering at the front door. He climbed out of bed, sighed, and trudged down the hallway. He opened the door and before it was even half open, Sally barged past him and into the flat.

'I should have known it was the cops from that knocking,' he said and closed the door. 'Do they teach you that in training?'

Sally turned around in the hallway to face him. She was taken aback and he caught her looking him up and down, with disdain, maybe even a little disgust. He was dressed in a pair of grubby and greyed boxer shorts, and nothing else. Above the waistline, his stomach swelled a little bigger than when they had last seen each other without clothes, which had not been as long ago as her partner, Steven, might think.

From the look on his face, it was clear she didn't want to see him this way again any time soon, but, of course, he knew she would see it anyway, just as he knew he would see her just as exposed and bare, when Amelia's birthday came around.

'Do you not answer the phone?' she said. 'You drag me out to god knows where to see god knows what and then you stop answering your phone.'

'No "hello"? No, "it's lovely to see you, darling"? "Aren't you looking well, sweetheart"?'

'Cut the shit, Peter,' she said and her voice quivered. She was a tough woman, a Detective Inspector who was well respected, but what they had discovered had gotten to her more than he had expected. 'How did you find that place?'

'Let me get some clothes on,' he said.

He returned to the bedroom and started changing into a fresh pair of boxer shorts. Sally followed him into the room and he gave her a look as she stopped in the doorway, looking at him, completely bare.

She crossed her arms over her chest and said, 'Don't act like I've never seen it before. Just please answer the question. There are sixteen mattresses in that basement but forty-five chains, meaning, if every chain was in use at the same time, there'd be three people to most single mattresses. There's blood and urine stains on each mattress from multiple people, so it's reasonable to assume it's been full at some point. What you've found is disturbing and it's huge. So tell me, how did you come across it?'

He hesitated.

'I'm not asking as a copper. I'm not even involved. I'm asking as your... you know.'

'I found it because I was looking for it. Because there was no fair in that park.'

'Because some brain damaged kid thought he remembered a fair? Come on,' she gave him a sceptical frown. She paced in front of him, wired and agitated like he'd never seen her. 'You're the most untrusting person I know. You're not going to believe a fair existed just because some kid claims it did, especially when the kid in question has mental issues. So why?'

Peter pulled on his socks, then his jeans and stood shirtless before her. He threw his arms out to his side, resigned himself to talking to her and said, 'Harold Tombes.'

She looked at him, questioning.

He told her briefly about Harold Tombes and the dates.

'That's his fairground I found down there. Tombes was

known for kidnapping people using his fair and when the staff were arrested, some of them confessed he was using the house of horror to play with them before he killed them.'

'And this list of missing people you've made matches his schedule? So, what? You think this guy's still out there travelling around and torturing people in a house of horror, feeding off their fear like Pennywise the fucking clown?' She laughed weakly. It was meant as a joke, perhaps an attempt to break the tension that had built up inside her but it seemed to make her feel worse.

'Well he was known to have an interest in the occult,' Peter smirked.

Sally sighed.

'I figured,' he continued, serious now, 'if somebody became interested enough in Harold Tombes, they might have started copying him and following the same pattern. That person would want a fixed location to feel close to Tombes, and where he could take his victims. That's how I found that place. I looked for Tombes's yard and I found his fairground.'

He pulled on a creased shirt over an equally crumpled t-shirt. He could feel her eyes watching and judging what he had become without a woman in his life.

'But what does it matter how I found the place?'

Sally swallowed and looked down at her feet. She closed her eyes.

'What?' Peter probed.

'Morgan will be coming to speak to you, for your statement. I needed to know what you were going to say.'

DI Edward Morgan, a man Peter hated more than any other on this entire planet, had been assigned to investigate the disappearance of Peter and Sally's four year old daughter, who vanished from their house one night while both of them were present, taken from right under their noses without a trace. Morgan had wasted valuable time treating Peter and Sally as though they were guilty of doing something to their little girl and she had never been found. Last year, he had been assigned the Treevale case.

If Morgan was coming to question him, it meant there had to be confirmation the fair he'd discovered was the same one William remembered.

He asked, 'What have they found?'

'A number of unmarked graves,' she swallowed. 'One of the bodies they've found has been positively identified as Julian Dobson.'

She paused. He waited, impatiently for her to say the words. She bit her lip. This was difficult for her because it meant admitting to a man who had grown to despise the police force even when that hatred ripped apart his marriage, that the police had been wrong.

Finally, she said it. 'You were right. William Campbell was taken to that fairground. Morgan is going to speak to him, then he's coming to speak to you.'

Peter sat down on the bed and started pulling on his shoes.

'You going somewhere?' Sally asked.

He marched down the short hallway to the living room and grabbed his denim jacket off back of the sofa. 'I need to get to the kid first, before that *dick* gets him in a room and treats him as though he's already guilty, just like he did to us.'

There was a stagnant moment as they both, individually, flashed on the memories of how DI Morgan had treated them, interrogated them, and branded them child-killers without any evidence to that effect. As though losing their only child wasn't hard enough.

'Then I'm coming with you,' she said. He opened his mouth to argue – she was, after all, another cop, regardless of who she had once been to him – but she added, 'It's not up for discussion.'

Peter's ankle still throbbed and walking was an aching chore, so he let her drive. Having Sally along could serve some use, at least. A few minutes later, they were hurtling out of Durham City Centre, headed for Treevale.

42

They drove in silence most of the way, neither of them sure what to say, despite there once having been a time when they could have talked for hours and hours.

Eventually, Peter asked, 'Was Steven angry at you for skipping out on the dinner party?'

She glanced at him, checking if he was preparing a joke or jibe.

'A little,' she said. 'He didn't push it though, once I told him what we found. He could hardly come out as the good guy if he acted like his dinner party is more important than a room where forty-five people may have been kept captive. I didn't dare mention you, though. He would have hit the roof, screw the kidnappings.'

They shared a smile. Sally driving out to meet Peter at the sight of mass captivity was the least of Steven's worries. He was aware of Peter and Sally's dinner once a year on their daughter's birthday, although he wasn't happy about it and he had tried to convince Sally to discontinue the tradition. What he didn't know was that Peter and Sally visited a hotel after their meal and spent a few hours remembering their old lives in fits of grief and passion, and the echo of old happiness.

They drove the rest of the way without any further words but the tension that had been building between them since Sally smuggled him that police file was broken.

As they reached Treevale, Peter directed Sally to the house William Campbell shared with his housemates. They pulled up outside and Peter was at the door before the engine was killed, knocking almost as hard as Sally had knocked on his door an hour before.

'Maybe there's nobody in? It's freshers week, isn't it?' Sally suggested, when nobody came to the door right away.

'It's the anniversary of his disappearance. I don't think he's going out clubbing,' Peter said and he realised the significance of his words, only after he'd said them. He knocked again. A minute later the door was opened by a young man dressed more like a businessman than a student. He looked Sally and Peter up and down with a harsh crease in his brow.

'What do you want?' he said.

Peter looked to Sally, who took the hint to take the lead.

'I'm DI Lincoln, this is my associate, Mr Lincoln.' She paused, likely realising how unusual that sounded.

The young man seemed not to care. 'Please tell me you're here about Will. They threatened to oust me from the house if I called the police on him but I'm so glad somebody has. Dude's a fucking nutcase. He's going to murder one of us in our sleep at some point. I just know it.'

Sally glanced at Peter.

'Who would call us?' Peter asked, ignoring the fact that he was not part of the *us*, in question.

'So you weren't called? What do you want then? You're not here to talk to me, are you?'

Peter wondered what the kid had to hide that made him so concerned and locked it away for later. He would discuss it with Sally once they'd spoken to William.

'We need to ask him some questions about his friends. That's all.'

'He's going to tell you he didn't kill them, you know. So why bother?' Xander said, and dove straight into explaining an incident in which Will was found brandishing a knife on the stairs right behind where Xander now stood, to justify his opinion.

This was going nowhere. Peter left Sally to listen to the young man, who, while he looked like a businessman, sounded like a snot nosed little brat who probably pushed kids from poorer families in the playground and pretended it was their own fault. He was probably an only child and wasn't used to getting his own way. He wasn't going to help them find William any time soon.

Peter tried to phone his contact but it rang off and went to voicemail. He tried again, but it rang only once before going to voicemail. He resorted to a text.

Really need to talk to you. Tell me where you are. It's urgent, he typed.

Then he returned to the front door where the kid was finishing his story of Will holding a knife, strangely, at the beginning, when they all went out for a night out.

'Look, kid,' Peter said, cutting him short. The young man's eyes flared and he glared at Peter, furious at his nerve to refer to him, a twenty-one year old, as kid. 'We really need to talk to Will. So tell us where he is, or I'll make sure you're on the front page of tomorrow's newspapers, as the sniffling, self-entitled little shit who stood in the way of solving the Treevale Five case. I'm sure your parents would love that.'

The kid stared at Peter for a long minute, during which Peter noticed the kid's eyes dart down the hallway behind him and he knew he was hiding something. Without hesitating, Peter pushed past the kid.

'Hey!' the wannabe-businessman called.

'Peter!' Sally yelled at him. 'We don't have probable cause.'

Good job he didn't need it. There was a door immediately on the left of the hallway and it was open. He looked in and glanced from what he saw to the kid in the front doorway. He shook his head.

Inside the room, a ball of muscle dressed in sweat pants looked at Peter like a deer in the headlights, while Peter took in the destruction around him. The wardrobe doors had been broken off, the chest of draw's emptied of clothes, which lay scattered around the room in ruined tatters. On the wall directly opposite the door, in bright red spray paint was the word MURDERE, with the R likely to have been added around the time Peter and Sally had knocked on the door. The spray can was still in the meat-head's right hand as his expression changed from concern to overconfidence. He was preparing to square up to Peter.

Peter left him where he was and approached the other one at the front door. He stood close enough that the kid had to back into the wall.

'You think this is funny?'

'Peter,' Sally said.

'Where's Will? If you tell me now, maybe I won't report you for the criminal damage you and your friend are doing in there.'

At the mention of criminal damage, Sally squeezed past the two of them and observed the bedroom.

Finally, the kid mumbled, 'They've gone to the fair.'

'The fair?' Peter and Sally exchanged a look.

'In Graham Park. They messaged about half an hour ago.'

They ran the few feet back to the car.

'Don't worry,' Sally called back to the kid. 'He won't report you, but I will.'

They got in the car without looking at his reaction. Peter tried his contact again but the phone went straight to voicemail.

'Fuck.'

43

On the other side of the smoke was a dark corridor with black on every surface, lit by weak lights on the ceiling. Will had to strain to see even a metre ahead. Where the corridor led was a mystery. He could see no turns. Only shadow.

After stepping through the smoke he came to a stop, while his eyes adjusted and he felt a tremor shake his heart. The slither of hidden fear he had begun to feel at the sight of the building was no longer hidden; it had come to the surface and made itself known.

'Will,' Beth said, coming up behind him with Ben at her side.

'You shouldn't have followed me,' he said.

'Remember what we were saying before about individual choices, yeah?'

His eyes adjusted as much as he felt they were going to but he didn't move an inch. He still couldn't see where the corridor ended, the lights were so dim. He saw an image of the Crooked Man waiting within that painful darkness, watching and waiting for him to step right into his grasp.

Something loud and close buzzed and he jolted. Then he realised it was a phone ringing. He turned to see the vague outline of Beth and Ben behind him. Beth fished a phone from her pocket and the two of them were illuminated in the light from the screen, which made them look plastic and grotesque, as though they were parts of the house of horror.

Beth stopped the phone from ringing and said, 'sorry.' Almost immediately, it buzzed, and she pressed to reject the call. A moment later the phone buzzed again, a single, elongated sound. A message.

Ben glanced over her shoulder. 'Who's Lincoln?' he teased. 'And why does he want to talk to you so bad? You got a new man we don't know about, huh?' He nudged her.

'Shut up,' Beth hissed.

Lincoln? Will thought, remembering the information the journalist had known, could have only learnt from somebody who had witnessed or been told about his hypnotherapy sessions.

'Peter Lincoln?' he asked, practically cried. 'Is that who you're talking about?'

Beth opened her mouth to say something, but no words came. Her screen went dark, leaving them as shapes in the poorly lit darkness.

'You told him what I remembered, didn't you?' he sputtered.

'Will, I,' she started, but Will was already walking away. He didn't want to be anywhere near Beth right now. She had welcomed him with non-judgemental arms, never asked him about his memories, never seemed to care either way whether he was guilty, and yet she had betrayed him to a journalist.

He heard their footsteps behind him.

"Will,' Beth pleaded.

Will came to a split turn, left or right. Without pausing to think, he took the right.

'Will!' Beth yelled, her voice urgent yet distant, as though screamed through a sheet of material. The panic in her voice made Will turn. He couldn't see either of them. He walked slowly back down toward the turn and struck something. He reached out and found a wall.

Right where he had turned.

'Will!' Beth screamed. It came from the other side of the wall.

Will hammered on it a few times to let them know he was there but the wall didn't move. It didn't even shake to suggest it was possible to move it, which it had to be. It had to

260

have gotten between them somehow.

'Keep going, mate,' Ben yelled through the wall. 'We'll go the other way and see you on the other side.'

'If we make it out at all,' Will muttered to himself.

A wave of light headedness overtook him. He put out his hands to steady himself. The walls were draped with black fabric. There had to be rooms between the turns of these corridors, behind the fabric. He worked his fingers to the edge of the sheet and yanked against the staples that connected it to the walls. The staples were strong but he was able to tear off enough of the fabric to reveal a small section of wood. But the wood had been painted as jet black as the fabric.

The Crooked Man flashed across his mind, stalking him up a very similar corridor, a gangly shape in the dim glow. There one second. Gone the next. As though he had melted into the house itself.

Will had found a way out once before, from wherever he'd been. He could do it again.

He took out his phone to use as a torch and continued down the corridor. The phone's torch was harsh and blindingly white but it obliterated the darkness and allowed him full view of the corridor ahead.

Flashes of memory told him there were greater terrors than the maze itself to contend with in this house. The suspiciously absent Crooked Man was among them.

He turned another corner. At the end of the corridor was a grey door, lit by a more powerful light, flickering above it. It was marked with the same kind of writing as the sign beside the entrance, filling the entire door: *No Way Out.*

Despite the words, Will barrelled through the door and burst into a small room covered in vertical stripes, stretching from the centre of the floor to the ceiling, lit in ultraviolet blue. The light pierced his eyes. Before him the lines seemed to twist and warp, as though the walls were moving in and out. The room felt alive, as though breathing. He swayed with the motion of it. He turned back toward the door but it had already swung closed behind him. The back of it was covered with the same warping, breathing stripes, and he could find no seams nor handle where the door should have been.

He spun back around and the room tipped. He stumbled with it, striking the far wall with his shoulder. His phone flew to the floor, screen side up, and the torch light was smothered. He closed his eyes to no avail. It wasn't merely the strange nature of the stripes on the walls. The room continued to move whether he could see them or not.

When he opened his eyes and looked over the room for a door, any door, he couldn't place where it was he had come in. The long, never ending black stripes blurred and shimmered as he moved, blending into one living shape. It morphed into something resembling a person and reached out toward him, drawing within inches of him before retreating back to the wall.

Will shrank into one of the corners, moving slowly so as not to lose his balance in the continually tilting and spinning room, and scrunched his eyes tightly closed. He clamped his hands over the side of his head and tried not to scream.

It was a trick, he told himself, created by the combination of the harsh ultraviolet light and the warping black and white stripes, continuing all the way around from floor to ceiling in continuous loops, as though moving, all working together to trigger a motion response.

If he could get his phone, he could use the light to offset the ultraviolet, but all he could see were the warping lines spread over every surface.

He tried Dr Phillips's breathing exercises but each breath shook and bounced with the trembling of his heart and it took a few attempts to calm it.

Will opened his eyes and removed his hands from his head, and stood up. The motion of the room had slowed and the stripes had separated again. He tried to keep his eyes from following the stripes to either the ceiling or the floor, where he knew the loop of them would set him off.

He placed his hands flat against the closest wall and walked slowly along it, feeling for any breaks with his fingers. He made it less than a metre before the room started its swaying and spinning again.

Within the blur stood Nicole, Julian, Craig and Tom, all stood close together and looking around the room, their eyes dazed and struggling for focus. They looked as though they were about to hurl, and they each swayed on the spot.

'I don't like this,' Will heard from his own mouth, without any thought of speaking.

Nicole sighed. 'It's a bit of fun, Will. Nothing's going to hurt you. There's nothing to be afraid of.'

'You aren't afraid to die,' Craig reminded him.

'You weren't afraid to let us die, either,' Nicole said.

'Why didn't you tell anybody where we were?'

'I thought you'd come back with help. Do you not love me anymore, Will?'

Will stuttered, 'I... I... Of course, I do.'

Nicole's face, already harsh and unforgiving in the purple glow, twisted into a mask of menace. She opened her mouth in a grimace and screamed in Will's face, *'Then why did you let us die?'*

Will screwed shut his eyes and continued along the wall. 'You're not real,' he muttered. 'This is just another episode. You're not real.'

He repeated it until he had done a full loop of the room and found no breaks, never once opening his eyes, fearful of what he might see. Finally, he opened his eyes again and the disorientation took him. The room tipped and he with it. He tumbled through the room, his foot catching on something and sending it skittering across the floor ahead of him. When he came to a stop against the wall, his phone was against his foot.

It was undamaged from the trip around the room and the light was still on. As Will lifted it from the floor, its cone of bright white light burst out, vanquishing the ultraviolet. In the white, the stripes on the wall remained still, as did Will's head.

Under the sweeping funnel of light, Will checked the walls again for any break. Finally, he found one. It was the slightest of lines within the black stripes, too faint to feel and with no handle. Will didn't know if it was the way he'd come into the room or the way he was meant to go out – *if* he was meant to go out at all – but he charged at it, shoulder first.

With an impact hard enough to send bolts of pain from his shoulder right down to his fingers, he burst through the door and onto the floor of another corridor, or perhaps the same one. He winced from the pain as he tried to get up and looked back at the door, which swung shut to reveal the same words as before.

It was the same door but it was not the same corridor. He scanned the way ahead with his torch. He had turned right before coming to this door, meaning, he should have now been faced with a left turn. Instead, he was looking at a right.

While Will had been spiralling out of control, the Crooked Man had been rearranging his maze.

44

There was a part of both Peter and Sally that never truly believed they would find a fairground in Graham Park, until it was before them, touching the night sky with enough light pollution to block out the stars for a couple of miles.

Peter looked up through the windscreen at the rides towering over the park, with wonder and many more questions to add to the list. There was a full fairground in operation here, yet he had expected the kidnappings were the work of one man, perhaps with the help of one or two associates. Not a harem of showfolk. And yet it was too much of a coincidence for this to be here, a fair in Treevale for the first time in more than a hundred years, on this night, exactly a year since the Treevale Five disappeared.

They got out together and approached the nearest of the park's four gates. On either side stood two men dressed impeccably in the kind of old fashioned suit an aristocrat would wear to dinner. They smiled at Peter and Sally and made as though to speak to them but neither Peter nor Sally acknowledged the men. Their eyes, as though one set and not two, were locked on something beyond the gate. An archway displayed a logo of a man in a top hat.

'My god,' Peter muttered. It was the exact same silhouetted profile as the one built onto the gate at Tombes's old fairground. 'It's him. We have to find Will.'

He turned to Sally to tell her she needed to call some units in but she was already turning away, her phone to her ear. Once she was off the phone, she would inform him that they both needed to wait out here until the units arrived but the kid and his new friends were somewhere in there; if they waited, it could be too late and they might later find three more bodies in shallow graves. And they might never understand how William Campbell had escaped the hell he had endured.

By the time Sally turned back to him, Peter was already through the gate and hobbling off into the park.

There were hundreds of patrons filling the paths between the stall, some walking, others grouped together in boisterous exclamations, some of victory, others of loss. To them this was nothing more than another exhibition. They would all go home to their warm cosy houses and they might never discover the connection this fair had to a dungeon and graveyard at another fairground many miles away.

He scanned the faces amongst the crowds, searching for Will or either of his two housemates. He thought about asking the stall holders but they had interacted with hundreds of different faces already, most of whom belonged to students, and they weren't likely to remember a specific three. Peter had worked as a bartender at a busy nightclub before his first journalist position and he knew after a while, all customers began to look alike.

Still, he had to try something. He picked a stall and decided to speak to the woman behind the counter dressed in Victorian dress, even if the most he got out of it was an understanding of whether they were in on the kidnapper's plan or merely hired puppets.

'Hi,' she said with a beaming grin. The stall offered apple bobbing. 'Would you like to have a go?'

'You know,' Peter started, making an effort to sound charming. 'I love fairgrounds. Always have. My dream is to own one.'

'That's a lovely dream, sir. I hope you make it a reality.' The sentiment was completely fake, the same way a supermarket cashier didn't really care if you had a nice day.

'Who runs this place then?'

'I... I...' the woman started but couldn't finish.

He rested his elbows on the counter and leaned toward her. 'Don't worry, I'm not here to cause any trouble. I just thought the best way to find out how to get to run a place like this is to ask somebody who already does.'

She backed away, afraid, although he didn't think it was of him. He smiled to himself. Fairs were rarely owned by one Barnum-like figure in the modern day, but rather stall holders tended to own their own stalls. It had been the answer the woman should have given to him, but she hadn't. This fair did have a leader, and he was bad enough to warrant fear.

'How long have you been with the fair?' he asked.

She swallowed hard, as if the answer were going to give her up and get her in some kind of trouble. She shifted further from him, until her back was against the back of her stall. As she moved, something clinked. Peter leant over the counter and peered down at the grassy floor. She was wearing a large skirt to her Victorian dress and it spread across the meagre expanse of the stall but Peter caught sight of something trailing out from underneath it; a thick, heavy chain which connected to a D-ring built into the side of the stall.

He looked up at her and her eyes flared in alarm.

He knew how the kidnapper had managed to pull off a full fairground. Leaving the woman behind, Peter took out his phone and called Sally.

'What are you doing going in there alone?' she yelled before he even had a chance to speak. 'You don't know what we're going to find in there.'

'The stall holders are the victims,' he explained. 'He's using the people he keeps alive to run the fair. There's a stall holder chained to the stall over here, just like they were in that basement. I'm betting the rest of them are chained up the same way too.'

'Tell me this is one of your messed up jokes, Peter.'

'He's made them part of his sick fucking game.'

She sighed. The stress was building now. 'Then you've got to get back out here, right away. I mean, let's not forget that

Morgan's on his way and he'll crucify you if he finds you in there, but there's also a lunatic somewhere in there, too.'

Peter hung up. He rushed on through the park, covering as much ground as he could, without causing his ankle too much further damage. He peered over more counters as he made his way along the paths, barging past and into people who were gathered at the stalls in order to gain a glimpse inside and confirm the woman he'd spoken to wasn't the only one chained up.

She wasn't. He saw a chain inside almost every stall he checked, and the ones where he couldn't see one, the skirt of the stall holder was too wide to be sure and the women unwilling to move for him.

There were too many stalls and rides to be able to count, too many potential captives chained to structures, which had not been there before and would not be there tomorrow. If they failed to catch him tonight, along with saving William Campbell and his friends, they could only hope the guy would not know that his yard had been discovered and was being watched for his return. The lights had come on via a sensor and Peter wasn't convinced there wouldn't have been another sensor somewhere, an intruder alert of some kind.

There could be no waiting for tomorrow. Peter needed to find the kid now and he had a feeling he knew exactly where he would be.

Peter needed to find the house of horror.

45

Will moved through the next set of corridors slowly, his light fixed before him as he took one small step after another. After the mind bending effect of the room back there, along with the moving of walls, he didn't want to barrel ahead and be caught unprepared by whatever else came at him.

If the Crooked Man was able to rearrange walls and move about this building freely, there was no telling where he would choose to come out. He could dive out right in front of Will.

Or behind.

At the very thought, Will spun in place and cast the light back the way he'd come. There was nobody there. He managed only a couple of feet before he half-turned again, casting the light behind him.

Get a grip, he thought. He had escaped the Crooked Man before, he could do it again. He tried to remember how he had made it out the last time, as though being here, in the territory of the Crooked Man would be enough to jolt him back to that night and remember – it was how they did it in the movies, after all, and there had to be *some* truth to it, didn't there? – but he thought only of his friends.

Where had they been when he had been escaping? Had they attempted to escape as a group and they had been caught, or worse? Or had Will selfishly escaped without them and left them to their fates?

He tried to picture himself, plumper and more unkempt, walking through black, barely lit corridors, his friends with him. He wouldn't have made it very far, even with his friends beside him. He had always been a fearful coward, who could barely make it through a mild horror film for the sake of his girlfriend – it was a wonder he had been able to go through with his suicide attempt – and he would have stopped somewhere in one of these corridors, slumped to the floor and tried to give up.

He could almost hear the words his friends would speak to convince him to keep going.

'Maybe this wasn't the best idea.' Craig.

'Is he having a panic attack?' Tom.

'You know, I used to have panic attacks all the time as a kid. My mam used to just leave me to it and I eventually snapped out of it. I would scream and scream myself hoarse but the best thing is to ignore it.' Julian.

'Are you stupid?' Tom.

'Seriously, give it a rest for one minute. A tantrum and a panic attack aren't the same things.' Nicole. He could picture her leaning in front of Will, forcing him to meet her eye.

Oh, how he missed those eyes.

'You can't give up. We have to keep moving and find a way out of here, okay? Just remind yourself that none of this is real. It's just a show, okay? We're going to get through this and we're going to go home.'

It would have taken more than that, and more than a few minutes to get him back to his feet and moving again but it warmed him a little to imagine his friends trying to help him, especially Nicole. It didn't matter that he likely made it up. It made him feel less alone.

He was brought from his thoughts by a sound behind him. A shuffle. A wall moving? A footstep? He came to a stop and listened, not daring to turn around lest he see the Crooked Man staring back at him. But no more sound came.

He didn't feel alone any more, not one bit, but he didn't feel good about it either.

Will started walking again, and there came the sound, a few metres behind. Footsteps. It was the slightest shuffle, a second after his own foot touched the floor, an echo. He stopped again, and the noise ceased, too.

There was no telling himself this was just a show. Not back then, nor now. There was something evil in this place, something which had hurt him and his friends. And it had drawn Will back to finish what he had started. He wasn't sure if his memories were actually real but this fair was laden with the same heavy, terrifying evil as the place he had been held before.

Taking deep breaths, he turned on the spot, moving the cone of light with him. Nothing. The corridor was empty. That didn't mean he could relax. Just because there was nobody there, caught in his light, it didn't mean there hadn't been. The Crooked Man could move walls and slip wherever he wished.

He turned back around and made his way to the next corner, where he paused. He reached the phone around the corner, casting the area ahead in bright light, and he fought back the image of the spider-like limbed monster filling the corridor ahead. He peered round, saw nothing and stepped around.

Something moved behind him and he jumped out of his skin, spinning to see. But there was nothing there, and no more sound.

'It's not real. It's just a show,' he muttered, although he knew that wasn't even close to the truth.

He walked for a few more minutes, in which time he made little progress and turned corners that made it feel as though he were walking in circles. With each step, he was sure he could hear somebody, or something, walking with him, matching him.

Beyond another corner, the lights dimmed further and Will trained his phone's torch on the space ahead with more determination. His right shoulder brushed the wall and he sidestepped away from it. It was only a single step but it sent his left shoulder brushing against the wall on the other side. He paused and pressed against both walls at the same time.

They were closing in on him, getting tighter with every step.

He checked over his shoulder with the light, to make sure there was nobody lurking there, and started back to the last corner, but the corridor came to an abrupt end. There were no turns and no other ways to go. He was at the Crooked Man's will. He could only do what was expected of him.

The walls continued to close in on him as he made his way through the narrowing corridor, until he felt as though he were in a coffin. The light from the phone lit less and less, and soon he had to turn sideways in order to fit between the walls, the arm holding his phone stretched out in front of him.

A few more steps and he could feel the walls pressed against his back and his chest. There appeared to be no end in sight, nor any indication of how narrow those walls would go. Was he going to keep on walking until the walls crushed him entirely?

Will turned his head to look back the way he'd come but all he could see was darkness. There wasn't even the glimmer of the dim orange lights emanating from the ceiling. He twisted his other hand so his torch would face the other way. The light struck the back of his head and pierced his peripheral vision, but what the light exposed was far worse than the pain in his eye.

Back the way he had come, the walls had started to close in, blocking his exit. He was trapped in a black cavern, a tomb. Where the narrowing ended, there was a slither, no more than a few inches, between the walls. In the gap beamed the half-smile of the Crooked Man, his dark eyes staring at him. Not a hallucination like the ones he'd had before. The real man, his face bleached white in the torchlight, watched Will with relish, watching at a rat caught in his trap, squirming to escape.

Will started moving again, frantically pushing his body through the tightening space. The pressure grew agonising but he rushed to escape the Crooked Man. He forced his body onward until the corridor grew too small to breathe in.

He pushed and squeezed and made himself as thin as

possible. And suddenly, the walls were gone. He fell forward. His knees struck the floor and then his shoulder and chest. He took a huge, gulping breath and threw himself to his feet, spinning to see where he was and whether he had escaped the Crooked Man.

Will found himself in a small room with a bright light overhead. The way he'd come was covered by a black sheet of material, a curtain made of the same fabric as the walls. He didn't dare look behind it. Instead, he turned to face his latest horror.

A short corridor led off of the room, this one made entirely of glass, which reflected the piercing lights back against each other, creating a stark white element to the room ahead, in polar opposite to the blackness that had come before. Will had to squint in order to see.

On either side of the corridor were two mirrors angling so that he could see himself in both. In dripping black, words were written over them.

Find yourself on the left.

Lose yourself on the right.

Behind the words, he saw his own terrified figure, his skin drained of blood.

It's only a show, he thought, although he couldn't help but return to the sight of the Crooked Man lurking behind him. It was a show. But it was *his* show and he was the one in control.

Will made his way into the hall of mirrors. Instantly, his vision was filled with tens of thousands of his own reflection, bouncing back at him and the other mirrors, distorting through prisms of light until there were near infinite amounts. Every movement he made sent a flickers across every surface he could see, and he shivered.

Straight ahead, he came to a tight turn, back on himself. Then another, the pathways wrapping around each other in tightly wound coils. With each step his many reflection moved with him, and he flinched.

He glanced around, all of his heads turning as one in all of the hundreds of reflective sheets of glass, to make sure what he had seen had, in fact, been his own movements and nothing else. He came face to face with himself, staring back, over and over and over, along with many versions that faced in other directions. He could see angles of his face he never wished to see.

He came to the first sheet of clear glass at the end of this stretch of corridor, creating a dead end. When he tried to go back, he found another dead end. The glass walls were moving too, shifting to block his return. He was trapped with his own reflection.

Find yourself, the entrance to the hall had said. He had spent so long trying to escape himself and now here he was, multiplied onto every surface in a room that seemed to stretch on forever.

He had no choice but to stare into the face of the man who had led his friends to their fates, and it was his own face. Hatred filled him. Hot tears stung his eyes. How could he have escaped the Crooked Man and done nothing to help his friends? How could he just forget it all and go on with his life?

What kind of a man does that?

What kind of a man, indeed. Will, staring at his own face, felt as much a monster as the Crooked Man. He had practiced his breathing exercises, had made plans for the future, had come to university to finally finish his studies. He had continued with his life.

'Will?' a voice called. A woman. Nicole.

He turned in the direction of the voice. He was met by his own face, reflected over and over, but there was another face inside the mirrors, as though trapped inside the glass itself.

Nicole hadn't changed a day. She was even dressed exactly the same, all in black, right down to her lipstick. The light burst brighter, disappeared and came back dimmer, and her red hair – *black,* black hair – shined. Before his eyes, the light burst brighter again and her hair was clearly the black it had always been, for as long as he had known her. It had been naught but a trick of the light.

'Will, are you in here? Please help me,' she called out and moved away, disappearing from sight.

The lights went out, and a new set of flashing blue and red lights replaced them. The disorientation of the striped room began to creep back into his mind. Through the flashes of reflection, he saw Nicole moving around, saw a figure, little more than a shape, shift behind her and then move away.

It crept up behind and reached out a for her.

'Nicole, look out!' Will screamed but she didn't hear him. She stalked warily between the glass. The figure touched her back and then was gone before she turned around. He reappeared, a black blur, but he was in all of the mirrors, filling them so fully, it wasn't clear where he was.

And then Nicole screamed. It was an ear-piercing shriek of sheer terror Will had never heard her utter before. He started searching the glass around him for a gap he could squeeze through, to run to her aid. He didn't know where she was in this mirror maze but he would find her. He had to help her, as he had failed to do before.

But he was sealed in. Four complete walls of glass were closed around him.

'No, no, no, no, no,' he pleaded. Slowly, he slumped to the floor, fell back against the glass. Nicole was gone from the reflections, as was the dark shape. He had failed to save her, again. All that looked back at him was his own reflection.

Something shifted and he realised the reflections were not his. They belonged to him, but not from here and now. They were of William Campbell a year ago this very night. Thicker around the midsection, shaggier hair but no less terrified.

The reflection was slumped on the floor in a similar way to how Will was sat but he wasn't looking at the mirrors. His forearms were exposed, and with his fingernails, he tried to tear open the puckered scar of his suicide attempt, to reopen the wound and spill the blood keeping him alive.

Footsteps echoed through the maze, accompanied by the taunting tap of a cane, and Will – the other Will – tore faster and more frantically at his arm. The Crooked Man was coming, and those fingernails would never be enough to open that healed wound.

The older Will snapped his eyes shut and blocked out the image.

'You have to play the game, if you ever hope to win.' The Crooked Man's voice drifted to Will and Will didn't know if he was talking to the present or the past. He kept his eyes closed and waited for it to end. The footsteps stopped and a gentle breeze, foreign in this environment, blew against Will's skin.

He rolled his eyes open. The powerful fluorescent white light had come back on, replacing the flashing headache of sickening colours. His younger self was gone. What had also disappeared were the multiple version of his own image, reflected back at him. All that was left of the nightmare was a single reflection in front and one behind. There was nothing visible on the other side of either pane of glass, but the panes to his sides had been removed completely.

On his left, was a small porch-sized area, the size of the area he had entered from. It wasn't possible, having moved through multiple different winding paths in the mirror maze, but he was sure if he went into that room, he would find a message on either side of the mirrored corridor reading *Lose Yourself* and *Find Yourself*.

To his right, stood a door in another small porch-like area. There was another sign beside the door, like the one outside the front entrance to the fair.

Goodbye, it read. Will wasn't foolish enough to think the sign was telling the truth and he would be awarded a way out, but the Crooked Man wanted him to go through this door, and so that was all he could do.

46

Peter moved quickly down the winding paths of the park, searching for the house of horror, certain that that was where he would find the kid. His ankle screamed but he didn't slow. His limp became more prominent but he hobbled swiftly on. His ankle could wait.

Finally, he came to the opening in the stalls in which the large and grotesque recreation of the burnt structure in North Yorkshire stood. His eyes were fixed on the building as he imagined what horrors might exist within it. Most fairground funhouses were filled with creepiness and jump scares but true terror would be acted out within those walls.

His attention was drawn to raised voices. To one side of the opening stood a young man and woman, clearly students, looking from each other to the entrance. Peter recognised them immediately. Their names were Beth and Ben. They were William Campbell's housemates. He took a quick look around but he couldn't see William.

'If we go back in through the front, how are we any more likely to find him?' Beth snapped.

'So, what? We wait for him to come out the other side like we did? He's probably having some kind of mental breakdown in there,' Ben argued.

They noticed Peter's presence and fell quiet.

Beth huffed. 'What do *you* want?'

'And here, I thought we were becoming friends,' Peter quipped and instantly regretted it. Everything about this set up suggested William was inside. Given what Peter had seen inside another house of horrors where William had spent a deal of traumatic time, he was in grave danger, not merely from his former captor but from his own unstable psyche. It wasn't the time for joking.

'Look,' he started again, shelving his sarcastic side. 'I think your friend is in trouble. We need to get him out of there.'

Ben said, 'Who are you?'

'This is Peter Lincoln,' Beth introduced.

To Peter, Ben said, 'So you want to help him? You? Mate, I thought you were just a leach, bleeding him for a story. Isn't that why you tricked Beth into giving you information?'

Peter sighed. 'I didn't trick anybody. Now I don't give a shit what you think of me, *mate*, but I'm going in there to help your friend.'

There was a stall a couple of metres behind them. The stall holder, free of customers, eavesdropped on their conversation. Suddenly, he said, 'All those who enter the funhouse can only hope to make it out the other side the same. If they make it out at all.'

Peter looked at the man and was preparing to accost him with questions when Ben spoke up again.

'Why? If he's in so much danger, why are you so eager to go in there and help him?'

Peter thought of his little girl and said, 'Not everybody's lucky enough to be saved.'

He didn't want to stand by and allow the kid to be one of them.

'Look,' Beth snapped at Ben. 'What does it matter? He wants to help so we're going to let him. When we're back inside, you and me can go one way and him the other, yeah? Cover more basis.'

Reluctantly, Ben agreed.

'What's inside?' Peter asked.

'Urm,' said Ben. 'A maze of black corridors but they're really dark, like there's only tiny, dim lights, like little orange circles and the walls in the corridors can move, so you can't go back the way you came. On the side we had to take, there were some rooms...'

Peter stopped him. 'You took a different side to William? Why?'

'He was ahead of us,' Beth said. Her voice was sour and she was speaking to him reluctantly. 'A wall fell in and separated us.'

Peter stepped forward toward the building but he wasn't going to enter it, not yet. The entrance, he noticed, was closed. He hobbled up to it and pushed but it was solid.

He turned to the students. 'How did you get out?'

Beth said, 'There was a door on the side of the building. You can't see it from out here but it looked like a proper door from inside. As soon as we were outside, it swung shut behind us.'

'Show me.'

They showed him the exact point where they had come out. There was only the slightest of seams to outline the door and no handle, nor any way of leveraging it open that Peter could see. He started around to the rear of the building and the two students followed. He found another outline of a door with no handle, but this one had a small hole where a handle would have gone.

He scoured his brain for any ideas on how to gain entry through this door. He was fairly certain this was a more important door than the other. While the other one, and any others he might have missed, were intended to dump the patrons out, this one was intended as a way of getting *in*.

If he could only think of some way to open it.

Something sparked as he examined the size of the hole and he turned, suddenly, to the two students. 'One of you find me a tent peg. There should be one holding the tarp down on one of these stalls.'

Beth didn't like that he'd told them to do something, as though he were in charge, but she headed off to the nearest stall and returned a moment later with a tent peg, which she handed to him, the snide comment she bit back evident in her expression.

Peter worked the end of the peg into the hole. It was a tight fit but he pushed it with as much strength as he could, meaning to leverage the door open with it. Once the peg was in, he heard a click and the door popped open. He pulled it wide and Ben grabbed it to keep it from falling back like the door that had spat them out of the building, while Peter stepped inside.

He immediately found himself facing a wall in a cramped space only fractionally bigger than the depth of his torso. To his immediate right, there was a ladder. There was no time to pause for thought. He gripped the ladder and climbed up.

Atop the wall a great emptiness stretched before him. Dim lights hung overhead, strewn along plywood beams that made up the roof. The floor was black and lined with thin beams of wood that were likely meant as walkways, between large stretches of empty black spaces, which contained small round holes cut in structured lines. He leant down and pressed his eye to one of the holes but all he could see beneath was black. Even so, he was sure these holes lined the corridors Ben had mentioned.

This was how the captor got around, and how he moved his walls. He was above them the entire time. He could almost guarantee parts of the ceiling could be moved as freely from up here as the walls, if you knew which spot to look in. Anybody beneath was a rat scurrying in a maze, unaware that it didn't have a chance.

47

Will stood, paused in momentary hesitation, in yet another black corridor. It was a couple of metres long, lined perfectly black and just as dimly lit so that Will had to return to his phone's torch function, but even without the torch, he could see there was a door at the end.

The message written on this door may as well have been laughing at him.

Goodbye, the last door read and as though to show him how foolish he had been – had he believed it – to think that the last door would lead to his freedom, this new one mocked: *There is no End.*

He had been so stupid to think he might have found one of his friends in here, or at the very least an answer. Even had he found the Crooked Man, it didn't mean he would find out what had happened to them. It would likely only end in his death. And now, here he was, destined to navigate this house of horrors via whichever route the Crooked Man decided, toward whatever ultimate destination he had chosen for Will.

The idea struck Will to not play the Crooked Man's game at all and ignore the door ahead, as well as the one behind. But as he hovered between the two, he felt as though he were already in a cage. The corridor was perfectly straight and gave him no view of both doors at the same time and he couldn't bear the thought of the Crooked Man sneaking up on him. A momentary lapse might be all the spider-like figure needed.

Will wrapped his hand around the cold metal handle of the door proclaiming *There is no End*, and turned. With a deep breath, he stepped inside.

It was a gloomy room lit by a buzzing, old fashioned lightbulb erected on a small table in the corner. The walls were pale wood. In the middle of the room was a wire cage, large enough for a medium dog. The door was open, waiting. In the next corner stood another small table. On top of it, slowly ticking with the seconds, was a metronome.

Tick.

Tick.

Tick.

Will looked at the room, at the cage and the two tables. The room was pretty tame compared with what he'd seen back in the mirror maze. Of course, there was a maniac pushing him through this maze and chasing him through it, so any room, especially one with a cage in it, was not something to take lightly. The very bareness of the room made him uneasy, as though there had to be something else to it. If the Crooked Man had wanted him to come here, there had to be a purpose.

As he watched, the metronome in the corner ticked faster, grew louder. It was the only sound in the room and it thumped in his ear like a pulse, quickening.

Tick, tick, tick.

Then the screaming started. It was an ear splitting sound created by a woman in both terror and agony. His first thought was of Nicole and he had to remind himself that it was a trick. The screams could have come from anybody. They might even have been made by an actress hired as part of the house of horror.

There was a high likelihood, he thought, that all of this was a perfectly innocent show within a fairground, which he, with his mental issues and past trauma, elevated to a higher level. One that felt real.

The screaming continued. The metronome ticked faster until it was a blur flying from one side to the other. *Tick tick tick tick tickticktickticktcktk.*

The screams grew sharper and they formed a word. 'Help.'

'He's not going to help you,' came a whisper in reply. 'Are you, William?'

Will froze at the sound of his own name. That couldn't be an innocent part of the show.

The unseen woman screamed help again. Will turned around and spotted a door beside the one through which he'd entered. Like all the others there were words scratched into the wood.

Find Your Mind.

He figured the woman being hurt had to be on the other side of this door but he made no move for it. Will was no hero. He was a coward at heart and even as the screams tore at his brain like an ice-pick thrust through his ear canal, he couldn't move. There was nothing he could do. He couldn't save anyone.

It's just a trick, he thought. *Like the striped room and the hall of mirrors.*

In the next room, the screaming would be gone, replaced by some other disorienting sight or sound. He tried the door. Locked.

The metronome was getting so fast now, the ticks sounded like a jackhammer. He turned his attention to the door he'd come through, where more writing had been carved.

The only way the pain ends is if you climb into the cage and lock the door. Time is running out if you want to save her life.

Another part of the show, he told himself but he couldn't deny the possibility this was real, that somebody's life was genuinely in his hands, and in doing nothing, Will might cause somebody else to die. He was a coward – the furthest thing from a hero – but he wasn't sure if he could live with any more guilt.

It meant giving himself to the Crooked Man, however, and resigning himself to whatever fate the murderer had in store for him. Whatever had happened the last time he was at the mercy of the Crooked Man had been so terrifying, his mind had taken measures to keep him from remembering it.

Could Will risk putting himself back in that situation,

whatever it may be, for the sake of what might be a trick? He hadn't actually witnessed any harm being inflicted upon anybody. The sound might have been recorded at some point in the past.

But what if he was wrong?

He went round and round, trying to find the answer of what to do, and all the while, the screams persisted. The metronome ticked faster, ticking away rapidly against a timeline Will couldn't place. There was no way to know how long he would have before the woman in trouble – if there was one – was killed.

Thoughts of his friends came to him, of what he would do to have any of them back, to free them from where they were and keep them from harm. He took a step toward the open cage, which was too small for him to comfortably fit in. It would be painful but he would get in there.

The room was plunged into darkness as the single, old fashioned lightbulb went out, and the room fell silent. The metronome stopped ticking and the screaming ceased. Will was so startled by the pure darkness that surrounded him that he forgot about his phone at first. He backed himself slowly toward where he thought the corner was. Only when his back was firmly against the wall did he remember it.

He fished it out of his pocket and turned on the torch. A cone of light penetrated the darkness and lit the cage. Will nearly dropped his phone at the sight of the wire meshed cage. It was no longer empty. Inside was a slumped figure resembling a person, crammed in against the walls.

Frantic, he cast the light over the rest of the room, swinging it back and forth. Somebody else had been in there with him. Somebody had come in, carrying that *thing* and shoved it in the cage. But in the light of the torch, the room was empty. He was alone except for the figure in the cage. Will leant forward onto his hands and knees and crept toward it, the torch before him. The cramped figure made no movement in response to the sound of Will moving, nor the brightness of the light, but it became more obvious as he grew nearer that the figure was, in fact, a person.

Or at least it had been.

Will reached the cage. The figure inside was dressed in thin, dirty, ruffled clothes that bagged in areas the cage allowed it to, hanging off the figure's body with less life than the body itself. The head of the figure was turned away and hidden beneath the hood of a large hooded sweatshirt.

Will needed to see their face. He had to know if it was one of his friends.

The figure in the cage was folded in on itself, hiding its face even from this side, chin pressed tight enough against its chest as though the two were trying to mould into one another. Will moved closer, angled the light in tighter, and tried to get a glimpse beneath the hood.

He glimpsed a bulbous nose that had been broken a couple of times and cracked lips that had probably seen adequate water the last time Will saw his friends. He could only make out these couple of things, along with the sunken shadows of a gaunt jawline, but he didn't think he recognised the person. It was a man, not a woman, so had not been the cause of the screams he had heard.

It was all just another trick.

Will relaxed, but only a little. He sank back from the body. There was no pulse point close to the mesh cage walls through which he could check if the figure was alive, but he had not been the emitter of those screams, the one the door explained would be killed if Will did not climb inside the cage. No matter whether the man was alive or dead, Will's conscience did not have to bear the weight of it.

It was bearing enough weight already.

That was such a horrifying thought and he didn't know where it had come from. A life was a life, and he shouldn't have thought immediately of himself when he knew he was not to blame. What would his friends have thought of him?

First, he had failed to think of them when it came to

his own death, attempted by his own hand, and now he was thinking only of himself in the face of somebody else's. At what point had he become so selfish?

A shadow moved, caught in his peripheral vision and he jumped, dropping the phone. The device clattered against the wood floor and he scrambled for it, to get the torch up and into the room before the shadow reached him.

His hands couldn't find it. He grasped in the darkness, scouring frantically and his hands moved too quickly. Something creaked, a footstep across the wooden floor. Will scrambled backward, abandoning the phone and the safety of the torch. He climbed to his feet. When he was confident he would be free of the cage, he sprinted for the doors. His knee caught the edge of the cage. Pain sparked up his thigh and down his shin, and he spun, striking the door, not with hands as he had intended, but with his back.

He was the wrong way round and in such a compact space, it would take seconds for whoever was in here with him to reach and seize him, seconds that had been wasted by his mistake. He should have ran wider through the darkness.

Still, he spun in place and searched for the handle. He found it, turned it and expected it to be locked, but the door inched open. Will pushed it wide and collapsed inward into another room.

He barely glanced at what he'd entered into, his mind still on the room behind. He turned in time to see the cage, lit by the flat fluorescents of this room, empty and open. Behind it, the figure in a hoodie unfolded itself, muscles stretching and joints clicking. Will threw himself up onto his knees and swung the door closed. There was no lock, despite the door having been locked to him before. He pressed his back against it and dug his feet into the tiled floor.

The room was cold and clinical, made up tiles, and pale blue curtains hung from the ceilings, closing off a smaller space within the room. It had the look and feel, and smell – cleaning products and death – of a hospital room, and through the curtain, Will could make out the shape of a bed and a person silhouetted there.

On the other side of the room was another door.

This is your Life, it read.

Will ran for it without paying attention to the room he was in. He was aware only of the impending doom coming from behind him. The figure in the bed might well have been the source of the screaming, a woman who lay dead because of him but there was nothing he could do for her now. All he could do was keep going and hope there would be a way out of this nightmare somewhere in this mess.

As he passed by the closed curtains, he couldn't help but notice the blood pooling on the floor and the razor blade that had fallen into it. Before he could even think of his breathing exercises, he was back in his family bathroom, a razor to his wrist, separating the skin, and moving on to the next forearm as the panic and the agony arrived. There was no warmth, no numbness within which he could slip away. There was pain and shock and, going against his own wishes, the body's thrashing instinct for survival.

48

Will collapsed through the next door, fleeing not just the figure from the first room but from his own memories as well. He stumbled into a living room, which at a glance, appeared totally out of place after everything that had come before it. Ahead of him, four figures filled a three seater sofa, each of them eating from plates on their laps while their eyes were transfixed on a television screen the size of the boxes from the eighties, which illuminated the entire room in an ethereal shade of blue.

The breath caught in Will's throat and for a moment, he was awash with disbelief. After an insufferable year of not knowing, he had found what he was looking for. Before him sat his friends. Julian, Tom, Nicole and Craig. They didn't look at him, didn't look away from the television screen playing static, but it was really them, huddled together on a sofa too small for the four of them.

They were still here.

If you make it out at all, the Crooked Man had warned.

As he watched them, none of them moved. He waved a hand over Julian's eyes but they didn't flicker. They were as perfectly formed in glass as the image he had recovered in his final hypnotherapy session. They were each frozen in place, food hanging from their mouths and streaming down their chins. On the plates resting on their laps, the food had turned to rot and mould. Maggots squirmed amongst the remains. The putrid smell of it wafted around them all and Will wanted to vomit, but none of the four still figures even flinched. The realisation that they weren't real was crushing.

Will made to move on, when, from the television, he heard his own voice. He turned around and saw the static start to break up.

'I want to go home,' Will cried from the speakers.

'Then go,' somebody whispered in response. The Crooked Man. 'If you make it out, you can go wherever you wish.'

The static gave way to a shot of a set of concrete steps descending into darkness. Will, a year younger and no less terrified, reached the top of the stairs and stopped on shaky legs.

'Go,' the Crooked Man hissed and Will set off down a corridor. The camera angle changed to show him running down first one dimly lit corridor, then another. The camera lingered a while longer on the corridor after Will left the shot and he could see the Crooked Man, without his cane or his hat, all gangly limbs. He cracked them, stretched them, and hunched over, his limbs bending in all the wrong places, giving him the appearance of a horrifying meld of an arachnid crossed with a large, skeletal ape. The Crooked Man began to run, a creature out for blood. A smile stretched from ear to ear across his face as he hunted Will.

Will didn't want to see any more. Even without accurate memories, he knew he was watching himself a year ago. He was witnessing the Crooked Man chasing him through a maze of his own creation, relishing his fear.

He rushed on toward the next door. It wasn't marked like the others. He turned the handle and went straight through. The walls were striped in red and white like the stalls outside, but the tarp was aged and dulled. In the middle of the room was an empty coffin. Sat in the furthest corner from the light was the slumped figure of a man, head down and, it appeared, without life.

There didn't seem to be any immediate trick, so Will kept his distance. It looked as though the figure was a model, like the life-like beings in the living room but he was not going to act on the assumption that that was what he was. If he ventured too close, he didn't want to find out it was alive when it leapt up and grabbed him around the waist, heaving him off the ground and forcing him into the open, empty coffin.

Beside the man, however, was another door. To get there without passing him, would require Will to walk all the way around the other side of the room, circling the empty coffin. Once he reached the other door, he would be a couple of feet from the man. Reaching distance. He wouldn't have very long to get the door open and get through it.

He circled the coffin until he was on the other side of it. It wasn't empty as he had thought. He peered over the edge. Inside the coffin was rotten and filled to the brim with bugs and writhing maggots. Arms shot up from inside and seized him by the sides of the head. The hands were impossibly strong and he fought against them desperately. The insects spread and parted, revealing the shape of a menacing, not quite human face beneath, rising up as it pulled Will inward.

Will pressed one foot against the side of the coffin and yanked back his head as hard as he could. At first it felt as though his head would come off his neck, and then the coffin tumbled to the floor. Free, he stood panting, looking at the fallen coffin, from which all the bugs should have spooled out onto the floor, along with whatever that *thing* had been. But there was nothing.

He cautiously retraced his steps back around the room and peered into the tumbled coffin. It was empty. There was no shred of evidence that anything had ever been in there.

He shrank back from it, more terrified by its emptiness than he was by the creature that had seized him.

What is this place? What's happening to me?

He crouched against the wall and suddenly he was in another room entirely. This one was covered in steel, and the walls lined with bones.

'*Roll up,*' he heard and knew the Crooked Man was coming. There was a door straight ahead and Will sat against the wall, terrified, and stared at it, waiting. He grabbed one of the bones off the wall, his stomach lurching at the odd feeling of it, not like plastic, but like actual bone. He held the thing in his hands and waited.

The tall shadow of his tormentor appeared first, stretching toward him.

He didn't want to die.

Will jerked up and sprinted past the coffin, away from the room full of bones and the impending arrival of the Crooked Man. As he reached for the door, the man in the corner leapt up and seized him by the arms. Will cried out.

'You have to help me,' the man said. His voice was a rasp but it twanged with a Scottish accent.

'Craig?' Will exclaimed. 'Oh my god, Craig.'

He was emaciated and unkempt, his cheeks covered by a long and scraggly black beard, cut away to nothing in one area, where a scar ran down his cheek.

He said, 'You have to help me. We have to get out of here.'

Will couldn't believe it. It was really him. His best friend was really here, alive. Will said, 'I don't know how to get out.'

From the previous room came the creak of a door opening and closing. 'Come on,' Craig said. 'He's coming.'

Craig unhanded Will and opened the door beside which he'd sat. No fresh room waited for him. Instead, Will found himself back in the dim black maze of corridors, but he had Craig by his side this time.

'You have to get me out of here. If we don't make it out, he'll keep us forever,' Craig explained.

They headed through the maze, hopelessly. Will knew they would only be able to go wherever the Crooked Man wanted. They were following a path he had set and there was nothing either of them could do to stop it. Or at least, there was nothing Will could do.

'Where do we go to get out of the building?' Will asked Craig, but the once strong man was frail and panicky. He rocked back and forth like some of the patients Will had met in the mental clinic.

'He'll make you stay forever. You'll become part of his group, and you'll do whatever he tells you to. You'll never see home again.'

Will wanted to stop and ask him what the hell had happened to them but he knew. Will had happened to them. He had led them to the park, he had led them to the Crooked Man, whether he meant to or not.

There was a sound behind them and Will looked back over his shoulder. He could barely see anything but he was certain he'd caught a glimpse of the Crooked Man stalking down the corridor toward them with his spider-like walk, before darting through a wall.

He wished he'd been able to keep hold of his phone back there in that first room. He'd give anything to see. The only other option was a zippo lighter in the pocket of Nicole's jacket. He dug it out and snapped it on. The flame flickered and shocked his eyes but it did little to light their surroundings. It was a comfort in his hand, however, so he kept it lit.

'He's gonnae find us,' Craig muttered, more to himself than Will. 'He's gonnae find us and then he's gonnae make us stay. Nobody ever leaves the fair unless he wants them to.'

Will pulled Craig to a stop. He didn't want to go forward and risk walking straight into the Crooked Man, nor did he wish to go back.

He looked into Craig's emaciated face.

'I left,' he said. He felt strange having to be the strong one. He had always been the coward to Craig's hero. 'I left, don't you remember?'

'But you're here now. If you left before, you won't leave this time. He'll come for you.'

'What happened to the others?' said Will. 'Nicole, and Tom, and Julian? Are they in here too?'

Craig looked at Will with eyes void of knowledge. His usually piercing blue eyes were a haze of confusion and loss.

'Craig? I need to know what happened to them. Tell me they're alive as well.'

Craig's head drooped. 'Everybody lives until he's done with them.' He started back down the corridor. 'We should keep moving. He'll be coming for us soon. He always comes for us.'

Craig passed beyond the limited reach of the lighter's flame and became a shape in the darkness. He moved with frail, fragile fear the likes of which Will had never imagined he would see in Craig. It had burrowed its way into him, making him a shell of the man he'd once been, and Will didn't like the idea of him disappearing off by himself. Nor did he want to be alone again. He rushed to keep up.

He never reached him.

The lighter flame flickered and before it went out completely, Will saw the wall beside Craig open up. A dark blur swept around him and disappeared. Will ran for the place where he'd been but the wall was back in place. He put the lighter back in his jacket pocket and hammered his fists against the wood.

He stopped only when the pain grew too much and blood slicked his hands, cold and wet. He slumped to the floor and began to weep. His best friend was alive, or had been, and now he was back in the arms of the monster in the walls.

'Roll up. Roll up,' the Crooked Man sang. 'Don't you want to know what's inside of you? I know I do.'

It came from back the way they'd come. Will took off in the opposite direction.

The corridors twisted one way, then another, pushing him this way and that, with no end in sight, nor any doors. Behind him, the sound of the Crooked Man's sing-song whisper chased him. His voice seemed to be everywhere. Behind him, on his left, on his right, moving around impossibly.

Will ran from it but it was always right behind him, prickling his ear.

He turned a corner, and there he was. The Crooked Man

filled the corridor ahead, and through the dim, almost brown light in the ceiling, Will saw him smile his crooked smile.

49

Will set off back the way he'd come. He turned the first corner and pounded down the corridor at an all-out sprint. Behind him, he could hear the movement of the Crooked Man, of the *thing* coming for him. It didn't move like a person, he could hear as much from the thumps of its limps, as though he were not quite running on all fours but using his hands on the walls to propel him forward.

It was not a man chasing him but a being plucked from a child's nightmare, garish and too frightening to ever exist in real life.

Will took another corner and expected to find the door back into the coffin room, where he'd found Craig, but he found only another corner. The Crooked Man had managed to shift the walls again, even while the sound of his hammering fists and feet hurtled after Will.

There wasn't time to slow and wonder how the *thing* had done it. Will took the corner at full speed. He sparked his shoulder against the wall and a burst of pain shocked through it, but he kept running, as fast as he could.

50

Above the maze of corridors, Peter Lincoln navigated a separate maze of walkways made up of crudely constructed wooden beams without any kind of banister or supports. Each step was a balancing act, one which could result in him falling through the floor, rendering him potentially trapped in an unknown area with no way out.

There were walls stretching to the roof, including a large section in the centre of the building, which appeared completely inaccessible to him, but there were great expanses of space where the wooden beamed walkways ran back and forth without interruption. On the floor, he noticed foot wide ravines running alongside what he assumed were the dark corridors Will's housemates had mentioned. At various points along the ravines, metal ladders descended from the walkway.

There was no way of knowing if Will was in the corridors or in one of the rooms, but he couldn't find any access to any of the rooms from up here, and so his only option was to keep walking and hope to hear or see something through the spaces in the ceiling. He came to a ladder and, not liking the sense of not-knowing, he climbed down into the space.

The gulley was tight. He had certainly put on a few pounds in the past few years but to be able to move through these spaces with anything resembling ease and efficiency, a person would have to be thinner than a skeleton.

He thought of what Beth and Ben had told him about the walls moving, separating them from Will. Whoever descended the ladder wouldn't have to be in the cramped space for very long, so long as they knew where to find the panels that moved.

In the narrow passage, the lights from above were of little use, and he was forced to get his phone back out and switch on the torch. There was little to immediately see. No doors were evident through which the Tombes imitator could enter the corridors.

He stopped and scanned the torch over the next panel of wall up from the one he stood pressed against. It was just wood, plain old plywood, nailed together in places and, in others, seamlessly slotted together. There were two small holes drilled into the panel, one on either side of the wood. At the very bottom of the panel ran a set of tracks, and Peter realised the holes were for rods or hooks, similar to the back entrance of the building.

He made his way back up to the walkway and began balance-walking in the direction of the rear entrance.

'Mr Lincoln?' A rasp, meant to be a whisper but louder than spoken word. 'Mr Lincoln?'

He should have known better than to trust the housemates to stay out of the building. He'd assumed at that age, everybody was more likely to be the coward than the hero but here Beth was, somewhere ahead of him, trying to get herself heard and killed.

Peter sped up and caught her before she hissed his name again.

'What are you doing? I said to stay outside and make sure nobody else came in,' he chastised in a whisper no quieter than her own. He realised right away she was going to argue back in full volume and put up a hand to stop her. Quieter, he said, 'Alright, he's your friend. You want to make amends, something. Whatever. If you want to help, I need you to do something for me.'

51

'It's useless, William,' the Crooked Man called. The voice surrounded Will, no longer a whisper but a deep boom, that came from all around, not just behind him. 'You cannot outrun me.'

Will ran, and the Crooked Man followed.

52

Using one of the tent pegs he'd asked Beth to retrieve, Peter gained access to an extremely dim corridor, if only to get a better glimpse of what they were dealing with. Facts. He needed information to act on if he was going to be of any help to the kid, but even once he'd seen the corridor and stood within its black walls, ceiling, and floor, he felt no better informed, no better prepared. If anything, he felt more hopeless.

If all the corridors were the same as this one, and there were as many as it appeared from up on the walkway, finding the kid would be a mammoth trial whether they used the walkways above, the corridors below, or both at the same time, and that was before taking into account the maniac showman's ability to move walls and rearrange the maze at will.

Peter climbed back up to the walkway where Beth waited, moving side to side with the same restlessness he felt. As he joined her, it felt as though he had more chance of finding the location of his missing daughter after seven years and across hundreds of miles of potential places, than it would be to find a single man in the maze below.

He was about ready to retreat and regroup his thoughts in the fresh air and the light of the fairground when the building erupted with cackling, maniacal laughter. Without even thinking, Peter set off in search of the source. And Beth followed.

53

Will spun around another corner, slowing just enough to not strike his other shoulder, and he stumbled to a stop. Dead ahead stood the Crooked Man. He was hunched over, creating a bulbous, round shape of his torso, from which his long arms stretched toward the floor. Were it not for his head sticking out of the curved silhouette of his chest and back, staring at Will with a grin upon its lips, he might appear as though he were transformed into a giant insect.

'I am everywhere,' the creature hissed. 'You cannot escape me.'

I did it once before, Will told himself in a rare moment of self-confidence. And he turned on the spot and ran.

But the Crooked Man's words followed him along with his laughter, proving true at every turn. Will found himself face to face with the Crooked Man's hunched figure again, and again. He ran and he ran until his lungs burned, turning and fleeing from the monster each time he found it standing ahead of him. No matter how far he ran, the Crooked Man was always there, waiting.

The sound of his inhuman movements followed Will down each corridor, along with a cackling laughter that made him feel physically sick, but then he would turn a corner and there the Crooked Man would be, having somehow cut through the maze to get ahead of him.

Still, Will didn't let up. He couldn't. He was face to face with the horror that had befallen he and his friends a year ago. Confirmation that he had not imagined the fair. He had found some truth. He couldn't let it all end now.

He had to get out of here. He had to survive. For them.

If only he could remember how he had managed the last time.

He racked his brain but there was nothing. Not even a glimmer.

Around another corner, the Crooked Man waited. As Will turned and fled back the other way, the Crooked Man laughed louder. It was the sound of a mad scientist bringing to life his most horrific creation, of a maniac slaughtering his victims and relishing the warm splash of blood against his face.

He ran from the ear-piercing sound, turning this way and that, following the twists and turns the Crooked Man had planned out for him, as he hopelessly tried to think of a way out. At any moment, he expected, he would turn another corner and find the arachnoid giant before him once again. His lungs burnt and a throbbing ache had settled into his limbs. He didn't know how much longer he could continue to flee. The sound of the laughter followed at his heels, never quietening.

There was no way out. He was destined to run until he couldn't go any longer. The only path he could follow was the one the Crooked Man planned for him. He came to a dead end, turned, expecting to see his tormentor behind him, but trapping Will like this would bring the fun to an end. Instead, he found that the corridor he'd just ran down had shortened, a corner added a few metres away, that hadn't been there before. Will was supposed to flee down it.

But he didn't. Will did the only thing he could that the Crooked Man didn't plan, didn't want. He stood, back against the dead end, and waited.

After a few moments, the Crooked Man appeared around the bend, stalking toward him. He beamed wider than ever but the smile was more for show. His frustration at finding Will stood there, like a lamb to the slaughter, was evident in his eyes, which stared out from beneath the pinch of his thick eyebrows.

Although he had nowhere to go, and he had brought this game to a stop intentionally, given himself to this wicked man, he tried to back away. He was supposed to have been chased until he ran out of steam, until the Crooked Man caught him. The anger in the deeply shadowed skull was evident despite the smile, and Will suspected he would imminently feel the full force of it.

Suddenly, he wished the wall against his back would give way and allow him the illusion of freedom that would come with another stretch of corridor. But it stayed solid. The Crooked Man stayed where he was, too, watching. He was cast almost entirely in shadow but still he appeared poised and waiting, eagerly, for Will to make some kind of move to pass him. Daring him to do so.

Enter if you dare, the sign had read, after all. To dare was what he wanted from all his captives.

The Crooked Man moved. It was a scurrying rush forward, so quick, Will saw the limbs move only once and then he was upon him. His long, bony fingers seized the bottom half of Will's face like a vice against his cheeks, and he pressed Will against the wall.

'I've been waiting an entire year for this, William,' the Crooked Man snarled.

Will could feel the tips of the Crooked Man's fingers against his teeth, his grip against the thin flesh of his cheeks was so tight, and he squirmed as much as the limited room between the wall and the Crooked Man's skeletal, spider body would allow.

He looked directly into the grimacing grin of the Crooked Man and he felt cold. He was exactly as Will remembered him in those recovered memories, but he was also identical to the photograph he'd found of Harold Tombes. It was impossible but it was true. All that was missing was his hat and cane.

'You won't get away from me this time, William,' hissed

the Crooked Man. His smile twisted to become more cruel, if such a thing were possible. 'I'm going to make sure you never leave my fairground again. And I'm going to enjoy every second I spend with you. Every moment of *fear* you experience. Tell me, William, do you fear me?'

Will urged himself to say no, but he heard the word forcing its way from his pressed mouth before he knew what he was doing. 'Y-es.'

'Good. You ought to. I am the master of fear. I can make you feel more fear than you ever imagined. When I am through with you, only then will you understand true horror. It will be all you know. And in the moments before your mind voids itself even of who you are, I will take your life. You will know, when you die, why it has happened to you.'

'Why?' asked Will, through a mouth misshapen by the fingers pressing into his cheeks. Immediately, he regretted it. He should have stayed quiet. That shouldn't have been so difficult for him, should it?

The smile dropped from the Crooked Man's mouth and his face was overtaken by true, murderous fury. His next word came as a scream, which echoed off the corridor walls. '*Why?* Because it is what you deserve.' He quietened before continuing, returning to the hiss he had opted for previously. 'This building is designed to terrify you. To change you. Those who make it to the end, who change and make it out of the house, become a part of my fair, as I had intended for you. It was a life of excitement and joy and the fear all people crave. My fair offered a place for you to belong, but you were ungrateful. You destroyed my house. You set it alight and left it to burn.'

Destroyed? So this wasn't the fairground he had been at a year ago, but there *had* been a fairground, another house of horrors. How had he managed to set it on fire?

Will bucked against the pressure of the Crooked Man's grip but the Crooked Man's other hand struck his chest, pressing him harder into the wall. As he bucked, Will slipped his hand into the pocket of his jacket and felt the cool lump of metal within.

54

Peter and Beth finally found the kid. They had chased down the laughter for what felt like an age and then it abruptly stopped, just as they felt they were right upon the source of it. There was silence as the two of them stood listening.

'*Why?*' somebody boomed and Peter bolted toward the voice, running as quietly and safely as he could across the walkway. He stopped and listened again, and then heard a voice, the same voice. He was close enough to hear it now, even without any shouting.

'You destroyed my house. You set it alight and left it to burn.'

Peter took another step closer to the voice until he felt he was right on top of it, then he stepped off of the walkway, being careful to ensure the ceiling of the corridor was strong enough to take his weight, and lay down on his stomach, lining his eye up with one of the holes designed to let in the dim, limited light.

Below, William struggled against a tall man with arms and legs far too long for his body. The man leant his head so close to Will's face, Peter thought he was going to take a bite out of it. Instead, he hissed, 'You set my pride and joy on fire, and for that, when I am done with you, I will make you suffer such intense pain, you will be begging for death. Then I will set *you* on fire.'

Set it alight and left it to burn, Peter thought. The kid had been found with nothing in his pockets except a zippo lighter. A zippo lighter, which Peter thought he could see in Will's hand.

He was going to do it again, with himself trapped inside. Peter couldn't let the kid set himself on fire. Not even if it meant ending the sick charade of this freakshow.

Peter leapt to his feet and stepped back onto the walkway.

'Well?' Beth whispered.

He nodded. Will was down there, it confirmed. But he didn't offer any other information. Instead, he asked, 'Is there anybody else in this building? Did you see anybody else go in or out?'

She shook her head. 'I don't think so.'

It was a fairly big risk with what he was considering doing, and what Will was considering, but he felt he could trust it. The entrance had been closed up, likely by the Crooked Man, no doubt to ensure he could focus all his attention on Will. He wouldn't want any interruptions. This was meant for Will, and Will alone.

Peter took off his jacket and handed it to Beth, who took it reluctantly, then he removed his shirt.

'What are you doing?' Beth demanded.

He ignored her – it wasn't like he didn't have a t-shirt on underneath the shirt – and took from his jeans pocket, his cigarettes.

55

'People don't crave fear,' Will said. He needed to keep the Crooked Man talking. The moment he stopped, it would come time for what Will was planning, and he would notice the Zippo Will had removed from his jacket pocket. It was the same one that he had been found with. It had belonged to Nicole and he had never understood exactly why he had ended up with it while he had lost his mobile and his wallet.

The half-smile returned to the Crooked Man's lips. 'You are a fool if you think that is true. Think of all the entertainment you people consume. The books, the films. They inflict on themselves things they know will terrify them. They want to be afraid and so they seek it out. It has been that way for eons. Freakshows were created for that very purpose, and, later, funhouses like this one were created to mimic the same effect. People far and wide have enjoyed a night at my fairground and hundreds of them have walked through the doors of my house of horrors, desperate to experience the darkest terrors it has to offer.'

While the Crooked Man spoke, Will flicked open the top of the lighter and placed his thumb on the metal circle, ready to spark. What he would do once the flame was lit, he would have to work out after.

'Your girlfriend craved fear. I could tell, even as the terror burrowed deep within her and replaced parts of her, that she was one of those lovers of fear. Am I wrong? And what of you?'

'Wh... What about me?' Will's voice was weak. The mention of Nicole had made his throat tight as though the

Crooked Man's bony fingers were clasped around his neck rather than his cheeks.

'You came to this house of horror even knowing it would terrify you. You came back to me. Only somebody who craves fear would willingly return, and I counted on that. I planted it within you and nurtured the seed. So if not for fear, why did you come back?'

'For my friends. To know... what happened...'

'Your friends are gone. There is nothing of them left, William. But don't go giving up on life yet. There's always something to fight for, always a reason to fear. Think about your new friends.'

Will did think about them and his thumb, about to turn on the wheel, hesitated. If they were still inside...

If the Crooked Man had them, then there would be no saving them any more than Will could save his old friends. He struck the wheel. A perfect flick of flame ignited and Will swept it toward the Crooked Man's body, meaning to pass the flame to his clothing as he had done with the candles earlier tonight. Passing the flame from the lighter to his friends' murderer would be a far better vigil.

But the Crooked Man slapped Will's hand away and the lighter fell to the floor, the flame extinguished. Will heard the thud of it drop and knew it was over. All of it. His search for his friends. His life.

He had lost.

'Did you really think that trick would work twice?'

As if in answer, a wall beside the two of them slid away to reveal another stretch of corridor. And the Stranger stepped into sight. From his hand hung a lifeless shape of blueish fabric, the bottom of which flickered with a small flame.

For a few seconds, the Stranger just looked at the two of them without saying anything, his eyes fixed on the Crooked Man as though he couldn't believe his eyes. Then, he managed, 'Let him go.'

The Crooked Man laughed. 'You are in my house now,

and you play by my rules. You do not give orders.'

'Let him go, or I'll drop it,' he nodded to the fabric. Smoke billowed from it, slowly filling the corridor. 'And this entire place can burn like your other one.'

The Crooked Man's face flickered. 'You will burn with me.'

'Maybe,' Peter said. 'But I don't have much to live for. The kid has a whole future.'

The smoke was growing thicker and the small flame spread rapidly. It had already reached halfway toward Peter's hand. He grimaced at the singe of heat against his skin. He wouldn't be able to hold it much longer, and then the three of them would be surrounded by fire and smoke, unable to control it.

Or at least two of them would be. The Crooked Man would escape behind another wall, like he always did and it would just be the two of them. The Stranger and the so-called survivor of the Treevale Five.

Coming to perhaps the same conclusion, Peter threw the material directly at the Crooked Man. The Crooked Man had no choice but to let go of Will if he was to avoid the fireball. Will fell to the floor, the wind rushing out of him. The burning material landed right beside him and a great plume of smoke blew through his mouth and nostrils, scorched his larynx on the way to his lungs.

He heaved and coughed but he had too little energy left to move away from the growing fire. Everything became black and he felt himself in the grip of hands again, pulled to his feet and down a corridor, but it wasn't the Crooked Man.

56

Peter looked from Will, hunched over and choking, to the freakshow act but the corridor was empty. Where the man who looked frighteningly identical to the historic serial killer had been a second before, there was nothing. He had already disappeared through another moving wall.

Peter forgot about him, for now at least, and focused on Will. The smoke was engulfing the kid, claiming him for its own, attempting to squeeze the life from his chest. Peter took his denim jacket back off and threw it over Will's head, covering his face. He lifted him to his feet and away from the fireball that had been Peter's shirt.

He pushed the kid into the next corridor and closed the wall behind them, closing the spreading fire inside that corridor, where it would stay long enough to give them a head start. He guided Will, the denim jacket draped over his head to protect him from the smoke as he attempted to cough it from his lungs, through another gap in the walls, into the gutter between corridors.

He eased the kid toward the ladder.

'Peter!' Beth called from above.

He placed Will's hand on the ladder and told him to climb it. Will managed a couple of rungs and then began to struggle. The smoke had already weakened him greatly. Peter became less confident about getting the three of them out of the building in one piece.

He placed the heel of his hand against the kid's backside and gave him a shove, helping him up the last few rungs, where Beth was ready to help pull him up onto the walkway. When

Peter clambered awkwardly to join them on his throbbing ankle, he became even less confident.

The air around them was filling with smoke, drifting up through the holes in the corridor's ceiling and he knew there would be more smoke coming from the other corridors throughout the building. Before descending to confront the maniac – who, he couldn't understand, looked exactly the same as Harold Tombes – Peter had lit three cigarettes, which he had, one by one, flicked in three different directions, where he expected they would burn against the wood and fabric which lined it, eventually catching fire, and ultimately, forcing the murderer and kidnapper out into the open where the police could apprehend him.

As they rushed away from the fire he'd set using his cheap polyester and cotton shirt, he saw the smoke filling the air in the direction of those cigarettes, and he realised the cigarettes had burned more effectively than expected. Now they were rushing through a smoke filled attic-like space, while Will continued to choke and struggled to stay upright on the thin wooden beams.

'Come on, William,' Peter urged. 'Just a little more.'

Carrying out Will's idea had not been the best idea, particularly when they were going to be escaping through higher ground. Most people who died due to a fire, died from smoke inhalation. Beth and Peter covered their own mouths with their arms and guided Will forward. The air was thickening and visibility within the smoky darkness was becoming difficult, even with the powerful white light of Beth's phone torch projected before them.

'I don't know which way to go,' Beth called back. Her voice was muffled by the crook of her elbow. 'I can't see.'

Will continued to cough. He wouldn't last much longer. Peter could already make out the sway of his movements and knew his head was growing lighter by the second. If they didn't get out of here soon, the kid would die and all of this would have been for nothing.

'Beth,' he called through the crook of his own elbow.

She called back that she was listening and he told her what he wanted her to do. Without lowering her phone, she navigated the screen and searched for Ben. She called him and, silencing his slew of questions – he was able to see smoke and desperately demanded to know what had happened, if they were okay, round and round and round – she reiterated Peter's instructions, and to be quick about it.

They crouched down in a hopeless attempt to limit their exposure to the gathering smoke, and they waited. It wasn't long but it was suffocating. Finally they heard Ben's call.

'Beth!' It was a hoarse scream of panic but it sounded to Peter, at least, like the beautiful singsong of a canary in a coal mine. Beth turned left and started toward the voice. Ben, in the back entrance to the funhouse, screamed Beth's name, over and over, drawing them toward him.

Will took a step and Peter could see right away that something was wrong. It was only by luck that he had seen the slightly more pronounced sway of that single step and caught Will with a hand on his chest as he lost consciousness.

'No, no, no,' Peter mumbled. He removed his arm from his nose and mouth in order to keep the dead weight of Will's unconscious body upright. He held his breath. He turned Will around so that they were face to face and he heaved him onto his shoulder like a firefighter would. The added weight made Peter's ankle scream and with his next step across the wooden beam, Peter almost toppled over. He held his breath, bit down on the inside of his lips, and rushed after Beth as fast as he could manage, hoping against all hope that Will was only unconscious and he wasn't carrying a corpse.

The carbon dioxide in Peter's chest burned until he was forced to release it and he took in a gust of smoky air, which made him cough the same way Will had. He didn't stop moving, though, even when Beth looked back with concern. He urged her to move quickly and soon she was almost running toward Ben's voice, with Peter hobbling behind her.

The heat rose around them, prickling Peter's skin. Burning hot sweat streamed from every pore.

Finally, they reached the edge of the building and the ladder leading to the back door. Ben stopped halfway through a fresh scream when he saw them.

'Oh, thank god,' he said.

'Thank him later,' Peter snapped, and almost pushed Beth onto the ladder in his urgency. When she was down, he, without warning, passed Will down, feet first. Ben and Beth both scrambled to take hold of him. When he was sure they had him, he yelled at them to take him outside.

He climbed down and fell out of the building. He stumbled far enough away to be safe before collapsing onto the grass. Sally was waiting for him with a couple of uniformed officers. She looked from the students as they laid Will down on the grass to Peter and back again.

'He needs medical attention,' Peter told her. 'He's inhaled a lot of smoke.'

'You need medical attention of your own,' she said.

Peter ignored her. He thought of the man – Harold Tombes, or a more likely a lookalike – and added, 'You need to make sure the building is surrounded.'

She looked a question at him but she told him the building was already surrounded, had been since the smoke started to stream out of it. She shouted for paramedics, who were already on scene to see to the stall holders the police had started the process of freeing from their shackles. In seconds, there was a group of paramedics surrounding Will. Beth and Ben backed away but were reluctant to go too far from their smoke injured friend.

Peter turned his attention to Sally. 'There's a guy in there. He's got the same limb disproportion as Harold Tombes had. He was about to kill William Campbell but we lost him when I started the fire.'

'You...' she started.

He nodded toward Will. 'He'd be dead if I hadn't.' *He still might be*, he thought. 'Anyway, I don't know if he was quick enough to escape.'

She nodded. 'Don't worry. If he did, we'll get him. We've got his other fairground, and helicopters have located the caravans they came here in. There'll be officers there in the next few minutes. He's got nowhere to go.'

Sally said, 'Morgan's going to be here any minute. You should make yourself scarce. I'll say I started the fire.'

But Peter wasn't listening. He stayed exactly where he was and watched the paramedics working on Will, and he waited for a sound to come from the young man.

57

After cutting open his own wrist, being kidnapped and escorted to a fairground miles away from home by a deranged serial killer, and eventually allowing himself to be lured back into the new fairground of that same killer, William Campbell finally died.

The doctors would share this news shortly after he awoke in a brightly lit hospital room a far cry from the last thing he remembered. The fair was like a distant dream, although he could feel a harsh ache in his chest and throat, a reminder of the smoke he had inhaled, deep inside the house of horrors.

He had stopped breathing, he was told, and then his heart stopped, but the paramedics were able to resuscitate him long enough to transport him the two miles to the nearest hospital. For almost a week, he had been intubated and in and out of consciousness.

Dr Phillips checked in on him when she heard he was awake but didn't pry too much, assuring him they would talk soon and that he should focus on getting better physically for the time being.

Ian had spent the week splitting his time between watching over Will's mother, who had not broken out of her trance even when told of her son's hospitalisation, and sitting at Will's bedside whenever he could get somebody else to watch over her. When he heard Will was awake, he came straight to him.

'You're awake,' Ian said, as though Will needed telling.

'I'm... alive,' Will rasped and winced.

'They tell me that will get better. In time.'

They were quiet for a long time. Ian noticed Will looking around the room, before his gaze settled on the door over Ian's shoulder.

'I know you wish it was your father here for you instead of me. And I'm sorry it isn't. I might not be your dad, Will, but I've always loved you like a son. I've done my best for you. I just...'

'I don't... I'm glad... you're here. Not him.'

'That means a lot, Will. I couldn't bear the thought of losing you. You know we could never afford to get your Mum the help she needed after David, and the NHS options weren't good enough. When you tried to... after the attempt, I couldn't risk not getting you help. I spent all of my savings on paying Dr Phillips to treat you.'

'I'm sorry.'

'For what?'

Will's eyelids felt heavy, as though he hadn't spent the majority of a week unconscious. 'For everything. I shouldn't have left the museum that night. I shouldn't have tried to recover my memories. I shouldn't have gone to that fair.'

Ian shook his head. 'You have nothing to apologise for. You saved a lot of people. They're calling you a hero. In the papers.'

'But... I didn't... It was... the Stranger.'

'You mean the journalist?'

Will nodded.

'He's been living in the waiting room most of this past week waiting for you to wake up. I tried telling him to leave, that you won't want to talk to any journalists but he wouldn't. Just because he saved your life, he must think you owe him an exclusive or something.'

The disdain in Ian's voice was obvious but Will didn't have the energy to try and subdue it. Instead, he said, 'I want to see him.'

'Will, come on. He's just going to try and use you. That's

all these people do. They take advantage.' As though the matter were decided, Ian added, 'You just get some rest.'

Ian left a couple of hours later. After he'd been gone long enough it was clear he was out of the building, Peter Lincoln came to see Will. He walked straight in without knocking and Will didn't object. He looked rougher and more dishevelled than ever.

'I'm so glad you're okay,' he said, and Will could see the same relief he had seen in Ian but, even though he was no relation to the Stranger, the relief seemed deeper, as though there was a part of his past that had gone in the other direction and somebody had not been okay.

'You saved me,' Will said.

Peter took the seat beside the bed and nodded. 'Like I said, I'm not one of the vultures. Some of them would have stood there and watched because it would make a good story.'

'But why?'

Peter rubbed his face with both hands and weighed up what he said next. 'I lost my daughter,' he explained. 'They never found her. I'd have given anything for somebody to come and save her from the bad guys. Everyone deserves the chance to be saved. Anyway, thanks to you a lot more people were saved.'

Will shook his head. 'I didn't do anything. I,' he swallowed. 'I went chasing shadows. Put my friends in danger. Again.' He paused, regained his strength. 'I would have gone there alone if I'd known Beth had talked to you.'

Peter rubbed his stubbled cheeks and sighed. Will remembered that social niceties and politeness didn't come naturally to Peter Lincoln, hence the name he brandished like both a shield and a weapon.

'There were hundreds of people like you, Will. People who were kidnapped and taken to a fair hidden in the woods down in Yorkshire and held captive. We're talking years. A lot of them are dead but there were a lot kept alive too. He chained them to the fairground stalls and forced them to run the fairground so he could force his fresh captives to play along. It was supposed to seem like an honest fairground and you're the VIP who had it all to yourself, until you reached the house of horror.

'They're all free now because of you. If you hadn't gone to that fair, I never would have followed you. And the police wouldn't have shown up. He'd have taken somebody else and disappeared again. Hell, none of this would have been possible if you hadn't been taken last year and escaped. And that lunatic would have gone on kidnapping and torturing and killing for years.'

Will's eyes went wide as he thought of the fire. 'The Crooked Man. Did you...'

'...get him? He didn't make it out. When the fire was out, they searched the wreckage and found remains that seem to match. The police share my belief that the man was a fanatic of Harold Tombes – I assume you researched him after our meeting? – and his interest probably grew from sharing the same deformity, the disproportionate limbs, which made him an outsider like Tombes was.'

He said the words as though he believed them but that belief didn't reach his eyes, and Will could see something there, which he also felt. It was the confusing, impossible knowledge of what they had seen, something they knew could not be true but was.

Peter continued. 'They haven't been able to identify him yet.' He paused as what he just said added to the conflicting knowledge in his eyes. 'No matter who he was, he's dead.'

'You said he tortured...' Will's throat ached and he wanted a gallon of water to drown it.

Peter nodded. 'Not in the sense you're probably thinking. It was more mental than physical. The police, along with psychologists including your Dr Phillips, have been interviewing the stall holders for the past week. She's a good doctor you've got there. I hear she waved your fee after your disappearance and she's waving the fees of all of the other victims too. The publicity it'll do her will be worth far more than money, and everybody gets the treatment they need. Everybody wins.

'Like you, the other victims' memories are not entirely reliable. Some of them don't even remember who they are because they've been brainwashed into thinking they're part of the fairground crew, even if they don't want to be. Some of them have been able to recall enough to piece together a little of what the man did to them.

'I've been gravely warned by your Dr Phillips not to talk to you or tell you any of this but you deserve to know. The man – the Crooked Man, you called him? – used the house of horror to terrify his newest captives. They would be drugged, I'm guessing with hallucinogens, and let loose in the corridors, and told to run and he would chase them through corridors and rooms that were intended to prey on their deepest fears and insecurities. He would make their own mind turn against them. He would torture them mentally for days and days for his own enjoyment.'

Will thought about his friends, imagined them tortured by their own minds as much as by the Crooked Man, and he returned to some of his own terrors in that house a week ago.

He said, 'I saw Craig when I was inside.'

'Nobody else was found inside except the... the Crooked Man.'

'So was anything I remember from in there real?'

'I don't know. Some of it might have been.'

'What about that night last year? How can I trust any of my memories? How do I know I'm even out of that house now?'

Peter bit the inside of his lip as he thought about it a moment. 'That's something you need to talk about with your therapist. You are definitely out of there, though. This isn't another one of the Crooked Man's tricks.'

'I went inside because I thought I saw Nicole and I thought I could find out what happened to them,' Will said, solemn and more to himself than to Peter Lincoln.

'I'm not sure you want that answer.'

Will shot him a look. 'You know what happened?'

Peter nodded. His head sank as he considered whether to answer. Finally, he said, 'I'm afraid only Nicole survived. But,' he added hastily, 'she doesn't remember much. She was recognised walking around the fair. So far, the only thing she remembers from her life before the night you disappeared is something about a suicide, but not her own.'

'It was mine,' Will mumbled to himself. 'I was going to try again that night. I've lived the last year living for the four of them, so I could try and find out what happened to them. What do I do now that I know?'

'I'm not the one to answer that question, I'm afraid.'

Peter reached into his jacket pocket – he was wearing a different jacket to the denim one which the smoke and soot had likely ruined – and removed a set of three envelopes. Will recognised them as the ones delivered to him, which had started this all. Peter handed them over and told him to open them.

Will had not opened the later letters but the envelopes were now torn open, the contents consumed by whomever had removed them from Will's bedroom.

As Will slipped a sheet of paper from one of the envelopes, Peter said, 'Nicole admitted she delivered those to you. She said Harold Tombes made her do it. So it seems the fanatic had actually convinced himself he *was* Harold Tombes.'

Will thought of the hooded figure he'd seen walking past the street at seven in the morning, on a day he received a note. Had he really been so close to her, all those times?

He unfolded the letter, expecting to see *roll up* written there to greet him.

Stay Away, it said.

He looked at another one and then another, finding the same message written in capitals with more exclamation marks, in larger, more urgent scrawl. She was trying to keep Will from going to the fair.

'She doesn't remember you,' Peter said, making sure Will understood that. 'She told the police she felt convinced after catching a glimpse of you coming back from your run after she delivered one of the letters, that you didn't deserve to become part of the fair.'

Nicole was alive but she didn't remember him. Will wasn't sure whether to be happy or sad, to laugh or to cry. He put the envelopes on the side of the bed. Suddenly, he felt a strong need to be alone.

'Thank you for saving me. And for bringing me these.'

It was clear in his voice what he wanted and Peter stood up but he didn't make any move for the door. He pulled out another envelope from his pocket and dropped it on Will's leg.

'Don't hold what Beth did against her,' he said. 'I found out about her dad's gambling problem and I used the information against her. I might not be a vulture but I'm not a good guy.' He tapped the envelope. 'This is the money I paid her. She wanted you to have it, by way of apology. She said you deserve it more than her dad does. She only wanted to help everybody. She realises now that's impossible.'

Without another word, he left the room and closed the door behind him, leaving Will alone.

For a long time, Will stared into space without touching the envelope of cash and his conversation with Peter Lincoln began to fade and dull. He was wondering whether it had actually happened or whether he was still somewhere in that house of horror, living through the Crooked Man's tricks, when he eventually fell asleep.

58

Dry, brown leaves were scattered on the pavement before the gate, and as far as the eye could see beyond. Where there had once been fairground stalls with red and white striped tarpaulin and beaming coloured lights streamed around and between each one, there was now only the discarded orange and brown of the deceased flakes cast down from the trees above. The sun was low but burning bright, revealing nothing besides a couple miles of park, where a section of grass near the middle was yellowed and damaged, charred from a fire.

Just a park and nothing more, despite what had happened here. And yet, Will stood across the road and watched the gate with the same trepidation as he always had on his morning run, as though to cross beyond that threshold would bring him closer to the danger that had befallen him the previous year.

'Are you ready?' Ian asked.

'Do you dare?' the Crooked Man had asked.

Will said that he was. Together they crossed the road. They paused for a brief moment at the gate as one last tremor of fear pleaded for Will to stop, to turn back and go home. To never come back here again. But there was no monster in there waiting for him. No Crooked Man. There would be only memories, and he thought he could handle those.

Fear still flooded through him, but he was done being defined by his fears. He stepped into the park for the first time since the night he died, three weeks ago. The leaves crunched underfoot, sounding each and every footstep. The wind blew, rustling through them. He wrapped his coat more tightly around himself and listened for any whisper upon the breeze.

Dr Phillips had suggested this trip. She had worked closely with Will in the past few weeks, along with the huge influx of other patients she now had – all of them pro bono as Peter Lincoln had said – thanks to Will. One of those patients was Nicole, who had since been able to remember who she was, although much of her life remained lost to her, including Will. That she didn't remember him didn't stop Will wanting to see her, and Dr Phillips had eventually agreed, but suggested it should be done in the park.

Dr Phillips wanted to not only have Will face his fears and come to terms with what happened to him, but also to rid him of the mysticism that he treated this location with. By having him meet Nicole again, here, was supposed to do that, showing him there was nothing here to be afraid of while allowing him to associate it with new, better memories again.

Will and Ian walked slowly through the park, Will's gaze tracking around him, unable to keep from looking at all the places where the stalls had been. His heart throbbed in his chest. They passed a couple of other people as they walked, but they paid Will no heed.

They came to the picnic benches on the east side of the park. At one of the tables sat a young woman with her back to Will and Ian. Across from her sat Dr Phillips who, upon seeing them approach, stood to greet them with a smile.

'Hello, Will,' she said, coming away from the table. 'How are you doing?'

'Okay, I think,' Will said, a little more of a tremor in his voice than he liked.

'You look calm, despite where you are. I'm glad to see that.'

Will nodded. 'It's hard not to remember.'

How things had changed, he thought. Only a few weeks ago, he was struggling with the desire to remember everything. Now, he was walking through the park that had terrified him for so long, and wishing he remembered none of it. Or at least that he could ignore those memories. That was, when he wasn't lying in bed at night, wondering if any of it was real, or whether he was still trapped in the Crooked Man's house, imagining it all.

He had once endured a horror film with Nicole about a man trapped in an evil hotel room. Some Stephen King thing, he thought. One part had returned to him lately, a scene in which the man thought he'd escaped only to find himself right back in the room, having never left at all.

Was that going to happen to him? Was he going to suddenly snap out of it and find himself back in one of those dark corridors? In the dead of night, there was no hiding from such a thought.

He focused on the figure at the table, who had not yet turned to face them, and it didn't matter to him whether this was all an imagining, so long as he never came back to reality.

'Why don't you come over to the table?' She turned her attention to the other woman. 'Nicole, this is Ian Stilt and Will Campbell.'

She turned around to look at them. Beneath her hood, her jet black hair had dulled and faded to her natural medium brown, which Will had never seen outside of photographs. She had grown thinner and the grey hoodie hung loose over her torso. The skin around her face had sunken inward, creating shadows where there hadn't been before, particularly around the eyes. Those eyes, so much sadder now than they'd appeared outside the museum. But they still sparkled a dazzling green that made Will's breath catch.

'*Take this,*' Nicole said to him and pressed something into his hand. They were crouched together on the cold concrete floor. And they could hear him coming. Will looked at what she'd passed him. Her lighter. She had kept it tucked in her boot, hidden, and the Crooked Man had not taken their shoes, even after the last attempt to escape. '*He's taking you up there more than any of us. You've the best chance. Use this to create a diversion. And then find a way out. Go get help.*'

As the light glowed at the top of the stairs and the shadow of the Crooked Man stretched down toward them, Nicole pressed her lips forcefully against his. He kissed her back for only a moment and tried to shut out the descending footsteps of the monster coming to collect his prey.

'Hi,' Will managed to say now. He remembered her wrapping her arms around him and holding tighter than either of them had ever had cause to hold the other before.

Nicole stared at him for a long time, her face searching his and then her expression relaxed into what he was sure was recognition. She said, 'Hi.'

Will looked into her eyes as they looked back at his, and whether she remembered him or not didn't matter. What mattered was that she was alive. Losing himself in her eyes, he felt some of the emptiness he had carried start to fill.

It wasn't much. But it was enough.

The wind whistled past his ears but if there were any words whispered upon it, he didn't hear them.

ABOUT THE AUTHOR

Michael Nunn

Michael Nunn is an independently published thriller novelist, living in County Durham with his wife and cats. An avid reader with a love of writing stories growing up, he discovered Stephen King at age eleven or twelve and became fascinated with writing about monsters, demons, vampires and all things dark and macabre.

This passion was temporarily set aside as he studied for a degree in Graphic Design at Teesside University. Shortly after graduating in 2016, Michael found himself drawn once again toward his love of writing, and devoted much of his spare time since working on his craft.

Echoes of the Forgotten is his first published novel.

You can connect with him on instagram: @michaelnunnauthor

Printed in Great Britain
by Amazon